A hero from a romance . . .

"You will bring your betrothed great joy, Clare."

"What will I gain from this man I do not know?" she replied with tremors of distaste.

"Geoffrey is jovial, amusing . . . attractive."

She appraised the Dragon's harsh beauty. "What does he look like?" *You?*

"Blond, blue-eyed. Tall and lean."

Not to my taste at all.

"He is the perfect picture of a hero from a romance."

"Not mine," she murmured. That shook her to her toes. Was she becoming too fond of a man she called her foe?

"Clare?" Jordan's hand touched her arm. "Clare—" His arm drifted around her shoulders.

Always eager to lead, she knew she'd found the one man she could follow . . . but not to another man's arms. That would be a mistake. Just as kissing this man would be. With sorrow, she drew away.

"Nay," he objected. "You need comfort and you want it from me. That which I can give you is that which you shall have. Here for one warm moment on a winter's night."

Books by Jo-Ann Power

You and No Other
Angel of Midnight
Treasures
Gifts
The Nightingale's Song

Published by POCKET BOOKS

JO-ANN POWER

THE NIGHTINGALE'S SONG

POCKET **STAR** BOOKS
New York   London   Toronto   Sydney   Tokyo   Singapore

This book is a work of fiction. Names, characters, places and incidents are products of the author's imagination or are used fictitiously. Any resemblance to actual events or locales or persons living or dead is entirely coincidental.

An *Original* Publication of POCKET BOOKS

 A Pocket Star Book published by
POCKET BOOKS, a division of Simon & Schuster Inc.
1230 Avenue of the Americas, New York, NY 10020

ISBN: 0-671-52997-8

First Pocket Books printing June 1997

10 9 8 7 6 5 4 3 2 1

POCKET STAR BOOKS and colophon are registered trademarks of Simon & Schuster Inc.

Cover art by Brent Watkinson

Printed in the U.S.A.

For all those who read, write, and publish romances,
affirming to the world their belief that through love,
much can come aright

This book could never have come to light were it not for the insights and advice of fellow romance writer and friend Susan King. She answered my calls, opened her library, and drank coffee with me as Clare and her Dragon struggled to spring from the recesses of my imagination to the pages of my manuscript.

THE NIGHTINGALE'S SONG

Prologue

Cheshire, England
November 1403

"In winter's snow, at umber hour,
he came most silent to my bower.
Stark in his need, he built the fire
with honor's ash for love's desire."

"MY LADY, THIS KNIGHT IS *DISHONORABLE?*" CLARE'S SCRIBE
lifted her quill from the parchment, dribbling black ink
upon the ivory expanse.

"On the contrary, he is his liege lord's right arm."

"But he intrudes upon his beloved's bedchamber? A lady
whom he should respect from afar? He even arrives in the
middle of the night, and clearly, he should not be there? My
lady, I do not think this will sell—!"

"This is one of those stories of chivalry, Mary." Clare
smiled tolerantly at the young woman whose skill for writing
extended only to her dexterous hands, not yet to her heart.

1

"We have created heroic adventures before, but never tales of love."

"I know, but that does not mean we can't."

"Nay." Mary shook her head, adamant. "But I thought you said we would next produce the life of our late King Richard."

"We'll begin that soon." *In a better place. Where I may write with a freer hand.* "I wanted to record this new idea of mine quickly. We'll warm ourselves on these cold winter nights with this fiction about devotion. Fear not, the hero will uphold his honor and hers."

"I am glad to hear it, my lady, for I do not want to write about men whom others cannot respect."

"Nor I. So, let us continue. We've introduced him and now we must meet him, see him as the reader does, and then enjoy him." *Does a man exist who can meet a woman, see her, and enjoy her for her mind? Clare laughed at that one!*

Mary looked at her as if she were losing her sanity again. Poor Mary. Being a scribe, she knew little about this imagination process and her tolerance for Clare's mental escapades was short.

Clare cleared her throat and pretended seriousness. "Ah, well . . . we must have a few lines about his appearance, shouldn't we? His hair and his eyes."

"Oh, my lady, that's a simple task. We give him the usual mien for these fables. Golden hair. Gray or pale blue eyes."

"I think not. This man is larger—" Clare spread her hands the width she'd wish his chest might span and knew no mortal man could match it. "*Much* larger than myth. Mayhaps, he is dark. Quite ruddy. With sturdy arms and thighs like—"

"Oak. The usual, I know." Mary was bored by this.

"*Trunks* of oak!" Clare corrected her.

"But if you give him black hair and eyes, no one will believe he is to be the hero. That is traditional coloring for an evil lord."

"Aye, but when he first comes to the heroine's castle, he is her foe. The darkness suits him, Mary."

"Well, I will try to like him. . . ." The girl shook her head, unconvinced, but applied her goose feather quill to parchment again. "What happens next?"

Mary was drumming her fingers on her tabletop by the time Clare spoke again. "I would like him to walk to her. When he stands before her, he should say something similar to

Bid me stay or make me go,
but tell me quick what I must know.
Can you love me? Will you have me
For one hour of bliss?"

"Oh, that's lovely." Mary was scribbling madly.

"You like this now?"

"Not his looks, I don't. He doesn't have scars or an eye missing, does he?" The scribe donned that look Clare called Ever-wary Mary.

"Only one scar that she can see. We'll put it across his brow, I think. But he lacks nothing. Save the ability to love."

"That's not courtly!"

"Mary," she chuckled, "he learns it here with the lady of the story, though he hates to acknowledge it. She has problems, too. We hear about them when she responds to his invasion of her bedchamber. This should be a sad summary. She should think to herself . . . something akin to

I rose, a rebel to sire, king.
Future gone with betrothal ring."

"Hmmm, I like the ideas. But the rhythm's wrong."

"We'll refine the meter before you must put it in good calligraphy on the vellum." Clare strode to her frosted window, looked out upon the falling snow, and fingered the loathsome paper that inspired this soothing shower of creativity—the latest of King Henry's orders to her father and, most pointedly, to her. "Mayhaps, that last line should read, 'Future cast off with gown and ring.'"

"She's *naked?*" Ever-wary Mary could certainly screech.

"Well, of course."

"My lady!" Mary plunked her quill upon her table. "This sounds too much like those scandalous French lais where passion overrules common sense."

"Don't you think that is what happens when one craves another?"

"I don't know, my lady." The servant stared at her, defiant as if she asked, How do you know?

Clare didn't. Among the suitors whom her father had paraded before her, none had ever attracted her eye and her head at the same time. No man had ever appealed to her heart, either. So whether or not she had the ability to love any man was a question that begged an answer. But just as she had not married one of her father's candidates, she could not allow herself to be dragged into a loveless union planned for her by the king.

She peered down at the document she had received less than an hour ago from Henry. She held her future between her fingers, decreed with a monarch's signature and sealed by his ring against her will. His sentence became hers. Marriage to a man—a younger man—reputed to be as lusty as her father.

Her sire's past certainly proved to her that desire for worldly pleasures could warp reason. Destroy others' lives. Make children, like her brother, John, and her sister, Blanchette, curse the man who ignored them as they watched their father sate his three hungers.

The first was for women, beginning with three heiresses whom he had married—and buried. Continued with two mistresses whom he had ensconced in this castle—until he turned them out for infidelity. Then played out with the procession of whores who spread across his bed for a night and scattered bastards into the countryside proving that he merited his reputation as a tyrant with a satyr's appetite.

His second greed was for regal favor, which swayed his loyalty with every breeze and shifted toward whatever army occupied his lands.

Whenever the soldiers planned to march on, Aymer de

Wallys, fourth earl of Trent, would exhibit his third avarice. His devotion to Henry of Lancaster or his predecessor, Richard II, could be counted upon—aye, *weighed*—by the gold each royal lord dropped into Aymer's purse.

Clare shivered in the cool November air. Never having witnessed love or even loyalty among noble men or women, she felt the irrational need to assume its existence and explore its nature by the only means at her disposal—in fiction. Her little troupe of women would help her produce this tale just as they had her other books. Her tiny band of six depended upon her for their livelihoods, their treasured independence and their shelter from the cruel world beyond the cozy tower workshop of Castle Trent.

Clare turned to answer Mary more fully. How could she encourage the young woman to use her imagination if she were not free with her own thoughts and reasonings? "We will imagine we know what passion is, Mary. We'll write of how extraordinary this hero is. Of his

> Fierce eyes, firm lips,
> moist flesh of rippling muscle
> Long shanks and longer—"

"My lady, you cannot write that!"

Clare sighed. "Now, Mary. . . ." *He's my hero and I'll create him as I want him.*

"'Tis not seemly, madam. The Nightingale has a reputation to uphold!" The apprentice cast wide her hands. "The Nightingale is a *man*—or so the world believes."

"Because more men are literate than women, and because we wish to attract as many patrons as possible for the highest price, we create the illusion that this enterprise is run by a man, Mary. But I care not who learns I am a woman."

"I know we use the pseudonym because most popular writers do it, but—"

"It adds mystery to a writer's allure. But if male writers can prosper under false names without public censure, I see no reason why a woman can't."

"Nor do I, madam."

"Then what is your problem here, Mary?"

"You must know that I am extremely proud that you have made such an impression on the world. But you have made it among literate people like dead King Richard and his cousin, the new king, as a writer of histories and fables and quests by purest knights. Minstrels may sing in the streets of . . . of *flesh*,"—she mouthed the last—"but we write for noble ladies' troubadours to learn our stories to recite after supper in the great halls. These women are refined."

"These women, Mary, have appetites for more rousing tales than poets tend to give them."

"But no English lady weaves a story of secular love so bawdy!"

"Then it is past time for the Nightingale to try her wings at romance."

"I am not opposed to writing more and earning more. I do like money, madam. But I doubt any Englishman will want to read this story from a woman's—a *dishonorable* woman's—point of view! No one will buy it! Even your agent in Calais has said we must be careful about how we construct the character of the hero and heroine for our patrons here as opposed to those on the Continent. For English readers, our characters in any work, adventure, or romance must be pure as driven snow! But for Frenchmen or Viennese, the more intemperate, the richer the sale! Nay, I say we will not profit from this if this romance is for an Englishman. Pigments, inks, vellum, and leather covers are very costly. I have helped you with the ledgers and I know our expenses."

"Mary, if you fear you will not be able to afford to send your share of next year's earnings home to your mother and her brood, cease your fretting."

The past year had been so profitable that Clare already had laid up enough gold coins in her coffer to pay her workers their annual stipend. Usually she paid them on Christmas Day. But she would not stand on ceremony this year. As soon as her father's illness took him from this world and she had seen him appropriately buried, she would dispense to her staff their rewards and leave Castle Trent and its problems forevermore. Then she would use the rest of her well-gotten gain to sail to France, where she would spend the rest of her life devoting herself only to her art. She would begin by using the precious collection of King Richard's handwritten memoirs to compose her life of him without interference from his successor, Henry. Richard had secretly sent them to her two months before he died, and she yearned to tell the world what torment he had endured at Henry's imprisonment. What's more, she'd do it with the French king's blessings, at his court with a new group of ladies to assist her who would be paid from that regent's pockets.

With the expectation of that artistic freedom and financial fortune about to become hers, Clare decided to calm Mary further by relating an embellishment of the truth. "No man wants this book, Mary. A woman has already commissioned this work. A wealthy countess who steadily grows richer. One who has always wished to meet a legendary man."

Mary wrinkled her nose, her rabbit's eyes warming slowly to the idea of her share of their newest patron's payment. "A man whose feats might rescue her from the burden of her dreary days?"

Clare did not believe that a man or a woman had the power to solve all trials and tribulations of their loved one. "I have seen a few partners who were joyful in each other's company, Mary. Their sharing seemed to ease life's vicissitudes and multiply its blessings. We will write that our lovers remain together at the end and live happily as possible ever after. Aye." Clare raised her palm against Mary's next argument. "I know that is not the favored convention for the conclusion to a romance. But the lady who wishes this tale told wants it that way. So shall it be."

Clare welcomed the challenge of producing a story she considered a fable. But she would also use the fairy tale to salve the wound carved by her belief that no man could cherish one woman solely, wholly, honorably till death parted him and his beloved.

She crumpled King Henry's letter in her hand. That man's decree made one aspect of her motive to write this romance clear. What she proposed to write was a story about a woman who could find a man to love and then surrender the course of her existence to him. Clare herself thought that real fiction, for she could never give herself to any man to control.

She was a woman who took the story of her life into her own hands. A woman who would foil her father after his death just as she had in life. A woman who would defy her king and this king's man—this Jordan Chandler, this fabled Dragon—who would come at Henry's command after the New Year to demand she marry his nephew.

But the Nightingale had a surprise in store for the illustrious Dragon. When he arrived at Castle Trent to carry her away and marry his nephew, he would find her gone. He could sit by the fire downstairs and hear the tale of the lady who had once lived in Castle Trent. One mortal woman who valued action above all and who flew away to create her own paradise.

Chapter One

SHE MUST BE PERFECT.

Blonde.

Blue-eyed.

Small-boned.

Harebrained.

But very well endowed.

The ideal woman for a wife.

Pretty. Please God, deaf and dumb. But filthy rich.

Jordan chuckled to himself, then spurred his horse. With a whicker, his black Flame objected.

Jordan could not fault the animal. It was torture to travel blindly through any blizzard. "Though these made of snow are more easily done than those made of men's and women's folly, eh?"

What an illusion to fashion this woman gorgeous!

"With my luck of late, I'll find myself betrothing my nephew to a harpy. No matter," he muttered to himself, "I'll do it even if she's bald, walleyed, and toothless!"

Though how could he in good conscience do that when he

knew the spark to this marriage's candlewick would be this issue of the bride's beauty?

But he must secure this union. He needed to conclude the nuptial agreement to burn brightly in his king's sight, just as he needed the bride's consent to come quickly to her marriage bed.

Certainly, there was little said about her to predict that outcome.

Rumor had made her legend.

Clare of Trent was the only wealthy woman along the war-torn Welsh marches who had managed to refuse all suitors since she was sixteen.

"Aged now," said one source.

Twenty-three, confirmed his own visitor to her father, the wily earl of Trent.

"A hermit," declared one companion of her sire.

"Silent," clarified his own friend, "when present. But so often absent from the great hall's table that people whisper she is given to much prayer upon her knees."

Jordan muttered so that the closest of his contingent might not hear him. "As long as she is given to much passion upon her back, she should become the model mate for a man who values such talents."

As a man who survived the turmoil of the past decade's civil wars, Jordan prided himself that he could look beyond his nose. It was the trait that helped him to see women and men for what they truly were. It was also this ability that forged him to his king's regard these past twenty-four years. As retainer. Adviser. Trusted friend.

Why should the matter of this marriage be any different from those other occasions when against all odds Henry the Fourth of England's Dragon had searched for facts, presented them, and dispelled the king's fears of treachery?

It wouldn't. He had assets to help him in most situations. For this journey, he had money, he thought, patting his belt beneath his cloak and breastplate. The leather was craftily folded and filled with fifty gold nobles from Henry's purse.

Jordan also had a dependable horse and two men, who were unfortunately less trustworthy than he wished. But in time of war, young men were at a premium, and these two would do for this marriage negotiation. Aye, he concluded, he had the means to accomplish his task quickly.

Still I would like to see her before I bargain for her.

But he wasn't seeing much. Not in this storm.

He yanked his cowl closer down his helm and brought his cloak more tightly across his mail tippet and breastplate. For this four-day journey, he had decreed that he and his two men should don light armor and put royal livery on the horses to scare off attacks by robbers, political adventurers, or Welsh raiders.

In this territory, so near the rebellious Welsh marches, Henry had wanted Jordan to take more men. But Jordan had argued that Henry needed every man he could for duties more dire than finalizing a nuptial agreement. In addition, his host, Aymer de Wallys, had a reputation for hiring enough men to protect his earldom from too much mayhem. But most important, Jordan wanted to make a wordless statement to the bride that he came without rancor to the bargaining table.

If only his goal could be accomplished so simply!

Ah, careful, man. The poison of your resentment against that sly fox Trent dyes the negotiations and taints the benefits to be gained from this quest.

Benefits.

Like peace.

And hope.

"Come along, Nathaniel," he bid the one of his two men who now returned from his rear reconnaissance to complain of the weather. "No grumbling. We'll be warming ourselves in Trent's great hall before long."

"I wish it to be so, my lord, but . . . how do you know if you've not been there before this?"

I was once. But few know. Not even the earl of Trent.

Jordan shot his newest retainer a withering look. For the boy to squeal like a stuck pig in the beauty of this soft white silence struck Jordan as irreverent. Nathaniel Pickering might be twenty, but in impertinence he was two. And nothing so roiled Jordan as a man's naivete in an atmosphere where one could die for it.

"Nathaniel," Jordan tried to take the ruefulness from his voice so that the youngster might learn to listen to everything that's told him—and remember it the first time. "I took the trouble to ask a few friends. We've come at a steady pace since midday. We'll arrive before supper is served."

"Lord Chandler!" Jordan's other man suddenly appeared, his cloak dusted so white with snow, he looked like a ghost. "I spotted a cottage ahead, across a little stream. There's a fire inside. We could ask shelter for the night!"

"Nay, Sir Wickham, we press on."

"But, my lord! The snow becomes more fierce with each breath we take! We cannot continue in this!"

"I say we can, Wickham, and we will. Did you find this lane passable?" he asked, memory serving up an impression that this area boded no good on a bright day. But speed was more important than comfort.

"Aye, sir," came the flat reply from Wickham. "As far as my mount could canter along such a treacherous path."

And you know much about treachery, coming from a family who benefited greatly from it, don't you, Wickham? Only after King Henry's victory at Shrewsbury in July had the Wickhams signed allegiance—and given considerable money from their overflowing coffers—to the monarch.

"The stream is shallow, my lord," Edward Wickham continued.

Jordan dug his spurs into his destrier's flanks and led the beast around his companions. They followed Jordan's lead down the ever-narrowing one-lane path through the forest.

Wickham would not give up. "But it is also glazed with ice. The rocks can be too slippery for—"

"We *will* press on, Wickham. I cannot tarry for a few flakes of snow. You know as well as I, our charge by King Henry is to conclude this negotiation for my nephew's betrothal and return to court forthwith."

"Surely, my lord, a night will be naught compared to injury or illness from exposure in this maelstrom!"

Jordan shut his eyes to Wickham's bleats. Would that he could stop up his ears, too. He disliked complainers, those who whined like wounded dogs upon the occasion of any impediment to their comfort. But in Wickham's instance, Jordan had to listen, didn't he?

"Watch this young man for me." Henry the Fourth of England had been explicit in his orders. "Record in that excellent mind of yours, Jordan, what passes in Edward Wickham's. Bring me back a betrothal for your over-amorous nephew, but return to me with an account of Wickham's every word and deed. Though my cousin Richard is dead, many still conspire to cheat me from my rightful hold on his crown. If the Wickhams band secretly with the Welsh rebel, Glendower, or other Englishmen against me, I must know. I weary of those conspirators who leave little trace of their desires but the cloud of their aspirations. It hangs over my head, over my throne and country. I must have more than the mist of their resentment. I must have evidence, Jordan. Proof to try and sentence those who would put me cooling in my coffin. If Wickham is one of those, I must place him molding in his grave. And quickly. Do me this service and know my finest reward."

Henry meant a greater title than the Baron Chandler. Yet he already owned a sizable plot of land along the Lancastrian shore which had brought him enough income to be comfortable. He considered doing nothing more for the remainder of his days than counting the profits from his wool trade.

Indeed, after his goals were accomplished in Trent, Jordan wanted no more from Henry than a rest from war and rebellion. A surfeit for the little that remained of his lifetime, because having passed his thirty-eighth birthday, he knew that most men his age were dead. Only a handful of years remained to him, if he was fortunate.

"Lord Chandler?"

Jordan concluded that obviously such a respite from his duties would not come here or now. "Aye, Nathaniel, what is it?" he asked, his eyes on the rush of the stream over the rocks.

"May I ask a bold question? I mean, I hope that over the course of this journey you and I have become enough fast friends that I might inquire. . . ."

"Do it, Nathaniel." This child's persistence outmarched his logic. Once trained to put the two in step, the lad might make an excellent retainer. Even a leader. "We have so little else to pass the time while we navigate these floes." Jordan had his black Arabian treading jagged rocks with the dexterity of a court acrobat.

"What if this Lady de Wallys is not as comely as her father's reports?"

"It matters not." *To me. Or Henry. Only to Geoffrey.* "The parchment is as good as signed." *Far from it, but I'll not say that to you or any man.*

"But your nephew is so often devoted to fair ladies, and this Lady de Wallys finds any excuse to refuse a suitor. She could reject him on the grounds that he likes women too well."

Jordan pretended to consider the gray sky. "I cannot speak for the lady, but I can say that my nephew, despite his appreciation for fair women, is ready to marry. At twenty, he is of the age, Nathaniel. Soon, I understand, 'twill be your turn."

"Aye, my lord. When this journey is ended, my father tells me I am to beg our king for leave to return home. My father has a match in mind."

Is that so? Jordan's horse emerged to the bank of the stream, and through the blur of snowflakes, he examined Nathaniel's petulant mouth. "You know the lady he has chosen?" *Odd that I do not. I thought I had the old earl's confidence in all matters.*

"Aye, sir. I saw her once years ago at a tournament. She had pimpled skin—but witch's hair, the color of spoiled cherries. Far from the courtly ideal or a man's desire, I swear."

"But Nathaniel, since then she may have changed, blossomed. I venture you were no picture of gentle knighthood then. You were—how old?"

"Fifteen."

"Ah. And she was?"

"Twelve."

"See there. She has had time to flower. Think back. She may have had other attributes. What of her manner? Her speech?" *Why did a young man not look beyond the outward evidences of a maiden to her inner virtues before he allowed his body to overrule his reason?*

Jordan grimaced, pulled his hood lower over his helmet against a sudden rush of snow and turned to lead his two men up the steep embankment. *Sweet hosannas, you should preach. You fell in love with a woman looking more at her appearance than her character. After she married your best friend, Malcolm, you took a host of other women to bed for their bodies not their ethics. Why should you fault this boy for his desire—normal but naive—to acquire a beauty in his bed?*

Jordan was about to ask her name when Edward Wickham chortled. "Aye! I remember a maid I met as a lad. She had two front teeth missing, a bird's nest of hair, and giant eyes, hellish as King Richard's coffin. Today she is a beacon of ebon beauty, outshining any blonde lady of lore. I prefer a dark lady to a lily white one."

Jordan narrowed his gaze into the gloom. Black tresses and glances comprised the reasons he had sworn himself off love. Diana Montaigne had cured him of professions of ardor with her lie that she loved him and would marry him above her father's objections. But her father had won that battle, declaring that Diana was his offering to his liege lord, Henry of Lancaster. What Diana had desired—Jordan for her husband—was no equal to the alliance of Diana's money and land with Henry's influence along the Welsh border. Jordan, loyal to his own feudal lord, Henry, and to his best friend, Malcolm Summersby, had accepted the marriage of the wealthy, landed Diana to the impoverished earl of Summersby.

Since that day Diana married Malcolm ten years ago, Jordan had coupled only with willing widows. Before he even spread them upon their beds, he put up his stipulation. He came to frolic only, never to marry. But lately, though his partners were eager and skilled, he found the exercise as exciting as a purgative—and just as draining to his soul.

That certainly made him think he approached his dotage!

He'd lost his appetite for love quite suddenly after the carnage of the battle of Shrewsbury. He didn't think his loss due to his lack of strength or technique or innovation. In fact, he knew a comely dowager marchioness who declared how well pleased she was with what she called his knightly services. She had demonstrated her joy to him repeatedly until she cornered him alone in the king's chapel one day, slithered off her cloak, and revealed her naked intentions. She'd offered herself there in a pew. He had refused. Mayhaps that had sent him hurtling into celibacy . . . and to this general boredom with any female.

Now, he yearned only to be at his duty.

Getting a wife for his nephew.

Gaining money—and an unwilling but necessary ally—for his king.

Obtaining his own permanent retirement from the fray of court politics. Intrigues. Murders.

In the vacant silence of the snow-swept night, he distinctly heard the swift hiss of weapons drawn.

He flung back his cowl and dropped his helm's visor across his face. He shot up one hand to halt his two men while his other slid into the leather strap of his traveling shield, then reached for the deadly comfort of his sword.

"My lord?" croaked Nathaniel.

Jordan sliced the air to stifle him. He felt Wickham come abreast, his broadsword at the ready. Jordan brandished his own long blade and reined his horse into position for attack. The three, as prearranged, formed a triangle of defense, swords drawn to their challenge in right hand, lethal misericordes in the left.

The minute sifted like sultry sands as tell-tale hooves on

slick ground whispered, picked, then churned the earth. Years of working Henry's will on far-flung fields from Ireland to bloody Shrewsbury had Jordan estimating the number, speed, and purpose of this band.

He counted.

Five.

Mounted.

Armed.

But *where?*

Two there. And there.

Two sprang upon them from the copse. The third and fourth drove at them at an angle that pinched them toward the stream.

The fifth?

Where could he be?

Jordan met the first of the four, bucklers clanging, swords crossing until he wore his opponent down and lunged, the sharp point of death's grace delivered to the brigand's bare throat. The man fell, a heavy blot upon the earth.

Jordan spun. Where was the fifth?

Not here.

So where? *Where?*

Nathaniel was too sore beset by one real man for Jordan to seek clues to a phantasm.

Jordan jabbed his horse, who knew so well this turmoil and how to best it. The animal performed his master's will with skill of years' bloodletting.

Nathaniel raised his arms, ducking from repeated blows. Fast to his side, Jordan advanced upon Nathaniel's opponent and, rising in his saddle, saw the man wore no mail! With a cry of righteousness, Jordan buried his blade into the man's tough gizzard. Surprise lit the fiend's eyes. He doubled, babbling in his blood, to hit the ground.

Jordan and Nathaniel whirled about.

Two brigands forced Edward down the bank so hard, so fast that his horse stumbled and slipped. In such uncertain footing, Edward could do naught but protect himself with one arm crossed over his head. That's when the other man sank an axe into Edward's thigh—and it stuck there. He swooned and fell from his horse, one foot caught in the stirrup.

Cursing, Jordan shouted to draw the two men from Edward toward him and Nathaniel. The outlaws turned in unison, one going for Nathaniel, one baring brown teeth at Jordan.

"To me, you dog!" Jordan roared.

The cur's cracked lips spread wide in a feral grin. "Never doubt it, Dragon!"

Jordan registered that the man knew who he was. Jordan vowed then that this man would die here and now for his impertinence and swagger.

But the man was big. As large as Jordan. Few foes had so well matched him. And where they had in height or weight, they had no agility to aid them.

Yet this man was quite different from any other man Jordan had faced. This man was Jordan's twin of evil's spawn. So equal, so exact that he wildly thought he fought some darker portion of himself. As if . . . as if someone had cut and tailored this contest to the two with cunning precision.

A cry of vengeance tore from Jordan's lungs as the absurd thought hit him. They clashed broadswords, blow to blow, a hefty challenge to the other.

Still Jordan forced him down the bank and at such an incline, he took the advantage. His adversary knew it. Fear flashed within his eyes. It was the only sign Jordan needed.

One moment's fail of arrogance and Jordan was sore upon the churl.

The man broke and turned his mount to flee.

Jordan would not allow it.

The brigand's horse was sure. Nimble as Jordan's famous Flame, but not as fast.

The man raced across the ravine, Jordan half a heartbeat behind him. But when he gained the top, the attacker earned flat ground's advantage, and his horse sprinted away just as Jordan's charger gained the precipice. Jordan jabbed his spurs into his mount, and the two united in the effort that had gained both man and beast renown in Henry's service.

Jordan grinned. Through brush and snow-laden thicket, he and Flame burned a path toward their goal.

As if stopped by a wizard's hex, Jordan's quarry skidded to a halt and backed to a notch of rock. Jordan noted the odd ploy but charged forward, brandishing his sword for the thrust that would end this contest.

But from his right side, he heard the fifth rider whom he had counted but never seen.

This man galloped forward—but unlike his companions, he wore armor—and he rushed toward Jordan with a lance bracketed against his breastplate.

Jordan blinked, cursed that his own buckler was so small a shield, and focused on the other man's long weapon, which was used only on battlefields. Not ambushes! But this lance's point—good Christ—was *blunted*. And the fool aimed the three-pronged weapon at Jordan's left shoulder when his throat or groin would have been smarter and . . .

Scarce had the idiocy of the man's target hit Jordan than he knew his intent!

No death for me! Not clean or quick. Capture's what this outlaw craves. . . .

Why?

Instinct made him raise his shield with left arm while his right hand wielded his sword to go for the only unprotected portion of the man's body—his thighs and manhood.

But before he could cut the man from his children, the blunted lance slammed into Jordan, ramming against the shoulder which had stood against so many.

He reeled and the world exploded.

He felt the familiar pop of ball from socket. The poker of pain that seared his torso, then his brain. A soundless cry of torment left his lips while his mind, logical beyond the frustration of his weakness, asked why he fell to this well-planned attack by a phantom in the snow.

He thudded to the ground. His sword fell from his hand. The snow chilled his helmet, but he swore he'd keep his mind. He would not faint.

Trussed quick as a pig to slaughter, he bit his lip to keep from screaming out his hatred and his anguish. But his attackers would never hear him. God's blood, they would not. Jordan offered his Maker words of praise for His good gift of his uncommon strength of will.

Never had any foe of Henry's Dragon doused his dedication! Nor would that change tonight.

Not as the fiends tore his buckler from his left arm and yanked his hands behind him. Nor as they twined ropes about his wrists and ripped his helmet from his head so fast he thought his nose went with it.

As they shoved a rag into his mouth, he rolled his head backward, the better to see who his attackers were. Before they could blindfold him, he realized he found no one he knew.

He forced the fetid cloth forward in his mouth and ground his teeth. Ropes and gags might do their will. But never would they bind his determination. Nor chain his mind to—

Horses?

Beyond dazed misery of dislocated shoulder and wrenching bondage, Jordan felt the earth pound with more hooves. There were more of these outlaws?

He froze.

His attackers paused. Ceased their struggles to lift his bucking body from the ground to the horse they'd drawn toward him.

"Who could that be?" spat one.

"We were promised that none of Trent's men would go in these woods when we attacked Chandler!"

"These are fairies then?" ridiculed the other. "Christ, gain cover!"

"But Chandler—?"

"Leave him!"

They scrambled away.

Through pain-glazed eyes, Jordan peered into the graying night. Ear to the earth, he heard the buzzing of the newest swarm of hornets to this hive.

Six?

No, seven.
Mounted.
Armed?
Not upon warhorses, but . . .
Oh, hell. Palfreys???
They thundered into the clearing, a phalanx on females' horses.

Jordan spit out the poorly tied gag and muttered about fantasies of warrior-women. As he picked at the ropes around his wrists and flung them away, his Amazons circled the troop who tried to take him. He sprang to a sitting position and inched backward into a thick bush for cover.

His eyes darted to the women's leader, a tall beauty standing in her saddle, shouting orders. He marveled at her tactics, her analysis of how to best these brutes and take them down with speed. She urged her women on into a fury of destruction, circling the brigands, squeezing them into a tight nut of panic. Two women shot arrows from horseback—and even in the blur of snow, they hit their marks. Two others sported daggers, tossing them with a nefarious ease that pricked two of his attackers like pincushions.

One brigand, scarce a foot away, sprang forward to bellow an order at his friends. The next second saw him sinking to his knees, an arrow piercing his throat and silencing all his future mandates.

Jordan snatched up the man's dagger with his good right hand and vaulted to his feet. Two females, who had sported small wood axes and dismounted, now found themselves sore beset by two men who believed hand combat their best defense. But women were no match for men in blood lust, and it took three women to try to pry one man off a friend. They clawed and gouged his eyes until one skewered him with her own dagger.

A cry pierced the air.

Jordan spun, seeing the leader yanked, kicking and screaming from her horse. Her attacker grabbed her by the shoulders to face him. She kneed him. He swooned, loosened his grip on her, and she sagged. But not far enough to leave his grasp. He whirled her around, struck her across the face, then shouted of how he'd rape her before he killed her. Trudging toward the woods, he dragged her backward by her braid, a brazier in the alabaster evening. Jordan could have found her in Hades for all the brilliance of her crown.

He grimaced, the taste for this man's guts filling his mouth with sour joy.

He ran bent, his left arm hanging, and in one roar, he threw himself upon him. They tumbled. In the roll, Jordan's shoulder circled in his flesh. The hot shock boiled his brain but not his warrior's perception. His right hand and arm prevailed by grasping the outlaw's. His left arm swung across the fiend's windpipe, gouging him and blocking his air. The man purpled. Jordan sank his entire weight upon his left arm, pressed the man's jugular until the churl's right hand weakened. Then, in one righteous stroke, Jordan struck his misericorde into the brigand's heart.

Jordan's nostrils flared. The stench of death nauseated him. Would he ever be free of it? Please God . . .

"Deliver him," the rescued woman prayed.

He glanced up. Stood.

She peered down at the lifeless body, panting, open-mouthed, hand across her chest. But he knew she saw nothing.

With anguish blazing through his shoulder and the rush of victory flooding the rest of him, he, too, looked—and gazed down upon a flesh-and-blood woman far more fabulous than words.

Chapter Two

A BRIGHT FLAME, SHE GLOWED AGAINST THE MISTY GRAYS OF winter's dusk. A vivid vision of yellows, reds, and whites. With a smudge of ashes on her sculpted cheek!

He shut his eyes. He shook his head. He almost laughed! That novelty alone had him reeling.

You are a warrior, Chandler, not a poet.

He forced himself to look at her again and view her humanity in cold terms.

She stared past him, transfixed in horror at the brigand's death.

She was no weak blonde, no watery-eyed waif, but those essences a troubadour would declare too lusty for any right-thinking man to desire, lest he lose his soul.

With that dark stain of ashes on her, she looked like a princess who stooped to stoke her kitchen fires.

She stoked his senses. His right hand burned to wipe the stain away while his gaze absorbed her.

Her eyes shown bronze. Her hair, escaping from her thick braid, tumbled in copper curls to her cloak. Her skin had been whisked pink by wind and dire exertion, while snow-flakes dusted her russet eyelashes with intricate embroidery.

She brought forth tears but did not shed them. Instead, she threw back her head in defiance of the circumstances.

But then she smiled at him. Compassion lit her beauty to greater radiance.

She was a sunbeam of a woman.

And her face grew red already from where that brute had struck her.

"Sir, I repeat you are not well. Your shoulder hangs at an odd angle. . . . Sir?" She placed a palm to his chest, and through his layers of breastplate and tunic he felt her concern.

"Aye," He found his tongue, his eyes falling to her hand. For blithe seconds he had forgotten everything except what pleasure he would feel to hold such glory in his arms. "This I can endure. But you are very hurt." His finger raised her chin so that he might look at the hideous sight of creamy skin marred by violence. "We must get you home to draw the swelling. He did not break your cheekbone, I hope?" He winced at the idea.

"Nay," she said, her eyes searching his. "You are kind to think of me, good sir, when it is you who has the more terrible condition. Mine is only bruising, but yours is a recurring problem, I take it from your nonchalance."

"Unfortunately, aye. 'Tis a dislocation for which there is only a temporary cure." Her hand lingered on his apprecia-tive body. He tried to clear his head, but the uncommon sight of a woman hurt and more concerned for him than herself dulled his pain.

"Will you allow me to assist you and put it back in place?"

Jordan cradled the limb, which hung oddly forward. About him and this bedazzling woman, her bevy of women sheathed their swords and daggers, shouting to each other of each outlaw's condition. The women's victory had made them proud and boisterous as men. "I assure you, my lady, after I have seen to my two men—and these who have attacked us, you may do for me."

When he strode toward Nathaniel, she kept pace beside him. "My women are quite able to truss any of these brigands still alive or indeed"—she glanced about and discovered what destruction her women had really wrought—"to pile up the bodies. They can also aid your two while I set you aright."

Jordan saw the truth of her statement as Nathaniel hopped up to him, supported by one accommodating black-haired woman.

The lad was shaken but whole and, by his wobbly smile, well pleased by his striking assistant. "It's my ankle, my lord. I twisted it myself in my haste to do that fellow in."

Jordan nodded. "You did well. Put no weight on your afflicted foot lest that injury grow worse. We'll get you tightly bandaged and—"

"We can do that for you and put him atop his horse." The woman beside Jordan persisted in her own purpose. "Let me see to you, good sir, before you faint."

"I assure you, madam, this has happened to me so often that fainting—were it even tempting—would be a temporary charm against this woe. Pardon me, but I have men to care for." *And an ambush to decipher. By men who knew my name. My location. And what else, only those who employed them could say.*

Jordan swung back to consider this gorgeous creature before him. His gaze narrowed on her features—her peaked brows, upturned nose, determined chin, and lips far too ripe for most to call true beauty. A new thought—and a malicious one—crossed his mind. *I do not know who you are or how you happened to come upon us so conveniently.*

"You whiten with the pain again, sir. I say you are too stubborn for your own good." She pushed back a lock of her glowing hair and peered at him through the lace of snow. Her cheeks flushed with an indignant anger and she jammed two hands on her hips. "What ails you besides your shoulder, sir? You look at me oddly, and yet I might remind you that you are the stranger to this land. Who . . . ?"

Something about what she'd just said made her stop and think. Then she shot a glance at the green and white livery of his horse. "My lord," she murmured, and Jordan wondered if she were cursing him or praying to God. "Who are you?"

She took a step closer and examined his features. "These woods belong to a kindly shepherd. I know him and his family. But I do not know you. Why do you and your small band pass here?"

Jordan had his wounded men to aid. "I am the king's man, so you can well understand my haste and my concern for my men." He turned to see to them.

She hastened to keep up with him as he walked toward the place where he'd left Edward. Jordan continued his reconnaissance through brush and gorse to find his man reclining in the snow. The ax that had pierced his thigh lay on the ground near its horrendous handiwork. Jordan concluded that the pretty blonde maid who cooed to him brought him as much relief with her looks as she did with her hands. Still had she done good service by Edward, stanching his blood with a torn bit of cloth. Jordan supposed it was this little dove who had also removed the ax from Edward's gaping wound.

Jordan knelt in the gore-stained snow. "Let me see him."

"He needs," insisted the lady in charge as she followed him down beside his man, "to be bathed, cauterized, set, and sewn."

Edward agreed between clenched teeth.

Jordan knew the damage such weapons could cause. They could not only cut major blood vessels so severely that the hurt man could watch his life drain from him in minutes but also they could hack bones so badly, the man prayed for death to deliver him some relief. Then, if he survived both those conditions, he had to hope no putrid matter formed to eat away his flesh. Through the long recovery, the patient needed a positive nature to bolster his efforts to once more sit, stand, and walk.

Jordan tried to give Edward some of that healing power in his words. "By the grace of God, man, I'd say this wound is not half an inch deep and only as long as my hand."

"Agreed, my lord. These ruffians were so poor at their

trade"—he tried to laugh but lost it to a grimace—"they used small weapons."

"Aye, Edward. You'll live." Though Jordan would not wager one penny sterling Edward would do so easily without a warm, dry room to welcome him—and soon. "We'll make an unexpected call upon those who live in that cottage you spied."

"We'll stop his blood first," said the lady of the bright hair and eyes. "Then we will take him to a far better place than the shepherd's cottage."

Jordan lifted both brows at her.

"My home is Castle Trent." Her pert nose tipped up in authority, and Jordan's years of experience in divining truth amid its camouflages declared who his sunbeam might be.

Trent. Of course, that would be where this lady lived.

Who else would wander woods at will in the middle of a winter's storm? Who else in this clime could afford to employ as many handmaids? Who could seize the strength of will or skill at arms to lead retainers in an assault such as he had witnessed here? Only a headstrong woman, used to her freedom, would dare to break such conventions.

"Then you *are* Clare de Wallys."

Her gilded eyes dashed to Flame's livery. Her expression crystallized. "And you are King Henry's Dragon."

He nodded once.

She shut her eyes. When she opened them again, she seemed distant, cold. Like a brilliant star burned out. "You have come earlier than we expected. Three months sooner than planned, Baron Chandler."

He nodded slightly, observing etiquette in such a delicate situation. Telling himself he did it for protocol, he ignored the voice which whispered that he did it to see her sparkle once more. "Aye, my lady, I am pleased to meet you."

Her nostrils flared. He might be termed the Dragon, but she breathed the fire here tonight. "I cannot say the same. Why are you here so early and unannounced? You come into our lands without many men to protect you and do not send us word? I never thought the legendary Jordan Chandler reckless."

Jordan sent her a look of reproof. The others were listening, trying to cover their interest by keeping busy. By such initial encounters were many judged. He would not be misperceived as weak or foolish. Yet, whatever else he was, he had always been temperate in the treatment of his foes. And while it was still questionable if she shared her father's double-dealing nature and, therefore, fully qualified as his own enemy, Jordan would not be underestimated by her— or her father. So he engaged her in a flank attack. "Even to an emissary such as I, manners are important, my lady."

She skewered him with narrowed eyes. "You avoid my question."

"And you, my lady, ignore the public circumstances."

"I have no secrets from my retinue about this marriage."

"Really?" He pursed his lips. "Is information about other matters here in Trent as free from you? I have a thing or two I need to know about you, and I would much rather hear it from your lips than anyone else's."

She was grinding her teeth. "You are shrewd."

"A requirement of my position." He arched a brow at her and saw that unlike most women treated to this superior attitude of his, she did not recoil. He smiled and relented a little. "I will reveal why I am here when I stand before you *and* your father. For now, you need only be polite."

"What care I for niceties when all I wish for in this world can be snatched from me with your slightest word?"

He lowered his voice. "I will not deprive you of your dignity unless you leave me no other choice. I bid you to have a care, madam, for what you say to me."

"Aye, for I have heard the tale that when the Dragon's anger is incited," she said as she turned to pass from one of her women to another a wineskin down to Edward's eager lips, "people die."

Everyone in the clearing froze.

But Jordan kept up his facade of indifference. "That is an old story."

"And true?"

"That depends on how you tell it." He smiled with the

grim grace he'd learned from Henry's French and Viennese tutors of diplomacy. Its power caused two women before him to cower.

But not Clare. "I must hear your version sometime."

"There is no need to discuss it, madam. Not even with my friends." His chilling tone made her vibrate with hot anger. *Good.* Her head snapped up from her ministrations. She was shocked, he knew, at the look of objectivity he gave her. 'Twas the one he gave any and all who dared to cross swords with him. Part of him was pleased that he had conquered her. Part of him mourned the cruelty of suppressing so worthy an opponent. "For now, I will say it matters not who I am or what my past may tell of me. I was told you agreed to this marriage to my nephew."

She shot up like an arrow, walked around him, supervising two of her women who tried to find the strongest tree limbs to fashion into a stretcher for Edward.

Jordan came up behind her. "Madam? If I have traveled four days through winter weather under false assurances by your father, Henry will be furious."

"What you mean to say is that Henry will take my land without benefit of marriage."

If he could have taken it without your consent or your father's cooperation, he would have years ago. "The king and I have been friends for twenty-four years. Many men do not even live that long. Fewer can claim a friendship of that length. So I can easily say I know my liege lord well and can declare that the man is fair."

Her eyes grew hard as her words. "Will you next tell me that this fair man did not imprison his cousin King Richard and then did not kill him to gain his crown?"

"Henry did confine Richard after he abdicated but still sought to stir up trouble among his former subjects. Henry would not permit that. But kill Richard? Nay. That story is popular fiction, and your summary is too brief to be an accurate portrayal of the real characters or plot."

Jordan loathed this subject, this everlasting question among the English about how the last king had died—and who, if anyone, had ordered his demise. He himself had investigated Richard's death at Henry's command and had found no definite evidence of murder. In fact, Jordan had left the scene of Richard's last days at Pontefract Castle with one troubling conclusion about how the thirty-three-year-old monarch had died. Within that conclusion was no suspicion, however, that Harry of Lancaster may have ordered his cousin's death.

"I tell you, lady, that the king is honorable. He takes nothing from anyone without just cause that they may try to take more from him. Your father is the proof. The earl, whose loyalty Henry thought he had purchased with many coins and favors, gave counterfeit in return, yet does your sire breathe. The earl of Trent should count himself fortunate that he has not lost his lands and titles before this. As for you, Henry does not ask you to relinquish your private wealth or your mother's lands. He agrees to let you manage them yourself."

"How generous of him," she chided. "What could make him agree now after I asked it of him for four years passed?"

Jordan cocked a brow. Henry could not dally with the de Wallyses any longer. During the past four years of his reign, Henry had tolerated too much independence from the earl of Trent. Now the Welsh rebels whom Henry sought to keep from England's door—and Trent's—advanced. Their leader, Glendower, was a crafty soul and might even try to align himself with the earl of Trent. If the earl or his wily daughter decided to cooperate with Glendower, the rebel leader and his army could gain access to the roads across the earldom into the heart of England. If such an accord were contemplated or had been signed, then Jordan's task was to nullify it by a marriage contract and possession of Trent by the king's forces. But he had to see first what this woman and her father knew of Glendower's actions so that he might gauge their loyalties. "You will have to ask the king why he agrees to this condition yourself. I know only I have a parchment in my saddle which confirms it."

"You do?" That paled her skin. But by the time he

nodded, she had recovered her composure. "Lord Chandler, those two stipulations my father presented to Henry as bargaining points."

"Delaying tactics," he corrected.

She widened her eyes at him. "And they worked well. It took Henry the four years he has been on the throne to get into Trent with one of his messengers."

"For four years Henry has held the Welsh rebel, Glendower, from England's door along the marches as well as dealt with northern nobles who wished to make Trent another bloody field like Shrewsbury. Now that Henry has secured some peace here, he wants more of it and quickly. Your wish to remain independent of Henry, England, and my nephew weighs very lightly against those needs.

"Believe me, Clare." His use of her given name surprised him and satisfied him as it slipped over his tongue with ease. "Your wishes will see *no* light of day unless you are amiable and try to gain Henry's favor. I urge you to a more agreeable tone because Henry is, despite all his military prowess, a logical and learned man who likes poetry, painting, and the fine points of diplomatic words. He appreciates good manners in men and women."

"Can good manners buy me what I want? I am, at heart, just the daughter of a marcher lord."

"You are a comely woman with stout-hearted supporters and friends"—he nodded toward her troupe—"who will outlive her parent's folly."

"Only if I agree to a living death by marrying—"

"My nephew? Give you a living death?" Jordan let out a sound he surprisingly termed a guffaw. "Geoffrey hasn't hurt a fly since he was ten. That summer he caught frogs and dissected them until he knew their insides so well he dreamt of them. One he willfully crippled and hated himself for the perversion. The next day he had warts—a hideous profusion of them—all over his body. The village physician said he'd gotten them from the frogs. The local witch declared he'd gotten them as a curse for killing and maiming wild creatures. After that, Geoffrey took to studying small delicate animals of all kinds. He collects samples of ones already dead. In fact, he fills his bedchamber with them—and books." *And girls.*

Clare de Wallys stared, clearly impressed at the last revelation. "Your nephew is a learned man?"

When he is not educating himself on the finer points of bedsport. "Aye. He reads, he ponders, he argues philosophy and religion with anyone who has half a mind to wrestle with him."

"Unusual."

"What is not is that he wants a wife." *A regular playmate he need not pay for in rare coin. A noble woman who will instead fill his empty coffers, his vacant nursery—and thus ensure his title does not pass to me.*

"I venture he does not want a wife who's aged."

"Twenty-three is a ripe age."

Shock of his knowledge about her made her blink. "But if your nephew is wise, he should desire a woman who is willing."

"Aye, he does that," Jordan agreed as he spread an open hand over his face to wipe pain's perspiration from his furrowed brow. "He also wants one modestly quiet."

Her full lips firmed. She tilted her head and her eyes danced. "Many wish I were dumb."

His mouth twitched with unexpected mirth. He liked her pluck if not the subject of her humor. "Only because you have loudly refused every man within a mile of you, aye."

"With good reason."

He glanced about at her retinue of females. A new thought on what that reason might be struck him as hard as had the blunted lance. That a glory such as she might find more joy in women than with any man suddenly made him suck in his breath. "Do you tell me that you do not care for men?"

"Now or ever have I found one to merit my respect or affection. They seem too bloodless. They want power, money, and women in profusion—and not to any end which benefits the rest of humanity."

"There are a few who crave none of that."

"I have not met one."

Ah, but today you have.

"Enough of this!" She waved a hand to dismiss their argument. "We debate over dead bodies—and fetid issues that need more discussion than the weather allows. Will you let me help you so that we might retire to a warm fire before which we might continue to bare our teeth at each other?"

He grinned, knowing full well the expression must have reflected the agony of his injury. "With such a view of men, how am I to know whether or not you will rip out my arm?"

"With such a view of me, how am I to know whether or not you will rip out my heart? Or do you think I have one?"

His features fell. "I have done with death and destruction, my lady de Wallys. Believe me or not, I really cannot care, but after these negotiations for your hand are done, I return to court, and only briefly. Then I retire to my long-neglected home. Fix my arm into my shoulder, if you will, but leave off with measuring me by other men's dimensions."

He glanced about, found a rock, and sat on it. "Please," he asked in recompense for his harshness. "Now."

She stood, wary of his sudden change of heart.

"For what you will do for me, I will be grateful. 'Tis a task I cannot perform easily myself, though when I was younger, the chore of repairing my crooked body was simpler. Now, like the rest of me, my bones are creakier."

Her eyes danced up his arms, across his chest, and up to his hair. "Sir, you may have a few strands of gray at your temples, but you are not yet elderly!"

"Oft times I think like you, but then with each succeeding injury to this shoulder, the manipulation to put it back in place becomes more painful. It becomes more unbearable, I do think, than leaving the bone out of its hole. But logic always overcomes the urge." He knew he was talking too much, but it took his mind from his pain. "The agony of its dislocation, while tolerable because I know to expect it, eats away at me—and I would seek relief."

"The injury happens more and more often then?"

"Aye, the last time was at the Battle of Shrewsbury in

33

July," he babbled. "I took an arrow in the thigh. I fell from my horse. The shoulder popped. The arrow broke. I blanked out. When I awakened, 'twas dusk."

"But the arrow was still inside you?"

"Aye," he said, remembering the torment of extracting it himself.

"Good God," she breathed, "you cannot tell me you removed it yourself?"

He nodded, the pain of this episode blending with the recollection of the last occasion. " 'Twas simple. I took a dead knight's dagger and cut a wider hole, reached in"—he fought to breathe—"and removed the shaft."

"Most men could never force themselves to such an act."

"Sometimes you must not think, only do what is necessary."

"But didn't you faint? What of your shoulder and arm?"

"Afterward, I walked about for God knows how long, unable to find a cohort alive enough and thereby strong enough to assist me. I finally decided to try to do the deed myself or else demand the surgeon amputate. But I was loath to lose even my left arm. I searched that wretched battlefield for a wagon big enough or one still standing that could brace my weight for the jerk of bone on bone."

"And did you find one?"

"I came upon two young squires in the surgeon's tent. 'Twas they who persuaded me to let them try to reset it in the socket."

"How did you withstand the pain? How can you every time?" she marveled.

"I am a fighting man, my lady. I have my ways." Over the years, he had learned to focus his ravaged mind on some fantasy. At Shrewsbury the only thing that saved his sanity was his usual diversion.

He gazed at Clare de Wallys.

Like lightning, he knew his regular distraction in such cases was insufficient. Creating bawdy verses appealed to him not half so much as visions of what he and this sunbeam might do if he could strip her to her flawless skin.

He warmed at the thought.

Irreverent, Chandler. She is a lady.

But what a woman!

She will never know your secrets. This—or any others. Do it! And see the end of your pain.

He raised a skeptical brow. "Setting a shoulder requires strength. I am not a small man."

Her eyes drifted across his shoulders, and she nodded. "Nor a cowardly one."

At her words and her gaze, the heat in his body flared higher—and lower. "Should I wonder that you know how to set my shoulder?"

Chastised but unbowed, she cast him a tolerant look, then looked to see that her women were still occupied. They dashed about to put order to the scene, cooing over his two men and collecting everyone's horses and weapons. "I once had a brother who suffered this same affliction," she explained. "I performed this relief for him often." She wafted one hand, and two of her contingent scurried forward.

"My lady, what will you?" asked one as Jordan's gaze shifted to the other. Only to snap back.

These two were twins.

"Mary, Margaret, help me with this man. His shoulder is out of joint."

One rubbed her hands in glee. "Of course."

The other frowned. "I can't."

Clare was not moved. "You can. You will."

He chuckled, surprising himself and stopping short.

Clare shot him a diminishing look, though she sent her twins away with an order to bring forth his horse. When they had gone to do her will, she cut him with sharp words. "You cannot be in too much pain, my lord, to laugh at one of mine who is insubordinate."

"Forgive me, my lady. 'Tis poor payment for one who has assisted me and mine so ably." He stepped nearer. In this brief space, he could inhale the musk of woman mixed with soap, geranium, and those infernal ashes!

He cleared his head. "Do pardon me, my lady. I see you dislike those who will contest you."

"'Tis no crime."

"I, too, value retainers who obey me."

"Then you'll not encourage mine in disrespect." She leaned forward to finger the point of his shoulder and run her hands down to his. Her touch became a balm—and a terrible delight. He flinched at his own weakness of the flesh.

"Don't move," she crooned, and continued her explorations.

What moved was far from his shoulder.

With eyes straight ahead and teeth grit, he watched while her twins approached, leading his giant Flame.

Clare pushed up his mail tippet from his shoulder to his throat and examined the contours of his breastplate. With the lady's movement nearer, he found the intoxication of her gentleness dearer than any other woman whose hands had laid upon him in many months. Indeed, if *length* were what impressed him, he could declare his body sprang forth with a rigor which tore his mind from the nagging limpness of his other limb. "We must remove your breastplate and tunic."

Quickly would be best.

"Can you do it?"

Never doubt it.

"Let me help you."

The best way.

Her fingers flew over buckles and laces, then went to his belt. He noted with satisfaction that she took great care with it and each other item, handing them to her maid, whom she ordered to hold them. When she had him bared to his skin, she bit her lower lip. Brushing the hair on his chest as lightly as an angel's touch, she splayed her fingers across the width of his chest. When he sucked in his breath, she curled up her fingers and swallowed at the sight of him. His skin prickled. One portion of his body stiffened.

"You're cold," she murmured.

On fire.

"Mount."

He blinked. *"What?"*

She inclined her head toward his horse. "Sir, do you or do you not wish me to put your bones to rights?"

He clamped his teeth to keep the guffaws down. "Aye, my lady." *One bone would be best.* "But I must have relief now before I ride anywhere."

She rolled those luminous eyes to heaven. "Of course. How do you normally do it?"

In any way you say.

She pressed her lips together, tolerance incarnate. "We should spread you like an eagle over a table."

I'd like to spread you like a bird of paradise over my bed.

"Face down."

Or up. Against a wall. In a chair. In meadows filled with sunshine, no rival to your hair.

"Lord Chandler?"

"Hmmm?"

"Have you never done it that way?"

"With you, I would try anything."

"Good. To let your arms hang is best, you know, so that I can get beneath you."

"My thought exactly."

"But since we're not at home and have no flat bed, we'll do the next best thing and use your horse."

He'd found good service from his horse on many a needy occasion of lust, but with this woman he'd want every indulgence he could buy from man and God. Silk sheets to hold her. Feathers to tease her. Ermine to please her. And time. Whole nights. Long hot days.

"I'm going to have to pull you into shape."

Sounds good but rather unnecessary at the moment.

"Are you ready?"

Like I haven't been in months.

"Good. Then put your foot in the stirrup and drape your body over your horse's back."

Jordan cast her a withering look.

"I know it's rather . . . ummm . . ." She toyed with a giggle, then cleared her throat. "Undignified."

He hooked his foot in one stirrup. "But something a king's man can endure."

She nodded. "You won't be sorry. I'm good at healing people. A better physician than many I've met. At least, I've never killed anyone."

"Not even a royal messenger?" he teased.

"If you don't climb up there, I will murder you to put you from your misery."

He chuckled as he swept up and down over his horse. In the doing, he forgot to have a care for that part of him he'd most like tended by her.

He felt a poker of pain from groin to eyeballs.

Damn, but this woman should rush. Besides, he thought as he shifted to rearrange his manhood and his taut testicles, he hadn't ever looked at Flame upside down. What a brute he was. Well hung. And eager for some female palfrey in this group. "Hurry, madam. My head pounds." *And it is difficult to keep my mind on bawdy doings while I am face to belly with a smelly steed who's earned a good rest as much as I.*

She came within his scope, flung out a blanket over the snowy ground, and slithered under him.

He liked her from this vantage very much.

"You're smiling," she said with satisfaction as she took hold of his upper arm with one hand and braced him and herself with a palm flattened to his shoulder. "That's vital to our work," she crooned. Then jerked.

He saw stars.

Millions.

Shooting. Flashing. Bright white bursts of pain that dyed to blue, then red, and all the yellows of the sun.

Her hands caressed his brows, his cheeks, his mouth. "My lord Chandler," she urged him to remain conscious, succeeding in catching his attention with his given name upon her lips. "Jordan. You are restored. I promise you. This is a terrible condition, but you have survived it once again."

Her voice flowed like sweet medicine to his stunned brain. And to his flesh—his face and shoulders—her hands brought honeyed succor.

"My lord Chandler, look at me. Aye," she soothed while her fingers brushed his rough beard, then traced his ragged scar across his cheek, "your trial is passed now. Let me help you down. At Castle Trent we have a fire fit for a man who rides so far, so fast, and fights for women with such fury."

He smiled down at her. Her hair, much loosened now with her activity, curled upon the blue blanket. The color put him in mind of his own family's azure. The velvet counterpane upon the baron's bed at Chandler Grove. Used too little for decades. But waiting for him—and a wife who never was.

"You have done me a great service, Clare."

His use of her name didn't shock her as much as it struck him how easily he uttered it. While he caught his breath, she returned his grin.

"See then, sir, you remember it as you visit us these next few days. I like my name better than my titles," she explained at his inquiring look. "My name is mine, a reflection of my individuality, not my paternity or politics. Come along." She pushed herself back and up to a sitting position, then stood and extended one hand to help him.

He was already removing himself from his horse and standing down. As she came around him, her joy at his recovery showed in her expression.

She commanded one of her servants to promptly bring over his tunic. "I don't think you should don the armor. It would require too much exertion. Besides, I will create a sling to rest your arm and protect it from strain."

He took his tunic and belt. "I agree 'twould be good for me, Clare." He liked the way her name tasted on his lips, and he crinkled his eyes at her in a warmth she returned. "But not best for you. Your woods do not seem safe, and should we come upon another band, you'll be glad I have some defenses left so that I might protect you." He donned his tunic but fumbled with the heavy belt.

She batted his hands away and scolded him, "You won't heal that shoulder that way. Let me." He inhaled the scent of geraniums as she smoothed his tunic down his waist and hips, then secured his belt. When she gave it an extra tug to tighten the loop, she backed away slowly. Her eyes were on the bulge of his belted purse. "I'm glad they did not steal your money. We've never had any brigands in these woods until today, Jordan," she offered so summarily it appeared to be true.

"Oh? Supposedly your father has in his pay the largest private garrison of men at arms in all of England, second only to King Henry's guard. Yet, today they were not at their duties to prevent this. Why?" He had to know if this attack was planned by her father's men. And if the rescue was planned as well.

Hands on her hips, she blew hair from her eyes. "I have no idea, but I promise you I will learn."

"I should think your father would be eager to thwart me in my mission."

"My father keeps his men standing at the ready to maintain his independence from Henry. But he has never done anything so treacherous as attack a visiting emissary on Trent's lands."

"That is probably the only ruse he has not tried, my lady."

She glared at him. "My father seeks to keep Henry from becoming too greedy and self-satisfied."

"And to keep the Welsh from plaguing your borders," he added as he tugged on his cloak.

"There are not many Welsh, I assure you. They have learned Trent is not an easy mark, and so they attack other holdings that are poorly fortified. You need not fear that there will be any more to strike us." She called to one of her women to find her a strip of cloth to make a sling for him. Her eyes delved into his gaze. "I speak honestly, but you cannot trust me."

Ah, if I could. . . .

"Well, what can I expect? My father's actions again color my own character, which is, of course, a taint I should be used to by now." She grew pink with irritation.

Jordan could not decide who rubbed her worse—her parent or himself.

"No matter," she said, but did not sound resigned. "I will still lead you inside my father's gates. We'll tend you and your men with a fine supper, soft bed, and more nursing for your injuries. Then you will feel better."

"I wish it were so simple to cure my problems, my lady de Wallys."

At his use of her full name, she looked sad. "So do I, my lord. I'd like the power to fix all our maladies."

He wished he could take his words back and begin again because he liked this woman's nature as well as her looks. But his primary goal here was to serve his king and discover who had tried to thwart that effort by attacking him, capturing him, and perhaps torturing him or . . .

Ransoming him?

He scanned the clearing, buying himself time to consider that astonishing possiblity before he spoke to Clare again. "Forgive me, I have work to do before I leave this scene."

"I told you my women could make arrangements for the disposition of the bodies of these men."

Arrangements? With whom? He hated the logical bent of his mind, which cried for answers to this mysterious attack on him and his men. "Aye, my lady, your troupe seems capable of much, but burying men in the frozen earth is no woman's task."

"Lord Chandler, a requirement of all who come to serve at Castle Trent is that they can ride and shoot a bow. We live in precarious times, and my women can protect themselves, but I would not expect my servants to do such heavy work as digging graves. I will send one of my women quickly back home to have a contingent of men at arms come to do what's necessary. They can help us get your two men home safely, too. You and your men need care. Stop worrying and do come."

"I will, but *first* I must satisfy myself and search the bodies of those who assaulted us."

"That is unnecessary. They are but knaves who . . ." Her eyes riveted to his. "Are they not?"

"If you say no robbers usually roam here, who am I to fault you?"

"What would you hope to find?"

He shrugged—and in the move noted that he could flex his shoulder with ease. Thanks to Clare de Wallys and her remedies. He owed her some explanation. "I seek some clue to their identities so that you and your friends and all within Castle Trent's domain may feel safe from harm."

She took that for the truth it was, partial though it certainly was. "I am grateful for your concern and your protection," she said as she turned toward the bodies but lifted her face to examine the horizon. "I will find out where the contingent of Trent's men at arms for this sector were. . . ." She turned back to Jordan, catching his questioning look and laughing lightly, the way he would always wish to see her. "Aye, Dragon, if I can satisfy myself about where they were and what they were about, I will share the facts with you."

"Thank you. You are generous."

"It costs me nothing to be kind in this regard. Clearly, you are perplexed about this attack. But so am I. I feel as much responsible for the welfare of Trent as any man or male heir. I care for my people—and my guests. Even those who cross my land unannounced and unwanted. I hate this war which plagues us along the marches."

"I am pleased to hear it, for that means I'll have an easier time of persuading you to my cause."

"I doubt it, but you may try."

Her merry nature, despite the odds against her, warmed him to his toes. He loathed the thought that he would have to foil her at all costs and give her to another man who might not praise her independent nature as vigorously as he himself. Curse Geoffrey and his need for a willing woman! This sunbeam outshone one hundred such fragile flowers of femininity.

She took his right arm. "Come. Let's see what evidence we can gather about these brigands before we leave."

Chapter Three

JORDAN FOUND NOT ONE INDICATION OF WHO THOSE FIENDS were. Or at least that is what he told her as he climbed onto his horse hours earlier.

Clare tapped her fingertips upon her armrest. She sat in her banquet chair in her great hall, eyes darting to the main doors where she expected Jordan to appear and join her for supper. He was late. Examining the condition of his two men, he took her at her word to come down to dine when he felt sufficiently restored and relaxed.

She gazed around the somber gray stone walls, hung with the silk and wool tapestries her father imported to lock heat into the century-old fortress and to impress his guests and his retainers with his generous attention to their comfort. Around the trestle tables, her kitchen servants took not just their usual care but a new leisure to set out Trent's best linens, plate, and goblets. She frowned on those late to a meal and those dallying to serve it. For a change of pace, tonight's tempo seemed to suit them.

Except for the captain of the day watch who drank his

wine far too fast and focused on her far too frequently with a distaste she would not soon forget or forgive. William Baldwin had thwarted her authority in front of Jordan and her own retinue a few hours ago, and she could not let him get away with his impertinence.

From the corner of her eye she observed him. Baldwin had come to her father's employ four years ago with the best and worst of recommendations. He was a mercenary. Like most of her father's three hundred retainers, Baldwin fought for any who paid him higher than his last lord. In Baldwin's case, his prior allegiance had gone to Harry Hotspur, a northern landed lord dubbed appropriately for his quickness to act—and slowness to perceive the results. Hotspur had won his final reward at Shrewsbury last July, when he died upon a field of battle to which his own treasonous activities toward King Henry had brought him. 'Twas even rumored that the Dragon had found the rebel on the field and delivered Hotspur's fatal blow. But whatever way in which Hotspur had died, Clare understood from her father's faithful servant, Raymond, that Baldwin mourned him. Because she rued rebels such as Hotspur, Baldwin's repeated lamentations of his loss had disturbed her.

Now it meshed with his failure to detect the five brigands who attacked Jordan today, and the combination created a fetid odor in her nostrils. She smelled disloyalty. Long used to ferreting out the acrid scent, she knew it when she whiffed it. But she would be fair and seek the evidence to confirm it. So when Baldwin had ridden into her courtyard scarce minutes behind her, her women, and Jordan and his men, she confronted him on the cobblestones.

He cared not for the public display. She noticed it in the way he bit his tongue and refused to put his ice blue eyes on her as she dismissed his first blithe answer to her questions.

"Enough vagueness, Baldwin. I want to know *precisely* where you were today."

"I told you, milady, we patrolled the river."

"The entire afternoon?"

His pale eyes shot to Jordan's two wounded men, one assisted but nonetheless hobbling up the broad stone steps to the keep of Castle Trent, the other being carried in a rough-hewn stretcher by her ladies and four burly house servants. "We heard a tale from the villagers in Crofton that a band of men roamed abroad."

"Aye, they certainly did. You see the results of their handiwork"—she gestured to the group going inside—"and thus do I witness your failure to perform your duty, Baldwin." She picked up her skirts and wheeled about, the wings of her cloak giving him the air she needed to let him know who commanded here. "I broach no failures in matters such as this. Neither does my father. Trust me to tell him."

She felt him dog her heels. "I cannot be everywhere, milady. I have men but—"

"You are paid well, Baldwin. Find a way to do what you must to merit your wealth."

"You threaten me?" He said in a tone of disbelief.

She never gave him the satisfaction to turn as she replied, "I state the basis for your continued employment here. Please me, Baldwin. It is in your best interest."

The stable servants had seen and probably heard her. Mayhaps even a few of Baldwin's patrol. Wonderful. Baldwin was a man who needed to constantly be reminded that she was chatelaine here as much as her father was lord of this estate. His audacity to stare openly at her now proved that. But suddenly, his head snapped to one side and he viewed someone he obviously liked even less.

Jordan Chandler filled the doorway with a Dragon's bold demeanor as he entered Castle Trent's great hall for supper. Though Jordan looked a little tired, she felt triumphant that William Baldwin found the Dragon incomparable. She knew the feeling well.

A greater thrill skimmed her spine when Jordan's quicksilver gaze raced to the dais to find her. Eyes locked to hers, he headed for her, his big brawny body eating up the space that divided them.

His swagger declared he had a goal. She reminded herself that it was detrimental to her and her own desire to flee to France. His smile assured her he had charm. She told herself that was not for her, either. Nay, he had asserted that he thought only of taking her to marry his nephew after he searched and found the identities of the five men who had attacked him.

So as much as she needed him to go and take his plans for her future with him, she heard her muse rejoice he stay. Here where she could study him. Find the facets of his character. Transcribe his essence to her written page—and in so doing, discover his faults. Please God that there were some, for each man had them. Afterward, with ample evidence before her, she could free herself of her irrational appreciation for him. Although she hated to admit it, never had she seen a man so perfect for the part of hero, and she struggled not to stare at him and once more admire him.

But tonight in candlelight, he shone more tempting than in twilight.

Her lips parted. Her heart paused. Just as it had bare hours before when she had first gazed upon this dragon. This myth come to breathing life before her appreciative eyes.

Sweet Mary, what a creature of fantasy he was! Worthy of more than mere words. Large and dark and silent, Jordan Chandler loomed more beguiling than he had in the stark contrast of a winter snowstorm. Tonight he wore a black velvet tunic decorated only by his thick leather belt and a gold Lancastrian collar of entwined Ss and swan pendant about his neck. In the amber glow of eventide, his hair framed his square face like ebony ink dashed with silver streaks. The straight black mass, unlike the bowled cuts of most men, flowed unfashionably to his shoulder blades, caught at his nape by a long leather tie.

Her mouth went dry at his outlandish appearance. Even having shaven his bristly beard, then bathed and richly dressed, he reminded her of childhood tales about marauding Goths. Verily, even without his breastplate and helmet, he seemed as huge as this afternoon. His thighs as sculpted and sturdy. His legs in black hose, even longer than she remembered. His power, more restrained in the cloth of civility, but just as raw. And now that she had time to note it, he possessed a grace she had not seen in many men. Certainly, in none so big. Nor so famous for aiding his friend Henry—and disposing of Henry's enemies.

But when he stood before her and inclined his head in greeting, she also remembered that he possessed manners. Suddenly, they didn't matter as much as the molten silver of his eyes. Or the satin swath of his voice as he greeted her in a confidential tone.

"My lady." His eyes seemed to memorize her gown, her mouth, her hair. Her heart drummed madly that he looked well pleased at her appearance until he frowned at the sight of her cheek, now black and blue from the brigand's abuse. "You look lovely," Jordan said as he gazed into her eyes. "I see you've removed your ashes, and I am delighted you did not don sackcloth to greet me."

She grinned, and in the move, a streak of pain along her cheek and jaw made her freeze in the pose.

"But that bastard hurt you very badly," he seethed. He put two fingers beneath her chin and cursed the man roundly. "What have you done to take down the swelling?"

"Cloths soaked in chamomile to draw the hot, dry humors."

"Have you nothing stronger?" He sounded impatient.

"If I do anything more," she said carefully, so as not to cause herself the pain again, "my skin will fall off!"

He laughed. "Then don't do that. I like your skin."

"The Dragon possesses much charm," she gave him with more boldness than she had ever before wanted to display to a man. When she wondered how well she compared to other women he had complimented, she betrayed herself when her palm skimmed the waist of her best wool in a sign of vanity.

He noticed and smiled so that his scar made a dimple appear. "Charm has little to do with this. I speak the truth. I like the pearl crespine and the burgundy gown, but I am displeased to see you without the ashes on your cheek. I liked that smudge. It makes me wonder what occupies your days."

She wasn't certain if he said "and your nights." But a

devil's glint danced in his eyes, and in her heart she wished he might have uttered such a sweetness. Her writer's mind skipped on, wondering what this Dragon did at night. Did he read, play chess, dice? Make love? How did he look lying down? As gloriously big and hard? Or was he less threatening brought so low? Was he tender? Could he murmur sweet words? Had he?

Of course, he had. And . . . to whom?

"Clare?"

Countless fortunate women had felt the bulge of his arms, the ridged wall of his ribs, the leanness of his hips against—

"Clare!" His hand was on hers.

"Hmmm?"

He frowned at her. "Do you have trouble hearing or seeing me? When that fellow hit you today, you didn't faint, but—"

"I am well," she assured him. "I am often preoccupied. Those who live here know I cannot sew or cook for too long without someone to assist me."

In disbelief, he examined her head to foot. "What do you do, prick your fingers or fall into the fire?"

"Once I got too close and my skirts caught flame. I forget where I am and what I do. My mind"—she waggled her fingers near her head—"goes faster than my body."

He looked relieved but fervent when he said, "A phenomenon I won't forget."

That, too, was praise. "Come to eat," she invited him, eager to sit and enjoy his company. "We've waited for you."

"I thank you for delaying your meal so that I might first see how my two men recover."

"It was no hardship for us."

"Lord Pickering's ankle is well bound by you, though he finds more comfort from one of your maids, I think. And Sir Wickham revives with good color from his wound."

"Sir Wickham is fortunate the ax did only shallow work. But he is very healthy and responds well to a compress of herbs, which will heal his injury and soothe his pain."

"He told me you sewed him closed, proclaiming you most proficient with your hands. He evidently saw no indication that your mind wanders from your tasks." Jordan was teasing.

"Agility in my hands was the first trait my good mother noticed about me. It serves me well in many arts, not just those of healing," she said with a meaning he could not mark, because though her family and staff here knew she was the Nightingale, few beyond these walls did. "Sir Wickham is a grateful patient. A good sign of his recovery. He'll need weeks of rest, however, during which his agonies and some of my less tasty potions might lead him to recant his kind words about me."

"I doubt that," Jordan said slowly while those eyes of his seemed to caress her. The spell broke when he clenched his teeth and extended his left arm to turn it this way and that. "I, too, have evidence you are expert in restoring people to health."

"You do not wear the sling."

"It restricts me. I must be able to move freely."

"A stubborn man. Do you feel any pain?"

"Not a trace," he said in such a husky voice she had to lean close to hear. "You are either an acclaimed physician, madam, or a witch."

The smile he gave her this time sent a frisson of remembrance skipping up her spine. Clare recalled the feel of his muscles beneath the old scar. How fast he was to grin—and try to hide it from her. She warmed now that this man whom so many feared could find humor with her. She had found slow wit—or no wit—in most men.

She beamed back at him. " 'Twas my pleasure to help you, my lord."

His lips curled, as he began to put a thought into words, but at some inner command, his face fell.

Lashed by the speed of his ever-changing emotions, she felt seared—and warned. Was it forbidden to smile upon the Dragon?

Clare despaired, seeking to retrieve the friendliness which fled for no reason she could find. She looked at Jordan with a nonchalance she did not feel. "You enjoyed your bath and the bed, I hope?"

She could have chuckled at her first choice of topic and cut her tongue out for the second! She cleared her throat instead, smiling . . . wincing at him.

He, infernal Dragon, struggled with a grin. "Does your mouth work faster than your head, madam?"

She drew herself up into her dignity. God knew, she appeared courteous to ask of his bath but, in truth, she envied what the water would have discovered about the Dragon's physique. She licked her lips, recalling how hot enticement had flushed her body earlier when she had offered to do her chatelaine's duty and bathe him. To measure the width of that extraordinary chest and to feel the sinew beneath the pelt of black hair were ambitions that caused her fingers to wiggle in anticipation. His winged black brows had quirked with wry mirth, but he had refused her ministrations with the politesse of a man of kingly acquaintance . . . a man used to women's admiration.

Now another glint twinkled in his large eyes. Try though he might, he could not dim this brightness. "I assure you, my lady, the lavish comforts of a huge fire and hot bath restored my good nature, but not half so much as the promise of seeing you again here in your hall."

Her cheeks flamed with his compliment. She chided herself that she blushed like a naive girl. Surely, he meant to imply no personal delight in her company but wished to lull her into submission and thus begin his negotiations for her hand. Aye, she must stop being so childish. So . . . *smitten* by a handsome king's man with a talent for talking and killing.

She pressed a palm between her breasts. Disappointment cut her foolish heart in two. But his eyes descended to her hand, swirled around the fullness of her breasts, and narrowed on one, then the other hardening nipple. She stiffened. Dropped her hand. Fantasy might be inspiring, even offering escape, but it solved no problems. "Supper awaits, my lord Chandler. Let us begin."

She took one step up to mount the dais and stopped at the harshness in Jordan's tone.

"But your father is not yet here."

"Nay. He is severely ill."

"Ill? Again?"

She turned to face him. "Continuously. You did not know?"

"He gave that excuse to one of the king's messengers weeks ago."

"It was the truth then as it is now."

"However, unlike the occasion when your father's condition discouraged that king's man from pressing for an audience, I cannot be deterred. I am here to speak with the earl, and it must occur tonight."

Clare lifted her chin. "I regret to say my father's condition makes it difficult for him to speak easily to anyone. I handle his business."

"Oh, what is this malady he suffers?" Jordan arched both brows. "For a man renowned for his desire to converse with any and all who would indulge his pleasures, your father seems to have lost his tongue."

She nodded not only at the Dragon's vehemence but also at his unwitting accuracy. "He suffers, Jordan," she said in frank appeal for mercy. "Only an hour ago he told me to ask you to forgive him because he cannot attend you. Mayhaps, he says, the morrow will see him better able to converse."

She knew that was not likely, but she did have to try to deal with Jordan herself as much as possible. Only that way could she control the negotiations for her hand. Only that way could she stall the proceedings until she had time to plan how she would escape marriage this time.

She bit her lip. But she could not easily control this king's man as she had others. Eventually, she might have to show Jordan to her father's bedchamber, and in that case, she needed time to prepare Jordan for the sight of her sire. None of this was easy. So with a nod, she indicated the largest cushioned chair behind the lavishly laid banquet table. "In the meantime, you have the place of honor."

Jordan Chandler did not move.

In his rigid countenance, Clare read his newest unrest

that her father insulted him by his absence. "I beg you, my lord, come to dine. 'Tis no slight of my father's that he is not here. He is, I assure you, a very sore afflicted man."

Chandler's nostrils flared. "Of that I am quite certain."

Most of her life, she had felt no love for her father. His vanity, his selfishness, his immorality, and his constant political maneuvering between Richard and Henry set a vivid example for her of the human male at his most undisciplined. Only last summer, as Aymer's condition worsened and he began his march toward death more visibly each day, did she discover that she possessed one odd feeling for him.

Pity.

Although she thought she camouflaged her sympathy for him with her efficient supervision of his care, those who resided in Castle Trent nonetheless perceived its presence.

She saw in their eyes their astonishment that she, who had never been affectionate with him, could tend him so diligently. They had the good sense not to speak of it, at least to her. Although she wished she would not display it for a king's man, Jordan Chandler was too intelligent to miss her sensitivities. Indeed, a king's agent, skilled in politics, could come to her home specifically to explore her weaknesses and tame them, then use them to his purpose, couldn't he?

So, though Jordan Chandler might be a model of knighthood for her literary endeavors, he was not a man to whom she could entrust her secrets. Nor would she permit the Dragon to reduce her resolve to ashes. If steady refusal would not work her will, mayhaps sweetness would.

"Please, my lord, do sit so that the servants may present you with the platters. My father has ordered a small feast for you, especially since he cannot greet you himself. He would not offend you, nor King Henry."

She stepped closer to Jordan and, though she was on the dais and he not, she still had to lift her head to look up at him. If his stalwart actions and his character had fueled her writer's and woman's fantasies of him upon that snow-swept plain today, tonight his height brought forth the admission that he could impress her with his boldness here or anywhere. While her mind warned her she should not want such from him of all people, Jordan's proximity brought her closer to a tempting body that dwarfed hers. A determination that rivaled hers—and drew her respect.

"Listen to me, Clare—"

She glanced about at her garrison of hired mercenaries, servants, and her six women. Baldwin scowled. Her scribe, Mary, stared. Solange gaped at this man's effrontery to use Clare's given name.

"We will speak after supper, my lord Chandler."

"Now." Something about the word, the way his mouth shaped the word, sent a jolt of lightning through her.

His mouth, that generous element of his features with its pouting lower lip, whispered for her ears, though she was sure her servants strained to hear. "I do not wish to cross swords with you in public and take your power from you in your home, Clare. Yet I must have my way on this issue. I cannot dally, lest Henry send a greater contingent to speed my progress with armed persuasion. I cannot spend the winter waiting for your father to decide to see me, though God knows I find attractions here"—he noted her hair and eyes—"which I never wanted to value."

Her skin flamed at his compliment. She dug into her mind for a response that was logical. "But you said you would look for clues to who attacked you. I promised my help. I need to know who they were as much as you do."

"Clare." He scanned the room while his fingers grasped her upper arms. "I beg you to lead me somewhere we might speak more privately."

Baldwin had advanced like a snarling bull, steps away. "My lady, what will you?"

I'll have none of you, she thought. Then aching to have done with this confrontation, she drew back and showed Jordan in a glance her own determination on these matters. "Come with me." She stepped down and led him off the dais, toward the corridor, the kitchen, and a small court-yard.

With him close behind her, she was passing the pantry

out of sight of others when he captured her wrist. She tugged away, but in two swift strides, he kicked open the door to the pantry, spun, and shot the bolt into its hold. Then he pressed her against the rough wood. It vibrated with their combined weight.

In the hell-dark pantry with the aromas of drying herbs and exotic spices, the Dragon became one with the blackness.

"Clare, I could not say these things in front of your people. Most especially that man who heads your day patrol."

"Baldwin is his name, but why should you care? Why do you care about any of my people?"

"Because they are yours. Because they care for you. Because they are English and that makes them Henry's."

"They will despise you no matter what you do."

"The classic case of killing the messenger, eh?" he said with ruefulness, his lips too close to her ear.

She had to stop breathing to block out the song of delight that trilled through her blood.

"Ah, Clare," he crooned, and she was certain he knew her body's reaction to him as he tried to bring her closer. But she put her knee into a strategic position. He perceived it and blocked her move by inserting his leg and forcing hers wide. The pose in daylight would have been obscene. In this void, the feel of his leg between hers was outrageous. And delicious.

She shifted to get away.

"Nay, Clare, stop and hear me. I think your villeins would hate me even if I came with no demands. They are so used to being protected by your father that they don't seem to realize this state of affairs comes to a close. Your people need to realize today is not yesterday. You say your sire is ill. Someday he will die. You will be married—"

"Nay," she ground out.

He shook her a little. "I brought you here because I have more to say, and I don't want to frighten your people more than they need to be! Mark me, Clare! I have much to accomplish here at Trent. I will begin by finding what facts I can about what happened today, but that search cannot deter me from my greater goal. I cannot sit or dine until I've met your father, because if I do not arrive at my nephew's home within two weeks, Henry will send a full one hundred lances to Castle Trent to accompany you there."

"Nay, he would not be so arrogant! That's six hundred men!"

"Aye," he said softly. "I doubt you want to see that much Lancastrian green and white coloring your courtyard or your wedding."

"My wedding," she whispered in horror. "Oh, God above, why should I be surprised that you would take me by force to a church door?"

"Clare—" He tried to put his arms around her.

She flattened her body to the door. "Two weeks! Why not two days or hours? 'Tis all the same when none will do!"

"Clare, you are obstinate."

"So this is the meaning of your legend," she said wearily. "The Dragon who breathes not only fire but ice. Yet ever did I hear that you always asked for justice to be served and this . . . this ultimatum is not just to me! Oh, why should I feel betrayed by a man I barely know?"

He sucked in his breath, astounded by her words.

"Nay, I think I do know," she hastened on. In the vacuum before her, she recalled his sharp features and found an answer she deplored. "I thought I saw in you a nobility of character. I thought that banned the barbarism which would compel a woman to take vows against her will. Amazing. I am not usually so blind."

She pushed at him with all her might. Surprised, he swayed backward a bit, jostling a cabinet filled with her little jars of potions and raining down upon them both a fragrant shower of drying dill and sage hanging from the rafters.

Jordan seized her wrists, pulled her forward, and curled his arms and hers around her back. Pressed to him so intimately, she felt his vehemence and discovered it

55

sheathed in a tenderness she'd known from no man. "Clare, I can explain. Henry has decreed this! He proclaims you must marry quickly or his army will escort you to the church door and my nephew's home. After you are safe, they will return here to guard Trent's lands."

"How considerate of Henry."

"Clare," he said with more equanimity, "Henry needs your marriage to guarantee this alliance."

"Why does he not simply march in and take us?"

"What a waste of precious men to make Englishmen fight Englishmen! Have we not seen enough blood shed at Shrewsbury and elsewhere? Henry has. He wants this alliance so that he can set up camp here for his soldiers who will fight the Welsh rebels raiding your borders."

"I don't want his help. I don't need it. I have enough men, well paid, well fed. Did you not see them in my hall? Brutes, each and every one. My father and I have stopped the Welsh with our care of our people and our money to hire men to defend them. Nay, I do not need Henry. And even if I thought I did, Henry has not the power to stop the Welsh."

The Dragon inhaled a mighty draught of air. "And well you know the reasons why, Clare. Because Trent has been the one territory which constantly changes allegiance to maintain its independence from all, the earldom has survived. But this state of affairs cannot continue. The rebel Glendower advances with his army coming closer to Trent each day—"

"He was still in the south at Carmarthen at last report. Weeks away from us."

"Mayhaps Glendower is, but what of his friends?"

"What friends? If you mean that ragged bunch today, they looked like no cohorts of a man who styles himself the Prince of Wales in defiance of English kings who stole the title for their oldest sons."

"Friends can come in many guises, Clare."

Her skin prickled at Jordan's implication that Glendower could have spies. That they could be anywhere. Even on her land.

Jordan tightened his grip on her. "Don't you see? An adventurer like Glendower gains any and all to support him. Thieves with a taste for more have no scruples, my dear. I need only point to that band of five we met today. What of them, Clare? Who were they? Neither of us knows for certain. Yet they are but a token of the others who have stung you for years. Whether these five came directly from Glendower or only on their own, you cannot deny they caused mayhem here inside your territory, close to your castle where they have never done such before. You have no answers for me, yet I know one. For whatever else you may say, the de Wallyses descend from a heroic Norman warlord who married a West Country heiress. You and all here are first, last, and always English."

"The de Wallyses are self-sufficient, paving our way with our own money—"

"That comes to an end, Clare. You know it, so do Henry, your father, and I. Your father must have Henry's support to drive these men away, else he would not consent to begin the negotiation for this marriage. *Aye,* I concede that your father is rich and pays his knights and archers in hefty sums to protect him, but that money runs like a waterfall from your treasury. One day it will drain dry, Clare. Then your father must finally choose a side. Why wait until your people are hungry, injured, and poor in spirit and in truth?"

She heard Jordan's arguments and silently acknowledged their accuracy. Her father's dwindling accounts reflected not only his generosity but also his need for a well-provisioned garrison of men at arms. She had always known the commissions she earned on her books could help replenish Aymer's funds. Thus far, he hadn't requested any supplement from his "chick" as he called her instead of the Nightingale. She had plenty set aside for the day when extra gold would be required to save her home from others' greed.

The need for regular income was one reason she accepted the invitation to France to become an honored guest of Charles the Sixth. That monarch had personally negotiated with her agent, La Croix, the particulars of her employment. Charles had agreed to all terms readily, requiring only two stipulations: that the Nightingale arrive before next April when he wished to open a new court with a new epic poem by her, and that La Croix reveal the Nightingale's identity. Clare had agreed to both conditions because Charles promised her agent that he would pay the Nightingale extravagantly well to produce books for his private collection. Three hundred English nobles per month—equal to a royal duke's pay for a full year of campaign—could do much to overcome homesickness, Clare decided.

Fearing that her father's money might one day run dry, Clare intended to send her monthly stipend home to Trent to her bailiff. He would continue to compensate her father's knights for their service. Then those she loved—her villeins, her shepherds, her household servants, and any of her flock of six women who chose to remain after the shop was closed—would still be safe. Protected by her funds—and, she hoped, united in allegiance to their new mistress, her sister Blanchette.

"Clare," Jordan pleaded, "I make good sense. Henry and England cannot afford to continue this conflict with Glendower because it costs too much in men and money, neither of which Henry has in any great abundance. I will be honest with you and tell you he grows poor with this war, going in debt even to his son, Prince Hal, whose Cornish lands and Hereford provide good income. Therefore, the king must secure Trent's extensive lands for England soon. Your marriage to my nephew, who has been a loyal supporter of Lancaster for many years, would fill the continuing vacuum of power here caused by your father's constant shift of his allegiance. Clare, think. I promise you, Henry's army comes. Would you rather they arrive as friends or foes?"

"I want no fighting here," she affirmed. "Neither did my father. That's why he always turned with the tide of fortune. He is a man of peace, despite what you might think. He told me often that when he was ten, he had seen his mother raped, then stabbed, and his father hung by Welsh raiders. He himself was ransomed from certain death by the kindness of old King Edward. My father's past made him fear blood lust. His constant recitation of this story here before this hall's fire taught me to hate the idea, too."

Jordan's tone held compassion. "I want to protect you from experiencing any such horror in your life. Don't you see that?"

No one had ever wanted to protect her. She had liked it that way. Encouraged it with her bold acts of writing books and riding about with her women as if they were her retinue. This man's desire to shield her from harm was the first she had ever considered. The only she had ever valued. "Aye, I see it, but in no way I call blessed."

"Sometimes we find joys in misfortunes. Mayhaps you think this act of Henry's as disastrous. Yet you might discover it has benefits. Look for them, will you?"

Her imprudent heart declared she had already seen one.

He must have felt some acquiescence because he set her gently to her feet. "Show me to your father. Bid the others eat. I need the satisfaction of putting my eyes on the man who has foiled two kings for decades and escaped the traitor's noose. For a cause which your father and I share with you, let me speak to him, and we shall end the procession of war and death that marches toward your home."

As he drew her aside and opened the door to the corridor, she saw the crowd milling about and muttering to themselves and each other. When Jordan and she approached the arch to the great hall, they overheard William Baldwin telling his companion that he couldn't understand why anyone would care to see the earl. "His appearance would disgust a dog of hell."

Clare saw Jordan take that in with equanimity. Diplomatically, he turned from Baldwin to lock his gaze to hers. She had to prepare him for the sight, as well as regain some of her dignity from this incident in which the Dragon had laid hands on her in the sanctity of her own home.

"Lord Chandler." She reverted to formality for the consumption of Baldwin and any others of his ilk who might test her ability to rule alone here. "My common sense says to let you in to see my father, but I will warn you that he is not prepared for visitors. Since July when he became much worse and—unpresentable, he has permitted no one near him but me and one manservant."

Jordan examined her. "He is that sick? Well, then, whatever else you may have heard about the Dragon, let me show you he can be kind."

Chapter Four

SHE CROSSED THE GREAT HALL AND HEADED FOR THE CASTLE'S oldest staircase and tower. At the first step, she turned with Jordan close behind her and paused long enough to wave her hand toward her kitchen staff, who waited for her permission to serve the meal.

"Where is your father's supper?" Jordan asked as they climbed to the top. "Should we not have brought him a serving?"

"Nay. He eats less and less. Broth, now and again, is the only substance he can swallow. Please"—she faced him when they stood before the portal—"allow me to go in first alone. He is not expecting you to visit him because I told him I would not let you in. Please understand that I would not have him embarrassed and raving at me for lack of notifying him. Any irritation is not good for him. Afterward he does not sleep well because his humors are inflamed and his skin . . . well, you shall see."

Concern suffused Jordan's face. "By all means, do what you must."

"Wrap this around your throat." She gave him a long swatch of thin clean wool from a small table outside the door. "Bring it up over your nose and mouth. I would not have you breathe in the fetid air to your own peril."

"You think what disease he has others may acquire?"

"I do not know for certain, but it is a popular belief that disease can spread through the air. Please, do this, Jordan, and do not argue."

"I will," he said as she wound her own cloth about her.

She rapped her knuckles on the wooden door four times in the cadence she and her father had decided would be her code to let him know she wished to enter his room. She heard footsteps inside and a quiet debate between two men.

When a gruff voice responded, she gingerly opened the door and took one step inside. She shuddered at what Jordan was about to see—and halted when she felt him tenderly squeeze her shoulder. Why did this man's touch fill her with so much solace and delight?

"Come, girl," bid her father from the darkest corner of his chamber where the firelight, purposely low, barely reached. She heard him fumbling to secure his bedclothes and bandages up about him, for even with her he was cautious that she not be horrified by his deteriorating condition. "Why are you here? Raymond brought me my soup." His slurred speech dissolved in a bout of coughing.

His servant Raymond greeted her with deference but frowned at the Dragon. Raymond, protective to the point of feral, moved to waylay her. She ignored him. Raymond could be too bold in his efforts. Many whispered he had more than one reason for it. He was a stocky man, but in that alone was he different from his once tall, lean master. Raymond, many observed, was of such similar appearance and demeanor to her father that the two were brothers. Raymond was the one born to the wrong side of the blanket in the same year as his legitimate sibling and lord.

"My lady, your father readies for sleep and I must—"

"Not this early, Raymond." She moved around him. "Sire?"

Raymond tried to block her, and she would have none of

it. This meeting was too important to their welfare for a servant to end it before it had begun. "I am here for good reason, Raymond. Give over."

"Do as she says, Raymond," her father managed between hacks. "She sounds determined and will not be dissuaded. I know that tone of hers well."

The servant was not happy, but when her father finished coughing, she took another step inside and sought to inform him of what his eyes grew too weak to detect from so far away. "Sire, I bring you a guest."

"What? Eh? *Who?*" He would be clawing at the sheets now to cover himself more, she knew. "I don't want him. You know that!"

Raymond positioned himself between her and her father. She frowned at his audacity but responded, "He insisted, Sire."

Long ago her father would have bellowed at her. Now he had not the strength. The sarcasm which came alone now did not offend her, either, because where before he was master of all he surveyed, she soon would inherit his domain. Then what he had fought to maintain and sought to keep free of any intruders, she would dispose of in a manner that she thought proper. Aye, he did not know her plan, but she would give his lands to the only one left who deserved it—the only one who had the right to hold it in the name of de Wallys. Her only remaining sibling. Her sister, Blanchette.

"Clare, shrewd girl. You found a man who will overrule you? Jesus, Mary, and Joseph—" Her father halted to pant, clear his throat, then spit into one of his jars. "I should see him, but I can't. Oh do be gone. I *told* you never to bring me anyone! Christ's wounds, girl." He would be squinting toward the door, unable to detect her clearly from so far because of the bloating of his flesh. "You don't hold a candle, do you?"

"Nay, my lord. I promised you I would never carry one. We agreed only you could light one if you so desired." She glanced over her shoulder at a patient Jordan. She felt great sorrow for him and the shock of what he would now encounter, but he had demanded to be presented here, hadn't he? She turned back to her father, hesitating to reveal the identity of their visitor now after keeping it from him ever since she'd received Henry's last letter more than a week ago. "Father, I have brought you King Henry's man."

"I can't see him!" he croaked. "Never—" He broke off in a fit of hacking.

Her instinct during such episodes was to fly to her father and soothe him. She was continually surprised that she felt the need to minister to the man who had so repulsed her with years of self-indulgence. Now, as his flesh reddened, oozed, and disintegrated before her eyes and she had yet one more reason to feel repulsion, she discovered only this desire to alleviate his suffering. But Aymer de Wallys, proud and self-contained even unto this bitter end, would have abhorred her touch. Discerning her pity, he would have banished her from his presence forevermore.

She shrank back—and pressed against the solid support of warm, hard man. Clare felt Jordan's strong fingers close around her upper arms. His comfort, like that a minute before, was unexpected and all the more welcome for its novelty. She certainly preferred he place his hands on her like this than in the frustration he had exhibited in her pantry. Aye, she could stand here, absorbing the Dragon's solace, for long years.

Meanwhile, her father's coughs rose to the rafters and he began to mumble about her breach of his orders. Raymond moved to his side to assist him, but he waved the servant's solicitations. "Be gone. Be gone!"

Raymond knew enough to leave but did so with a slam of the outer door.

"Lord de Wallys." Jordan advanced on the bed. "I insisted your daughter show me here. Caught between her duty to you and her need to be respectful to me and King Henry's wishes, she brought me to your door only because I threatened her."

Her father laughed. A hoarse noise, it soon turned watery, then became another spasm of coughs.

"Please, my lord," she begged him, "do take a drink to stop that fit."

He groped for the water urn. "Aye, girl," he sighed when she thought she heard a sound that indicated he might have sunk against the headboard. "I'll do this for you so that he can leave us both in peace. What did he threaten? Marriage again? Soon? Bah. He's a jester to try to drag you to church, isn't he? Tell me, Clare, what is this heathen's name, eh?"

Jordan's real name meant less than his legendary one. "This is the Dragon, my lord."

Beneath his ragged breath, Aymer droned, "Harry, Harry, Harry. A pest. Never stops. Nibbles at you like an ant to your feast!" He contended with more phlegm and spit it into his jar. "That's why he's on the throne. Not because he's more swift or crafty. Just . . . persistent."

In a few sparks from the fire, Clare saw him beckon Jordan with a gnarled and poorly dressed hand. "So do approach me, Dragon. I have heard of you. Who has not since you saved Harry from himself often as a boy. Ha, even protected his son Prince Hal when King Richard imprisoned the boy in Ireland. Let me—if God is kind—see some of your face. Come to the end of the bed."

The polite man who had stood with her left her to walk into the black hole. In a flash, the flames leaped high, and in that light, the Dragon pulled away his cloth. He freely gave her father the sight he wished.

The old man barked in laughter. "The devil's own man! And Henry's! Ahhh, Dragon, Dragon, the fire is good to you. It sharpens your strong bones and evil eyes. Come closer still. Ah, you *do* have a scar on your cheek. Is it from King Richard's poor aim of his knife at Hal, as people say?"

"More a result of my quickness to duck, my lord."

Clare's mouth curled at the Dragon's wry humor.

Her father, who was usually quick to laugh, saw no joy in the subject. "Not easy to be Henry's man, is it?"

"But satisfying."

"Really?" He found great mirth in that. But it, too, resulted in a copious expectoration into his jar.

Clare walked forward into the gloom, easily sensed Jordan, and put a hand to his arm. Why did she wish to see these two have an honest discussion? She had always honored her father in public and private despite his failings, but why should she feel so inclined toward a king's man she had met only hours ago? Because he had saved her today from rape and death at outlaws' hands? Maybe so. But also because she wanted his integrity preserved—and she knew her father could test it in many a creature.

Jordan covered her hand with his own, and in a tone that told her she should never have questioned his ability to defend himself, he disarmed her father in a few potent words. "Just as you have performed your duty to maintain your independence from all intruders to your lands, my lord earl, so have I acted on my knight's vow to serve a man who saved my widowed mother from poverty, my only brother from King Richard's pettiness, and my only living relative, my nephew, from a life of indolence."

"Pretty speech, Dragon. Did you learn that from Henry?"

"With Henry from his tutors, my lord. Here in England and abroad."

Aymer coughed. "So what they say of you is true? That you have traveled by Henry's side since you were a lad?"

"I became a squire to his father, John of Gaunt, when I was fourteen. Henry was then thirteen."

"It was said you were already a giant at that age with a reputation for saving people from themselves."

"That, my lord de Wallys, is a vastly inflated legend. I have not saved all those whom I wished to." He said it with such remorse, Clare felt his loss and wondered who it was he had not saved from harm.

"We must live with our human frailties, and I could wager you are but a mortal man, Dragon. Besides, rumors say you have so many victories that it must be easy for you to balance your scales."

"Nay."

"But is it not true that your own brother lived because you walked through fire to rescue him?"

"My brother was enjoying a liaison in the loft when the

flames broke out in our dovecote. He was trapped. I helped him down, that's all."

"From that moment on you were dubbed the Dragon."

"What people say is difficult to control, Lord de Wallys."

"How well I know. But tales of your heroism seem to be accurate. They spread beyond your home in Lancaster. That's why Gaunt thought you useful to protect his heir. Though Henry was the firstborn of his mother Henry was said to be puny, a runt. Was he?"

Jordan stiffened at this search for gossip and deflected it with diplomatic words. "My lord Henry was active for his age. Alike as we were, we became fast friends."

"But Gaunt wanted more than friendship from you, didn't he?"

"'Twas my responsibility to teach the art of self-preservation to Henry without dampening his natural inclination for discovery."

"I would conclude then you taught him well, Dragon, for Harry now wishes to discover the benefits of holding Trent for himself."

"And England."

Her father offered no reply but silence.

A log in the fireplace crackled in the heat, casting a glow so wide that Clare could see the Dragon's angular profile.

"'Tis why I am here," Jordan told him in a soft but determined tone. "You cannot play off one power for another any longer, my lord de Wallys. Richard is dead—'"

"Killed by Henry!" Aymer shot back.

"There is no reason for anyone to think that. And I should know for I was the one Henry sent to investigate the scene at Pontefract Castle and examine Richard's body."

Clare went still. Richard's memoirs, which she had read repeatedly, showed a man tormented by his own inadequacies. A man ready to die. But also one afraid of those who might poison his food or sneak into his bedchamber and dispose of him to the benefit of his cousin Henry. Clare feared Richard may have died in a perverse manner. But she had no proof. Only his words, his suspicions.

She had to know if they had any substance, and she

turned to the Dragon. "And what did you discover about how Richard died?"

"I found no foul play."

"None?" she asked, having read in Richard's own script how he had deliberately deteriorated his own health.

"Only by Richard himself! In truth, Richard's servants told me he starved himself out of perverse belief he would purge himself of earthly misdeeds—namely the one of abdicating his throne to Henry months before."

Clare's heart clenched. So Richard had succeeded in his goal to waste away as penance for his weaknesses as a ruler. He had committed a slow suicide to salve his conscience.

"There is no motive or proof of murder," Jordan affirmed. "Besides . . ." Clare felt the hair on her arms and neck rise as he continued. "Don't you think that if Henry had wanted to murder Richard, he would have sent his Dragon to do the deed?"

Her father paused, then admitted, "Aye, for it is well documented by witnesses you were in Cheshire working Henry's will on another aged nobleman who wished to keep Lancaster's hand from his door—and his daughter."

"My lord, Henry wants peace for England and for you."

"Enough to ask you to find the traitor Harry Hotspur on the field at Shrewsbury and kill him?"

"I met Harry there, aye. But it was an accident we faced each other."

"And was it an accident that Harry died?"

"Hear me, my lord de Wallys, I always fight to win. Especially if I think my opponent a dishonorable creature who is a rebel to his king."

"I fight to maintain my own power, Dragon."

"But the time draws nigh, too, when you cannot supervise your estate and your heir must."

Clare admired the way Jordan had turned the argument aside. She smiled at the idea of a dragon who could mediate.

"Ah, my dear Dragon," her father rasped, "I have always known I was mortal. In fact, my daughter can even tell you how my love of carnal pleasures has turned her from me and diminished whatever happiness she might have found in our mutual company."

"Then in the name of compensation for what you did not have in life, grant her *now* those benefits you might. Sign my document for her marriage. Give her protection, a husband, and family."

Clare bristled at the arrogance of men to make such intimate decisions for a woman. "I want no man or family."

Her father crooned, "Ah, Clare, don't do this," and in a disarming move, diverted to Jordan. "Tell me, Dragon, how old are you?"

Clare shook with rage, used to her father's tactics and knowing how well they worked to confound opponents. Oh, how she wished she could see Jordan's face more clearly as he adjusted to her father's diversion.

"Thirty-eight," he replied quickly.

"Only ten short years between us, Dragon."

Jordan said naught.

"When I die, I can count three wives and many other good women in my bed, but rumor says you have never married."

"That is true," Jordan affirmed.

"Nor do you have children. Not even bastards."

"None about whom I was ever told."

"No one to fight for, then. And no land of your own, either."

"There you are misinformed, Lord de Wallys. I hold a barony given me by John of Gaunt."

"So then, is it large enough you would fight for it?"

"I suspect I would, had I good cause."

"It is attacked by no one? Coveted by no one?"

"Coveted, it might be. Attacked, nay. Many know I am the king's man and would not risk his wrath to offend one of his own."

"You think Henry is powerful enough to help you keep it by his blessing alone?"

"I think so. Supporting him faithfully, I know I serve as an example for others to do the same."

Clare felt more admiration for this man burst open like another bud flowering.

The earl tried to chuckle but wheezed. "You believe in the power of devotion?"

"Aye."

"Yet you know it only from one vantage."

"Oh, how so?"

"You know only how to give it."

Clare felt Jordan turn to stone.

Her father continued. "Rumor says you do not get it—not from your only living relative, this nephew you would join to my daughter—and not from your lifelong friend, Lord Summersby. Now why is that, I wonder? Can a Dragon not inspire love?"

Clare sensed Jordan's tremor, like a wild beast straining to attack. "My private life is no concern of yours," Jordan declared. "My public life with the Lancasters speaks its own tales. What and whom I have loved will never be food for the masses, my lord."

"Have you ever loved?" Aymer insisted. "A woman? Madly?"

"Aye!" The Dragon raged in a bright fire of anger that made Clare's heart burn with shock, admiration, and compassion. "I could not have her because she was to wed my best friend! I drank to drown my sorrows. But I soon learned that was foolish to kill myself for love. I never drink wine now. *Why* can any of this matter to you?" Jordan's ire had banked, but not his focus on the main issue.

Her father was his match. Even weak as he was, he remained wily. "I wish only to know if the capacity to give and get love exists within your family, Dragon. You want me to hand over my heiress to you—and though she holds no great affection for me and, therefore, would not care to hear this next from my lips, I do tell you I value her. What is your Geoffrey Chandler like as a man, Dragon? I need to know before I sign your parchment. I must give your nephew to understand that when I lie cold in my vault for eternity, Clare should not lie cold in her bed for want of a

man who should ignite her virgin's body and fan the flames
in her sweet heart."

Clare reeled, never having heard such sentiments from
her parent. Had disease made mush of his brain?

"My nephew has his faults, sir. But I assure you he can
love a woman. Moreover, he has promised me he will love
his bride."

"Even though she is older than he is?"

"Three years is not so much, Lord de Wallys. And your
daughter has many fine qualities to tempt a man and keep
one. Wit—"

"Willfulness."

"Beauty!"

"Skin wrinkles, withers, *dies,* Dragon."

"The loveliness of soul endures eternity."

"Cease!" Clare cut the air with one hand. Her cloth fell
from her face. "My lords, I do not wish to leave my home.
Only this political matter makes it necessary—and that in
your eyes, not mine."

"Clare," her father said in a soothing tone, which shocked
her. He usually ended arguments, especially with women,
by fiat. "We have talked of this. After I am gone, you will
contend with the same problems I have. Yet you are a
woman and this marriage is best—"

"This marriage grows more heinous by the minute, Sire."
She spun to Jordan and saw his mouth turn down in
sadness. "Lord Chandler comes before you, Sire, three
months earlier than planned to persuade you to agree to the
union."

"Why so, Dragon?"

"Henry demands the wedding within two weeks."

She expected anger. Instead, the sound of an animal in a
trap reached Clare's ears. 'Twas her father. Anguished for
her. She stilled, overwhelmed by the joy that he cared so
much for her and repelled by the prospect of having to leave
him before he died.

"I understand your sorrow, my lord," said Jordan.
"These arrangements are not what you or your daughter

would have liked. Now that I am here, I understand many reasons why that is so, yet I cannot change the timing of Henry's preparations to come here to Trent."

"He comes?"

"With a portion of his army, my lord."

"How many?"

"Six hundred."

Her father cursed, coughed, and groaned. "Ah, Christ, this life does hurt. Why, Dragon, does Henry decide to advance now? Does he know I am at the hour of my death?"

Jordan inhaled, that slow draw of breath that Clare knew would make his chest expand like bellows. "Nay, my lord, he put no credence in reports of your ill health. He thought it one of your diversionary tactics, used once too often. I am loath to say the very worst reason why I am here so early is because . . . Glendower advances."

"Glendower, Christ upon His cross. Another ant! How close? When?"

"He sails north toward Carnavon and Beaumaris."

"If those two castles fall," Clare speculated, "Cheshire can be easily attacked."

"Aye," Jordan agreed. "But we have indications of another event more dire."

"What?" her father asked.

"The French have sent a fleet of ships up the Welsh coast to raid English fortifications."

Clare recoiled.

Her father swore. "The French have allied themselves with Glendower?"

The shock of this news rattled her senses, yet could she detect Jordan tense. Why? To measure how much her father knew about this. Why would the Dragon think that possible?

The odd thought hit her that Jordan might know she had corresponded with King Charles. But how? Who would have told of it? Not her agent La Croix in Calais who was English through and through and totally devoted to her art and her prosperity—and therefore, his own rising percentages of her commissions. Only one trusted guard carried her letters from here to a Flemish cloth merchant in Chester, who further arranged to send them to La Croix in Calais. La Croix then dispatched them on to Paris. Her guard had never spoken of being waylaid or questioned on the road on any of his journeys. Unless some correspondence between them had been interrupted . . . intercepted . . .

Did Jordan and his king interpret this flow of letters as Trent's collusion or—dear God—political conspiracy? Did Jordan think her father had conspired against Henry? Nay, impossible. Ever had her father aligned himself with one and then another English king, never a Welsh rebel.

But to a Dragon the possibility could look real.

If Jordan knew she wrote letters to Charles, he might even suspect her of betraying her country.

She tasted bile at the hideous idea. She was a writer, an artist. Her work could be bought. Not her body—nor her *allegiance!*

Jordan stepped around to the side of her father's bed before she found sense enough to keep him away from her father. "We are not certain what the French and Glendower discuss. Do you mean to say you know nothing of this cooperation between them?"

Nay! Clare wanted to shout.

"Not a word!" Aymer forgot himself and shot forward. In the dancing firelight, his bony face appeared swathed in pus-soaked strips of cloth. He shot an arm across his visage. "I am no traitor! Never! Get back." He waved in disgust, then shrank into his pillows. "You think of me unnatural things! Get out! You come too close!"

"Aye," declared Jordan. "I knew it before I entered your gates, my lord. But you cannot turn me out. Forgive me for my bluntness, but your days upon this earth diminish. Your mercenaries know no loyalties longer than their arms, which reach into your coffers. Your daughter—even with her six women who fight like demons—cannot keep the hordes from your walls. And they do come in all guises to your door."

"Who? How? What do you torment me with now?"

"Did she tell you about the attack of five men this afternoon?"

Clare stilled.

Her father shifted, his voice a rasp. "What is this? Clare?"

"I was at the shepherd's cottage this afternoon, discussing the spring's lambing. As my maids and I returned home, we came upon five men who had waylaid Baron Chandler and his two men."

"And who are the five, Clare?" her father asked.

"I do not know, Sire. I have never seen them before. All now are dead, and so we cannot ask them from whence they came."

"And there are no indications of their identities?"

"They were poor men, Sire. Without purse or rings to signify them."

In the flicker of a flame, she could see her father fume. "Who had the watch? Why did the men on duty not detect this band and end the mayhem before it began?"

"'Twas William Baldwin, Sire. He says he did what he could but could not be everywhere, especially in a snow-storm.'"

"Baldwin. A bull of a man. I have not known him to miss an opportunity to engage in conflict before this. Why now?" he mused.

Jordan advanced. "Are you saying you think him capable of conspiracy?"

"Any man or woman is capable of it, Dragon."

"What would Baldwin's motivation be?"

"What it always is. Money."

"What are his appetites," Jordan persisted, "that he might not be satisfied by what you pay him?"

"Women. He is an ugly beast. Unlike you, Dragon, and unlike what I used to be, some men must pay for the privilege to take a woman to bed."

Jordan cast a glance at Clare, sorrow in his countenance for the indelicacies of what she had to hear. "My lord de Wallys, these events declare that you must take greater securities for Trent's safety—and for your daughter's. Give over, my lord de Wallys. Settle her future before you die. Sign my documents for her marriage. Clearly, she cares for you, and for that alone, she deserves to live out her life without fear of attack and with a bevy of children around her."

Clare swallowed hard. Children. More people to care about, more to die too easily and leave her alone, loveless.

"Nay, I would make a terrible wife. A virago!" She grabbed Jordan's sleeve. "I do not want these things."

"I do not believe that." Jordan dropped each word like a stone.

"You need not, only hear me refuse you again!"

Her father moaned. "She has avoided marriage for years. It is because she has nursed too many who have died on her. Her mother, pretty lark that she was, died after the surgeon had to cut her open to pry the baby from her. That child was her third who died, Dragon. Clare has also treated but buried two more wives of mine as well as two mistresses I was well fond of. But mostly Clare misses the children who were given us. *Christ,* more infants than I remember. How many were there, Clare?"

"Two of Rosemary's and two of Adelaide's," Clare whispered. Memories bleaker than this foul-smelling sick room rushed to her head. "My brother, John, too."

"Her only brother," said her father. "He taught her how to ride like a man and shoot a bow like an outlaw."

"He urged me to be bold, Dragon," Clare added in defiance. "But he was kind and gay, so much like our sister, Blanchette." She pictured beautiful Blanchette, who had survived childhood maladies by the grace of God and sought to pay Him back by her secular devotion to Him in a convent close to Chester. Because Blanchette had never loved her Heavenly Master enough to take nun's vows, Clare hoped the girl had the desire to take Trent under her wing once Clare was gone to France. If only Clare could convince her that preserving Trent's integrity was worth the trouble to emerge from the convent's walls and take on the world's woes. Clare had tried when Blanchette had come home on a visit to broach the subject and failed to interest Blanchette sufficiently.

The earl scoffed. "Ha, I thought Blanchette was weak, but John was the sillier of the two. He ate wild berries he thought would be a treat. Clare gave him an emetic, and he vomited within minutes, but the poison was faster than Clare's cure. She held his hand as he died."

Suddenly, Clare heard countless moans and shouts and death rattles she had closed from her mind. Now they pulsed around her like the wailing of old ghosts.

She covered her mouth with her hand and the odors of disease wafted about her. She remembered how death had stalked her only hours ago and how Jordan had killed her assailant so easily with a dagger.

Not all deaths were so quick or easy as that man's. Her mother's hadn't been. Nor her stepmothers'.

Were disease and suffering the only components of life? Sometimes, such as now when the faces of departed loved ones appeared before her, she believed it to be so.

Tears obscured her vision. "Forgive me, I don't feel well." She hastened to the door.

"She never cries," she heard her father tell the Dragon.

She fled them both, their passions, their needs. She had her own. She needed her privacy, her tower chamber. Her refuge.

"Clare, wait."

She couldn't. She ran toward the stairs, flinging the wrapper away.

He caught the end and spun her to him without apology.

"I take my leave of you, my lord," she told him as she lifted her chin higher, noting with horror how tears dribbled down her cheeks. "You anger me with your impertinence to follow me and put your hands on me again."

"But you're hurt."

"Did you not think I could bleed?"

"Aye," he agreed on a ragged whisper. "I feared it from the first second I saw you."

"Fear no more. I assure you I always recover from the terrors I encounter."

"And always alone."

"'Tis no concern of yours."

"Though I do not wish it so, I feel your pain, Clare."

"Don't," she said, but wanted to ask *why*.

His hands framed her cheeks. "Look at me."

She shut her eyes.

"Very well. You cannot escape listening to me." His voice dropped to a husky resonance she felt to her toes. "I have combined these recent facts about you with the respect I learned in the forest earlier today. I am very glad I know all these things."

"Why?" She quivered, wild at his pursuit and thrilled at his compliment. "These revelations you have just learned only make me a better candidate for a wife, am I correct?"

"Aye."

"I am not pleased at all then."

"I know. Clare." He said it like a prayer against her temple. "I wish you wouldn't cry. Wish I weren't part of the cause. But I am and I can't change it."

She moaned and the dam of her sorrows broke. "I do not weep in front of anyone. Why you?" She was outraged at herself, raising her eyes to the crossbeams while tears cascaded across her temples.

"Because"—he wrapped her close—"you must sense this compassion I feel for you, Clare. I think so many assume you are self-sufficient like your father that they never consider how needy you are."

"That sounds like pity, and you may have it back."

"What I feel for you is the opposite of pity, dear woman. It's admiration." He thumbed fat tears from her lips. "And I can't seem to keep myself from touching you. Why is that?" he asked himself more than her.

She shook her head, her lashes fluttering downward as his nose traced patterns on her cheek and his lips brushed across her jaw. "Don't," she ordered, but wished she could have said, *Don't stop.*

He did her will. "Clare, all things beautiful." He trailed his mouth down her throat to nestle in the hollow between her collarbone and shoulder. "You smell like so many things I love. Apples and herbs and geraniums. You feel like so many things I have lost. Youth and certitude."

Shock rippled through her, drying her tears. Her hands drifted over his shoulders, down his arms, around his back. "You feel stalwart to me. A man of great conviction."

He made a sound that was pleased but rueful. "Time and circumstance have taken their toll on me. I approach my old age, and I want only quiet for the end of my days."

"You are not so old. I saw you today battle like the avenger of God. What's more, you fought for me. Yet were you injured. Most men would have let that man have me."

"I could not allow any man to take you," he said with soul-devouring succor, and urged her closer to his steely body. Against him, she felt hard evidence he was vigorous as any man half his age and just as lusty. "Men's avarice to take what is not theirs, like that man's greed to have you today, make me want to retire from court alone."

Without wife or children? "Surely you have friends. You are the king's loyal man."

"Aye, but my friends are not so loyal as I would wish them to be. I am disillusioned with their jealousy of my friendship with King Henry. As for my enemies, I weary of the constant fray. Duty has filled my life—and now I must end it before I become bitter in the bargain."

"You are too sweet to sour," she insisted, and caressed his devastating handsomeness with appreciative eyes. But clearly from the sideways glance he gave her, he did not believe her. "Jordan, you are so healthy that you *can* have life and have it abundantly. You are not that old!"

"Many men are grandfathers at my age, Clare! Most men are dead before thirty-eight! I even watch Henry sicken lately. Christ"—he seethed and gripped her arms so tightly that he shook her—"can't you see that I have no one to turn to as most men do. I only want a little peace before I die!"

"Surely then, if Henry is your true friend, he knows this desire of yours and would grant it."

"Aye, he will. Once I have accomplished my purpose here."

He drew away.

She should have argued her own cause, but she could not help herself. She reached out to cup his cheek.

He froze.

With her fingertips, she traced his scar, the brand of his devotion to his liege lord and his son. She outlined his mouth. How could a man whom God fashioned in so mighty a mold possess two lips that tantalized her with their softness?

He crushed her fingers, pressed her palm to his flesh, and graced her with a swift, hard kiss. Then he gently lowered her hand and stepped backward.

"We will not touch again, I promise you. You are a sensitive woman, and I am too attracted to your sweetness to dishonor my king and my nephew. Prepare yourself to leave, Clare. We depart as soon as my one man's ankle heals enough for him to mount a horse. Ten days at most." He pulled away and descended the stairs.

She wished she could have stopped him. Reminded him of his need to search for the identities of those five who had attacked him this afternoon. Or delayed him with an injunction to stay and watch his other more severely wounded man, Wickham, recover.

But she watched Jordan go and grieved over her own problem. Her lack of time. Lack to tend her father in his dying days. To set her house in order. To send for her sister, Blanchette. To notify the French king that the Nightingale needed to fly to him much sooner than the New Year. To ask him to turn his ships from Cheshire and her home . . . her country.

She had scarce days to accomplish all these tasks.

Hours available before she had to escape a Dragon. Before she learned so much more about this unique creature that she could be consumed in his fire. Kept in his thrall.

Chapter Five

"So as snow mantles earth
  And night disrobes for dawn . . ."

Clare walked in circles, dictating to herself. She usually did her best work deep into night when most in Castle Trent had gone to bed. But no lines came after those pitiful two. Her problems began with the hero, who had become Jordan, and the fact that this romance she wrote resembled too many aspects of her life. No matter how she tried to disentangle them, they only entwined more. And if dangerous memories of Jordan's lips did not burn her creativity to ashes, fears about leaving her home did.

What if Blanchette could not be persuaded to become chatelaine over the estate? What if she were not crafty enough to manage it? The girl was feisty and intelligent, but their father's imperious manner had hindered her willingness to hear another person out. She judged people and circumstances instinctively. Too much so to make Clare comfortable. What made Clare more accepting of Blanchette's ability to rule here was that Blanchette usually analyzed people and situations correctly. However, she was sixteen.

Clare's other worry was King Charles of France. Why had he really approached her to come to his court? Was it merely because he admired that book of prayers she had produced for his cousin while that man had served as emissary to England two years ago? Or did Charles have a more sinister reason to patronize her?

Suddenly, Clare suspected even the timing of his first letter to her through La Croix, the month after King Henry won the Battle of Shrewsbury—and ended hopes that the marches on the English border of Wales, Trent included, might go over to Wales. Why did Charles offer her so generous a stipend? Was he buying her artistic talent to glorify his own name as a patron of the arts and add to his famous library? Or was he conveniently, mayhaps even benevolently, trying to remove her from her home before he and his ally Glendower overtook it?

"My lady Clare! Wake up!" A rapping came on her door. "Please!"

She ran to fling it open to her father's harried servant.

"Raymond, what—?"

"He's torn the bandages off in his need to scratch! Then he fell in his rush to get to the garderobe to relieve himself. He raves so at me, I do fear he's broken his head this time! Help me. He'll listen to you."

She found her father curled on his side, pounding his fist on the floor, cursing God and His Right Hand, Harry of Lancaster. Adding Glendower to his list, Clare persuaded him to cease his mutterings, allow her to clean and bandage him, then crawl back to bed.

Breathless from lifting his lax body, Clare was again amazed that a man once so burly and now so pathetically lean could feel like such a dead weight. She needed to seek her own bed, and hoped from this exertion, she would fall into the featherbed.

But as she bid her father good night, even that possibility fled like a blackbird. He clamped her hand in a death grip. His words were lucid as his eyes. "I want to die, Clare."

The man who had enjoyed his carnal nature wished to end it. In one way, she was not surprised by his statement. If she ever suffered as he did, she would want to be delivered. But she had never enjoyed herself with abandon. Envied those who had a taste of it. So since she had only partially lived, how could she care to die?

She didn't.

"Help me, Clare."

"You cannot mean that I should—?"

"You have plants in that kitchen pantry of yours. Herbs and deadly flowers. Holly berries seize a man's brain, don't they?" A shade of who he once was—the infamous libertine Aymer, Tupper from Trent—smiled at her from his body's decay. "Hemlock would be my choice, girl." He wheezed, then deflated so completely, she leaned forward to see if he still breathed. "Aye, but you'd have it on your soul, wouldn't you? Oh, just to think what comfort it would give you on a cold night to know you had helped me into hell." He grinned with cracked lips to bare brown gums.

"Father." She had no idea if she meant to say "You're right" to both his alternatives or if she simply wanted to cry. Again. The idea was intolerable.

"I beg of you." His chin trembled. "Think on it."

Appalled that she would consider it for his sake and that after years of his blustering Aymer could weep—nay, *sob*— she hastened from his presence and stood in the hall, sagging against the frigid stones.

She wanted to be finished with illness and death, tension and war. She wanted to laugh with someone. She wanted to live her days in peace, doing work that she loved with people whom she respected.

A dragon flew into her thoughts. A large black beast with long, gentle fingers and terrifying ultimatums.

"Nay, there are other men as admirable," she whispered to the void.

None, however, sprang to mind.

She desired and admired what she could not have—a protector, a man to honor her, love her, keep her. And she could return the same devotion to him. If only this world were her fantasy and the Dragon could defend her from Glendower, Henry, or the Devil.

Her throat tightened, burned.

"You will not cry."

She went straight to her workroom. Wildly angry at herself for imagining the one man she could not crave, she lit every sconce and candle to drive him from each niche and corner of her mind. But even as she opened the stopper to a vial of ink, she was reminded of him.

She sat down at Mary's workbench and table with a quill in hand. But deprived of rest and filled with trepidations, she was not capable of performing even the simple task of writing two letters, one to Blanchette and the other to King Charles.

Creating them became a bigger nightmare than her father asking her to kill him—and Jordan Chandler transforming into some hero from a romance.

To Blanchette, Clare had once expected to write only "Your day has dawned when you may come home and rule Trent in my name." But now that events spun out of her own control and she had to leave Trent sooner than planned, Clare must influence the girl to arrive here before the father whom Blanchette hated lay cold in his vault.

But that took summaries of complicated events in Castle Trent to a young woman who had visited here only once in the eight years since she'd left. Blanchette, who had retired to her Benedictine convent at the tender age of eight, went with their father's blessing. Aymer rejoiced to pension off the child who quaked at his every word and clung to her mother's or Clare's skirts each time a mouse ran through the house. When Blanchette's mother, Rosemary, died, followed closely by their brother, John, the child mourned them both fervidly with prayers and tears. She became hollow-eyed, lank-haired, and so thin she resembled more a broom than the blonde blue-eyed angel who once made people halt in their tracks to admire. Begging to become a nun, Blanchette left home with that intention but never fulfilled it. Instead, she lived as an honored guest of Saint Ann's, reading and writing, gardening and avoiding her father.

Clare had seen the girl a few months ago in August. She had regained her beauty to a ravishing extent and possessed three additional attributes to make her hegemony here at Trent a strong one. Like her father, Blanchette was stubborn and proud.

But unlike the simpering child she had been, Blanchette knew how to control men. Precisely how she had learned this at a convent baffled Clare. But when she had visited her sister at Saint Ann's, Clare watched Blanchette deal with the villeins who came to work at the nunnery or the tradesmen who came to sell their wares. Invariably with men, Blanchette need use only her appearance to influence them. A look, a sigh, and she could melt a man at her feet. Those that didn't dissolve at her coyness she could bend with stern wit, which the nuns had encouraged in imitation of their own. Blanchette's imperious nature reminded Clare of Aymer's, and so this girl-turned-woman could rule here. With Clare's money. In Clare's name. And with Clare's consent and power.

Thus had Clare expected Blanchette would do well by them all because she could maintain respect and power with an aura of feminine mystery and sensual promise. Until this latest news that Glendower came with Frenchmen at his heels, Clare had rejoiced that Blanchette, young though she might be, could order a contingent of men anywhere. But in the neatness of her plans, Clare had become too complacent.

Now a Dragon appeared months earlier than forecast.

And French ships sailed up the coast of Wales to threaten Cheshire, Trent, and all of England.

So to King Charles, Clare knew she had to write a letter filled with diplomacy. She desperately wanted to negotiate with him. She even envisioned the words: "I will come to you sooner, but only if you cease your raids closer to English shores."

But who was she to ask for political considerations? She

was a writer. To be appreciated, her manuscripts—costly as they were to produce—had to be purchased! But her body did not have to be bought.

That sent anger, sour and hot, through her blood.

As an artist, she had to be free. Like the Nightingale she called herself, she needed to fly above the winds of petty politics. But her only hope to save her home was to bargain with her artistry. To hope Charles would want her enough to promise to spare those whom she loved.

That was a petty pawn to play, and she knew it. But she had no other. She held no power other than her land and her money. If she left the first to her sister and earned the second from a foreign monarch, she would be defenseless. Her devotion to her art had allowed her to think she could leave and work for anyone. But now she reeled at her naivete. What did her wishes or her art weigh against the will of the French king? They counted only differently to the English one.

Where was her succor?

Like Jordan, she wondered if any existed. She paused, her quill midair. Only with him, for brief minutes, had she found any sanctuary at all.

Her lifelong belief that she did not need a man to find peace within her soul surfaced. She needed to discover it within herself!

But suddenly a new thought danced at the edge of her mind. Could she create her own sanctuary independent of anyone? Free of father, sister, Welsh, English, or the French?

That was an interesting fantasy! If only she could. . . .

But her illuminator appeared at the door to the workshop.

"Madame?" Solange Dupre blinked in surprise. "You are never here at dawn. You are writing early, too. *Incroyable."*

"I do wish it were possible, Solange!" she said far more gaily than she felt. She was a much worse mummer than a writer. She put down her quill as she watched the pretty woman begin her day's work by arranging her quills, brushes, stencils, and tiny jars of precious pigments. Soon a steady stream of Clare's assistants followed, crowding the cozy workroom with their chatter and bustle. Wishing for solitude, Clare dashed off the best words she could find.

She sealed each sheet of parchment with wax and ring, left the tower, and searched for her most trusted guard. When she found him on the battlements, she led him to her solar and closed the heavy door. She asked him if he had ever talked to anyone on the road to Chester about where he was going or what he carried for his mistress. His answer was a predictable nay.

She quickly pressed into his meaty hand both of her newest letters along with a purse filled with enough gold to get him to Blanchette's nunnery near Chester and beyond, to her agent in Calais. This time she'd take no chances passing her correspondence through different hands. La Croix had never done her wrong, never cheated her, always praised her works, and she knew through him that her letter—unopened and undefiled—would arrive at Charles's Louvre in Paris.

Afterward, she bathed and ate. She avoided morning prayers, the shorter service of nones ever more to her liking. She had found God's will worked best when she went about her own business with speed and dedication.

She hastened to the apartments of the east tower where guests were housed. Passing by the Dragon's door on silent feet, she headed to the next, where she knocked and looked in on a serenely sleeping Edward Wickham. A very fortunate man, he had only a slight fever and awakened quickly at the touch of her hand to his forehead. Cleaning and dressing his nicely healing wound, she left him for Nathaniel Pickering, who also slept soundly. For him, she went to her alcove storeroom off the kitchen, measured out a dose of an elixir meant to lessen his swelling in his foot, gave it to a maid to administer, and returned to her warm workshop. There her women broke into two groups. One set of three prepared to produce a copy of an older commissioned work by cutting green sheets of varnished vellum parchment, now dry from a bleach of quicklime and a second bath of bright emerald verdigris. The other three set to their individual tasks for the romance they produced.

But Clare could not work. Her worries about her future and all of Castle Trent's loomed—and she prowled the room cluttered with tables, chairs, woodcuts, old pattern books, piles of sheepskin vellums, and people.

Solange, the illuminator who was Clare's newest recruit, sketched a few patterns as possible borders for the book and then mixed a large bowl of yellow pigment to complete them. Soon the woman dragged a hand through her hair, confessed a lack of inspiration, and asked if she might look in on the knight who had sprained his ankle yesterday. Clare let her go, silently hoping Edward did not recover well into the next millennium.

Her eyes drifted to Solange's designs and the tight little scripted notes of Solange's apprentice, Ella, a novice from Blackpool. Their manuscript borders were usually very delicate, but these yellow flowers appeared garish, and their tiny black vines looked evil. That furrowed Clare's brow. Both artists were more talented. Why were they slacking in producing the finest quality?

She glanced up at Margaret Frank, Mary's twin, who sang, oddly happy for once in her irritable life. She mixed lampblack ashes and gum to make a new supply of ink, interrupting her song now and then to ask her sister what she thought of the consistency. Mary, never one to be effusive in her praise, was usually less than charitable in her rejection. Today she gave Margaret a tongue-lashing she did not deserve.

Drained of tolerance for the constant conflicts between these two, Clare strode toward the door. "Continue without me. I must see how our sick and wounded fare."

Mary frowned at her, then glanced over at Margaret. Clare did not have to see the look that passed between them to know they questioned why their mistress was losing her ability to write a coherent story.

"I tell you she had trouble writing this morning."

"Could you see what it was?" Nathaniel Pickering asked. Jordan halted in the hall to better hear the smoky female voice inside Nathaniel Pickering's bedchamber. His door swung open wider from crooked hinges.

"Two letters."

Jordan knew who this woman was with the French accent to her fluent English sentences. She had helped Nathaniel on the field after his injury yesterday, and she had been here last night after supper when Jordan came to see how his man fared. Jordan also knew for certain this woman spoke about her mistress, Clare. He was not surprised that the lady who could fight as she had yesterday could write. What bothered him was that he could venture a guess why Clare could not perform her normal functions easily this morn.

He had frightened her last night with his revelations about Glendower and his orders from Henry.

What Jordan did not know was to whom Clare had written two letters. And for what purposes.

"I do not read your English," the woman was scolding Pickering. "I told you that before. Not French, either."

"How can you not, with what you do?" Pickering was chuckling.

But the woman must have poked him because he stopped of a sudden. Then she spoke with seriousness. "That medicine she sent makes of you a cretin. I say that I am worried. She never comes into the workshop before the sun is high, but when she does arrive, her thoughts always flow like water. Yet when she wrote these two letters, I saw her start and stop countless times."

"To meet the Dragon," replied his man, "is an unnerving experience for many women. Even for a warrior like your lady, he is a challenge."

Jordan scowled, questioning the tone of this conversation between two people who had not met until yesterday. He could not decide which particular note jarred him. Or did he not recognize simple harmony between two people when he heard it?

He pondered instead how well he himself knew Nathaniel. The young man had joined his service last month at the request of his father, who was Henry's lifelong supporter. Yet now Nathaniel did sound as if he knew Jordan well, enough to embark upon those oft-old tales about his prowess with women, wine, and song. The boy's words made Jordan cringe.

"I have seen women pant for him like a dog."

Never enticing.

"I see the reasons, *mon cher*. His visage. His disposition."

"Aye, though I haven't seen him with a woman since I've joined his service." Nathaniel seemed confused by that. "I have heard women offer themselves to him. I have it on good authority, too, that he is the one who taught Prince Hal how to wench and drink."

Hal needed no teacher.

"Some women dream of taming a creature like the Dragon," she grumbled, "and make him—how do you say, water at the mouth?"

Pickering hooted. "I assure you, Solange, the Dragon never drools."

Enough of this! Jordan retraced a few of his steps and made much noise to the door so that the two ceased their banter.

"Good morning," he bid to Nathaniel as he ducked his head to enter the sunlit room. "I see you are awake. You also have good reason to recover speedily." Jordan took in the provocative black eyes and hair of the woman and felt immediate revulsion for her.

Nathaniel did look hale and hearty from a good night's rest, laughter, and the woman's company. "Aye, my lord, I feel stouthearted. The steward and a kitchen maid came with porridge and strong mead this morning. Lady de Wallys sent a potion, too." He stuck out his tongue like a child. "This kind lady just now brought me some broth from the kitchen. You saw her yesterday upon the field. She is Solange Dupre."

"You are French, Solange?" Jordan asked as he inclined his head in greeting.

"Non, my lord. I am from Bruges, and I serve here as a maid."

"Bruges," Jordan said slowly. " 'Tis a long way to come to serve as a maid."

"My mistress pays me well for what I do, my lord."

"I see. And what is that?" Jordan detected the slow slide of Nathaniel's gaze toward the petite lady he obviously found so attractive.

She smiled. "I assist her with her writings, my lord."

He wanted to shout, "How can you do that if you do not read?" He chose instead to ask, "She has so many?"

"To keep the accounts for an earldom of this size," came Clare's explanation from behind him, "is no easy task."

Every time Jordan saw her, he created more fantasies of her which had nothing to do with enduring pain of a dislocated shoulder but began with discovering where her latest smudge of ashes rested.

This morning's collection was on both hands.

He cocked his head. He challenged his intellect to find the reason for these spots. Did she build fires, make candles, assist the farrier? What did she burn to gain these odd decorations?

He wanted to ask her, help her so that she could avoid them . . . or . . . could he mayhaps burn with her?

He jammed down the urge to laugh and to simply walk over, embrace her strong, firm body again, and make off with her to some dark pantry where they might speak of happier topics than war.

Damn his wandering eyes, she was even more enchanting this morning in the rays of sunlight than last night in candles' glow. Then she'd pulled her curling tresses up her high brow into a pearl coil. Today she'd caught her hair back in emerald ribbons too weak to control the loose copper braid. Last night she had donned a burgundy gown, which had contrasted her pale skin but was not as complimentary to her complexion as the emerald wool gown she wore now. This style hugged her shoulders, revealing the hollows at the base of her throat, at her collarbone, and the entrance to the valley between her breasts.

Mentally stripping her of her clothes, he pictured how he would enjoy her naked. His hands would trace sleek skin, overflow with creamy breasts. He'd thumb her nipples before he laved them. That made him wonder if they were blossoms or buds, silk or linen. He rolled his tongue around his mouth, shaping whatever they were into diamonds of delight. Pushing down a groan, he shifted from one foot to the other and forced his eyes to her face.

She looked weary.

So . . . she had not slept.

Neither had he.

He disliked the shadows under her eyes. Just like her tears, he hated the idea that he had put them there.

Solange rose from her place on the edge of Nathaniel's mattress. "I can return to my duties, if you wish it, *madame."*

"Of course not, Solange." Clare trained her smile on Nathaniel, her lips more generous in their mirth than the rest of her strained features. "How do you feel now, Lord Pickering?" She stepped around Jordan as if he were not there and lifted the blankets to examine his man's splinted foot.

"Last night it blew up like a dead fish. But it grows no more. See there. I tell you, that draught of celandine you sent this morning made the throbbing stop. It must have had a drop of oriental poppy juice in it. Will there be another, dare I hope?"

"One more is the most you'll need, I think, Nathaniel."

"And no surgeon to bleed me. I won't let you."

"I have seen one use his knife like a butcher to a slaughter. I would never allow one into Castle Trent. Not even to sew up your companion, Sir Wickham. Rest easy, will you?" She offered a sweet smile to his man, and Jordan felt a stab of jealousy.

She bent to Nathaniel's ankle, adjusting the wooden splints wider against his leg. "You have big feet, sir. I think I will have my men split a log and fit you for a sturdier brace, Nathaniel. You don't mind I call you that, do you?"

"Nay, my lady," said the lad, flushing red with her attention. "I am honored."

"You look much like my brother."

"Oh?" Nathaniel frowned, his gaiety as dead as if it had never been. "I did not know you had a brother."

"Had a brother is the right word, Nathaniel," she said as she wound the cloth more tightly about his leg and tied it off. "He is dead more than eight years now."

"But you loved him well, my lady," Nathaniel concluded.

"That I did."

Jordan traced Clare's smooth brow and upturned nose, her ripe lips—and when she moved, behind her he focused on Solange.

Arms crossed and leaning against the wall, Solange stared at Clare with narrowed eyes.

A shiver skimmed Jordan's spine. What ailed the maid?

He shot a glance at Clare and found no reason for the Flemish woman to resent her. Clare certainly was treating Nathaniel as if he were her brother. And yet, the look on Solange's face was not that green-eyed possessiveness of a lover, either. It was quite simply hatred.

Clare flipped back Nathaniel's covers. "There. That should support you until the new brace is cut. In the meantime, stay off your feet, Nathaniel. See that you encourage him, Solange." She made a line for the door.

In the hall, Jordan caught her arm. "Wait, Clare! I would know about your father's health this morning." *I wish to search your eyes for any sign you stayed awake because I walked your mind, as you did mine.*

She whirled and jabbed a fingertip into his chest. "He is worse for the anger aroused in your meeting last night. I am no better," she announced with a toss of her head. "Not that it would mean much to you. But let me tell you, you put your hands on me enough last night, my lord. I remind you of your vow not to do so again."

Ah, she had thought of his hands on her. How? Slowly, as he had envisioned? Completely, along every crest and cavern where his errant mind traveled leisurely. He looked down at her palm, now flat to his heart. One brow arced. "I concede the joust, my lady."

"What would it take to make you concede the entire tournament?" she asked boldly and obviously without forethought of where this debate might lead.

He glanced at her eyes, her mouth. "I have a few

suggestions that would cause you to blush and me to lose my honor."

That startled her a moment, but she taunted him. "And let England go to the Welsh?"

"For one hour alone with you, my sunbeam, I think I'd let the whole world go to hell."

She stared at him while her cheeks flamed. Then she huffed, "Think no more, Dragon. I am not weak or simpering."

"What man—or Dragon—wants a woman that way?" He couldn't cage his need to step nearer. He cupped her neck, splaying his fingers into the heavy mass of her hair there where her moist skin covered her strong spine. His nostrils flared with the intriguing scents of geranium and musky woman. "You're so bright with life to watch you hurts my eyes." He brought her so close that through the superfine wool he memorized her lithe curves. "You renew my joy in living."

"You are too eloquent," she objected, but in her eyes he saw she was awed and succumbing to his praise.

"My words cannot begin to praise you," he said against her ear and ran one open palm down her backbone to press her loins flush to his thighs. She could make a man turn to water. Turn to drink. Die for a taste of what he craved.

That slammed him back to reality. He'd lost himself in wine for more than two years after Diana Montaigne married his best friend, Malcolm Summersby. He'd sworn to never take another sip. He wouldn't now.

The similarities between both situations pierced him like a dagger. Like Clare, Diana had been a titled, landed, wealthy heiress destined for another man when he fell for her charms. Like a boy, Jordan had not stopped to think what heavy price in lost self-respect he might pay for loving a lady destined for another. Luckily, he had not lost Malcolm's friendship entirely. Malcolm had been cool to Jordan for many years, but in the last two, he'd become Jordan's confidant as much as he had in their youth.

With Clare, conditions were only slightly different. The man who had claim to the woman Jordan cared for was his nephew. Simply because Geoffrey and Jordan had not ever been friends did not mean Jordan had a right to seduce this sunbeam.

With remorse, Jordan stepped back.

She swallowed hard.

He wanted to kiss her confusion and embarrassment away, but *Christ,* he had assaulted her and learned the details about her exciting body against her will. Luckily, Solange had not emerged from Nathaniel's chamber—and grief ate at his guts.

He deserved it if Clare slapped him.

Today unlike yesterday, words would work as her weapons. He watched her collect them, like David collecting stones against Goliath. "You are an intolerable man, Jordan Chandler. You come to my home and assault me, order me about, and then handle me as if I were goods at your disposal. Unlike other women who may have fallen into your arms at the flick of your lashes, I am not at your beck and call. I am my own master. I make my own mistakes! And plenty of them! Trust me, sir, allowing you to use your charm on me will not be my newest!"

Hands clenched, she strode away.

Alone, he brooded on her uncharacteristic self-criticism. Had he caused that? He doubted it. She had done nothing here to encourage him. The thought that she assumed he purposely charmed her thrilled him and enraged him. She was the first women in months he had even looked upon with interest. The only woman he had seen in years with integrity.

Worse, he also realized how easily he had breached the wall of honor separating them. Could he fill the rift?

He would spend at least two or three weeks with her, waiting for Nathaniel to recover and taking her to Geoffrey. Could he leash the animal who ached to touch her?

He would. For his good and to the benefit of nephew, king, and country. To keep safe a woman who had ridden across the cold terrain of his past, driven boredom from his days, healed his body with her care—and his sad turn of mind with her own positive nature. Clare de Wallys had caused him to witness that a woman could be assertive and honorable. That she could be dedicated to those she loved in spite of poor treatment at their hands. That she could be courageous in the face of danger—and against odds that assured she would not win her way.

He could feel her pulsing in his blood. And he wanted more of her. In his hands, in his mouth.

But he'd *not* take her!

Instead, he would focus on the other problem that chewed at his brain.

His mind circled back to the sickroom. To Nathaniel Pickering and Solange Dupre.

Aye, he planned to return often and at unexpected hours to check on Nathaniel's progress. Something was askew about the relationship between his man and Clare's maid.

Why would these two, who had met only yesterday, talk in so familiar a manner about Clare?

What did they share?

What did they hide?

He was halfway across the courtyard, headed for the stables to check on Flame, when he halted, remembering the point of their conversation. They worried over two letters Clare had written.

Why? For a lady who could write, composing letters was no extraordinary matter. He knew quite a few women who carried on extensive correspondence with each other. One had even written a small story for the entertainment of her friend.

What would Clare write of interest to her maid and his man?

And to whom?

Chapter Six

THE NIGHT AFTER SWATHING HER FATHER IN CLEAN BANDAGES, Clare administered his regular dose of two drops of opium in his nighttime ale to ease his pain.

He clawed at her skirts. "Did you do it?"

One look into his yellow eyes told her he asked if she had found the nerve—and administered the means—to kill him. "I wish I could."

He cursed and fell to his pillows, staring into the barrenness before him.

She saw his despair and fled it.

She ran the length of the castle to her tower and her chamber and snatched at her cloak. She sought the battlements. The night and the air. Solitude.

In the stillness, she gazed instead upon one huge silhouette which blocked the moonlight.

She had found the Dragon.

When she hesitated—and loathed her weak need to commune with one who seemed forever stalwart—she would have left, but his voice drew her to a halt. He sounded as tired as she.

"Stay. I would not deprive you of fresh air to clear your mind. It would not be a mistake," he said, reminiscent of her words that morning to him. "You see, some say I am not poor company."

She wrapped her cloak more securely about her throat and over her unbound hair, rejoicing at the dark which hid her face from him. She would not want him to see her delight he was here. That might lead him to think she approved of his behavior when he had stopped her in the hall this morning. She didn't . . . but she could still imagine how his big hands covered her and held her to him. A shocking stance. Riveting as a bolt of lightning singing through her blood. But she could not tell him in words or imply now by her demeanor that she had enjoyed it.

Nor did she want to spar with him. She was too drained by recent events. She would only stay here to enjoy the night and the few minutes with an intelligent, intriguing man.

"I apologize for my outburst this morning. I was . . . overwrought. I am certain many value you, else you would not be here on this mission for Henry." She looked out upon her land to change the subject. "'Tis not often a winter's night is quiet."

"Aye," he said on a hushed voice, "I like it when no bough bends."

You value strength and resolve, she thought, but cast that aside for the communion she sought here with him. Concentrating on the delicacy of a Dragon's observation, she smiled to herself. "I enjoy it, too, and come up here often in any season. Else, I walk the courtyard."

"You are an owl?" Laughter lurked in his bass tone.

"Aye, another peculiarity to add to my collection. I prefer the darkness to daylight and need the silence and the solitude," she told him, revealing a portion of her loneliness to him. Surprised she had—and that unlike others, he was not repulsed by her frankness—she added on a more mundane note, "Snow comes after such nights."

She could hear rueful laughter in his words when he said, "I suppose you wish for a blizzard."

"Up to your eyeballs!" she shot back merrily.

He made no response.

What could she expect? That the camaraderie she had experienced a minute ago was a permanent part of their relationship? He would not agree with her to delay their departure past the day his man Pickering could stand on his sprained ankle. To the Dragon, it did not matter if snow reached this wall walk—or if she and he became fast friends. But then why ask what he had?

She closed her eyes, listening to the silence—and a Dragon's breathing. She refused to leave her own battlement because he was less friendly than she hoped.

Footsteps approached. Four of the guard changed. The new watch bid them both good evening and strode to their posts around the parapet.

After a long minute, Jordan said, "I missed you at supper."

"The minstrels I hired were not terribly entertaining. At least that's what my women told me. I am sorry."

" 'Twas not your fault. The minstrels used too many bells to cover poor singing. The food your cook prepared was much better. Unfortunately for me, the company—which would have been the fairest of all tonight's pleasures—was not available."

She rejoiced, she despaired. "Jordan—"

He pronounced the next words on so civil a note, she took a few seconds to understand his meaning. "When I left my bedchamber for supper tonight, I found two guards on duty at my door."

She did not comprehend how this could have happened.

"Am I your prisoner, Clare?" he persisted, cool and sharp as cut glass.

She shook her head from the shock of his news—and his implication that she may have ordered him to be watched. "Nay! Did they detain you?"

"Look at me." He spread his arms wide. The pose which

on any other man would have indicated crucifixion, transformed him into a dragon with wings outstretched to attack.
"I am unharmed and still here."

"I did not know of this. I swear I did *not*."

"Would your father know?"

She thought long on that. Aside from her, only three
others had the authority to order a guard. Baldwin, his
equal for the night watch, Gruffyd Fitzroy, and her father.
Would William Baldwin dare to post men at the Dragon's
door and for what reason? To flaunt his power, mark his
territory, or spite the English emissary from Henry? The
man was surly, impulsive, but never so much so to be
termed stupid or totally insubordinate. Then there was
Gruffyd Fitzroy, a mongrel of a man with a mother from
Wales, a father from Chester, and a wife from Trent. Never
had that man been impertinent, though he seemed to trust
no one, English or Welsh. "It is possible my father could
have ordered this, though I doubt it."

"I must ask him."

"Nay! You will not disturb him again! I cannot allow you
to see him."

"Allow?" Jordan pronounced the word like poison sat his
tongue. "Clare, you will arrange it."

"You cannot tell me what to do. This is *my* home.

"And my life is at stake."

"I will inquire who ordered the guards!" she insisted.

Once more, Jordan changed tactics on her. He spoke with
serenity as he said, "Clare, I have been attacked in your
woods, just as you were. We do not know who they were,
unless you have discovered news you have not shared."

"Nay, none. I checked my captain's story that a few
villagers feared an attack of outlaws. They did and Baldwin
took his men to scour the forest there. My men cannot be all
places at once. Unfortunately."

"Aye, and for that reason, my two men are down. I am
alone. Here. With you." She thrilled to the intimacy of
Jordan's tone as he swept out a hand to define the wall walk
and her home. "The Dragon is in your keep."

Aye, his welfare—his very life—was her responsibility as his hostess. "'Twould be against all honor to offer you our home and see you hurt."

"Are you saying that those two men kept me *safe?*"

"Nay!" *Not that I know.* "I will ask my father, I promise you. 'Tis not like him to be rude. Never have I known it of him."

"Do you mean to tell me that your father *never* set guards on guests within his own halls?"

"Aye, he did once. But only then. Long ago when another messenger came from Henry. I was small and heard my mother tell the tale. It was when King Richard was alive—and Henry was only the earl of Derby and wished to parley with my father over common borderlands. Henry sent a retainer of his with conditions. The man acted shamefully with one of our maids, and my father imprisoned him."

She paused, remembering something familiar about the man's giant appearance and his commoner's name. Chandler. Aye, she was most certain. Matching vague recollections to the man who stood before her, she cocked her head. "Rumor went to Henry that my father would ransom the knight if only Henry would retreat. But Henry sent a spy here instead. This intruder invaded the dungeons, killed the guards, and escaped with the prisoner. To this day, my father will not admit the breach of his defenses. He says only that Trent's mice learned how to make way for a Lancastrian rat."

She wished she could see the Dragon's face to know if this story meant anything to him personally. Then she perceived him smile. "Do you know that man who was imprisoned, Jordan?"

"He was my brother."

"And the spy?" she asked, knowing the answer already.

Jordan was chuckling. "I confess I never did think of myself as a rat." His laughter died abruptly as it was born. This time his voice filled with concern. "I hear in your hall that your father is even worse tonight."

"Aye, his angers and fears combine to put him in misery."

"Is it leprosy?"

She leaned forward to rest against the parapet. "I cannot be certain. His flesh"—she would try to be delicate—"decays but does not mortify in the same way as those who wander homeless with clackers in their hands to ward off others. He has not lost any fingers or toes but his skin withers. . . . He weakens from the constant itching and makes himself more at misery to scratch. At first we thought his malady temporary and curable, but other afflictions appeared—deteriorations of lungs and heart and stomach."

"How long?"

Clare knew he meant how long did her father have to live. "A few months at most. Mayhaps a few weeks. He wants death badly since he cannot sleep or eat or see very well." She pulled her hood forward and gazed out upon the land that would be entirely hers after her father died. In the rolling horizon of grays on black, she saw the reason to stay blur with the reason to leave. She loved her home and wished to see its people survive and prosper.

"Clare, for your sake, I wish I could remain indefinitely. Your father deserves succor from his family as he dies. Any father deserves that from a child."

Remorse tinged his words.

Clare lifted her face to him. How many human emotions did the Dragon possess? "Your father is dead?"

"For five years now. I had to leave him when he was dying, and my brother refused to come to console him." Jordan inhaled, that act he so often used in place of words. "My father was very much like yours. Proud and self-serving. Demanding. At his end, he was endearing because he embraced me for the first time and told me how and why he cared for me."

"Why could you not stay with him?" she asked, feeling Jordan's grief and thrilling to the knowledge that this virile man would want—and take—affection from his father.

"For the same reasons you cannot. I belonged to Henry of Lancaster, and he had been banished from England by his cousin King Richard. I had to go when I did or see the inside of one of Richard's dungeons. My father understood politics. He played them often enough when he was young and strong, but he wept when I left. He regretted, he said, how he had not taken time to truly father my older brother and me. He told me he often wished he had shown us how he loved us, simply because we were his. I saw in that encounter that on his deathbed a man changes."

"Aye," she breathed into the night. "I see it every day and stand amazed."

"My older brother, Gerald, did not forgive me for leaving."

"Why?"

"Gerald courted a second wife in Kent. She was an heiress, and he had debts to pay for dicing and bad investments in shipping for the wool trade with Flanders. He had won the woman's heart but not her father's. Gerald thought negotiations more important than attending our father in his final days."

"And?"

"This is not a pretty tale."

"I like stories. 'Tis the only thing I had from my father for many years. Please tell me . . . that is, if you like."

Jordan faced the parapet. "Our sire often told us of a fortune he had collected when he invested in a smuggling ring out of the Cinque Ports. He taunted Gerald and me often with the tale that he had hidden an enormous number of gold coins somewhere on his lands. When he died, he said, he would reveal its whereabouts and divide the contents according to the degree to which each of us warmed his cold and lonely heart."

He gave a short laugh. "My father's problem was that Gerald, whose first bride came to him with less money than he expected, wanted Father's gold too much—whereas I did not want it at all. If Father even possessed such a fortune, I asked myself who would want it, tainted as it was? The old gentleman couldn't lure me to his game. Since I needed to leave his side and England before he thought he was *in extremis,* he told no one where the gold was hidden.

Gerald, until he died two years ago, dug and picked at every nook and cranny in Morning Star Manor to find it. I swear to you, he would have torn the walls down had he the money to build a new home. But he never found it. His son Geoffrey does not follow his father's lead, that I know. Geoffrey lives frugally off his inheritance and seeks to make his fortune in another way."

Clare nodded. "Like his father, Geoffrey seeks to marry a wealthy woman."

"Oh, I think Geoffrey seeks a few more assets than money."

She froze at the idea of what this unknown husband might ask from her. "What more can a woman give than her freedom? Her body?"

"Affection. Children. Peace. You can give him those and more."

"He could acquire them from another, too."

"Aye, but sadly, without the king's approval—and not to the king's benefit, either. Geoffrey is a good match for any woman. He may not be rich in gold, but he has much land— land near my smaller barony in Blackpool along the coast of the Irish Sea and bounded by much of the duchy of Lancaster. With the addition of Trent to his domain and the protection of the Montaigne lands to the south, Geoffrey will stand as a bulwark for Henry and England against the Welsh rebels. *And* he'll have the money to do it well." He came closer to her, and she warmed at his body heat, if not his words. "Clare, I know Geoffrey well. He will adore you. You will bring him great joy."

"And what will I gain?" she replied, crossing her arms against the tremors of distaste.

"You will find him active, jovial, amusing. What's more, he is attractive."

She turned to look up at the profile of a dragon. The moonlight conspired to show her his angular symmetry, his sweet quicksilver eyes. "What does he look like?" *You?*

"Blond, blue-eyed. Tall and lean."

Not to my taste at all.

"He is the perfect picture of a hero from a romance."

"Not mine," she murmured. That shook her to her toes. Was she becoming too fond of a man she called her foe? A man she could never marry, enjoy? One she should never desire? She squeezed her eyes shut.

"Clare?" His hand touched her arm. "Clare—" His arm drifted around her shoulders.

Nothing had ever come so easy in her life as going to his embrace. Always fluent with words, she found none to describe this euphoria she felt against his rock-hard chest. Always filled with the need to be accomplishing some task, she wanted only to stand here till the earth died. Always eager to lead, she knew she'd found the one man she could follow.

But not to another man's arms.

That would be a mistake. Just as this was.

She drew away.

Hands to her waist, he slowly pulled her back. *"Nay,"* he ground out like an animal in pain. "You need comfort and you want it from me. That I can give you is that you shall have. Here." He enfolded her like a vise made of iron. "For one warm moment on a winter's night."

Her body expressed what she dare not try to translate into speech. She buried her nose in the folds of cloak and tunic, which could not conceal the strength of him. Beneath her mouth she felt his heart beat a frantic rhythm. She flowed against him, circled her arms around him, and noted for the first time that she could not encompass him as he so easily did her.

He ran his open hands along every inch of her back, massaging her muscles, lifting her tension, and easing the way to mold herself against him, breast to belly to thigh. He breathed raggedly, nuzzling his lips against her crown, pulling her cowl off, and spiking his hand into her hair.

If she moved now, he would kiss her. But if she felt the Dragon's brand, could she escape the conflagration of wanting more from him?

She would never know.

Grief shrieked at her to do this, have this one pleasure in the dark on a lonely night with a man worth tasting. She let her head fall back into his hand.

The shock of his expression stunned her.

She thought she'd see a man who was entranced.

She found a dragon who was heartbroken.

"Do you hunger for a hero?" he asked.

"Aye, though I never knew that until . . ." Her fingers traced his lips. "Now."

"What I want to do with you is not heroic," he said between clenched jaws. "It is villainy, and I cannot stop, though I told myself we would never do this." He lifted her against him. "But the air need only fill with your fragrance, and my body screams to have you."

He carried her to a darker corner where the guards could not see, she vaguely thought. Though she stood in the shadows, she saw his face full in the moonlight. He appeared in torment.

She wished she could spare him, but how could she when she couldn't save herself from wanting him?

"God assoil me, Clare, but my desire for you eats at my honor," he proclaimed in a hush, and put two hands to the opening of her cloak. "And still, I do not care. Tomorrow in sunlight, I'll chastise myself and take a new vow to stay away. But for now, let me do this my way." He asked permission but did not wait to spread her garment wide.

To be undressed by him was an ambition she had not known she possessed. She rejoiced in it, thrust modesty aside, and undulated to his hot velvet touch. She bit her lip to keep from crying to the moon in joy.

His open hands spanned the neckline of her gown, the top of her breasts, and slid deliberately up her bare skin to cover the hollows at the base of her throat and over her collarbones and shoulders. She circled her throat, both thumbs raising her chin. "Last night in my cold bed, I told myself you were a woman who needed wooing. I even practiced at words to persuade you to allow me to put my hands all over you." He exhaled beneath her ear with such force of his passion that she swayed closer to him. "But who needs words when I want to put my mouth on you . . ." She trembled. "Everywhere."

She dug her nails into his cloak and wished she could sink them into his skin. "Kiss me."

"Do not doubt it. But be warned, I mean to make it memorable for us both. Geoffrey will have to work his damnedest to surpass what I intend to do to you, my sunbeam."

"Don't speak of him."

"Nay, none but you."

Words could work no more magic than his had. She put her open mouth a breath away from his and waited for his lead.

"My sweet woman," he spoke upon her flesh, "has no one ever taught you how to kiss?"

"I never wanted any man's initiation, but now I do wish for the Dragon's fire."

"'Twill be my joy, then, and my torture."

"Not your pleasure?"

"Aye, mine and yours, together more than God allows." His first sip of her lips was a whisk of angel's wings. His second taste was a slant, the sting of a bee. His third began when his fingers puckered her lower lip and his mouth nibbled at her. His fingers intruded to trace her mouth, take her moisture, and outline his own mouth in preparation. He licked his lips and grinned wickedly.

She clutched at him, expecting this time he'd give her the fuller taste of him, but she objected as he pinned her to the wall and trailed the tip of his tongue down her throat. She was not sorry. He dipped into the hollows he had bared to his view, then found the cleavage of her breasts.

"Tell me," he said against her pounding heart, "what do you feel?"

"Strange. Exotic!"

He uttered an anguished sound akin to laughter. "What else?"

"Hot and tight."

He groaned. He moved lower.

She stopped breathing.

He paused above one breast. She thought he'd put his mouth there, where she felt the pointed need to have his warmth. The same way she had wished for his attentions whenever he looked at her with narrowed eyes. The same way he lifted his head and gazed at her now. "Describe your breasts to me."

She dropped her jaw.

"I won't taste them so I must know what they are like as compensation for what I'll never have."

"I—they are—" In the dark she blushed madly.

"Melons?" he suggested.

She wanted to chuckle. "Cushions!"

For reward, he hugged her. "Your nipples?" he asked against her throat, his hands kneading her waist, never drifting upward to the begging crests they discussed.

"Round."

"Their color?"

She ground her teeth.

"Like raspberries?" he suggested.

"Nay, ripe peaches."

He trembled. "And as large?"

"Aye, very. Too big!"

He crushed her against him, his mouth to her ear. "I could make them small, hard."

She sagged.

He held her tenderly, his mouth skimming her cheek.

"Kiss me," she demanded, one hand diving into his hair, loosening his leather ribbon and filling with thick silk. "Now, before I die."

"Ah, sunbeam, before you expire, let me show you what it is to live."

He showed her what it was to fly. He placed his mouth to hers like the caress of a spring breeze that quickly surged into a raging storm. She rose amidst the fury with his arms around her, weightless, mindless.

Then he took her to where the fires of heaven began. He sent his tongue into her mouth and took a fast fierce taste that shook him to his toes. He yanked away.

She called his name.

And then he taught her what it was to burn. He caught her chin, licked the outline of her lips and plunged inside once more. Her legs gave way, he held her up, then gave her air. She brought him back, and this time she sampled the surrender of a Dragon.

He melted. "Clare," he repeated her name as he dropped kisses to her willing mouth, his fingers in her hair, his lips to her temple. "Darling, we will not continue."

She made a small ignoble sound.

"I know," he whispered. "Passion like that is meant to flame, but ours would only render us to ashes. We are too used to facing ourselves with pure natures."

She wanted to pound her fists into his chest. To scream at God, Henry, and—

She felt like laughing! A mad woman. That's what she was.

She was a woman who wrote stories, who fantasized, and yet the one time in her life when reality surpassed any fiction for glory, she would have to end the tale before it had begun.

She sank against the stone wall, snapped her cloak around her. Her breasts throbbed. Her loins ached. Her lips chilled. She faced the giant shadow in the night. "I will notify the guards at your door that they are relieved of their posts."

That was the only positive thing she could do when the knowledge eating her alive was that she had just kissed the Dragon and made the biggest mistake of her life.

Chapter Seven

THE NEXT MORNING A YOUNG LAUNDRESS NAMED ISOBEL AR-
rived at Jordan's door. She ushered in two servants, carry-
ing the water and a tub for his bath. As she loitered,
Jordan's first thought was to send her away. He disliked
servants doing tasks for him he could perform himself.
Especially the intimate one of bathing. But he rejected the
impulse as he wondered what he might learn from her.

She seized that moment to plead with him. "Don't send
me off as you did the other night, milord. 'Tis my assigned
task to do this service," she appealed to him with a
suggestive widening of her eyes. "I swear, milord, the cook
ordered me here and will beat me if I fail."

Suspicious of many in this castle now, Jordan speculated
on what particular job the cook expected Isobel to perform.
Whatever their plan or lack of it, he had not been able to
create one of his own.

He was alone, at Clare's mercy and others like Nathaniel
Pickering, Solange Dupre, and even Edward Wickham. He
needed more than brawn and brains to survive in this nest.

He needed information. As a guest, and an unwelcome one, he had tried to talk with the staff, but no one spoke with him freely. Clare did not even come to the table to dine with him, let alone converse with him. Then whenever he was in the great hall in the presence of William Baldwin, that man glared at him as if Jordan were a disciple of Satan. Though Jordan expected that attitude from most in Trent, Baldwin's antipathy seemed particularly rabid. Yesterday in the stables, Jordan had asked a more amiable fellow about Baldwin's surliness as well as more probing questions—who might live in Chester of such importance to this household that Clare might send letters to them. But the boy brought no light to his search. It was clear to him now that he wouldn't discover to whom Clare might have sent letters or anything else unless he took advantage of what was offered and let this laundress in.

"Very well." He opened the door to her and her expectations.

She glided in, directing the two men and dismissing them as soon as they had the tub arranged before the fire. Her saunter, tawny hair, and small-breasted body gave her the mien of a wiry and hungry cat. Clearly, she meant to offer herself to him if he so desired.

He didn't. His eyes had been struck by a sunbeam two days ago. Dazzled by Clare, he found it ironic that the one woman who stirred his senses like no other had in months—or years—was one who belonged to his nephew.

"Come, Isobel," he beckoned as he removed his clothes without ceremony and carefully tucked his money belt beneath the folded garments. He stepped into the water with pleasure. "I am in need of a good soak."

From the servant's constant swallowing and smacking of her lips as she soaped his body, what she required was a man who supplied satisfaction. Jordan leaned back in the water, lifted a leg, and gave her conversation.

"How long have you served as laundress here?"

"Since I was ten." Applying herself with eager attention to his toes and calf, she told him a tale of an orphan among itinerant minstrels who put herself in service to a prosperous lord. When her hand rose to Jordan's thigh and came perilously close to the most private part of him, he clamped his hand over hers and directed her to his stomach. He smiled smoothly at her. Why be coy? She wasn't. "I would enjoy a description of the castle." He arched a brow. "Can you do that?"

"I can tell you much," she promised.

He wondered if the old sapper tunnel he had traveled years ago to rescue his brother still existed. If the odds continued to mount against him here and he needed to get out quickly, he had to have a route. Unfortunately, Isobel had never been below the kitchen.

"Should I know something about the dungeons that is interesting, milord?" She tried to compensate for her lack of knowledge by tracing the muscles of his hip upward to his chest.

"I do wonder what they look like. Your lady ignores me so completely that I thought I should be prepared lest she lock me away."

"Lady Clare would not do that. She is kind but blind when it comes to men." She lifted her brows. "I am not like her, milord."

"I see that," he led her on.

With her fingers tangling in the hair on his chest, she inquired about his view of Castle Trent.

The place was comfortable and lovely, he told her, gritting his teeth against the itch to rip her off him. "It is huge." He tried to sound suggestive of other attributes he himself possessed. "I have never seen so many Arras tapestries and Luccan silks or panes of colored glass in one home. How can these de Wallyses pay for such fine goods?"

"The earl married three wealthy women. Lady Clare however earns more than her keep."

"Oh, how so?"

Isobel lathered his shoulders. "She and her six women are employed by many. Lady Clare writes books. She calls herself the Nightingale. Did you not know?" Her deft fingers plunged to his scalp and washed his hair.

"Nay, I **did** not." He congratulated himself that he

sounded nonchalant. Many writers took pseudonyms because they sounded mysterious or romantic. What was Clare's reason? "Does she hide her real identity because she is a woman?"

Isobel fairly hummed as she bathed his arms. "I do not think so. She is proud of what she does and talks often about it. I think she took a name because it is the accepted practice and makes her work worth more money."

That sounded true enough. The Nightingale was famous among English nobles for his—nay, *her*—production of illustrated manuscripts. In a time when most landed nobles could write and read, many of the merchant class now learned, too. The demand for books increased, as did the need for more original works of fiction, like those of his old friend Geoffrey Chaucer. The Nightingale's production of others' tales and her own original stories filled some of that need. Even King Henry had recently borrowed a book produced by the Nightingale from Malcolm Summersby. Afterward, Henry extolled the quality of the heroic adventure in text and form. He told Jordan and Malcolm that he would like to employ the Nightingale to write a piece for him, just as his cousin King Richard had repeatedly wooed the writer via letters to come to work at his court.

Jordan closed his eyes, trying to remember Henry's last comments regarding this bird whose eloquent voice had enchanted him. "But this impertinent writer would not go! Even telling Richard no night thrush has ever sung in an English royal domain since Edward the Confessor banished them for disturbing his sleep almost four hundred years ago! Richard was livid, of course. Proud fool that Richard was, he thought no one could endure without him or his beneficence. He envisioned himself the supreme connoisseur, irresistible personally and financially to starving sculptors and writers."

A smile came to Jordan then. His sunbeam was really a spellbinding bird! With an enthralling song that lured patrons to her art. And pulled a dragon to her with a simple smudge of ashes on her cheeks and hands. Her charming stigmata obviously came from mixing and using ink.

He frowned and wondered how long she toiled, how hard ... and how much money she earned. Could she pay three hundred men here and along Trent's borders with the income from books? At some point she might have to, for inherited money went only so far for so long.

"Unusual for a woman to produce books," he pondered aloud to Isobel. "You say she earns much?"

"With her last commission, she bought the gold plate you ate your supper from last night."

"What kind of book brings that much money?"

"It's said that King Henry's half sister, Joan Beaufort, bought a copy of some tales from a man named Chaucer, and she paid one hundred nobles!"

"Geoffrey Chaucer's works could fetch a goodly sum, that's true. If the copy were illustrated, it would command an even greater amount."

"Oh, it had pictures. I know because I saw them. That's why Lady Clare hired that French woman."

"Oh, who is French?"

"Solange. Solange Dupre. You met her. Your retainer likes her well. She's the one with black hair and——"

"Aye. I thought Solange was from Bruges."

"She told me she was born in Rouen. That's France, isn't it?"

"Absolutely." Solange Dupre could paint but did not write ... or so she said. She was from Bruges ... and Rouen, which was not far from Paris. "Does your lady write other kinds of books?"

"Many things. Letters. Histories. Heroic tales. The bailiff said at supper last night that he hears her next project is a life of King Richard."

"Ambitious. Who would patronize your lady to do that?" *And would the words be fact or fiction?*

"I can only guess about that, milord."

"What would you venture then, Isobel?"

"Any opponent of King Henry's."

This laundress was more sophisticated than the average manor servant. If she came to him this morning with more in mind than a liaison, she would want to return to whomever had sent her with information equal to her gift to him. What would he give her?

Crumbs. Only if he had to.

"Tell me then, are there many here in Castle Trent who favored Richard over Henry?"

"Nay. Only William Baldwin has a passion and that for a dead man. Harry Hotspur. Most here in Trent like their independence, like the earl and his daughters."

Jordan kept a blank expression at these two bits of vital news.

Baldwin had followed Harry Hotspur? Christ in His grave. Hotspur had aligned himself with Glendower the last year of his life. He had even urged King Henry to negotiate a peace with the Welshman, been refused, and then turned on his king and England . . . before Jordan himself had sequestered him on the bloody field at Shrewsbury, drew his sword, and buried it in Hotspur's guts. It was well-known fact the Dragon had killed the traitorous northern border lord. Did Baldwin have a score to settle with Jordan for that act of war? And if so, when had the man decided on his course of action? The afternoon when Jordan's livery may have declared who he represented and he was attacked by five brigands? Was this why Baldwin had failed to detect the band? Or was Baldwin in collusion with someone else who knew the Dragon secretly came to Castle Trent? That was only three men: the king, himself, and Malcolm Summersby. Jesus in His Tomb. How had word gotten out?

"You look stricken, milord," the laundress ventured.

"I am. The earl of Trent and his daughters are formidable foes."

Isobel chuckled. "The old man, aye. His firstborn, surely. But have you ever seen Lady Clare's sister?"

That was the subject of the second revelation which struck him. He remembered a description of Clare's sister during his encounter with Aymer, but he had the impression that the girl was dead. "Nay, but I have forgotten her name . . ."

"Blanchette," Isobel quickly supplied. "A pretty girl, if you like blondes. Do you, milord?"

"I care more for what a woman does than what she looks like, Isobel."

"I could do for you, milord," she cooed, and his stomach revolted.

"I am certain you could, Isobel. What would you bring that Blanchette might not offer?" To get a picture of the sister, he let his eyes speak of erotic delights. Too bad for Isobel that he could consider them now only with Clare de Wallys.

"Oh, milord, I am eager. No dry fish or flat board."

"Does that describe Blanchette?"

She pouted. "She's small and thin, without good breasts or hips like me." Isobel smiled. Jordan didn't. She went on, unhappy. "The men in the garrison here used to talk of her beauty even when she was a child. She would have been a gem, too, if it weren't for that foot of hers."

"What was wrong with her?"

"She was born with a clubfoot. She always limped, but well . . . if a man has three good legs, a woman doesn't need any, does she?" Isobel had leaned close to virtually whisper the last in his ear.

"Indeed not." He made his voice sound amenable, though his skin began to crawl. "So where is this lovely Blanchette now? I have not seen her here."

"She's in a convent, milord. Near Chester."

Chester. "Intriguing. To what order does she belong?"

"She doesn't." Somehow that amused the laundress. "Her father pays the Benedictines a healthy sum to keep the girl well housed."

That happened often. Many lords who had sired a surplus of daughters paid an annuity to the church to keep them. Most of these sheltered women, however, took vows and had no reason to be interested in politics. Yet, according to this servant, Blanchette's preferences were her sister's and her father's. "If Blanchette lives there, how do you know so much about her?"

"This past August she came home to visit once all the armies had left the area after the battle of Shrewsbury. Her father does not know she was here. Lady Clare does not tell him, especially since he has become so ill."

"Why not?" he cast over his shoulder. "Though Lord de Wallys blusters, I think he appreciates his eldest daughter's care of him. Why not his second daughter, too?"

"Blanchette de Wallys is very different from her older sister, milord. She gladly fled to her convent. You see, her father disliked females who were afraid of him, and Blanchette shook like an apple on a tree whenever he passed. She begged to leave after her mother and brother died." Isobel became grave and her fingertips massaged his scalp more slowly. "When you take Lady Clare away to marry your nephew, what will happen to us?"

Although the maid's concern was normal, her question meant that those in Trent knew the reason for his mission. Good. He and Henry wanted the news of Clare's impending marriage spread abroad to Glendower and his rebels to deter them from any forays.

Henry had never kept the marriage a secret. Only Jordan's journey here had been a closely guarded one. Or so he thought.

But, of course, someone had told it.

Who?

He had asked himself that for two days now. Now, more so since he knew about Baldwin's affection for Hotspur.

Jordan recalled the last meeting of the three who had known he was coming here. Henry, Malcolm Summersby, and himself. They had met privately in Henry's bedchamber a week ago, their topic of Trent's security already chosen, its fate decided. Jordan described his meeting with his nephew Geoffrey the day before and how the young man had announced that provided Lady de Wallys was easy to his eye, he would wed her. Henry had handed over his gold to Jordan and bid him godspeed. Malcolm, too, had wished Jordan well and embraced him, telling him to return quickly so that they might see to the last preparations for the army's march toward the border between England and Wales.

The success of this mission depended upon utter secrecy.

Henry would inform no one and had no reason to. Jordan himself had said nothing to anyone, not even revealing their destination to Pickering and Wickham until they were on the road. The three of them had slept at an inn one night and, on the second, took the only room available together in a hostel at a nunnery, speaking to no one out of the ordinary.

That left only Malcolm Summersby, whose loyalty was questionable. Malcolm, his own friend, and Henry's Master of the Horse for twenty years.

Malcolm had ever been as true to Henry of Lancaster as Jordan. Through two decades of conflict between Henry and Richard, Malcolm Summersby had given his advice and much of his money and many of his men to Henry's causes. Malcolm, like Jordan, had followed their liege lord into exile five years ago; returned with him to claim his lands, which Richard had illegally seized; stood by him as Richard abdicated in his favor; fought with him; wept with him when his first wife and later his father died.

What reason could Malcolm have to turn on Henry?

Jordan shook his head. He knew of none. None!

But someone was responsible for the intrigues Jordan had met on this journey. He had been attacked on the road. Called by name. Trussed like a chicken. And for what reason? Afterward, in the luxury of Castle Trent, Jordan discovered collusion between Nathaniel Pickering and one of Clare's women. He found a mercenary named Baldwin who favored a man he himself had dispatched to hell. In addition, two guards had been mysteriously posted at his door. And though they had left last night—he assumed by Clare's order—this morn he felt the probes of a laundress, less cunning a cat than she needed to be to pick information from a dragon.

He was so tired of treachery! Sinking backward into the tub to rinse his hair, he rose in such a rush that water ran down his naked body like a river.

Isobel went to stone.

He stared straight ahead, pretending indifference to a display which had seemed natural before today and now felt like . . . betrayal. He prodded his mind from his astonishing discovery to the subject at hand and the woman before him.

"As far as I know, Isobel, after Lady de Wallys weds, you remain where you are." He held his arms out, awaiting her to dry him in a towel, and tried to sound appealing. "Don't you want to?"

"Oh. Aye." She could not seem to find his face, so focused was she on elements much lower on his body.

She could do that till eternity drew nigh, and still she would not get a rise out of him. But she could hope . . . and he could tempt her for a little more information. He hated every minute of it. "You like things here?" he asked, and put his hands low on his hips. He could tell by her glazing eyes what specifically she saw that she liked.

"Very much."

He led her to his purpose with a devilish grin. "Would you stay, even if Glendower came to roost here?"

"Oh, nay! He is a ragged Welshman. What money can he give a poor girl? I work to make my way in the world," she announced proudly. "I want to be as rich as Lady Clare."

"Smart," he told her, and wondered if she earned anything to carry news of the Dragon's topics of conversation. "I grow cold, Isobel. Do give me that towel."

"Here." She came close and put the cloth to his shoulders. "Allow me to dry you, milord."

He shut his eyes to this woman's offer, yearning for the caress of Clare's agile hands. "So you don't want Glendower. Who would you have here if you could?"

"Ha, that's easy," she purred as she rubbed his chest downward to his ribs and hip bones. "I'd have anyone who could ensure a spark of fun and a little peace."

He extracted the towel from her hands and his vision filled with Clare. "Ah, 'tis a pity we cannot always have what we want." He nodded toward the door. "Good-bye, Isobel."

She was stunned. Furious. Muttering about his ingratitude as she stomped away.

Minutes later, he went down to supper and once more sat alone on the dais next to Clare's empty chair. He took one bite and pushed his plate away. 'Twas then, in view of all one hundred or more of the house garrison and servants of Castle Trent, he saw the folded parchment.

He scanned each person at the table and those before him in the crowd. Young, old, healthy and not, none of them looked expectant or joyous that he found it. Refusing to permit any one of them the satisfaction of seeing his face when he opened it, he took it and left the hall.

He headed toward the stables. Alone there in the stall with his horse, he greeted the stallion and unfolded the message. The succulent scent of geraniums wafted to his nostrils as he read the cramped black script.

"Leave tonight and take Clare with you."

When he looked up, though, he realized that even if he decided to react to this injunction, it would be difficult. From his saddle draped over the post someone had stolen his stirrups. The thief was certainly someone other than the note writer because their goals were opposite.

He suppressed the impulse to ball the parchment in his fist. Cursing, he folded it and tucked it into his money belt for safekeeping.

In this castle, numerous people had tried to isolate him, ignore him, imprison and intimidate him. In some cases, he knew who they were and what they hoped to achieve. In other instances, he had only suspicions.

He did possess one asset about which no one knew. He put his hand to his belt and felt the fifty nobles. He had ridden into this domain and, by all that was holy, he would ride out. Stirrups or their lack could not keep him imprisoned or detour him from his mission. Nor did he need retainers to assist him. He had walked alone through life's perils before, and he could do so again. For this last time, for his king and country, he would do what he must.

He would leave Castle Trent.

Tonight.

Because clearly the contest between factions supporting Henry of England and Glendower of Wales grew more virulent in this border castle, he would go before he could not. The opponents—numerous, diverse, and puzzling in their loyalties—became bold enough to approach him secretly. When they found they could not deter him, their next step would be an open assault on him. And if they attacked him, they might soon try to persuade others in the same ways. He could not chance that they might fail in their persuasions and move on to more nefarious acts.

So he knew he could not stay.

Nor dare he go—without Clare.

"Madam," a kitchen maid announced as she opened the door to Clare's bedchamber, "Tom, Lady Blanchette's messenger from Saint Ann's priory, just rode into the courtyard and begs to see you."

Clare took a look at the maid's offering of a covered platter that would contain her supper. She knew she could not eat. 'Twas nothing new. Since the Dragon had come here, she had not been able to sleep, write, or think of ought but him. She welcomed the chance to be planning her escape. When and how and now, with this knowledge of French attack on English garrisons, she wondered where she might flee with her integrity intact. But she had to settle matters here at home before she planned anything, and she praised God that Blanchette's answer to her offer had come.

"Thank you," she told the girl, and flew down the winding stairs.

The courier stood outside the doors to the main hall, where she knew everyone would be dining. Indeed, she saw no one in the corridor. Wishing to avoid any who might leave early, especially the Dragon, Clare greeted Tom quickly and led him toward her cluttered little pantry. There, behind a closed door, she lit a candle, offered him a stool and a smile.

He did not respond, and her heart fell to her feet.

"What's the matter?" She knew Tom the gardener well because he had been employed by the prioress as one of the caretakers for the grounds of Saint Ann's since long before Blanchette went there to live. He seemed young, carefree, as those who lived near godliness often do. The nuns liked his lack of guile. So did Blanchette. Early in her residency, she asked him to perform small favors for her. Over the past eight years, he acted much as Blanchette's retainer, including escorting her here in August when she had visited. Tom was lanky and shaggy but bore that golden coloring her sister extolled. Rolling his ragged liripipe hat in his nervous hands and shuffling back and forth, he looked as if he had been chased here by the hounds of hell.

Alarmed, Clare put a hand to his arm. "Tom, is something amiss with my sister? If she is ill or—" *Has she refused my offer to come preside here?*

"She is well, madam." His blue eyes held shadows. "Better than me. She said she would reward me well with a noble if I arrived here before nightfall and returned on the morrow. I have come half the way, but at much cost."

"What do you mean?"

"Soon after I left Chester, I found a dead man on the road. He'd been robbed, beaten, and thrown in a ditch. I kept to the forest and picked my way to the next inn, where I told them of the man. They say Glendower is coming to Chester. I must return quickly then to help the nuns prepare for a siege. Lady Blanchette relies on me, too, for news of the world—and pays me well to bring it."

Tom gave Clare a watery lopsided smile, proud of his responsibility but worried over events. Though he appeared untutored, he certainly possessed enough intelligence and ambition to arrive here quickly, safe and sound. Clare was impressed with her young sister's shrewdness. Blanchette knew how to pick a man—and then knew how to motivate him.

Clare wished she shared that trait and could persuade a Dragon to her own desires. But for now, she would reward this man for his devotion.

"May I offer you some supper, a tankard of ale, and a good bed, Tom?"

"Aye, madam. I'll take the first two, but not the last. I'm going home tonight. Before I do anything, you'll want this." He dug inside his cloak and extracted a letter, sealed with the vermilion wax Blanchette used.

Clare took it, suddenly afraid of its contents. Suppose

Blanchette had decided to stay in her convent? Clare could not blame the girl. Aymer had never been kind to her, never treated her like a sensitive child. But then Aymer never treated anyone to what they needed from him. He gave only what he wished—and took what he required. Blanchette, snubbed by the man she was told to respect, had crossed him from her existence, coming home to Trent only once last summer at Clare's request and her promise that their father could not appear to mar the visit. All had gone according to Clare's hope that Blanchette might inspire some loyalty among Trent's people and that Clare might introduce the subject of Blanchette reigning as mistress. Her little sister had agreed to consider ruling but stipulated she would do so only after the death of their father.

"I wish to read her letter alone, Tom. Do you care, Tom, if I leave you to your supper?"

"Nay. I can find my way to the kitchen. Will you have an answer for me to carry back for my lady?"

"I will. I need only as much time as it will take you to eat."

She turned for her tower and solitude. Breathless from her run and climb, she sank against the door, her letter clutched to her chest.

'Twas then she noticed how only one candle burned in the sconce nearest the door. The rest of her sitting room and her bedroom lay swathed in darkness. When she went to meet Tom, she was certain she had left four tapers burning. She stepped forward, confused but curious. Was her mind failing her now at the very time when she needed all her wits about her?

She crossed the threshold of her bedroom. The purple coverlet glowed magenta in the flames from her fire.

Her ears pricked. Her skin shivered.

"Come in, Clare." The bottomless bass voice engulfed her in turbulent seas of delight. In the farthest corner, where her armed chair caught the warmth of her blaze, she detected the form of umber on black . . . in a Dragon's guise.

"Why are you here?"

"You ignore me, Clare."

"I have nothing to say to you."

"Nothing you want to say. But much to relate, pretty Nightingale. *Aye,*" he crooned, and rose from his seat, "I know who you are, what you do. 'Tis no sin to sing for your supper, my sweet bird. Why hide your true name from the world? Is it for effect? Or a deeper reason, mayhaps because secretly you fear men and would rather control them by words from afar than deal with them in your own nest, darling?"

"Get out."

"I come too close?" He stepped nearer and though she could not see his face, she felt his magnetism and turned away for her door. He caught her before she took one step.

She whirled from his embrace. "Your presence here is beyond the bounds of propriety."

"So is most of what occurs in this castle."

"What do you mean? You speak in riddles."

"We *live* in a riddle, lovely thrush."

She sank a hand into her hair. He confused her, surprised her, appalled her to come here to her bedroom. She would not let him rattle her nerves. "I cannot fathom what you speak of."

"But we will untangle what we can of this and we will begin now." He stepped into the light from the hearth. If any man looked like Satan, this Dragon did. It took all her will to resist such temptation since last night when he had put his hard, sweet mouth to hers. But his eyes, glittering and blank, fell to her hands. "Let us hear what your sister has to say."

With her mind a riot of questions about how he knew she was the Nightingale, she panicked that he knew this missive was from Blanchette. Speechless, she stood her ground.

He stalked her and gave her the information she craved. "I left dinner early and went to the stables. When your sister's man arrived from Saint Ann's, I heard about Tom there from your servants. Open your letter, Clare."

"This is mine," she said, and cursed her illogic.

"I know you wrote to her, darling. Open it."

"Nay. How could you know? What are you? A magician?" Her messenger had left the castle quickly. Who had seen him go? He would not have told anyone of his destination . . . or would he? And who would have related such news to the Dragon?

Jordan took another step to stand so near she saw the sorrow in his eyes and the determination of his jaw. He wore his cloak. Over his arm was hers.

"What are you doing?" she asked, her eyes roaming his features for clues. "Why do you have my cloak?"

His gaze narrowed, pulled her into his silver charms. "You are joining me, shall we say, for one of your walks in the moonlight, Nightingale."

She understood his rationale and his finesse far too well at this point to underestimate him. "I will not go with you freely, so I hope you've provided yourself a means to bend my obstinateness to your goal. What did you bring? A dagger?"

His nostrils flared. "Christ, you think I'd hurt you?"

Nay! she wanted to scream but bit her lip. Heartbreak that she had criticized the only man whose honor she had ever admired had her stepping backward. "I won't go with you, Jordan. There is nothing that can make me do this!"

"You won't know until you've heard me out, Clare." He walked her backward to the wall, then pinned her to it with his body and a hand to the stones at one side of her head. "I fear for your safety and—"

"For your own, you mean!"

"That, too, but as a paltry second, sweetheart."

"I ordered the guard away from your door. My father had set it there, though God knows why, and he won't tell me. But as for this other you speak of, no one would dare to hurt me in my own home!"

"This place is such a hotbed of intrigues, I am surprised you have fared so well for so long, Clare."

"You fantasize. How would you learn of intrigues?"

"I have means. Not all people are silent in this castle, and some have come to me to tell me tales which you would not share. Worse, a few have left messages for me that bode no good for you or me or anyone else here."

"What messages?" She was wild with anger to hear her staff had loose tongues.

"One written. One not."

"Ma-aa--daaam!" A wail of someone running in the hall made them both turn their heads to the shouts coming through her door.

"My lady, my *lady!* Please come!"

"It's Raymond," Clare whispered.

Jordan pulled away.

"My father—" She slipped away from him and tore open the door.

"He's dying, my lady. He calls for you *now!"*

Chapter Eight

HE WAS DEAD WHEN THEY GOT THERE.

Clare swayed backward at the sight of her father, his eyes staring open, his head flung back, his mouth hollowing his cheeks as if he still gasped for his last breath. Jordan's hands gripped her shoulders, though if she could have spoken, she could have sworn she didn't need his support.

Raymond was sobbing.

She moved forward, dreamlike, and tugged the sheet over her father's face. She didn't want to see him like that any longer. She wanted to remember him acerbic and proud, the way she thought she'd always hated him.

"Clare?" Jordan asked when she stood there for eternities.

She turned slowly, her eyes drifting to his. She tilted her head, listening to the sounds of a world without her father.

Raymond was now babbling and suddenly, she—who had ordered this castle as if it were a palace, a fortress, she who had created many a fictional domain—had no idea how to proceed.

She walked straight into Jordan's open arms.

She didn't cry. The way he enfolded her so tenderly, she somehow realized he expected her to do that. When she didn't, his hands kneaded the contours of her spine and plunged into her hair, gently drawing her head back. "Sweetheart, you won't faint, will you?"

But she had no idea, and couldn't say, could she?

He bent, caught her beneath her knees, and swept her up in his embrace. She nestled her nose into his shoulder, squeezed her eyes shut, and clutched his cloak. Vaguely, she knew a crowd of servants gathered at the door. Some curious, some wailing and afraid to go too near the sick room.

Jordan strode the length of the castle without stopping and made for her tower, her chamber, where eons ago she and he had faced each other in conflict.

He nudged the door open and then closed. Inside, the single candle sputtered and burned low. Even these rooms, which had been her first and favorite sanctuary from her earthly woes, took on a different glow in light of Aymer's passing.

But from the darkest corner where the Dragon had once awaited her she heard another wild beast stirring. She knew him well. His name was grief.

"Don't go!" She seized a bigger handful of Jordan's mantle as he set her on her bed.

"I promise I'll return, darling. Let me find a servant."

"Nay! I don't want anyone. Just you."

He dropped a fierce kiss onto her knuckles. "I would not leave you. I want only to get you some wine."

He left and returned quickly, swirled off his cloak, sat on the edge of her bed, and took her hand to count her pulse. Satisfied, he put a finger beneath her chin and examined her eyes. His gaze traveled to her trembling mouth. "What can I do to help you, Clare? I am at your service."

"I—" She shrugged and scanned the room. "I am in a fog."

"We should get a priest."

"Of course, a priest. . . ."

"Clare, look at me. You must not worry over your father's absolution. His end came so quickly that I am certain a priest may find a way to discharge him of his sins, even though he died before confessing them."

Jordan's tenderness salved her wounded heart. "How adorable you are, fierce Dragon, that you should be more concerned for my father's soul than he was."

"You compliment me too much, madam. I am devoted to your welfare more each glance I take of you. I want you to survive this loss with relative ease, and if God will let me alleviate some of your burdens, then I will praise Him that I am most fortunate to aid you."

Cocooned by his sentiment, she marveled at him. "You are most eloquent, too, my lord."

"High praise from the silver-tongued Nightingale."

"And no fiction, either."

"If you think so, my beautiful thrush, then I will agree." He raised one of her hands and pressed his lips to her skin. "Where might I get a priest, sweetheart? Have you one for the castle? If so, I have not seen him at meals in the hall. Mayhaps, in the village?"

"Neither place. Our cleric for the castle and the village went to Chester to visit his sister last week. I didn't think that my father was so ill that he would go so quickly. . . . So when Father William asked if he could leave, I said it would be weeks or months before . . ." She frowned. "How could I have been wrong?"

"You cannot predict God's timing, Clare."

"But I have seen death come to countless others."

"Each man's death is unique to him."

She shook her head. "I know. My father had so many problems. He could not breathe easily. There was a liquid there." She drove her fist into her chest. "He had lost most of his teeth, and his eyesight was dimming, but still—"

"He was weak. Who is to say what could have suddenly afflicted him?"

"Aye," she whispered, and recalled how distraught he was when she refused to help him escape his infirmities. A man like her father did not accept disobedience, even on his deathbed.

A maid rapped at the door and declared she had wine.

Jordan let her in. She poised upon the threshold, and he peered down at her to ask what she required.

"Raymond, milord, milady. He's raving like a dog. He's yelling that he won't let anyone in to take the body. He's barred the door!"

Clare lifted her shoulders. "I don't know what we can do." She hadn't the strength or the imagination to find answers to this newest challenge. She ran a hand into her hair and tried to recapture her questions about how Aymer would have reacted to her rejection to aid him in his quest for a merciful death.

"Well, then," Jordan told the girl, "let Raymond grieve in his own way. He's harming no one, least of all his master."

"But, sir, the body will begin to—"

"Aye. Thank you! If Raymond continues overlong, I will see to him. Good night," he firmly bid her, and shut the door behind her.

Would that Jordan could sequester her from other miseries! From this animal, this bull who pawed the dust of her emotions for a father she had never revered. And from this other creature—this snake of apprehension whom she had first glimpsed minutes ago in this room and who could poison her belief that all in Trent could be loyal to her. If only Jordan could support her attempt to remain impartial in politics. Then, even though he might put aside his loyalty to his king for her, no one could mistake that two kings maneuvered to sacrifice her as pawn in their game and one Welsh would-be king threatened to take her castle, her knights, and all else she loved.

"Drink this."

Clare glanced up at the one man who played no game with her. The Dragon who moved her with the force of his incorruptibility—and his concern for her. She vibrated with the sudden knowledge that he could become to her more important than anything and anyone else she had ever adored.

"You're cold, darling." He held a full goblet of wine out to her. "Take this and I'll stoke the fire."

She accepted it, grateful, and drank deeply. Closing her eyes, she sank against the bolster. She could hear Jordan adding a log to the blaze and bringing a chair close to her bed.

"I should comfort Raymond," she said after another healthy draught of the wine and a decision to try to focus on pertinent matters.

"Nay, you should not. He is old enough to deal with death himself. Because you are chatelaine here does not mean you must attempt to cure every ill that exists."

Her eyes opened to rest in his. He sat, hands steepled beneath his chin, brooding over her. "You are sweet to worry over me."

"And you are very sweet to contemplate."

Her breath came thick and slow. The death of her father was a subject that could be put at bay by this fascination with a dragon. "You're not drinking," she observed.

"I never do."

She raised both her brows.

"I once drank so much, I thought I'd drowned in wine. Then I discovered I didn't need to live in a haze to find satisfaction."

"Satisfaction is not happiness."

He moved a shoulder. "Happiness is a fleeting condition, dearest."

"And for you, very temporary."

"Nonetheless for you, it would seem," he said pointedly.

That he could see this and define it so easily struck her hard. She took another drink of her wine. She'd rather talk about him than herself. "Would you change any part of your life to gain more happiness?"

"Some things I might have done differently, had I the choice. But for the most part, I can say I am easy in my skin."

She wanted to ask what his choices had been, but she knew that was very bold. Yet, she wished to know the answers and thought of another way to probe. She ran a fingertip over the rim of her cup. "If you could rewrite your life's story, how would you do it?"

He snorted. "I cannot say. I've never pondered the impossible."

"What then are your dreams made of?"

His face went lax. "I gave them up with youth and self-recrimination for loving a woman I should never have wanted."

Jealousy rose like a holocaust in her brain. Burned, her reason could not hold her tongue. "So then you have never wanted another woman since that one."

"I have wanted many. Had them, too. But not given myself. 'Tis a dangerous act to give your heart away."

They stared at each other for a long minute until he murmured, "It robs you of the ability to make rational choices. And whether we like it or not, we do not live in a world where all our choices can be freely made without regard for other people."

She smiled ruefully. "I have lived under the delusion that I was free—" She put two fingers to her temple. "At least here. But I see that even in there what I create speaks of what I am, what I experience and value. Most of all, I have made certain decisions about my life which were not actions, but reactions. To my father. To Richard and Henry whom I have never met." *And now to Glendower and Charles.* "I have not flown as free as I thought."

She went to take another sip of her wine and stopped to stare at it. She put it from her, tears clouding her eyes.

He took her goblet and then her hand. "Come here," he whispered, and she went gladly to his arms. He gathered her close, arranging her thus so upon his lap. Her legs over the arm of the chair. Her hair behind her ear. Her head against his shoulder. Of her own accord, her hand went to his heart.

"Cry," he urged her, his lips buried in her curls. "You usually do not allow yourself the luxury, but tonight it will do you good."

Here, in her dark room filled with the aura of death, she

saw a new light dawn. She did not feel like crying but rejoicing. Enjoying. She should be mourning . . . and yet the emptiness she'd felt at her father's loss was now filled up with the tenderness she felt for a dragon.

"You worry, lovely bird, that I cannot fly above earthly conditions, and yet you will not reach down into your soul to release your grief," he said, and sighed. "Very well, we'll see what an embrace can do to ease the sorrow."

She pulled away to observe this man of many talents, this dragon of gentleness and honor. "I feel that power already." She licked her lower lip. "I would sample what a kiss could do to ease the pain."

He caught his breath and gave her a warning look. " 'Tis but temporary succor."

"I'd rather taste the knowledge than merely hear the description of the fare," she said, then quickly lost her mettle because he looked so opposed. She pushed away.

He pulled her back, cupped her cheek, and whispered, "Ah, but so would I."

The other night upon the wall walk, they had kissed in simple passion. Dishonorable as it was to them and Henry and countless others, that expression of desire had burned fast and hot. When he put his soft lips to hers now, this kiss flamed slower, sweeter for its compassion.

His mouth moved gently against hers, salving her sorrows. But then too soon, he broke away. He rose with her in his arms and put her to her bed.

"It breaks my heart to leave you on such a night as this with you, my darling, in such need of all the comforts I ache to give you, but it will be so."

He put her hands firmly to her chest and stepped back from the bed. "I will send someone to sit with you," he said, not looking at her but at any portion of her room that took his eye. "Is there one special person whom you prefer?"

"Aye," she told him, bitter at his choice to go and hers to let him, "but he is not mine to want. I wish for no one in his stead."

* * *

Long into the night, Clare rose from her bed and lifted her cloak from the chair where Jordan had placed it before they had run to her father at Raymond's summons. She did not doubt Jordan had come here last night to take her away. To be married to his nephew.

She turned away, sick with worry and lack of hope.

Her eye caught the parchment near the door. Blanchette's letter, long forgotten in her confrontation with Jordan and his terrible implications, beckoned, and Clare hastened to open it with shaking hands.

She sought her chair and read it in haste. Ah, Blanchette was coming. But at her leisure in a few weeks!

Of all times for Blanchette to be dallying! Hadn't she heard that Glendower approached? Didn't she understand she needed to be quick and determined?

Well, Blanchette must come sooner now. She had a sire to put into his grave. And a sister to bid farewell. . . .

The question was would the sister go to a foreign king who may have lured her to him for intrigues or to a husband who might want her only for her inheritance.

She frowned into the fire.

What if . . . she did neither?

She laughed. The surprising sound had her raising her eyes to the shadowed ceiling and blinking away tears.

What if. The game she often played when writing fiction. The mental exercise that led her down new paths and made her characters unique, their paths—their *plots*—through their stories vibrant.

What if she went neither to France nor to Geoffrey Chandler?

Suppose . . . she journeyed wherever she wanted? Whenever, however she chose? God knew, she had enough money to disappear into an Irish bog or a Scottish hillside . . . or better yet, some Continental city-state, independent of the machinations of France. Mayhaps a tiny town in the Lowlands near Amsterdam or in Flanders, where a growing community of artists created for their patrons everything from lace and embroidered velvets to tapestries, sculptures, paintings, and portraits to display their wealth and power. She could use her savings of gold to set up a workshop, liberated from any who might wish to manipulate her. *Aye,* Flanders might be the very place for the Nightingale to nest and finally become free!

She could ask Solange, who had been born and raised in Bruges, to tell her more. Solange could add the small facts about Flanders that only a former resident could reveal. That way she would know if it were truly the peaceful, prosperous artistic community she had heard lauded by La Croix from his vantage in English-owned Calais.

She rose to pace before her fire. She could do this. She would! After all, money could buy much. Why not her independence?

In her mind's eye a Dragon loomed.

Aye, he was her challenge.

How to be free of him and his eternal vigilance?

How to leave Trent to her sister, with enough money and men at arms to defend the earldom? Clearly, she had to wait until the girl arrived. But she could speed that process, couldn't she? Tell Tom the gardener to bring Blanchette hence with due haste. Send Tom back to Saint Ann's with a guard or two to soothe his harried brow and escort Blanchette here safely, lest Glendower's men and the French come closer.

The idea of leaving sang through her blood. But the reason she could not fly away now awaited her in the other tower. She would bury her father with all due ceremony, not only because as lord he deserved the rituals and she needed to say goodbye to him in the finest way but also because to speed the funeral would be out of character for her. She needed time to mourn her sire and to plan her escape.

She whirled for her door. She'd get Raymond out. . . .

But she couldn't. Try though she might, the servant would not talk to her, much less comply with her wishes. He wailed, he moaned. He cursed at God.

Dropping her forehead to her father's bedchamber door, she rattled the handle and pleaded with Raymond for another countless time. "Oh, why won't you let me in?" she asked, loosing patience and heart. "Will you let in another?" An idea came to her, sparked by Jordan's words to her minutes ago. "Mayhaps, a priest?"

The old man finally came to the other side of the portal. His voice sounded crackly as parchment. "I fear, milady."

"Fear what, Raymond? Your master is dead. I must be let in to prepare his body for burial."

"Nay! You must not touch him!"

"Raymond, please. I told you for many years I was not certain if my father had leprosy. I touched him often. So did *you!* Neither of us is contaminated and yet—"

"He is!"

She put a hand to her eyes. What was he babbling of now? "He will be all the worse if you do not let me in to ready him for his funeral."

"Nay. He cannot have one. Well you know it, madam. *He—was—not—shriven!* He died so fast he could not confess his sins. They were many. He *needed* to be cleansed!"

She remembered Jordan's comfort to her on this matter. "The priest will find a way to allow my father's soul to rest. Surely, many people die before they can recite their faults. Is God one of mercy or hate? Raymond, I choose to believe He is the former. Let me in."

She waited a long tiring minute as she heard him fumble with the bolt, then draw open the door. "Thank you." She put a hand to his arm. He hung his head, yet did she note his puffy eyes and tear-streaked cheeks. "Please do not torment yourself so much. We knew his time approached."

He looked at her with glazed eyes. "Aye. He became more wild these last two days. Ever since the Dragon came here."

Her father was not the only one who had changed since Jordan's arrival. Had it been only two days? It seemed centuries ago when she had first met him and he rescued her from rape and murder.

She and Raymond walked toward the bed where already the rigors of death o'ertook her father's body. "See you, he looks peaceful now," she told Raymond, who had been her father's friend since both were babes born to this manor.

"Aye, better than when he argued with Baldwin. That killed him! I know it did. He should not have been so excited as he was, but Baldwin insisted he have an audience and—"

"How could my father have argued with Baldwin?" Why had the captain been to see her father? He had not been allowed in before. No one gained entry. He must have had an extraordinary reason, and he must have worked great wiles on Raymond for the servant to even consider letting him inside the door. "When was Baldwin here?"

Raymond sniffled and rubbed his nose with his sleeve. "I don't remember."

She examined Raymond closely. This fellow was a simple man whose major characteristic was that he had been faithful only to his half brother, Aymer. Now that his lord was gone, Raymond needed a new allegiance. She might not qualify in gender or age, but she certainly did in kind—and she meant to have it from him. "It is imperative you recall, Raymond."

Something else tickled the back of her brain. Had not Raymond been the one to tell her that Baldwin mourned the passing of Harry Hotspur? Ever was Raymond a good source of rumor for her father. Now he would do such for her. "When was Baldwin here?"

He did, but he avoided looking at her. "A few times."

"List them."

"Tonight before supper. This afternoon. And the first night after you brought the Dragon to see your father, Baldwin came to me to ask admittance."

"Why? What reason did he give that could so persuade you to even consider breaking my father's strictest order?"

"He wanted to post a guard at the Dragon's door."

Her father had posted the guard at Baldwin's insistence? Aymer rued doing anything unless he could proclaim he had thought of it first. "Lord Chandler is a guest in our home. What reason could Baldwin give my father to become such a knave as to post sentries?"

"I do not know. Your father bade me leave while they

talked over it, milady. I only heard Baldwin say that he had evidence that the men who attacked the Dragon in the forest were king's men."

"What evidence?" And why would king's men attack their own? That was, dear God, treason. Committed against Jordan. If this were true, it was no wonder Jordan was wild to discover who had planned that raid by those outlaws, who were in themselves of no consequence. And if treason were behind the attack, then the rumor in Crofton of brigands in her forest was one planted for cover. But by whom? "I asked you, Raymond, what proof did Baldwin have?"

"I did not ask and I was not told, milady."

"If that were so, then are you implying Baldwin and my father tried to protect the Dragon?"

Raymond shrugged and moved to the side of the bed to put a palm to her father's bandaged arm. "He is so cold. It's like touching wood, isn't it? Or glass."

"Raymond, answer me. Why did my father post the guard, and why did he and Baldwin argue?"

He skimmed a hand over his wild gray hair. "I told you, milady, I do not know. They made me leave!"

"You did not listen behind the door? Come, do tell me, Raymond, why did you not engage in your usual eavesdropping?"

"Because I had other tasks to do, my lady! I am not an idle man!" Taking umbrage was the normal way this servant cheated the noose of responsibility. Just like her father.

"I did not think you were lax, Raymond."

"Nor am I immoral." He sniffed.

"I never said that. Listening at doors is hardly an offense I would ever equate with the venial sins, Raymond, so I absolve you—"

He cackled like a demented man.

This debate was a waste of time and effort with a man who was as stubborn as the one he had served. She had much more to do than to try to chip information from a stone.

She advanced around the bed. "Raymond, please try to be calmer. Help me, won't you? I require someone on whom I can rely. We'll need one of his more lavish tunics. The sapphire velvet would be appropriate. What do you think?"

"Aye. 'Twas a favorite of his. He said it matched his eyes." He barked in laughter, then swiped his nose. "He liked the pale blue hose with that. I laid them away for the day he might recover. But he never did. . . ." Raymond's mouth crumpled as he began to sob. "I'll get them." He lurched around and went for the alcove where her father once bathed and dressed.

Raymond's behavior, normally so composed, could be explained. Ever when death presided in this castle had she noted that people took on a different mien. Those who cared deeply for the one who had passed on could oft display aspects to their character not seen on any other occasion. Raymond could be understood because he had just lost his best, mayhaps his only, friend. Albeit that her father was Raymond's lord, not his equal, it mattered not. The affection had been real.

Like the rest of us, Raymond will just have to bear the loss in his own time and his own way.

Baldwin's behavior was the one that needed explanation. She meant to have it, too, as soon as she had prepared her father for his eternal rest.

She turned to the body and began to recount those tasks she now must do for him. She had accomplished these tasks so often over the years, she could do them in her sleep.

She sighed. Sleep, which eluded her on normal nights, was the one thing she suddenly craved tonight. But she knew she would not gain it for long hours.

She strode around to the side of the bed, and her foot kicked something that rolled across the floorboards. Habit made her bend to reach for it, pick it up, and frown at it.

'Twas a vial from her kitchen pantry.

An empty vial. Which had once been filled. With what? She smelled it. Stared at it.

Glazed black clay. The color of death to indicate its ability—

Nay!

Yet her eyes confirmed what her mind could not grasp.

Around the rim stood tiny crystals. Whoever had used it was not as careful with it as she had always been. Knowing its ability to kill insects and weeds in her vegetable garden, she always used the substance gingerly. Upstairs in her workshop stood another vial of the same gray substance. That supply she had purchased for Solange and Ella to mix with oil and, thus, obtain a glorious yellow color for their paintings.

Both containers held the base element of arsenic.

In horror she looked down upon her father, now unable to answer the final question she would ask him. *Did you take this poison?*

She still stood there, unmoving, examining her father's lips for traces of the crystal when Raymond reappeared, her father's rich clothes spread across his arms. He looked more composed. His usual self.

"What know you of this, Raymond?" She opened her hand.

His face fell. "Nothing."

"It was on the floor."

His eyes rounded. Fear and confusion danced in their depths. "How did it get there?"

"That is what I'm asking you."

"I know not, milady. It looks like your other little bottles from your storeroom. Is it?"

"Aye. How would it get from there to here?"

"I do not know, milady! Why ask *me?* I am more a creature of this domain than downstairs."

More a man to follow my father's commandments than God's?

She could imagine a scene in which Aymer had confided in his loyal friend, Raymond, that he wished desperately to die. That he had asked his daughter to assist him and she had refused. That he was in constant agony and the means to his relief so close at hand, if only he had someone to help him. To take from his daughter's herbal store a substance that would cure his woes forevermore.

Aye, Raymond could do this. Indeed, it might explain his torture over the state of Aymer's soul as it passed from his body into purgatory.

"You can't think that I would kill him!" Raymond looked shocked. "Nay. You would make of me a murderer?"

A liar and a truer friend than many have.

"How could you think that of me?" He was screeching.

Because you have always done my father's bidding. Because you are like him in so many ways. Wily. Self-serving. Irreverent. What would it cost you to offer your best friend the means to make him happiest forever?

"I loved him!" Raymond was affirming. "I *loved* him and you insult my years of service to him to—"

"Please." She put up a hand, suddenly weary of trying to change so many things she could not. "I do not wish to bicker with you." If he had done this, she'd never get a confession from him.

But she could not ignore the other possibility that her father might have been murdered. She had to investigate the likelihood that another man had forcibly fed this poison to her father before his supper. The only other person admitted to see Aymer. Baldwin.

She must confront William Baldwin for his audacity to demand an audience with her father, persuade him to post two guards at Jordan's door, and then argue with him about their removal. She must look into Baldwin's eerie blue eyes and detect what else he may have done to move events to his own goal. Whatever that goal was. . . .

What a tangle. Where to begin to unravel it? She had to know now. "Continue here, Raymond. I shall return as soon as I can."

With the vial in her hand, she went to the corridor, down the main stairs, and awakened one of the servants from his pallet by the fire in the hall. When she told him to bring her William Baldwin from the barracks with all due haste, the man rubbed his eyes, blinked, but scurried off.

Minutes later, he stood before her, wincing at her incredulous tone.

"Baldwin would not come?" She was outraged at the mercenary's effrontery.

"Nay, my lady. He *could* not."

"Why? I will have him!" For defying her authority, she would have him thrown into chains without the opportunity to explain himself! She was coddling him, being judicious with a man who had breached the rules of proper conduct and perhaps even committed murder.

"Baldwin has fled, madam. His men say he took his horse and armor and disappeared."

"When?"

"After supper."

Reeling with anger and despair that Baldwin may have slipped between her fingers, she said, "Bring me his five subordinates. I want them immediately before me."

She debated whether to have this interview before her staff but thought it best to make a display of her power, especially at a time when she needed to gather her father's unto her to complement her own.

Within minutes, Baldwin's men stood before her. Bleary-eyed but strangely proud, the five men who reported directly to Baldwin stood shoulder to shoulder in the hall before her and an audience of wide-awake servants. "Where has your captain gone?" she asked them.

"Away. Anywhere, my lady," announced one.

"We threw him out, madam," said another with a smile of satisfaction, eyes focused beyond her.

A third finished with an explanation of his friend's words. "Because we had heard him speak against you and your father too often, we told him tonight we would listen no more. Nor would we ever be persuaded to his cause. We said we wished to serve you as you paid us so well to do, Lady de Wallys."

No guile marred any face of these five men. The lack warmed her chilled heart. So did the murmur of agreement that went around the room among the household staff. Clare dared to hope Baldwin's treachery was unique unto him and that her people returned to her the affection she bore them. But she needed to hear more before she felt safe. This brought to mind Jordan's hints of mysterious doings in this castle as he attempted to persuade her to leave here with him earlier tonight. She would ask him to explain those hints as soon as she heard the rest of this unsavory matter.

She pursed her lips. She must be methodical and wary, lest she lose everything she valued. "Baldwin has spoken against us before?" she asked the five.

"Aye, repeatedly since he came four years ago, my lady," offered the first man.

"Lately, however," said another, "Baldwin's words became more impassioned. And since we hear tonight in the hall from your sister's man Tom that Glendower's army attacks English garrisons with the help of the French, we wish to preserve you and yours, Lady, as you pay us so well to do. We hope to do it without a traitor in our midst. Especially a man who favored that Judas, Harry Hotspur, over a good English ruler like Henry."

Clare's heart paused at the name of the king whose protection she must now court to save her sister, her home, and her villeins from the likes of the Welsh and the French. Henry seemed her best hope to secure a safe future for them all. Her father was dead, and with him had gone the most vibrant reason to pledge allegiance to no other above him. She was left to deal as best she could with the results of Aymer's years of indifference to royal politics. She needed to be bold, brave, and rescue her own future in the process. She would give this castle to her sister, entrust her welfare to loyal retainers like these men, and please Henry as much as she could by pledging her faith to him. But in the manner of her doing, she would keep faith with herself.

She would leave this castle with Jordan, bound for Henry's hegemony and Henry's planned marriage for her.

But she would never utter marriage vows to Geoffrey Chandler. Since she had met the Dragon, to even consider another man in her heart and bed had become a flight of imagination not even her fanciful one might take.

She would take whatever opportunity she could find to

escape the Dragon. Barring that, once in Geoffrey's domain, she would demand an audience with the king, pledge her fealty to him, and honor it for the rest of her days. She would convince Henry with her ardor, her adamance, and if that did not work, with her money. In spirit, but *in absentia,* she would remain true to the English king while encouraging her sister to follow suit. Meanwhile, she herself would forevermore fly free as she had always longed to do and never known quite how.

The prospect was invigorating.

Terrifying.

To effect this farce, she would need to convince a Dragon that the Nightingale would surrender totally to his care—and she wondered if she, who was such a poor actor, could succeed at this dire mimicry.

To delude this Dragon would be to anger him. And to enrage this creature had never been a prudent act for any man. So then, to betray the beast might destroy the bird whose breast beat too frantically at his sight and whose mind now bellowed that she loved him too much, too tragically.

For when she did escape him somewhere along the road to marriage with Geoffrey Chandler, she would commit her own crime. She would murder any hope that the Dragon might remember her fondly. Aye, he would forever curse her name.

Ah, but why should she be surprised? From the start, this whole affair had rolled into a ball of mysteries.

A tear trickled down her cheek. She cast it away.

Nay, she must not weep at the one certainty which now wrung her heart.

The Dragon could never love the Nightingale.

Chapter Nine

"I'M WILLING TO GO WITH YOU," SHE TOLD JORDAN WHEN HE allowed her inside his chamber. She watched him put his dagger down. He must have picked it up and concealed it in the folds of the coverlet he had draped loosely about his lean hips before he answered her knock at his door.

The idea that he would need a weapon inside her castle walls shocked her—but not as much as it would have before the questions raised by her father's death.

She repeated her statement to him.

He stood still as a figure on a crucifix. But the fire in his chamber gilded his bare chest and sinewy arms with a sheen that inspired new life into her longing to caress him naked as she had when first they met. "This is a drastic change of heart for you, darling," he said softly as he examined her too coolly for her needs.

Why had she thought he would welcome her to his room? Why had she thought he would embrace her and comfort her as he had scarcely an hour ago after her father died?

Why could she not foretell a Dragon's emotions? It maddened her.

She would have to become much better at predicting his emotions and actions if she meant to carry out her plan to leave with him pretending to marry Geoffrey—and then escape to Flanders. Mayhaps if she became closer to him, she might learn the workings of his mind more intimately. Yet, to merely gaze upon him like this—half nude, but staunch and imperturbable—she confirmed what she had learned so well these last days. He was the second man she had ever met, aside from her father, whom she could not dominate.

With her father, her approach had been simple. She had become as strong, as dedicated to her pursuits as he was to his own. They had clashed, each going his and her separate way until illness influenced them to call a truce.

With Jordan, the conditions of their personal conflict seemed similar. They disagreed, each demanding his or her prerogative. But there was no solution to their strife. He wanted her compliance, and though he would gain it in her allegiance to King Henry, he could not win her hand in marriage to a man she did not know or love. She simply had to accept the fact that she and Jordan could find no common ground. Whatever delight they discovered in each other, whatever respect they harbored would die with her deception.

But she could make no other choice now. She had already told him she would go with him.

"I know my change of plan may seem odd to you, Jordan."

He crossed his arms, the rippling muscles of his chest and shoulders affecting even his long, blunt fingers.

Air clogged her throat, but she stepped nearer with the audacity her plan required. "After you left me, I could not sleep and went to my father's chamber."

She was omitting her reason for her inability to rest, and it cut her that she was not as forthright with him as he had always been with her. But she had to go on, didn't she, to save herself, her sister, and her home? "I wanted to see if I could persuade Raymond to give up his custody so that I might cleanse and dress the body. Amazingly, he did let me in. When I began, I found this."

She extended her open palm to display the black vial. "I discovered this under my father's bed a few minutes ago. It comes from my kitchen storeroom and it is now empty, though once it did contain arsenic."

Jordan's gaze shot from her hand to her eyes. "Why do you have arsenic in your possession?"

"It kills weeds and insects quickly. I keep a supply in my pantry storeroom to make my garden productive."

"But then how did it get from your storeroom to your father's chamber?"

She put a hand to her head, suddenly buzzing with visions of her assistant, Margaret, mixing pigments and Solange Dupre and her assistant, Ella, using them to paint ugly yellow flowers. All three women understood the power of arsenic.

"Oh, Jordan, I don't know! I am afraid because I am not certain how my father died."

"Who can enter that pantry? Anyone?"

"Aye. I have never forbidden it, never had to worry before about who had access. I was always the one to cure the sick and tend the dying in this domain. That store was mine and all here respected that. But now . . . conditions have changed. Yet do I know this—my father was too weak to go down to the kitchen to get this bottle, and the vial did not walk into his chamber by itself."

"And Raymond is the only other person who you said goes there?"

"Aye."

"Are you implying that Raymond might have killed your father?" Clearly, Jordan thought that impossible. "The man seems too devoted to murder his friend . . . but then, we can make mistakes when assessing people's loyalties. . . ."

"Raymond would not hurt my father. Gossip and sycophant the servant might be, but traitor he is not."

"Of what precisely then do you suspect him?"

"My father underwent a crisis of conscience since you arrived. I know not all the particulars, but I do know this. He begged me to be merciful and give him a potion to let him die."

Jordan's expression tightened. "How could I be so intimidating to an independent earl who had not been swayed by any king or rebel in the more than twenty-five years he ruled here?"

"But you are impressive, my Dragon."

He cast her a sidelong look. "Come, sweetheart. There is more to this explanation than that. Give it to me."

"If Raymond did not assist my father, I think William Baldwin, the captain of the day watch, may have. But I know not his motive, whether it be mercy or . . . murder. Baldwin is—"

"I know. A very questionable character."

She lifted both brows at him, but another thought checked her inquiry. Another piece of information about Baldwin nibbled at the back of her brain. Some important fact about Baldwin and the attack on Jordan. What was it? Prodding herself to remember, she probed Jordan about the mercenary. "How do you know, *what* do you know about this man?" she asked Jordan.

"I told you, Nightingale, you are not the only one in this castle who weaves tales."

"What tales? Who else am I not to trust here in my own home?"

"Your laundress."

Saucy to the men but respectful to Clare, this servant had never caused her any trouble. "Isobel. I cannot think of any incident when this woman may have acted against me or my father. What did she tell you?"

"Much. For one thing, she said that Baldwin did favor Harry Hotspur, a turncoat to my king and yours. Because I did end Hotspur's time on earth, I think Baldwin would not wish to see me live too well for too long. But why would he hurt your father?"

"I have no idea! I wish I did. But I cannot ask him anything because he has left my domain. Invited by my own men, *his* five direct subordinates, to depart Trent because they rejected his authority."

"Why?"

"He spoke against me and my father, so they say. Tonight after supper was the worst of his diatribes and with the threat of the Welsh and French attack, they sought to cleanse Trent of one who would not defend it wholeheartedly."

"And this man's defection and possible involvement in your father's death leads you to accept Henry as your rightful king—and Geoffrey as your *husband?*"

"Aye," she said with hot conviction when Jordan did not believe her. "Forces collect against me and my hope to see Trent free of any other yoke. Conspirators abound. Not just William Baldwin but those others whom you hinted at earlier when you came to my room. I see clearly now with my father's death that I cannot fight them all off. I can remove every other poison I own from my kitchen storeroom. I can order a lance of my men to search for Baldwin and bring him back to me—"

"You have done these already?"

"Aye, before I came to you now! I recognize I cannot control everyone or maneuver to save my people when I do not even know what forces exist!" She advanced on him. "I must know more of what you did not tell me hours ago in my room. I admit to you and will to Henry that I cannot combat these people alone."

He stared at her.

Did he not believe her? On this issue of her allegiance, she *was* being honest.

"Oh, Jordan, chaos is not a choice that would bring any prosperity to my people. Anarchy implies every man for himself. By remaining independent, I invite that here, particularly now because the French and Welsh advance. You were right the other night when you said that above all else, Trent and its people are English. Henry and the protection of his Crown is not only a logical choice, it is one

I choose based on common blood and tradition. I will go with you. Willingly."

Still, he was too stoic, and she needed him to react, give her more information by which she might gauge how well she might succeed at aligning herself with Henry and then escaping him.

She stepped even nearer to Jordan and let her admiration shine in her eyes. "Why would you come to me like that? In the dark of night with my cloak and yours? Why would you abduct me—but tell me first?" She placed a hand on his forearm, and he dropped his gaze to it. "I know you, Dragon, and you must have had good reason to do such a deed. Abduction is beneath your pristine code of honor. Something must have driven you to make a mark against it. What was the cause?"

"I feared someone would hurt you. I do now even more so than hours ago." He lifted the arm she touched and trailed the backs of his fingers up her throat and then sank his whole hand into her curls. He circled her waist and brought her entire body close to his. "You are too precious a creature to lose, my pretty thrush. It pained me to tear you from your nest, but I thought I had to do it."

Her fingers in the thick hair on his chest splayed and paused, paralyzed with the impulse to measure the muscles beneath his skin. Fires igniting in her blood flashed to bright intensity and nearly blinded her mind to the subject she pursued.

But his lips brushed her ear, and with his words, she forgot her own. "I bought two barbs in the village. Healthy enough horses. One for you and one for me."

She tried to look at him, but he held her so that she might not see his face as he continued. "I wanted you safe," he explained, and kissed the hollow beneath her ear.

"You would not wait for your men to recover and accompany us?"

"If I delayed, I thought harm might come to you. I could not risk it. Especially since tonight someone left me a note to leave and take you with me."

She pulled away. "Why?"

"A puzzle, certainly, for the note came on parchment scented with geraniums. I assumed from the fragrance that the sheet was from your personal store of writing paper. Is that so?"

"Aye," she told him and was rewarded with a little hug to ward off the terror of his revelations.

"But the secrets multiply. Within minutes of receiving that note under my plate at supper, I went to the stables to see to my stallion. I knew, you see, that if someone meant to harm me, they might well begin by destroying my means to do it. So I was surprised when my horse was well, but not my saddle."

"What was wrong with it?"

He smiled sadly. "Someone took my stirrups. The two acts quickly topped a list of suspicions I have kept since I was attacked in your forest. In this castle live many forces. Some seen and others unseen. You, who wanted me to leave without you. Another, who bade me go and take you with me. A third, who wished me to stay without reservation. And who knows how many more exist here? We can only act on those we know. So tell me, darling, who do you think would do any of these things?"

"I am at a loss. I—I feel foolish not to know. Nor to have the vaguest notion. . . ." She checked his silver eyes for ridicule.

Their diamond-hard glitter melted with compassion as he said, "I will list the few I know. Raymond is suddenly suspect as a man of mercy killing. Isobel, whose job is to wash clothes and bodies, comes to me gladly to see if she can soak information from me."

Clare stiffened at his implication that the maid had seduced him.

He felt it and pressed her close, his lips to her cheek. "Do not worry. She got nothing from me, sweetheart. But I took much from her. She says a lot about you. She reveres you and your women in your tower. She envies them, I think. What's more, she knows a lot about them. She must speak with them at meals, I would guess, especially your woman from France."

"I have no lady from France among my—" She broke off, confusion filling her breast, because the only one among her ladies who was not English was Solange. "You mean Isobel thinks that Solange Dupre is from France? She is not. She comes from Bruges."

"Is that so?"

"Aye! She became known to me through my agent in Calais. He has met many artists in that Flemish city. They have a guild, you see. A famous one and—You do not believe me."

"I have reason to doubt Solange, Clare. If the woman comes from Bruges, why did she tell Isobel she comes from Rouen?"

His mistrust of the artist blended with her growing one.

"Sweetheart, I see horror in your eyes. Tell me what scares you."

"Arsenic." She licked her lips. "As a simple element, it works wonders in gardens, killing bugs and weeds. But in a mix with oil, it creates a glorious yellow color."

"Does Solange Dupre use this pigment often?"

"Aye. As recently as the past few days."

"Does she know the use of the color's main ingredient?"

Clare recalled Solange's steady handling of her tools and supplies. "Aye, she knows why and how I apply it to my garden soil. She is also quite careful of the crystals when she makes the liquid color."

"Can the color mixture kill?"

"I do not know. I have never tried to use it in my garden and Solange . . ." She frowned, remembering what the woman had done this morning. "Solange mixed a new supply of yellow pigment earlier today. She emptied the workroom vial of all arsenic and asked my accountant, Mary Frank, to order more."

"Why does that worry you?"

"We had a new supply last week. Solange cannot be using yellow that quickly. She is painting very tiny flowers."

"Perhaps she planned to use the workshop's supply and saved some of it—"

"But then could not get to it?" Clare asked. "Nay. That is

absurd. Unless she planned to use my kitchen supply as a diversion . . ."

"Darling," he spoke low and firm, "you must dismiss her."

"Aye," she said after a long minute of thought.

"Why do you hesitate?"

"It pains me to act on suspicion. I have no evidence to point to her involvement in my father's death."

"How many years have you had this vial in this castle?"

"As long as I can remember."

"And no one here has ever died of mysterious causes before this?"

"Nay."

"Clare, when more than one suspicion attacks your mind, my dear, I have learned 'tis best to cut the infection from you than to let it linger and decay the whole body."

"But Solange is the very best illustrator I have ever employed and I—"

"*I* have a third suspicion to add to your two, Clare."

"Nay. What?"

"She speaks intimately with my man Nathaniel Pickering. They appear to desire each other, but I doubt it is really affection that binds them. I came upon them together the first morning we were here in Castle Trent. I have tried to catch them talking since then but have not been so fortunate as I was that time. As Solange sat on Nathaniel's bed, she was familiar with him, talking to him in a tone of equality more than one of a woman in love. She also told him things about you, which I at first found odd but interesting . . . and disloyal."

"My God. What did she say?"

"That you were so disturbed the first morning after I and my men arrived here that you were up too early for your normal routine and that you could not write easily but had finally written two letters."

That Solange had noted the odd hour of her toil—and that she took note of what her toil was—made Clare tremble.

"Clare." Jordan lifted her face with a fingertip so that her eyes met his. "I know now one of your letters went to Blanchette. I do not know the recipient of the second."

Nor will I tell you. If you ever learn, you will think me and my father traitors, when of that heinous crime we are innocent.

"Clare. Will you not relent?"

She shook her head. "That letter is irrelevant." Which was true. She had no intention now of flying to Charles or the French. She would be free, independent of them all.

Jordan narrowed his gaze on her. "Very well, then. I will tell you what is relevant, my sweet. If Solange had access to your storeroom, knows the uses of arsenic, and has reason to lie to you about her place of birth, then we have more reasons to suspect her of killing your father than we do Baldwin or Raymond."

"Except Raymond did not say he had seen her anywhere near my father."

"Clare, will you take the chance that Raymond sees all there is to see?"

"Or that he is honest."

He nodded.

"You are right. I can't risk that she is a snake in my nest, can I? I will have her taken from here tonight." Her mind whirled with necessities of how it should be done. "So that no one may have any advance indication, I will have a lance take her from her bed and under guard take her to Chester. I will pay her but instruct my men to put her on a ship bound for . . ." Clare tilted her head at Jordan. "Where?"

"Any enemy of France would seem a prudent choice."

"Spain. Let her work her way back to Paris, if she wants. If she can."

"I like your author's turn of mind."

"Devious?"

"Necessary."

She nodded. "What of your man, Nathaniel? He will miss Solange and ask for her."

"He cannot follow her because his ankle has not healed yet. But when he asks about her, and he will, you must be quick to see he gets a fulfilling answer."

She smiled, but the effort was too weak to go to her eyes. "I will. I'll say she disappeared in the middle of the night. That will be true."

"It will also confuse him. I do need him puzzled, Clare. Cut off from any who would assist him."

"So shall it be, Dragon. I will place a secret guard near his door night and day. No one will come or go but that you and I know who it is and why they arrive."

"Thank you."

"I do offer you the same thanks, Jordan. You have given me much here tonight."

"Would that I might give you more."

His generosity eroded her gratitude, and suddenly she was afraid that he could see through her duplicity. She faced his fire, trying not to knead her hands. "I must see to my father's funeral, Nathaniel's guard, and Solange's disappearance." Was there aught she had forgotten?

She shivered. There was an important fact she meant to tell him. What was it? Baldwin had said something . . .

But she could suddenly think of nothing when at her back she felt her Dragon move against her. His hands traced the length of her hair from her crown to her spine, catching it up in his fists and wrapping it about her like a lining to the warm cloak of his body. "Aye, lovely bird, do those things. Call on me for help if you want, for I am yours. After all is said and done, then you may fly away with me." His voice was rough magic against her ear.

Her eyes closed. She drifted back to his charms. "I go to Henry's protection. For my good and the good of all my people."

"I thank God you see it, darling. Henry's banner and his men will only make Trent impregnable."

While I pretend to become pregnable to another man.

"You will not be sorry," he gruffed. "I will ensure it with Geoffrey. Though God knows, I wish I did not have to deliver you to anyone, save me."

His admission had her melting against him. "I wish it were so, too," she declared on a ragged breath as his hands forged her back to him. "Never have I known a man so worthy of his name and reputation. Yet is my Dragon sweet."

He made a tortured sound, his hands lifting a breast, one sliding down her ribs past her belly to cup her between her legs. Her knees buckled. He held her up, growled, and nuzzled her nape. "Christ, you are so strong and sleek, but everywhere you should be merely rounded, you are lavish, temptingly plump." His fingers massaged her nether lips, now swelling and throbbing into his care. "My Nightingale, you are such an opulent creature. Colorful. Intricate. Intriguing."

Breath eluded her as she lolled her head against his shoulder, and the gentle torment of his fingers made her shudder and gush in a rush of longing. "Jordan . . ."

"Aye, darling, 'tis wondrous how you react to me. Wild and wanting what I might provide." He braced himself more firmly, and she could feel that his coverlet was gone. His iron thighs girding her derriere and legs, his fingers—joined by those of his other hand—gathered up her gown. They combed into her secret hair, diving between her moist flesh and spreading her so that he might sluice tender but hungry fingertips along every fold and rise.

"God," he beseeched, but she wished for no intervention to end this ecstasy, "you are so wet to have me."

Unthinking, only needing him, she tried to turn to do just that, but he clamped her securely to the wall of his body. "Nay, radiant bird. If you face me, we shall both be undone. I am so high and hard in want of you, I hurt. Put your flesh against mine, I will want to come inside you. And nowhere is it written that a dragon may make love to a nightingale."

She ground her teeth.

"Here," he said, "let me give you what I can—relief."

"Nay, I don't know—"

"Hush. Feel. Learn." His fingers felt like a lure to fly to heaven. "You have been through hell tonight. Let me do this service for you. Enjoy it."

One hand opened her wider, anchoring her thigh back against him, forcing her loins forward in a pagan offering to her beloved captor. With sure fingers, his other hand traced her rises and valleys, then found with thumb and forefinger some point that jolted her back more surely to his embrace. He secured his footing, and with a dragon's groan rumbling in his throat, he teased her to a flowing slickness, swirling sweetly over the brazen crest of all her needs. He brought her quickly to some blaze where nothing mattered except that she flame in the conflagration. She gasped, crying to him for release, begging for it, and when it came, she burst apart, her body a shower of cinders, never to be the same.

She whimpered, flailed her head against his massive chest. His lips went to her temple to still her. "Darling," he whispered as he let her hem fall and his hands wound around her waist, "you burn so beautifully that were I less a man of Henry's, I would take you to this bed of mine and never let you leave it."

Tears stung her eyelids. Air soughed into her lungs. Sorrow flooded her enjoyment of him, sweeping away the pleasure which had soothed her body, but drowned her soul.

She turned to him—wondered if she turned *on* him— angry for sampling rapture she knew she had barely tasted.

The sight of him nearly sent her to her knees. Utterly naked to her, he stood revealing everything he was to her. Incomparable warrior of sinewed might. Unfulfilled lover of giant proportions. Heartbroken Dragon of sweet yearning. "If I could, my darling, I would never allow another man the joy of what I have just discovered." In graphic illustration, he swept a hand down his torso, past his hard evidence, palm out to her. "Though God and I do know you are a virgin, sweetheart, I tell you no woman matches you for ardor. I am honored to have brought you that once, but I take full blame for whatever dishonor it casts. I ask nothing more of God than that he punish me for this."

She swayed with the force of his nobility—and his audacity to show her paradise then rip her from it. "I ask only that you see me to Henry's care"—she found enough sanity to state her case—"after I bury my father and my sister is ensconced here in my name. I will write to her, urge her to come home."

"You will tell her about the threat of Glendower and

Henry's hope to ally Trent and win the war against the Welsh?"

"Aye. As much as I need to tell her to gain her compliance. Blanchette is . . . independent." *More than I have been. As much as I aspire to be.*

He looked pained. "You must write quickly and persuade your sister to act with speed." He stepped forward and she knew he meant to comfort her.

She stood her ground and glared at him, defiant.

A fleeting threat passed her mind. She stifled a laugh at what she could not add to this discourse. She would not order him not to touch her again. She had tried that once. It hadn't worked. Nor would it now. For she realized what she had not before—she wanted him to touch her. Though the demons of hell might come to claim her for such an admission, she wanted more than his hands on her. More than his lips on her. She needed that portion of him that had risen to her wildest need. She wanted him inside her. Where no other man had ever been or ever would.

She swept from the room without another word. For she might become Henry's, but never Geoffrey's.

She had tasted a Dragon's caress, and any other man seemed as insignificant as ashes in the wind.

The sun rose outside his windowpane when he emerged from the stupor to which her visit had confined him. He sat in his chair before his dwindling fire and steepled his hands before him. The scent of her was still on him. Geraniums and musky woman.

He put two fingertips to his mouth and bit back the urge to suck in the only essence of her left to him.

Judas, he'd been a traitor to handle her so intimately. He could not resist her. He had not from the first.

But he must exorcise the devil who drove him to have her. Especially now that he would take her away . . . to Geoffrey.

Jesus wept! Of all base ironies to have to give her to a man who had not the depth to understand her, appreciate her, honor her.

He stood and went to the window. Naked still, the

morning air drifted over his skin. What temporary succor he had given her body had stolen peace from his mind and drove higher this aching erection he longed to give her.

How could he give her to Geoffrey?

He would, though.

He swore he would, no matter that he craved her like the intemperate beast whose name he bore. No matter that she wanted him like a wild bird tamed to his hand, for his hand alone. No matter that she had no intention to marry Geoffrey . . . or mayhaps honor her pledge to Henry as well.

Exactly what she planned to do, he had no inkling. He only knew she spoke in terms of aligning herself with Henry, only implying her agreement to marry Geoffrey. In the telling, she was honest with him. That he knew.

In that lay the greater irony. For under any other circumstances, he knew she would speak sincerely with him. She was at her core true, bright, clear, aptly christened. His Clare. Proud, intelligent, creative. His fondest desire.

But not his. Ever!

He ran a hand over his mouth and down his torso to the part of him that defied his logic to tear her from his heart. He cursed himself roundly and swung around to brace himself against the mantel. Like a man stretched on a rack, he punished himself because he wanted her lush body and her rich mind and her tender heart in spite of everyone and everything that stood against it.

For though she professed herself eloquently, he knew her too well.

She wanted to be free, this gorgeous bird of his. And she would do much to make it so.

His task was to discover her plan—if she had one—and her means—if she could create them.

For he was certain that she had told him all she knew, except for one small fact. She had not told him to whom she had written a letter days ago. She had not told him who else was her confidant. He had not asked. He would.

The knowledge roiled him.

But did nothing to make him love her less.

Chapter Ten

"SHE'S DEAD, MILORD."

Jordan wheeled away from the sight of Clare's lifeless palfrey and the elderly nun bending over the animal. God in His heaven, what a disaster this journey was!

His own black Flame whickered in agreement in the next stall.

"No use to fret, sir. Let's leave the body here fer now and get ye inside to warm ye by the fire! Think brightly. Mayhaps on the morrow, the sleet will stop and you can hire a boy from the village to send news of your delay to your nephew."

And to my king.

Would that he could remain here, make Clare healthy again—and hide away from everyone who meant to tear her from him. *Even the person who has been following us.*

From the start, when Clare agreed to come with him, events had gone awry. Solange Dupre had been escorted from Castle Trent bound for Chester, but her two guards returned, saying she had escaped them in the night along the road. Though Clare had ordered another lance to accompany the first to return and search for the woman, they had come back the day before Aymer's funeral empty-handed.

Then Blanchette took her sweet time about attending her father's funeral, and the day of the event, Tom the gardener arrived at Trent's gate with a letter from her. The girl blithely declared she had decided not to come.

Clare had paced as she read the missive to Jordan in the privacy of her chamber before Aymer's mass. "'If I honor anyone in this family, my dear sister, it is you. Therefore, if winter weather permits, I will make the effort to journey forth. Otherwise, I shall attend you when I can do so easily. Besides, I do enjoy weddings more than funerals and the earl of Chandler lives closer to me than you.'"

Clare crushed the parchment.

"Blanchette can be too willful! Failure to pay respects to our father will not go down well for her among Trent's people. Our sire may have been arrogant and independent, but our people loved him! My sister will pay prices for this, I fear."

Why their people's respect for Blanchette was an issue of import to Clare did not puzzle Jordan for longer than a minute. He concluded that Blanchette, as Clare's only living relative, was to be Clare's heir or, at least, her surrogate in her absence. Aye, his bird meant to fly from him along the road to Geoffrey's manor in Lancaster. And she intended to leave her nest in the care of a sister who would not tend to her domain as selflessly.

Jordan admitted to himself that he cared not to ever meet this sister who would shine less brightly than her nobler sibling. Yet he thought Blanchette might inject herself into a wedding where she would not be necessary or even wanted, lest her interfering ways be too much for king or country.

Thank God, Blanchette had not changed her mind about attending the funeral. The day after Aymer de Wallys's earthly remains had been lowered into his chapel sepulchre, Jordan and Clare had left Castle Trent alone. Waved off by well-wishers, most of whom had tears in their eyes, Clare sat her own palfrey with a dignity that made Jordan's heart expand two sizes in his chest.

She had insisted that Jordan and she would go without any of her maids, regardless of what anyone might think of the impropriety of an unmarried woman riding with an unmarried man. She declared that if Henry and Geoffrey trusted Jordan in such a situation, she had more reasons to do it herself. So, just as Jordan wished for neither of his two knights to accompany them, she wanted to worry over the loyalties of none of her own people. She already had enough of that. She needed to ride fast and hard to outrun any attacks on Cheshire by Glendower or the French, of whom they had heard nothing in the past week. Clare also claimed she wanted to travel quickly to her new home, unencumbered by excessive amounts of her clothes and her jewels, for which she could send later. Indeed, her bulkiest baggage consisted of two velvet bags of nobles, by which she said she would feather her new nest. She never said "with Geoffrey," but Jordan knew what she really meant.

He took these signs as more proof that she would try to leave him before they arrived. He also welcomed the opportunity to have her to himself and enjoy what they could of each other before he had to hand her to a man who could not appreciate her in the myriad ways Jordan himself did.

But hours after they set out, the skies grayed, the wind cut into their garments like knives, and snow began. In the incomparable silence of a storm, he had detected the footfalls of another horse. So had Clare.

Urging her to take cover, Jordan had left her. Armed with a small bow, arrow drawn ready to find its mark, Clare had backed to a brace of trees. Jordan completed his reconnaissance to come back to report no sightings of man or beast. Just as he would have waved to her that all was clear, she led her mare out—and was greeted by an arrow. He had turned, scoured the underbrush, heard a horse pound the frozen earth, but discovered no one. He feared for Clare alone and galloped back to her.

She knelt beside her palfrey. The arrow was an odd one because it was extremely short, less than a forearm's length, but made of good ash wood with four gray goose feathers. It had grazed the mare's foreleg but left a puncture wound that ran and seeped, though she and Jordan bandaged it. Without any herbs to speed recovery, the animal's wound became infected. Jordan feared another attack and urged them to press on.

Traveling more stealthily, Jordan had taken them from the main road north toward Morning Star Manor. Knowing of this convent because he and his two men had hosteled here on the way to Trent, Jordan had sought it out—but not soon enough to protect Clare from ill health.

Now scarce hours after they had arrived, he praised God that they had arrived before the palfrey was completely hobbled. Jordan yanked his cowl lower over his head and gazed sightless at the interior of the rickety stables. He must find Clare another mount in the tiny village when the storm abated. He must also hire a messenger to send to Henry and notify him of their delay.

"Best ye come inside quick, milord," crooned the hunch-backed nun as she rose from the carcass of the horse. "The ice storm gets worse, an' there's nothin' ye can do for this creature. I can't even make glue from him 'til a thaw comes and the caretaker can trek up from the village te help me. Let's save yerself an' yer lady."

Aye. The horse could freeze but Clare need not, should not with the terrible malady she'd contracted and suffered these past two terrible days.

He opened the ramshackle door for the kindly woman. "Ah, sir, yer a good man, fer fair, but if ye huddle with me, ye'll not make it inside 'fore ye turn to ice, too!"

"Come, Sister Freda. I'll help you in as you have helped me."

"Incorrigible man. God does love ye."

Of that I have had little evidence, he thought to himself, but took the lady's arm as the two of them picked their way across the courtyard of the rambling old convent. Skating more than walking, they arrived at the huge front door with relief and praises for each other's agility.

"Get ye gone to yer lady, sir," ordered the nun with a gnarled finger toward the stairs which led to the public hostel's chambers. "I have a good broth brewing of licorice and barley fer her. Ye might do with a bowl yerself, milord. Fer warmth and vigor, lest ye get her malady."

"Thank you, Sister. I will attempt to stay healthy and lead us out of here." He was grateful that the nun did not preach to him about staying away from a woman who was not his wife. The nun did know, and so did her prioress, that his noble companion could not be his mate.

When he had arrived hours ago with a feverish Clare lax in his arms, Freda flung wide the convent doors to welcome him and immediately remembered him from last week when he and his men had slept here. The kindly nun, who acted as portress, cook, hosteler, and stable hand for him and Clare, did so because most of the other twenty-two in her community were down with winter sicknesses themselves. Only Sister Freda and her prioress walked strong in this place, aside from him. Because she was overworked to get her sisters well, Freda had declared Jordan would have to tend his lady himself. He would not have it other.

Nor would he now. He sped toward Clare.

Since they had left Castle Trent two days ago, he had not left her side. This past hour or more, when he had gone to see to the ailing horse, had been his first absence. He rued the day he'd taken Clare from her home and set her on this path to hardship and now sickness.

He took the winding stairs and long corridor, dark and dank, and in a few swift strides, he thrust open the rough hewn door to the room they shared.

He stood on the threshold, his heart aching for the lady who lay limp on the straw pallet he had pulled before the fireplace. If he had taken her from her home only to kill her with exposure to these chilling elements, he would forever writhe in hell and deserve it wholly.

He shut the door gently and went to her on soundless

footsteps. She reclined, copper hair waving across the coarse gray linen sheet, beautiful eyes closed, her russet lashes fringing high cheeks too gaunt, too red for health. He cast off his cloak, knelt, and put fingertips to her forehead.

Christ. He hung his head. She burned higher than before.

At his touch, she turned her feverish face into his hand. "Dragon," she breathed, and licked her lips so that in the doing she tasted his palm.

"Aye, my love." He trembled for her pain and his delight in the feel of her. Even though she was sick, he wanted her and could not scourge her from his heart.

"Don't leave."

"Nay." She tore him open with her need and her sweetness.

"I was searching for you. In a fire. The flames surrounded me and I could not find you—"

"I would find you anywhere, anytime you are in peril."

"Aye," she said hazily, satisfied and then not. "I called to you. You would not answer—"

"I'm here now. You were dreaming, darling, because you are too hot. Let me loose your clothes. The nun comes with soup."

"Not hungry."

He reached for her blankets and flung them off. Her undertunic clung to her every rise and plane, damp with her perspiration. He would not argue with her. 'Twould sap too much of her strength. Besides, she'd eat. He'd see to it.

"Burning," she objected, grabbing a fistful of her gown and lifting it from her body. "Wet."

"Aye," he mourned as he pushed her clothes up her long legs past her hips and waist, then hooked an arm behind her and lifted her upright so that he might peel off the gown.

Naked, she shuddered and lolled her head so that she looked him straight in the eye. Then she grinned. In her ravaged mind she must have known what he was doing but thought he had a more sensual intent.

He fought to return a comforting smile to her—and not survey the wonders of her form, which he had so long yearned to admire. Was it not enough that her skin felt like moist butter against his own?

"My Dragon." She pressed her plush breasts against him, her hands tangling in his hair and undoing his leather tie. "You always make me feel hot and wet."

He choked. "Do I, darling?" He tried to lay her down, but she would not go.

"Hold me," she beseeched him.

He squeezed his eyes shut.

"Don't you want to?" Her voice gave a small catch.

He snapped open his eyes and saw tears in hers. "Aye, my love. I want to do that and more."

She sighed and rolled her head back, her parted mouth a temptation for the beast in him. "Then kiss me."

"Sweetheart, you are so ill and this is not the proper time or place." *Or circumstance.*

She smacked her hand to his chest. "You ruin my romance."

"You, madam, do make mine."

She tossed him a saucy smile and rubbed the tip of her nose across his cheek until her mouth spoke on his. "Kiss me."

He shook his head. Kiss her and he would not stop.

"Why? Because I am not for you?"

Nay. For Geoffrey.

"No one will know," she whispered like a conspirator. "I'll never tell, and God knows, you won't."

"That path leads to utter damnation."

"I'd rather burn in hell with you than live without you."

Whether or not this was truth in delirium, he'd take her words to his grave. But while he lived, he could not acknowledge them. He could only hug her.

She enjoyed it for a minute, then accused him of "Not enough." Out of her mind with fever, she had enough sense to yank away from him. "Go away." She turned her elegant back to him and sank like a stone to her bed.

His rebellious eyes roamed the sleek length of her from bared nape to nipping waist to flaring hips, firm heart-shaped buttocks, the dark juncture of smooth thighs, then down to shapely calves and ankles.

He saw her burrow into a more comfortable position.

At odds with himself, he spied her gown and spread it over the back of one chair to dry before the fire. He heard the nun knock and announce her delivery of their soup.

Grateful for diversion, he answered her summons. He shut the door, walked to Clare, and told her she must eat.

She said nothing.

He noted her even breathing and thought she slept. For long minutes, he did not disturb her but put the tray upon the table next to her two bags of money. He had left them in clear sight of her pallet because he wanted her to see he would take nothing from her . . . nothing that he hadn't already stolen. Her kisses. Her freedom . . .

He yanked out the chair, plunked himself in it, and tried the soup. It went down like rocks. He pushed the bowl away and, from the corner of his eye, saw Clare roll to her back.

He turned his head, suddenly quite deaf and dumb. Only his sight worked—and the errant part of him that demanded her regardless of loyalty or the dubious welfare of bloody England.

She was far lovelier than he ever had imagined.

He pushed back his chair and, heathen that he was, he went to stand at the foot of her pallet, throbbing, reveling in the wealth of skin and hair and lips laid bare to him.

He told himself to go slowly. Not devour her in one scan. But he quaked with the conflict between honorable man and irrational animal.

He clenched his hands, and only then did he permit his greedy eyes to flow over her.

Her neck was long and swanlike. He had noted its nobility before. Her shoulders were wide but trim and vaguely muscular, as were her shapely arms. Her collarbones, even as she reclined, jutted prominently. The little hollows they created were ones he had first appreciated days ago. They still beckoned to his desire to dip his tongue into the valleys.

But, oh, she had a greater valley. A deep one between her

two plush breasts. She had been so right to call them cushions. Even reclining as she was, their ample contours promised a man or babe generous succor. His blood roared in his ears, demanding that no other man must suckle there—and no other man's child seek nourishment there, ever.

He braced himself against the storm that traveled from his loins. He put his hands out, madness in his method. From this vantage, if he narrowed his eyes, he was touching her in more than his mind. Her breasts were bigger, better than a man had a right to desire. They overflowed his palms. His thumbs could circle her blush nipples, make them pucker, make them reach for his tongue, and make them yearn for the nip of his teeth.

He fought back a groan and an insane urge to lay his head down on her. To banish time and place, Geoffrey and Henry.

To have her. To make his only life's ambition to put his mouth on every inch of her skin, his tongue into every crevice and lave every plane and peak. Suck her into him, absorb her, get lost in her. Forget his body, lose his mind, and unchain his honor. Live to love her, make her grin and give her experiences she could never write about or sell, because words could never describe the thousand and one ways he'd bring her to novel climaxes. Aye, he would because the innumerable examples of how he adored her were real expressions of how intricately love and lust combined. He and she would make a marriage . . . and babies. Countless babies.

Though he had never sired any, he knew he had the stamina—and the imagination—to make love to her so often and in so many ways or die trying to get her with child. For he dearly wanted now in this ripe moment what he never had required. A wife. This woman. A family. A *huge* family. Children to prove to the world how every night **he craved his wife. This wonder in his bed.** This darling of his days for all his remaining ones on earth.

For a man who had concluded he was too old to want

anything except peace until the end of his life, he vowed he desired this Nightingale to nest with him. He would lay her in a home filled with the simple but splendid comfort of his devotion . . . lay her nightly in broad beds where he would tantalize her for hours. Fill her full of him during the day in chairs where he could spread her strong legs over the wide armrests. Satisfy her quickly at any convenient minute against any wall or on downy toweling before a fire, no match for the one he'd build inside her—and tend until he died.

He ground his teeth. *What fiction was this?*

She shifted, as if she knew his need to run and in her anger at his rejection countered it with a better view of more of her. She thrashed, arched, and extended one leg.

Open to him, she was this madman's fantasy. With her athletic thighs wide, she spread her feminine treasures before him. Inviting him in her fever. Tormenting him in his perversion. Copper curls, paler than on her head, coiled about the entrance to those heavy lips he had massaged the other night. Pink skin peeked out, magenta folds beckoned him closer. He could see himself spreading her apart and hearing her liquid declaration of how she needed him to sample her creamy readiness.

He rooted himself to the floor, remembering how she felt. Soft and warm. How she smelled. Spiced and wanton. How she tasted. Like no other woman.

He spun.

He needed to *feed* her, not consume her with his eyes!

He must save her.

From himself.

For Henry and Geoffrey.

God damn them all.

She contemplated the two red velvet pouches of money. Sitting precisely in the middle of the only table in this room, her coins taunted her to rise up and use them.

Ha! How? She could barely move, let alone leave here, buy passage, bribe someone to aid her . . .

She closed her eyes again, listening to the utter silence of the night. Even if she had the strength to get up from this bed, she had not the will. She wanted other things more. A bath. Food. And the comfort of one man.

Once again, Clare's eyes shot from the crackling logs in the fireplace to the giant creature who slumbered before it. A dragon in repose, she thought in her cool euphoria of the fever's aftermath, can be an enchanting sight.

Where were they?

The room was certainly no princely palace. Spare but clean. One pallet, huge but hers only. One table, two chairs. Stone walls, one adorned with a large crucifix.

Ah. A convent. Its hostel.

Alone with the man who was her greatest temptation in a place where people removed themselves from all temporal seductions, she suppressed the urge to writhe in her own torment.

She reached to cast off her covers . . . and discovered she had none! She glanced down at her body, naked as the day she came into the world, and chuckled.

She clamped a hand over her mouth, lest she wake him, and felt the sting of tears.

What irony to be here with him, alone, without the trappings of clothes and politics—and be entrapped by their own loyalties. Jordan's, to his king. Hers, to her people and herself.

She moved and felt the lingering ache of her illness in every muscle. How long had they been here? She had no idea. She could not remember how they had come by it.

The only visions she had were ones of a dragon's solicitude. His worried face and anxious hands as he lifted her from a stumbling horse, seated her upon his own, and held her tightly as they traveled forever in pelting snow. Of this place she had no memories.

She ran her tongue over her lips. Cracked.

Dragged a hand through her hair. Filthy.

Tried to rise. Failed.

She fell back to her pallet with a small cry of defeat. Done in by her body, her mind seethed at the circumstances she could not control. How could she escape a dragon if the creature was ever watchful and she was loath to leave him, sick or well?

She pounded her fist into the straw and, by force of will, rose. She stood, weaving on aching feet, and wondered what the infuriating man had done with her clothes. When she spied her tunic spread over a chair, she gnashed her teeth at how very far away it was. And how it lay under his hand.

Damn man, he thought of everything.

She would show him a new trick or two.

She tried to tiptoe and only succeeded in making her head spin. So she put her whole foot down and a floorboard groaned.

He was out of his chair, around it, teeth bared and grabbing her up before she took her next breath.

"Jesus!" He quaked, then froze as he gazed down into her eyes, as surprised as she that he held her in his arms.

The shock drained her of any energy she thought she possessed.

"What in hell are you doing?" he bellowed as he caught her before she sagged on watery knees to the creaking floor.

"You needn't shout," she told him, wincing.

He said no more. She knew he couldn't, not when he realized he held a totally nude woman in his embrace. His touch changed from anger to reverence, speed the only constant to his actions.

When he had secured the coverlet to her chin, he asked in a quieter tone, "How far did you think you'd get?"

"Evidently nowhere without you," she taunted, and turned her back on him. *Your honor and your vigilance combine to make my romance a classic tale of purest love and ripest frustration. Why I should adore you does not escape me—just as clearly as I cannot escape you.*

Chapter Eleven

CLARE GOT LOST FOR ANOTHER COUNTLESS TIME IN GEOFFREY Chandler's blue eyes. Since she and Jordan had arrived this noontime at his nephew's manor, Clare could not seem to cease admiring this attribute of the young man. Indeed, if his large, lushly lashed orbs could be duplicated by any earthly pigment, they would have made the most perfect cerulean color for a hero's portrait. They sparkled at her now as he delivered yet one more compliment to her hardy nature . . . and her beauty.

She laughed lightly. Geoffrey Chandler tried to be as facile with his tongue as his other attributes of courtly manners and blond good looks that most women would admire.

That was, of course, unless they had already seen and been enraputred by the darker allures of a dragon.

Geoffrey's mouth, so similar to his uncle's sweet lips, spread in a seductive smile. "Have more wine." He lowered his voice to bare levels and leaned closer. "You need it, I think, to sleep well and deeply. I'll not have you too tired for the wedding." He raised his brows and let his glance define the line of her bodice. "When Henry and his court arrive in a day or two, I've planned a great reception and feast to celebrate our union. You'll enjoy it." He winked at her.

She snapped her attention to the ruse of mollifying this man, who by his bold manner already imagined himself as the husband who would soon bed her. "Thank you, my lord, I will have one more cup. 'Tis hearty stuff, and I am pleased to be in warm comfort after the terrors of the last days out in this bitter cold."

"I trusted my uncle treated you well." Geoffrey smiled as he poured fine Bordeaux into her cup. Over his broad shoulder, Clare could see the man in question next to Geoffrey, looking straight ahead at the servants gathered in the hall of Morning Star Manor. By the way Jordan rolled his tongue around his mouth, she knew he took note of every word of this conversation.

"He did take good care of me. The very best." She lifted her cup to her lips.

"But he did not use the king's livery to ward off mayhem!"

"We both thought that best. We wanted to travel with all due speed and without anyone asking questions about our destination." She drank deeply, pondering her next words if he should ask for an explanation of this.

Geoffrey arched a blond brow. "If you are ashamed to let the world know you are marrying me . . .?"

She nearly choked on laughter. Why would she have worried that Geoffrey would probe further about this matter of the livery and the need for secrecy? His vanity, which obviously came before any other consideration, demanded stroking. "Nay, my lord. Pride or shame never entered into my deliberation of this marriage to you."

He looked deep into her eyes and appeared appeased. "Very well. But I am still concerned about this journey. You were so ill. When Jordan's message arrived, I worried that I would lose so beautiful a bride."

I'm certain that, since you had not yet seen my face or form, you grew anxious you might lose so bountiful a dowry.

"And now," he crooned a little too cloyingly to suit her, "*now* I learn that you had to buy another horse because yours died! I tell you, madam, I am undone!"

She hated this inherent insult to Jordan's charge of her and vowed to deter this young man from trying to sink any thorns into the flesh of the man she adored. She did not understand the animosity between them, but even if she had, she would not contribute to it by ignoring Geoffrey's tone. "The horse's death was caused by a combination of the loss of a smithy's shoe in the ice, a flesh wound on one leg, and some disease that made him froth at the mouth. Those conditions could not be controlled by your uncle, I assure you." *The best control your uncle has is the one he exerts over himself, for which I praise God and at the same time offer him no thanks.*

Geoffrey laid his big warm hand over hers. "I promise you, madam, I will make that horror up to you."

Beyond him, Clare saw Jordan wince.

"You need not, my lord."

"My name is Geoffrey." He squeezed her fingers. "Use it. We will soon move from formality to familiarity, my dear, and I find you not only lovely and congenial, but worthy of my attentions." He raised her hand to his mouth.

She wanted to hoot and howl at his self-admiration but bit her lip as he pressed his flesh to hers. God. 'Twas too civil, nothing like the hard cindering kiss of a dragon.

"My dear Clare, let us begin the journey to a happy marriage now."

If she could have uttered a sound, she was certain she would have eeked like a mouse. Instead, she cleared her throat, fixed her sight on Jordan's taut profile, and thought only of her mission for later this evening. Aye, she had to take in all aspects of this small oak-lined hall, note where servants came from the kitchens and any other alcove she could discover. She had to find a way out of this manor house so that tomorrow she might bribe a servant to say nothing as she departed. Then she'd buy a horse from some discreet but hungry person in the tiny village. And she would ride away. With the wind. Toward the sea. The nearest port of Blackpool—or so she thought, if her good sense of distance served her right. In Blackpool she'd find a ship to Flanders. Or any passage she could gain to the Continent, to escape this coil, this cage of politics, wars—and hopeless love.

All of that she would do, of course, after she left her copious document pledging her loyalty and that of the people of Trent to Henry of England. Thus would she solidify the agreement by leaving money in lieu of her body.

"What do you say, darling?" Geoffrey said against the skin of her hand. He looked quite boyish as a shock of blond hair dipped over his brow.

In the silence she heard the grumble of a dragon.

"I think you are right, Geoffrey. We'll start now on the road to our future." She tried to beam at him but failed when beyond him she saw an injured dragon turn and gaze at her with pain.

"Pardon me, Geoffrey." Jordan pushed back his chair with an ear-splitting scrape of the floor. "I am weary of this. I will retire."

"But I hired minstrels for the week, dear uncle. I planned for us to dance. Do stay and—"

"I cannot dance, Geoff."

"But I have seen you, sir! You are superb and there is many a servant woman here who—"

"Geoff!" Jordan said in such rough anger Clare was certain as he rolled his eyes to the crossbeams that he wished to roar. "I bid you good night."

Clare stared at his vacant chair after he had gone.

"Look at me, Clare. . . . I wonder . . . was my uncle too good to you?"

Now her ire rose, but unlike Jordan, she could speak of it and deal with this twenty-year-old. "I will be plain, Geoffrey. If you mean to ask if he seduced me, the answer is no. Your uncle is the most honorable man I have ever met, bar none. I assure you that when I go to your bed"—she searched madly for a way to say this delicately and found none—"you will find me a virgin."

"Oh, madam!" In his blush, his youth did show. "I never meant—"

"Aye. You did, Geoffrey. Let us play no games in this relationship of ours. Never lie to me. Never cheat me. Never underestimate me. Between us there will ever stand truth. I will show you how by starting with the blatant facts of our marriage. I am here to wed you against my will. I do it to gain Henry's protection for my people. And you do wed me for my money."

"Ah, but madam, don't you like me?"

His innocence spiced with the dash of coy self-assurance made her smile at him. "Aye, sir. I do. You are a handsome, charming man. But you could do with a little more discretion in your words and much more respect for your uncle. Why is it that the two of you are at odds?"

"I'd rather talk of us."

"Geoffrey, I will speak of your relationship with your uncle *first* or of ours not at all. What of this antagonism between you and your uncle? From where does it come?"

He shrugged one of his shoulders. The move made him look like a petulant child. So similar to a gesture of Blanchette's.

"'Tis an old irritation. My father and my uncle often fought."

"Are you telling me you took up the gauntlet your father dropped at his demise and threw it toward your uncle?"

Geoffrey pursed his lips.

"I see," she said. "For what reason?"

"My uncle Jordan knows where some gold is hidden."

She ransacked her memory of the description of the gold Jordan's father and this child's grandfather had illegally collected and had supposedly hidden somewhere in this house. "I have heard this story, and it seems there is great question if the gold exists at all. And for this, you nettle Jordan? Good God, Geoffrey. That is rather petty of you, don't you think?"

He whispered, lest someone overhear his lack. "The money is important. I am not rich."

"You will be if you marry me."

He looked as if she struck him. "Really, madam, I expect more discretion in your choice of words—and in public, too—from my future wife."

She shot to her feet. She would not let this boy have any inch to rule over her. "I demand more adult behavior from my future husband. Think on it, sir." She lifted the hem of her train in a pose of control, yet did she smile benignly at him. "I wage my money on your better nature."

Hours later, she clutched her cloak about her and crept along the upstairs corridor on cat's feet. She'd brought no candle, relying on the glow from low-burning sconces and her memory of the manor house's architecture to lead her down the stairs from her small bedroom to the great hall. Instead of going for the main door where, surely, a guard would stand watch, she turned for the kitchens and any other egress she could find to the courtyard.

Morning Star Manor was no century-old castle like Trent. Her home had been constructed during the time of Edward the First of England when that man's assault upon the Welsh made him dot the marches and the interior of that wild country with the strongest fortifications he could design and then grant them to trusted retainers. One of those had been a de Wallys.

However, Morning Star was at most twenty or thirty years old and situated well inside the shire of Lancaster, which was long allied with the Crown of England. The building was constructed mostly in oak, reflecting the Chandlers' background as nobility of recent ordination and mediocre financial means.

For her to escape this place, she need only open the door and walk out into the byways of the village. There was no long causeway to cross over a moat, no manned barbican, no grilled portcullis to raise. In fact, only a few guards defended Geoffrey and his people by standing watch on the parapets of one huge but broken gate at the entrance to the village. As she and Jordan had ridden past the gatehouse, she had seen that it was the remains of a wall which had once surrounded the village. When she asked Jordan why it had never been repaired, he told her that there had never been a need.

"No rebels or conspirators come here. Morning Star is not rich or strategically situated. It is simply a quiet place to live," he told her as they dismounted. "That virtue is difficult to duplicate."

She remembered the look in his eye as he said that, and she recalled his desire for peace himself. Well, he could have it, she hoped, although she knew it would come to him after he accepted the fact that she had escaped him. Provided, of course, she found a way to do that!

She suddenly smiled to herself as she entered the kitchen and spied a door beyond two smaller rooms. One was probably the buttery and another, mayhaps, an herbal pantry like hers at Trent. She sailed over and cursed quietly that the only obstacle now between her and the greater freedom she sought was this damn heavy bolt!

"Allow me to assist you, darling." Jordan stepped from one room to surround her and put his hands atop hers.

When she stopped shuddering from fright, she dropped the iron and wood bolt into its brackets with one thud. She spun in his embrace and sank backward to the door. "Are you *everywhere* I go?" She ridiculed his vigilance and fisted two hands against his chest.

"Always."

"Well, prepare yourself. I won't give up!"

In the variegated golds shining from the blaze of one nearby wall sconce, she saw his mouth curve in a wry gesture. It put one dimple in his scarred cheek and made her want to trace his features with fingertips. "I would be disappointed in you if you did, pretty bird. Besides, I like your spirit." He lifted one hand, appearing to lead her back to the hall, but impetuously drove his fingers beneath her hood into her hair. "I love your curls. I like them unadorned and tumbling down. Like this." He pulled them taut so that his hands smoothed them over her arms.

Her breasts ached for a similar caress. Her breath grew

hot in her throat. Her fingers encompassed his wrist to end this torture. "I'll return to my room. You need not worry."

"Oh, but I do. I think of you every minute." He was whispering now, drifting closer, his legs nailing her to the door, his hips following . . . and then his chest. His nose trailed her cheek, and she felt his breath hot upon her face. "Did you dance with him?"

She felt paralyzed and wanted to taunt him for doing this to her. "You might say I did."

"Is he good?"

"Not as proficient as I."

Jordan chuckled. But the laugh soon died, and he gripped her arms so tightly she thought he'd bend her bones. "You like him."

"Not as much as another."

He stilled.

She edged away.

He let her go, but in the ambers and indigos of night, she heard anguish in his voice. "Living with you will make him a better man."

"Not probable, but possible *if* I can refrain from acting like his mother."

Jordan snorted. "Darling, the only thing you need do is offer him the richness of your companionship and he will be enchanted."

"A man like Geoffrey needs a woman totally devoted to keeping him fascinated only in her body and, therefore, only in her bed."

Jordan sighed. "Christ, you see that already."

"Aye. And I am not happy that you did not tell me this yourself."

"It would not have sold the marriage to you."

"I haven't bought it anyway!" she said too fast for prudence. Then in anger at herself, she whirled for the main hall.

She fairly ran, but she could perceive him behind her, catching up to her too easily by his long sure strides. She considered herself relatively successful at staying just beyond his reach until at the entrance to the hall, his words gave her pause. "I never thought you had agreed to this marriage, Clare. I know you better. You want to leave me, Geoffrey, Henry, England. I just wonder where it is you want to go."

"Where I *want* to go!" She laughed ruefully and spun toward him, poking two fingers into his chest. "You know where that is!" She meant anywhere on earth with him.

"Tell me."

"Flanders! Are you satisfied?"

"Nay! I want more for you. I want you happy!"

"Since I have put myself into the Dragon's keep, happiness is not possible for me!"

"God above, Clare. I will die mad with grief to know I brought you to this pass!"

"Aye! But what comfort to go with your honor as your shroud!"

"Christ, you kill me with my own sword and shield!"

"So be it, Dragon. Live with your satisfaction over this."

"How could I be satisfied to know that you leave—"

"Oh, *damn* us both." Bitterness for what she could not have—would not once she left England—had her rising on her toes, cupping his nape, and making him gasp as she kissed him squarely on the lips.

Her anger sparked a firestorm of mutual passion. With one hand, he tore open her cloak and dragged it off her shoulders. With the other, he hauled her against him, crushed her close, no part of him held in abeyance from the glory of his desire for her. She mewled and grabbed his hair. He lifted her off her feet, nibbled at her mouth with fierce little bites, and then trailed his tongue down her throat. She arched, braced herself against his shoulders as he found the crest of one nipple beneath the thick wool of her gown. His tug seemed too shallow for the hard wild ways she craved his mouth on her. Of a sudden, she felt herself pushed against the wall as his hands pulled up her skirt and he sank to his knees.

"I want you," he declared against the quivering flesh of one thigh. "And I am vain enough and jealous enough to need you to remember me."

She tried to cry out in ecstasy as she felt his fingers skim her calf, her knee, and trace the inside of her leg so that she had to open for him.

"You are so lovely, my Nightingale." He tugged on her secret curls and rolled her nether lips apart. She froze in the shock of cool air . . . and then flew in the euphoria of him kissing her needy flesh, his tongue diving and flicking and swirling on some special spot that made her moan and buck.

With one hand, he pushed against her hip so that she braced herself to the wall. "I'll never forget the taste of you. Or your scent." He sucked her into his mouth in one deep eddy, and helpless in the whirlpool, her hands fluttered to his shoulders.

She gulped and lolled her head against the wall. "Jordan, don't do this." He growled and sent a finger up inside her traitorous body. She marveled, somewhere in her brain, that this was the tiny place he had touched the night her father died. What his fingers had brought then, she decided was prologue to what his tongue could expound on now. "Oh, my God, Jordan, don't stop!"

"Open wider for me, my love," he gruffed. "I don't want to rip your virgin's shield. *There,*" he crooned when she had spread one leg and curled her hips forward in a wanton pose for which he rewarded her fully. A fingertip circled inside a throbbing place while his tongue licked in homage against a flaming little point. "Jesus, but you're good. Give me more."

Gladly. "Here."

"This?" he whispered and circled the hot nub with strong swathes.

"Aye, aye . . ."

He used his talents to her raging benefit. "Christ," he cursed between swirling mouthfuls of her, "how can I give you away?"

"Don't!" she sobbed, and hated herself for the misery she would bring on both of them with such an admission.

Her head throbbed with need for the release she wanted from his lips, from his body . . . from his accursed quest.

The drumbeat became louder, fiercer.

Suddenly, she knew it was the sound of horses outside. Shouts and conversations ensued as guards spoke with those who arrived. There was a furious pounding at the front door. "Open up, I say! 'Tis late and we're tired and hungry."

Through the roar in her ears Clare understood the tone of this entreaty. The voice grew familiar. Tom? Tom the gardener!

Her body pulsing, she sank her nails into Jordan's shoulders. As if she had talons, she wanted to rip him apart and make him end this torture. He pulled away and used his fingers on her. In a few hard circles, she had flown, soared, dived to earth. She dragged air into her lungs, her eyes shut against reality.

Jordan let her gown drop, smoothed it down her legs, and with a brazen kiss to the juncture of her thighs, he took to his feet. His hands tangled in her hair as he framed her face and offered her the delicate homage of his lips. She sampled her own fragrance as he whispered, "I adore you, madam."

She wound her arms around his neck, but he pulled her away and warned her with his eyes. Tears pooled in hers.

He thumbed a few drops from her cheekbones.

She wanted to laugh hysterically at her folly but collected her thoughts for the necessities of the moment. "Should we open the door?"

Upon the main stairs, footsteps proclaimed neither of them need respond. One of the house staff ambled forward with a candle. In one glance up and down their two forms, the elderly man seemed to understand the tenor of what had passed between them, and he smiled sadly. "Shall I open 'er up, do ye think, Lord Chandler?"

Jordan nodded. "If the guards at the gate let them through so easily, they must be friendly visitors, Harold."

The man repeatedly banging at the door gave a fuller answer. "My name is Tom, and I'm in service to Lady Blanchette de Wallys. We come for the wedding. Let us in!"

Chapter Twelve

HAROLD OPENED THE FRONT DOOR AND GAPED AT THE SIGHT that greeted him. Jordan snapped his own mouth shut and marveled at the comedy played out before him.

Tom the gardener, the man he had heard about and seen at Castle Trent more than a week ago, carried in his embrace none other than the Lady Blanchette de Wallys—and he did so as if he held the Crown of England.

The blond girl, who had wrapped one arm around his shoulders, clutched his cloak with a nonchalant hand, which illustrated her trust of him and her belief she merited the devotion of his actions.

She glanced at Harold and dismissed him as insignificant. Then she trained her sights on Clare, but for only a second. Her pale eyes found Jordan and concentrated on his form as if she mapped him for a plan of attack. When she had scanned him from feet to crown and back again, she beamed at him with twinkling eyes and then deigned to greet her sister.

"Good evening, Clare. I know we're very late, but I did

want to sleep in a good bed tonight. Most hostels are so barren and cold, don't you agree? You look oddly flushed for this hour of the night. Are you well? Now, don't start to reprimand me, dear. I had to attend your marriage, didn't I? Tom, I see a chair over there. Do put me down, will you? I think you must be tired, poor man."

Jordan wrestled to hide his grin as he felt Clare bristle. Her hands clenched. Her mouth moved, he could have sworn, in words no lady spoke aloud. That her willful sister had decided to come to a wedding that Clare herself had no intention of attending would make her angry. In Clare's case, the move was a tragic one.

Suddenly, he found no humor in this situation. It was one thing for him to thwart Clare's ambitions to escape him, to save her from someone who tracked them from Castle Trent and then to watch the weather and sickness combine to make her effort more difficult, but it was more roiling to witness her own sister drive this stake into her heart's desire. He ached for her.

She saw it in his gaze, thanked him silently, and left him to walk toward Blanchette.

Harold, doing his servant's duty, was inquiring about the new guest's needs for food, drink, and accommodations for her servants.

All the while Harold asked, Blanchette was pulling aside the hem of her cloak and arranging her skirts well over the clubfoot she took great care to hide. Only when she was quite satisfied with her gown's drape did she flip back the hood of her mantle and shrug out of it to display a low-cut sapphire gown, which was but a shade darker than her eyes. Jordan noted now the buttery yellow of her hair. It offered no comparison to the rich copper of Clare's, but certainly when complemented by Blanchette's exquisite profile and petite form, made a picture of a woman ideal for most men's romance.

But not his. His love went out to Clare, who stood before her sister, trying to contain her ire.

"I will not ask why or how you decided to come here,

Blanchette. I suppose I should have expected it. You have always done as you wished, when you wished."

"Well, of course, darling, why would I not want to see my own sister married? Tom, get me my gift for Clare from my saddle, will you? Thank you." She settled back into her chair, hands hanging gracefully from the chair arms, her flawless skin and perfect almond-shaped nails a testament to her idle hours and care of her person. Still, shining in her eyes, Jordan noted, lived a deep adoration of her older sibling. "Shall I speak in front of this man?" She indicated Jordan with a tilt of her jaw.

"Aye," Clare said with a nod in his direction. "This is Lord Jordan Chandler, King Henry's man."

Blanchette acknowledged with a sensuous curve of her lips how acceptable she found this information. "The king's Dragon? How appealing. I heard from Tom, who took it from Trent's servants, that you, my lord, have cared well— very well—for my sister. I thank you. She needs succor, especially at such an hour when she is made to marry"— her blue orbs turned cold and sharp as cut glass—"against her will, albeit that the bridegroom is your nephew." She turned her attention to Clare, her manner solicitous, even deferential. "How could I not come to investigate if this impoverished earl is worthy of you, sweetheart?"

Clare swallowed hard. "'Tis not a marriage made in heaven! Well you knew it, too, from my letter."

"Certainly. But for my sake nor none of Trent's would I see you die, Clare, in a marriage made in hell."

Jordan reeled that this girl, this vainglorious child, should speak his worst fears. Oh, God, he knew Geoffrey would never abuse Clare. Never physically. Never verbally. But in the omission would Geoffrey hurt her.

Jordan had witnessed Geoffrey's actions tonight, and he knew the boy too well to ignore what lay before him like an illustrated manuscript. Jordan could read the signs of the future. Geoffrey took delight in Clare's beauty. Christ, what man would not want to lick his lips over the long strong body, suckle two firm full breasts, and wrap those elegant legs around his waist in the throes of ecstasy?

But Geoffrey's vanity and youth meant he was no match for sensitive, intelligent Clare. One day—mayhaps very soon—Geoff would resent her maturity. When she demanded—and she would—that he grow into a more sensible creature, Geoff would balk. Then would he walk into the arms of another woman. And to darling Clare, who believed in holding fast to principles and honor, this adultery would wound her. Gravely. Though Geoff's desertion would never kill her—for she would have to love the boy for Geoff to wield that power over her—Jordan wanted no man to injure this divine creature who should belong to him alone.

Clare seethed at her sister's declaration. "I thank you for your desire to protect me, Blanchette, but that is all it can ever be. I must"—she worried her lower lip and the light went from her eyes—"must marry Earl Chandler. You cannot change that, no matter how you wish it. Conditions are not such to change it." She walked into the shadows of the room.

Jordan felt Clare's frustration as keenly as a knife in his belly.

Blanchette turned her own anxieties on him. "How *can* you make her do this? You and your king can afford some largesse! Do you not have the means to protect Trent without forcing a woman to spread her legs for a man she does not know and cannot hope to love?"

Across the room, the man they spoke of put his foot to the bottom of the main stairs. Geoff was running a hand through his disheveled hair and tying the belt of a robe about his naked body. A servant or the sounds of voices must have awakened him.

Jordan was too angry, too roiled by the odds against Clare and her happiness to care how Geoffrey might feel about what he must say to this girl.

"My lady de Wallys," Jordan said between clenched teeth, "I assure you that if I had a choice, I would never force your sister to this union. I believe two people should want each other madly, love each other dearly to consider conquering the joys and sorrows of daily life together. I also know they should respect each other, a condition I see too little of in arranged marriages. But England is in peril."

Blanchette flicked a wrist. "Glendower again, 'tis all."

"'Tis much!" Jordan roared. "He wages *war*. Spills human blood. Burns villages. Steals horses, cattle, goats . . . anything he can get his hands on! Have you seen the effect of battle on men? Nay. Not from your convent! Well, I have, and it is not pretty. Not polite. I tell you the Welshman comes and now he has an ally. The French!"

"Nay." Blanchette paled, appalled. "I did not hear that."

"Believe it," he shot back. "And whether you see this or not, I will repeat what often I have told your sister." He stepped forward so that the child's eyes would not stray to Geoffrey, who had stepped into her line of vision and drew it despite the direness of this argument. "Your father would not align himself permanently with King Richard or Henry, and for that, like it or not, Trent and all in it must now pay the price for their prevarication."

"So you take my sweet sister as hostage to your politics?"

"Aye!" shouted Clare, just beside Jordan. "Call it what you will, Blanchette, *but—I—am—Henry's!*" She shook so violently that Jordan curled an arm around her waist and, undone by the panoply of her emotions, Clare turned her face into his shoulder.

Jordan could not help himself, so rife was his torment for her that he did not care these two saw it. He brought her securely to his embrace, his lips buried in her hair.

"My lady Blanchette," Geoffrey's voice pierced Jordan's misery. "Allow me to assure you of my desire to wed your sister."

Jordan scowled at his nephew's sensuous tone and shifted to watch this encounter. Clare, unmoving from his arms, raised her head.

"You are Earl Chandler?" Blanchette's tone held censure, yet Jordan noted that she smiled like a queen at this boy whose appearance kept drawing her gaze to his nearly naked chest.

"Aye, none other." He threw her a ravishing grin and sat in a chair across from her, allowing the robe he wore to gape open dangerously past his waist, his long legs set before her to inspect at her pleasure . . . and leisure. "I am glad you have come."

Clearly. Jordan suppressed a groan, indignant at Geoff's enchantment with this girl who said nothing and did not need to when she tossed her curls and let her eyes run down his form in saucy admiration.

Geoff pursued the girl more. "Your presence, dear lady, will make this event a more glorious occasion."

For whom? You?

Clare dug her nails into Jordan's wool tunic. He squeezed her fingers, anguished that she should see what he had predicted would happen—and this soon! God forgive this callow young man. Geoff would preen for any woman who showed the slightest regard for his face and body! Satyr that the boy was, Geoff would strut like a cock to lay any chick he sought to savor. He'd even do it to Clare's little sister—and right before her eyes!

Clare straightened. "I am weary," she told them all. "I know you will be shown to a comfortable room, Blanchette. Forgive me, but I must retire."

When Jordan would have gone with her, she stopped him with a fierce look. "Leave me alone. Please. I *am* going to sleep."

"I never thought other." *I have deterred you from leaving only to witness this. Have I foiled your efforts to escape too often and in the process robbed you of your hope?*

He saw her go up the stairs, listening to the bill and coo of the two young people in their chairs. He welcomed this new and unexpected role as chaperon while Harold returned with an urn of wine and four goblets.

Geoffrey took over his duties as host and waved his man off to bed. "You may go, too, if you like, Uncle."

Jordan merely met his nephew's gaze with his own. The boy lifted a corner of his mouth in recognition that Jordan would not do as he suggested.

Blanchette saw the exchange and adroitly took up a string of conversation which led her to gush over the beauty of Geoffrey's land and village. "Although I saw it only in the moonlight, 'tis quaint. So lovely in fact that I do marvel at how like my inner vision of a place I once dreamt I'd like to live."

"You have an imagination," Jordan commented before Geoff could respond in some cloying way, "just like your sister." He'd be damned if he would sit here and let them forget why they were here and to whom they owed their lives and their futures.

"Ah, Dragon, you have learned she is the Nightingale then? Good."

"What is this nightingale?" Geoff asked of both of them.

"A writer," declared Blanchette with pride. *"The* writer whom Richard sought to bring to his court."

Geoff looked bewildered, then disdainful. "The one who writes in the common English?"

"Just as Chaucer did," Jordan announced, "and he made a great deal of money from it."

"Oh, well then," Geoff smiled, relieved by the idea of wealth justifying some act he clearly had at first questioned as suitable for his intended wife, "that makes it interesting. But why would a king wish for a writer at court?"

Jordan thought sometimes Geoffrey could be block-headed. "Because Richard valued the artistic endeavor."

Blanchette giggled. "My father told Clare that Richard valued clothes and painting, sculpture and wine. Anything effete, he said! But Clare is very smart to use the common English language. So many now do. Even the nobility. Is that not true, my lord Dragon?"

"Aye. Even King Henry uses it instead of Norman English. So does his oldest son. They both say it will be the glue that binds us as a people."

Blanchette's face lit up. "Aye, of course, I am certain. Do you know Prince Hal? Wasn't it said that you—*aye, that the* Dragon did protect Hal in Ireland?"

"Aye, my lady, I did," Jordan responded, noting her peaking interest in the heir to the throne and Geoffrey's dislike of her questions.

She leaned toward Jordan. "Is Hal as wild and handsome as they say?"

"He has a taste for wine—"

"And women, too. I have heard many tales of his conquests. Gossips say he is very charming. Is he?"

"Of that I cannot be the best judge, madam."

"Come, come." She waved a hand in excitement. "Do tell me. I hear he is tall and well formed." Her long fingers, so similar to Clare's, undulated in the air as if she ran them down a lithe body.

Geoffrey rearranged himself mightily in his chair, his gaze on those hands of hers as they went to nestle in the vee of her lap.

What this child knew about luring a man, a legion of oft-bedded wives could not impart.

Jordan grew more angry that Geoff could be so enraptured. "I assure you, my lady, that Prince Hal is very much a ladies' man."

"He has had many, I would think." She picked at her skirts coyly. "Do you think he'll come to this wedding? Mayhaps to confer with his father, if no other reason? I do hope so, and I wonder, as so many do . . ." She tapped a finger against her lower lip. "Must he marry a foreign princess? Many say he should wed an Englishwoman and avoid international intrigues in his bed."

Why did Jordan feel there was more method than curiosity in her query? "I do think he must find a wife abroad, madam. He and his father wish to secure the French territories so long disputed, and the prince will want allies to wage his suit."

"Ahh, 'tis a pity. For there is much good to be had in an Englishwoman's embrace, don't you agree, my lord Chandler?" she inquired of a silently fuming Geoffrey.

"Aye," he said gruffly, and thrust a goblet of wine at her.

"Oh, nay, dear sir!" She sighed, then put a hand to her mouth and feigned a yawn. "I cannot drink a drop. I am quite exhausted and unable to manage your stairs." Her gaze met Geoff's in steamy invitation. "Won't you do me the greatest service and carry me up to my room?"

Her helplessness—coupled with her forwardness and intense feminity—brought Geoff to his feet in a nonce. He scooped her up as if she were one of the small, rare specimens of the creatures he had collected and mounted in his solar upstairs. He smiled at her like the sun to earth. "Aye, madam, I will put you in one of my best beds—and I assure you I do have many worth a try."

"Geoff!" Jordan rose, shocked speechless by the pair.

"You might go to bed yourself, Uncle. I will do well by this lady because she is my guest, and thus, you need fear nothing goes amiss with her."

Blanchette tipped her head against Geoff's shoulder while one hand caressed the blond fuzz upon his chest. "Thank you, good sir. I am so tired, and I wish to help with the wedding preparations. There must be much to do, and I am very good at setting tasks for servants. The king will come, won't he, Geoff?" she whispered in great intimacy. "I want to look my best for him, so do take me to bed." She snuggled closer, if that were possible, and grinned serenely at Jordan. "Good night, Dragon." As Geoff carried her up the stairs, she called back. "Sleep well."

Sleep?

Jesus wept!

He circled the room. Prowled it like one of Henry's tigers in the Tower of London. But unlike those beasts whom English kings kept locked for the amusement of themselves and their court, his own imprisonment was a thing fashioned as much by his own hand as by a code of honor set upon men, by men, *for* men. Aye, he believed a code was necessary, beneficial! Common values made for peaceful living among men and within each man's soul. He had enjoyed contentment with observing the rules of right conduct. He had found satisfaction with himself, his king, and his God.

But Clare had been right days ago to observe that satisfaction was not the same as happiness. And down all his days, he had found none so bright, so right as that ecstasy he claimed with that woman in his arms.

He dragged both hands through his hair.

This agony was so useless. There was no relief for him, no release. He would not abandon every principle he'd ever upheld. He would not act in haste, unwisely, immorally to grant himself succor. Christ, he doubted he even knew how to do that!

He felt like tearing down the house with his bare hands.

His eyes scanned the hall, seeking solace, answers, a way out of this torment. He found one on the table.

The jug of wine.

He went to stand before it.

He had not been tempted by wine in so long, he had forgotten how to drown in its depths. Now he forced himself to remember its sharp flavor, its rush of giddiness. Its glow of serenity.

He poured it to the very rim of his cup. If he lifted it, the liquid would spill. Like his life, it would pool and run upon the table in the whorls and groves carved by natural events and other people. If he sipped it, he would drink more and quickly. Gluttonous, he'd turn into an ugly monster, grizzly and grim. He'd drink often and without regard to codes or peace, king or love. He'd lose a sense of time. Hell, he'd lose whole days . . . and more than his mind. He would become bitter, wild, and sick, and *still* he would possess no Clare. No clarity to his days. No reason to go on.

Wine changed nothing. Cured nothing.

He picked up the jug and strode through the hall to the kitchen and with one sure hand lifted the heavy bolt Clare had tried to raise less than an hour before.

Outside, the winter night was crisp but silent. Like that night he and Clare had met upon Castle Trent's wall walk and he had first kissed her and knew he craved her, the stars twinkled brightly like diamonds upon black velvet.

He threw the wine from the jug. In the quiet evening, the sound of it splashing to the frozen earth made him think of money dropping upon glass.

Money.

One cause of all these troubles.

If Clare had none, she would not have tried to leave. Or would she?

Of course, she would. She knew the value of her soul's delight, and she set a high price on her own happiness.

But he had no money. Was that perhaps why he had never learned what she did? That there is no money equal to the joy of being true to yourself?

Aye, it was certain that he had no money. Not any to call his own or in any amount that could buy anything he wanted. Of course, there was now only one thing he wanted more than life itself.

He wanted Clare's happiness . . . and that meant Clare's freedom. That's what she desired above all else. And in this love he bore her, if he could never have Clare, by God, he'd ensure she'd enjoy her heart's desire.

What if . . . ? What if he helped her purchase the freedom she so desired? What if he traded upon his only asset—his friendship with Henry?

Certainly, he had never asked any favors from Henry. What did he ever want from life but things Henry could never grant? Peaceful daily existence this king could not find for himself, let alone one of his retainers. And the love of one good woman no monarch could grant him, either.

Suppose then he argued Clare's case as her advocate— and ceased to act as her gaoler? Suppose he assured Henry that England's Nightingale needed to sing in peace, unfettered by political concerns, and reassured him of her allegiance to her own king?

Then could Clare fly free—and Geoffrey could go to hell.

Chapter Thirteen

"GOOD MORNING, JORDAN. OR FROM THE LOOKS OF YOU, should I ask that?" The king, who had surveyed the court-yard from his horse, glanced down at Jordan. Henry's personal guard rushed about to take up their positions to surround him, allowing only Jordan close to the king. From their dishevelment, the army and Henry had ridden here quickly and early—and Jordan bemoaned the coming wedding he had to stop.

"Are you not well?" the king persisted. "Your delay along the road was not caused by your own illness, was it?"

Harry, who had never liked riding and enjoyed it even less on campaign, looked haggard as he accepted Jordan's hand to help him dismount. His stocky body had never sat a horse well, and to travel at such an early hour for him as noon added nothing to his comfort. Unlike most men, though, this man was a rational being. His physical discomfort did not often affect his mental acuity.

Still, Jordan would have liked conditions better if Henry

had never come this way nor so fast. "Sire, I was never ill, only Lady de Wallys."

"Ah, but as is your wont, I trust you saved her." Henry wiped a hand across his perspiring brow. His complexion, from riding in the sun, had blotched, which meant that beneath his layers of cloak, tippet, and tunics, his larger skin lesions itched and oozed. Jordan knew his king yearned to scratch himself to death when this happened, and he pitied his friend this malady no physician could seem to cure or even soothe.

Jordan turned his mind to what he could correct. Clare—and her bondage.

He answered ruefully, "I wish I had saved her. Henry—"

Behind him he heard the jangling of the spurs of numerous of the king's guard.

"Jordan! You look well."

He turned to face Malcolm Summersby. As tall as Jordan, Malcolm had thinned over the years. Nonetheless, his features resembled those of a lean but hungry bear. Round-faced, sweet-eyed, snub-nosed, Malcolm looked eternally jovial. He appeared an incongruous mate to the petite black-haired raven who was his wife and who, like now, seemed ever at his side. At least, during the days.

Jordan put out his hand, but suspicious of Malcolm's involvement in the ambush on the road to Trent, he did not embrace Malcolm fully as was their custom. "I enjoy good health, as do you, it appears. Good morning, my lady Summersby." For this company of king and cohort, Jordan never addressed Diana by her given name. Her title put a distance between them that he wished to keep, now more than ever. To her would he give only a polite nod.

She bristled. "I, too, am well," she gave him at his lack of inquiry.

She was affronted. More than that, in her eyes stood the memory of their last encounter in the castle at Kenilworth, just before he left for Trent. She had surprised him in a dark corridor, accosted him, and offered him—for another countless time—her body in his bed. When he rejected her, she had acted like a woman scorned. She had threatened him with retaliation.

He concentrated instead on saving Clare. "Sire," he said to Henry as they crossed the courtyard, passing the wooden outbuildings of dovecote and smokehouse. "I wish to speak with you. Much has happened at Castle Trent that you need to know, and I have many unanswered questions."

"Aren't there always?" The king sighed. "In good time, Jordan, we shall talk." Henry gave him a wan smile and raised his chin toward a guard. The man jogged forward and Henry handed him his gauntlets. As he and Jordan mounted the steps to Morning Star's great hall, Henry turned back to survey the courtyard. "Christ, the sun is hard and oddly warm for November in the north of England. What happened to the snows of last week, eh?"

"Melted as if they never were," Jordan replied, wishing he could have remained cloistered with Clare far away from here and the necessity of her marriage.

"Damn, damn," Henry mourned. The sun irritated Henry's sensitive skin, more so as years went on. If Henry disliked war, he hated going to it. But fighting in the sunlight, he loathed. And most wars were conducted in the summer and harvest months, when the heat was high. "What do you suppose they roast in that house this morning?"

"'Tis the season to smoke hams and bacon."

"It turns my stomach."

One of Henry's peculiarities since he had become ill these last four years was a delicacy of his digestion. His diet was indeed bland, made more simple by the fact that everything he ate was not only tasted by two people before he dined, but the preparation was rigidly supervised. The pervasive possibility of regicide poisoned his appetite for food or friends or fun. Remaining to him was the joy he found in his wife, his children—and less and less in ruling.

"I will order them to cease, Sire."

"Nay. We will move on to Trent and to meet Glendower as soon as I am rested from this trip. The road here was a nightmare, Jordan."

At the doors stood Geoffrey, with Clare and Blanchette at either side of him. Jordan frowned at the young man. Geoffrey should have known better than to put himself between the women, on this occasion, especially. Clare was the senior and deserved the place of honor at Geoffrey's right hand. After her should come her sister, if at all.

Geoffrey should roast in his own smokehouse for what he was trying to do here! Jordan had ordered his nephew not to present Blanchette to the king and, thus, disregard the petulant girl's request. Catering to Blanchette's whims could earn the boy the rack or, worse, the block. Henry would want to get to the main issue once he arrived here—and that meant the wedding. It also meant Jordan had little time or patience for Geoffrey's antics.

Yet the boy had done as he wished, as usual. And from his expression, Geoff had donned his customary self-confidence. He bowed to his king with a triumphant twinkle in his eye to Jordan.

Jordan scowled and directed his attention to the one for whom he was more concerned. Clare glowed this morning in the sunshine. Despite her abject fear that stole the blush from her cheeks, she seemed serene as she sank in a sign of homage, and Henry spoke to her.

"You are far lovelier, my lady, than legend gave you credit."

"Thank you, Sire," she murmured, eyes to the cobbles.

"I am pleased to tell you that I have enjoyed your manuscripts, too." Clearly, Henry had known the Nightingale was a woman when Jordan himself had not.

The king smiled. "I have borrowed many of your works from my aunts and cousins. You have a talent for words, madam, that I admire. Would that I could persuade you to sing for me, Nightingale. But of course, I would prefer if you came without rancor."

Clare lifted her face to Henry then—and loving pride burst through Jordan's veins. She showed pleasure and honor—those emotions Henry savored for their honesty and scarceness in his life. So, too, did she reveal her dislike of the idea in her response. "Your praise salves many wounds, Sire."

But before she and Henry engaged in any discussion and possibly locked in any controversy, he would have his time with Henry.

"Sire," Jordan appealed to Henry when the introductions were done. "Let us speak together. I know you must rest after such a long journey from Kenilworth, and my words will not take long. But I need to talk with you . . . privately." He uttered that last word under his breath because the Summersbys hovered so near.

"Oh?" asked Malcolm with congeniality. "What can I not hear in times of war?"

Geoffrey, eager to appear the convivial host, intervened. "Sire," he said to Henry, "allow me to describe the menu for dinner."

The king knit his brows together. "Please, do me no favors in that regard."

Geoffrey looked crushed. So did Blanchette.

Clare opened her mouth to add her own comment.

But Jordan intruded. "Sire, I promise to take short minutes of your time."

"Aye. I must speak with you as well, Jordan. . . . Earl Chandler," he said to Geoffrey, "I beg you, show us to your most private and most comfortable room—with thick walls and no squint holes for spying or listening."

Jordan breathed more easily. Years of working together did bear ripe fruit instantly. He prayed that in his tale of the ambush along the road to Trent and his suspicions about William Baldwin and his own man Nathaniel Pickering, he could get Henry to see the complexity of this situation. In the process, he hoped to establish that Clare was innocent and should be allowed to avoid this marriage and go to Flanders.

Soon Henry sat in a cushioned chair in Geoffrey's upper solar, the sunlight's refractions off the oak walls lending him more color of health than he naturally possessed. One squire scooped up the king's cloak and tippet, then promised him to return with wine.

"Not so early in the day. Bring us both some juice."

Jordan waited until the boy shut the door before he looked at his friend. To speak of Harry's deteriorating health was a sore subject. In public, the king could be stalwart about his affliction, but in private to Jordan, the man was becoming more weary and superstitious about his condition. Harry wondered aloud—and only to Jordan, he was certain—if this agony were recompense for taking his cousin's crown. But Jordan could not dwell on that so much as the mysteries at Castle Trent, which threatened Harry's hold on Richard's domain.

"Harry, I have much to tell you about what happened with the de Wallyses."

"Aye. No hasty message from a convent's walls can relate such things as negotiations, death, and conspiracy with any justice. Tell me about Aymer and your Clare."

The last two words told Jordan his friend was perceptive, as ever. Jordan had said nothing in his curt note to the king that indicated he cared for Clare. Yet this man knew Jordan's feelings for her in only a few minutes of observation. Therefore, they would converse without preliminaries, knowing each other deeply as only lifelong comrades could.

"I am sad to report that I have three mysteries to solve. The first lies in the story of my journey to Trent."

"You said in your letter you were attacked by robbers."

"That was a description laid down for brevity and fear someone could waylay the messenger and read the longer truth. The fact is that I was attacked by five men, Harry. Well armed in a snowstorm, they came at us suddenly and knew our destination."

"Mayhaps in such a clime they found the only ones who traveled in a storm."

"Nay, Harry. They were clever, but they were also very well informed."

Harry tilted his head. "Meaning?"

"They not only knew my name but also they had one man fully prepared to engage me in combat and ram my shoulder with a blunted lance. My left shoulder, Harry. After that man had dislocated it, they did not search my body for gold or trinkets nor did they try to kill me but bound and gagged me. They wanted to ransom me, and I never learned why because I was saved by Clare and her band of women."

Harry pondered for a moment and asked, "This rescue by the lady did not appear to be planned? To ingratiate her to you for saving you from brigands?"

"Nay, Harry. This was a real attack. All five outlaws died in that encounter. If the attack and rescue were some sinister plot, I do think they would have planned to allow the five men to escape. They died. Furthermore, I inspected each body, Harry, and no mark, no livery, no item of clothing, or trinket gave any evidence of who they were or by whom they were employed."

Harry pursed his lips. "And you learned nothing at Castle Trent about who they might be?"

"Nay. Inside the de Wallyses' domain, I found a few clues, but also more mysteries. Never have I felt so beset, and I do believe the retirement I sought with your permission is now quite timely."

"We will debate your retirement later. I would hear instead about these other mysteries you encountered."

Jordan came to sit opposite his friend and leaned forward, elbows on his thighs, hands clasped. "To do that, I must tell you the story in order. After the attack, we went to Clare's home with her women caring for my two men."

"Aye, you wrote they were injured, but how badly?"

"Severe enough to leave them at Castle Trent." Jordan left off for the moment the issue of how he questioned Pickering's allegiance—and why Jordan had decided to travel to Morning Star Manor without an escort. "Wickham received the worst blow. He took an axe in the thigh. He mends slowly but well, I am pleased to say, and that last because of Clare de Wallys's skill with herbs and medicinals. Pickering, too, was afflicted during this ambush, but he suffered a sprained ankle. Again, Clare bound him, splinted him, and sent him potions to relieve his swelling and discomfort. He will heal quickly, but not soon enough for me to take him as escort here to Geoffrey and you. And then, there is the other matter of Wickham's and Pickering's loyalty to us."

These words were sparks to a fire Henry had so long tended that only his eyes flared in outrage. "Tell me everything."

"Wickham, whom you instructed me to watch for signs of disloyalty, showed none throughout the trip. Nathaniel Pickering, whom I had no reason to doubt, became my bigger question."

Jordan sat back and relived the ambush . . . and recalled a detail which had escaped him ere this. "Just before we were attacked, Pickering had done reconnaissance ahead of us along the trail and river into the forest. I never thought of it then as an opportunity to signal anyone. But he could have been communicating our position. . . ."

"You have no proof?"

"None. But at Castle Trent I soon discovered I had more reason to distrust Pickering. The morning after I arrived, I went to look in on him to see how he fared from his injury. I overheard him talking with a woman who was one of Clare's helpers. She and he had struck up a relationship the day before upon the field where he lay injured. At first, I thought their attraction to each other was sexual—and I was preoccupied with learning the identity of the five outlaws. But the morning after the attack, when I went to Pickering's room, I overheard him converse with this woman and I became disturbed and wary. Their discussion was of Clare, and their words showed they were familiar with each other not in any physically intimate way but as if they were"—he loathed this word as did Harry—"conspirators."

Harry's dark eyes took on a dire glitter. "Who was the woman?"

Why Harry should be more interested in who the woman was than in what she said was not logical, but Jordan answered anyway. "Clare's manuscript illuminator."

"And her name?"

Jordan's focus narrowed on his friend. What was wrong here? What was Henry hiding from him? "Solange Dupre."

"Dupre." The king tasted the name and found it indigestible.

Why? Did Henry know of this woman? Could he possibly have her in his custody? But how might he have learned of her—and why was an illustrator important to this king? Unless Henry had learned she was more than that, and his friend was extracting information from him to confirm what he already knew. Jordan's mind whirled with fears. He simply would tell Harry everything and see if he could pry loose those facts from Harry which threatened him—and Clare. "She told Clare she came from Bruges in Flanders. But later I learned from Castle Trent's laundress that the woman told others she was from France."

Harry seemed to lose all tension in his body. Sad and suddenly older than his years, he stared at Jordan solemnly. "Do you believe in Lady de Wallys's veracity?"

"Aye."

"Did you from the time you met her?"

Jordan reflected. "At first, I suspected anyone of having set those five brigands upon us. Yet as I grew to know her, I found Clare de Wallys one of the few people in this world I could trust."

"Ahh, I see. Should *I?*"

Jordan stared at him.

"From the way you stop, I would conclude you have reason not to recommend it. Why?"

"Not because she has done aught against you."

A commotion began below stairs, and in the wooden manor house, sound gusted like the wind.

Jordan continued though Harry glanced toward the door. "I hesitate because Clare seeks to live in freedom."

"Not with Geoffrey?"

"Nay! She wants to be free of politics."

"I'd say she should have thought of that before today, Jordan."

A pounding came upon the door. "Sire! Please!"

"It is Malcolm." Jordan raked his hair in displeasure. "Let him wait a minute. I have more to tell you, Harry. Aymer de Wallys died in a strange manner. He was ill, probably with leprosy." Jordan knew he touched a nerve with Harry, but he had to proceed. "However, the way in which he died was too sudden for any complications of that disease."

Harry had often conjectured privately to Jordan that his own affliction might be leprosy. Its mention now had him writhing in his chair. His other pervasive fear of regicide made him hoarse as he leaned forward to ask, "You think Aymer was murdered?"

"Sire, we must speak with you now."

"That's not Malcolm, but—"

"The captain of my guard, de Quincy." Harry waved a hand impatiently. *"Was* Aymer killed?"

Jordan told him how Clare had found the vial. "Aymer's servant suspected one of the mercenaries, one of Aymer's captains of the watch. The servant said this man brought the poison—or at least delivered it to Aymer. Aymer did wish to die, Harry, and had asked Clare to assist him. She refused. But Aymer, as you know from years of dealing with him, could be resourceful. Soon after Aymer may have obtained the poison, this mercenary captain disappeared. He was a cold creature. William Baldwin, by name and a former friend of Hotspur's, no less. We are not certain of all his motivations, but then I must tell you that another suspect is Solange Dupre."

"How can that be?" Another knock came. "Ignore them."

"The illustrator had access to pigments, of course. One of them is yellow. Its base element is arsenic."

Harry clutched his stomach as if he himself were the one attacked. He grew pale and short of breath, fear of the unknown eating at his vitals.

"Sire!" de Quincy called. "We have found a brigand in the smokehouse. I must see you. He has French papers on him!"

"Christ does bleed!" Harry straightened of a sudden and

began to scratch at his hands. "I will ever live in torment. Open the door, will you, Jordan?"

Angry that he had so little time with Harry before Malcolm intervened, Jordan crossed the room and cursed Malcolm's increasing tendency over the last few years to never leave him alone with Harry for long before he intruded. But when he opened the door, his anger went from Malcolm to the man who stood between him and de Quincy.

William Baldwin glared back at him with icy eyes.

Malcolm shoved Baldwin inside to stand before Harry. "De Quincy found him running from the smokehouse to the dovecote. He will not give his name or where he lives."

Jordan could. "This is the mercenary who was hired by Aymer de Wallys, Sire. The one I spoke of a few minutes ago. William Baldwin. Also known as Harry Hotspur's friend."

"How came you here, Baldwin?" the king asked.

Jordan had an idea of that. The man was filthy from days of hard traveling. Had he been the one following him and Clare? "What of his horse? Have you found it?"

"Aye, my lord Chandler, the animal is near death with fatigue," replied the young viscount de Quincy who had performed two years of loyal service to Harry. "Sire, I think he was caught in his hiding place when we marched in so quickly. I knew you would want to see him. I have searched him and his saddle. He carried this bow and quiver, these two misericordes—Italian, I do think for all their sharp elegance. And these." He held out two folded but crumpled sheets of parchment toward the king.

But Jordan examined the short arrows inside the leather quiver. These ash wood weapons bore the same distinctive fletching of four gray goose quills that had pierced Clare's palfrey's leg. He stared at Baldwin, no doubt in his mind the mercenary had tracked them through the woods.

But at whose order?

His gaze landed on Malcolm.

"Have you read the papers, de Quincy?" Harry asked.

"Aye, it is part of a letter written in French, but I could translate them easily. They speak of Glendower's allegiance with the French king, Charles, and of the coming attack upon the Cheshire coast. The sender thanks the recipient for all the help given."

"Is that so?" Harry examined Baldwin as if he were a plague. "By whom is it signed, de Quincy?"

"It unfortunately ends with only the words *your friend.*"

Jordan went to stand next to Malcolm and, in so doing, felt that man's seething tension.

Baldwin, meanwhile, glowered at Henry.

"Vicious beast, aren't you?" the king said beneath his breath. "Well, do not let us wait longer! Time is precious, and your life grows shorter each precarious minute. Tell us, man, who is your friend and when will Charles's men arrive?"

"I do not know," Baldwin spat, his eerie eyes going round at his four captors.

"Come, come," lured Harry silkily, "I have little patience for your diversions. You can imagine that my decision about *how* you shall die, will, of course, be based on the length of time you make me wait for useful answers. I have a thousand ways to make a man squirm and wish he'd been more prompt."

"Like drowning Richard in a vat of wine?" Baldwin taunted.

"Aye . . . like that." Harry used the old rumor whenever he wished to build fear in an opponent. He closed his eyes to slits, and Jordan knew that in his mind, the king looped the hangman's noose for this audacious mercenary.

Jordan hated that years of such accusations had made Harry cruel. No matter that his cousin Richard had most likely died by his own plan to starve himself, Jordan had no proof of that. But neither did Harry's opponents have evidence that the former king had died by rough means.

"I'll tell you nothing," Baldwin vowed.

Harry nodded toward the door. "Out! Take him *out!* He'll never hold another parchment, and to be certain of it, start by separating him from his fingernails, de Quincy."

Baldwin froze. "Those papers are not mine."

"Oh?" said Harry. When Baldwin did not reply, the king smirked. "After that, I'd like his fingers, one by one."

Jordan swallowed bile. Harry had become coarse over the years. He had watched it happen, knew why, and could do little to save his friend except serve him faithfully. Yet now that steadfastness meant he could not have the one thing he wanted in this world.

Baldwin gulped. Cowed, he looked at Harry. "Nay, do not do that to me."

Harry stood. "Well, then. . . . Do—not—make—me—wait."

Baldwin regretted his outburst, hung his head, and bit his lip. "That letter is not mine."

Harry laughed. Tears came to his eyes and rolled down his cheeks to his jowls. His was the gaiety of the ill. "Astounding. Wonderful ploy, Baldwin . . . but useless."

Jordan loathed Harry like this.

The king lifted the two sheets of parchment. "Take him outside, de Quincy. I want to hear his cries for mercy."

"Sire!" Jordan stepped forward. "This brutality is not necessary."

"Really? We shall see, won't we? Bring me the Nightingale."

"Sire, why? What has Clare to do with this man's failure to tell us about a few pages of a letter?"

A letter. Good Christ. Had Clare written those pages? He stepped forward, needing to see them, but even if he did, he did not know her script. He took small comfort that he also knew one more thing: She would not invite anyone to come into her land, her home. Not Henry, not Glendower, and not the French.

But Henry did not know that. He turned a shrewd eye on him. "We will let her listen to this man howl while we hear her song, Jordan. And she must give quite a performance to continue to live."

"You will not hurt her!"

"I will do as I must. You know that better than any. Bring her here. Now, Jordan."

Chapter Fourteen

WHEN JORDAN STRODE TOWARD HER, CLARE HAD SAT FAR TOO long waiting for a summons to the king. But from the fright on Jordan's face, the audience she had dreaded would now occur. "What is the matter?" she asked as she shot from her chair and could not refrain from putting her palm to his cheek. Let Blanchette and Geoffrey see her action, if in their mutual infatuation with each other the two youngsters even noticed. She loved this man and he needed her succor. She would give him what she could for as short a time left to them.

He dropped a kiss into her hand and seized it. "Listen to me, darling, and do as I ask. Do not lose your temper from this moment on. Promise me."

"Aye," she vowed solemnly. "Why, Jordan?"

"Harry is not well. You must do this."

"I will. I swear it."

Jordan tucked a stray curl behind her ear and then led the way toward the stairs.

A few steps up, she tugged at his hand and brought him

around to her. "Hold me," she whispered. "For whatever evils I now face, I need once more to feel your embrace before I go."

Jordan seized her like a man aflame. "Darling," he breathed into her hair in ragged voice, "would that I could carry you away with me. I wish I had. I was so wrong to bring you here."

She trembled. "What does he mean to do with me?"

"I will see he never harms a hair on your head." Jordan pulled away and raised her chin. "Trust me, Clare. Do it as you have never done before. Say you will."

"I do."

"Good." He gave her a wan smile. "Now come."

When once more she stood before her king and bowed to him, Clare felt a chill she had not known upon the manor steps. Odd, she thought. Henry did not look like a man who could murder his cousin. Or quell a rebellion. Or unify a war-torn country.

Clare recoiled from the jolt of her second and closer observation of this man. When minutes before the glimpse of Henry had stirred her compassion for his political burdens and for his illness, now his intensity terrified her. More so as Henry bid Jordan to come sit beside him, her hale and hearty Dragon did put the king to shame. Henry, who was one year younger than Jordan, appeared two decades older.

"We are honored to have you here, Lady de Wallys," he offered after a thorough examination of her face and form. "I have often thought my cousin Richard was astute to want you to write at court for him. Now that I meet you, I wonder if I could make you the same offer and if you would refuse me."

"You will not learn until you ask, Sire." She smiled, hoping she made it clear she wished to be polite more than diversionary.

Henry lifted his hand to beckon her closer, and as he did, she saw his skin was dotted with the same lesions her father had manifested when his disease began. This awakened her pity for his torments.

Henry took his good time about responding to her. In the awkward silence, Clare waited.

From the corner of her eye, she could see Jordan, unmoving, worrying. Next to him sat another of Henry's retainers, whom Clare had often heard of as a good military strategist—Malcolm Summersby. Beside that man sat his wife, the Montaigne heiress to the lands that bound Trent's to the south. This was the first time Clare had ever encountered Diana Summersby, and Clare acknowledged that the woman lived up to her fame as a black-haired, black-eyed beauty of great charm. Although to Clare, Diana showed no smile, no warmth. Nor had Diana graced Blanchette or Geoffrey with any in the hall. Nay, from her idle chatter now to fill the void left by their king, this woman spent her emotion on three men—Jordan, Malcolm, and her king. And surprisingly, she did it in that order.

Once Clare enjoyed more time and less precarious circumstances, she promised herself she would ponder this woman's fawning over Jordan. Even more, she would rejoice in his indifference to the lady. As to why the woman was so important to the king that she should attend this interview, Clare could only assume that the rumors of Diana Summersby's wealth brought her here. Henry was poor with his wars. Diana's fiefdom, under the Lancastrian and later the Crown's protection since she married her husband years ago, was a rich one. Plus, that land did sit to Trent's south, strategic to the defense of England from Wales.

Their monarch, shrewd and cautious, examined every hair on Clare's head, every feature of her face and facet of her eyes. "You do not like the idea of working for a king, lady?"

His lack of use of her title chilled her. Never had she met one born so high with manners so low. But then he had the ability to flaunt his power, didn't he? "I do not like the idea of working for one person only. In truth, I prefer to labor only for myself."

"You will continue to produce manuscripts after you are married?"

Avoiding the debate over marriage, she focused on the main issue of her art and simply said, "I will."

"How many women can gain a husband's consent to neglect their family and home to make a profit in business?"

"I know a few merchants in Chester and a good dyer and tailor in London who are women alone heading businesses for a good turn of coin. They are married and have many children. None of them suffer because the women work."

"That's only four or five. What makes you think you will survive and prosper?"

"I have had practice combining the running of a business with the running of a castle. And during troubled times, at that." She said it without rancor, but it brought her that in triple.

Henry was seething when he spat, "You, madam, and your father created much of that trouble."

This interview was a gladiator's contest to the death. Henry had no reason to be kind to her. Jordan, who had known this man most of his life, was afraid—and afraid for her. No matter that she was powerless caught in his web. What a fool she was to hope a man who was so sore beset by conspirators at every post and highway would offer courtesy or kindness to a woman who had defied him and sought to run from him.

But Henry did not know that last. Not unless . . . she turned to Jordan . . . not unless he had told his king about her attempt last night to leave the manor. Jordan might be loyal to his liege lord, but he was prudent . . . and he cared for her. Nay, he would not reveal this to Henry. The king had other cause to treat her thus. She feared now for the first time that she would die for her father's perversity.

Lest she be sent from Henry's presence, she had to seize this opportunity to state her case and win Henry to her cause. She polished her finesse. She gazed at him, taking in his looks with more objectivity than a few minutes before, and explained, "My father and I thought we were acting in Trent's interests, Sire. Or at the time, we did believe it so."

Henry's nostrils flared. A man who may have once been comely, his face and form ran now to fat. In the chair, he appeared weary and paunchy. His dull red hair was graying and thinning. His skin was milky, livered, and diseased. Then, too, she feared other ills beset his mind. She would be cautious as she had promised.

"And now, Countess, you believe conditions have changed?"

"Aye." She grew angry that Henry drew out this confrontation with coyness. She was no simpleton to be led into a debate. She welcomed it! "You, Sire, have changed them and so has Owen Glendower." She tilted her head toward the courtyard where Henry's army—God, it had looked like half of England—camped out there. "Trent cannot stand independent in such a fray."

"You see it rather late, lady."

She would not give him the benefit of a verbal answer when she knew it would only reaffirm his power over her.

"You and your father, with your thirst for independence, have cost me much. Because of you, I have had to retain more knights and archers at great price. I have had to go around your lands and instead use this good lady's." He pointed to Diana. "Her estates do not offer the best route to defend my kingdom, but she and her people have died in great numbers and suffered pillage and rape because Glendower's raids concentrated there. South and west of Montaigne, my crown lands receive blows from Glendower. These attacks drain my people and my treasury more than they would have if you, madam, and your father had aligned with us. Do you have *any* idea"—his voice was rising, wheezing as she stood stoically before him—"any *concept* of what you have done to this country?"

Perspective was what this gentleman needed. "*I*, my lord?" She bit her tongue, lest she use it and lose her head. *I did not insult my cousin nor imprison him. I did not demand he sign abdication papers in my favor. I did not raise the fury of most of England by putting on a levy of taxes that took what few pennies they had in their little jars.* "What I did in one tiny corner of England was what any English subject has done since King John signed the Magna Carta. I indulged my own right to defend my own lands in my own way with my own money. What's more, I—and my father—paid you our taxes."

He would have yelled at her, but with a mad look at her, he schooled his features to moderation . . . and cunning?

Jordan sat forward, an animal ready to spring.

Clare braced herself.

Henry inhaled and sighed, his jowls wiggling. "Madam, your sin is no bigger or no worse than many in England over the past four years of my reign. You thought you could do as you wished in your little domain, thought I would not notice, but I needed to when Glendower decided he was Prince of Wales and God's right hand. And when the French king decided—rather oddly, too, I might add—that he would ally himself with the Welshman, I came to the realization that Trent's ambivalence was a continuing phenomenon I could not abide."

"And so you have me," Clare said, and swept out a hand to indicate her presence and surrender.

"Do I?"

Why was he so argumentative? "I am here," she insisted.

"Against your will."

"Not totally."

Henry hooted, just as Jordan shot her a pained look. "What evidence do I have for that?" the king insisted.

"None. But I wish to give you reason to believe me."

"Really? *What?"*

"Money."

"Countess, for what trouble you and your father have caused me, a little money cannot buy my pardon."

"That I knew, Sire."

"How much do you think will?"

Not bashful, was he? "A sizable payment and then a yearly annuity."

"How *much?"*

"I will open the discussion at—" She projected what it had cost her father per year to arm, feed, and clothe his mercenaries and estate villeins, then added a bonus to whet the appetite of her king. "Six thousand nobles."

Summersby and his wife gasped.

Jordan moved not at all.

Henry pursed his lips. "Is that the advance or the annuity?"

"Both."

Henry's face went lax. "Generous."

"Sufficient to pay to man an entire garrison like Carnavon with one thousand men for a year."

"What, madam, do you want?"

"My freedom."

One corner of his mouth curled. "You do not wish to marry Earl Chandler, I take it."

"He is a comely young man, Sire, but he is not for me."

He chuckled, but there was no humor in it. "Is *any* man?"

What could she say? *There is one man. That man. Your man. No other man will ever do.*

Henry struggled from his chair, and on shaking limbs, he stood. "You, lady, have refused every man ever presented to you by me or Richard or your father. Can you tell me you do not like men? Mayhaps you prefer your women for many reasons, eh?"

Jordan stood.

Clare did not move.

Henry took a step forward, his hands punctuating his words. "You think I do not know who you are? *What* you are? The Nightingale may have freedom in her words, madam, but I do tell you now and forevermore, that bird will sing only by my order and only in my kingdom!"

She wanted to scream at him, but somehow made her thoughts come slowly to her lips. "What do you mean to do with me then?"

He seemed to salivate as he rubbed his hands together. "I want to put you in a dungeon and forget you."

Jordan stepped forward. "Nay, my lord."

Henry did not look at him, though he spoke to him as he smiled sardonically at her. "You are right, my friend. She will not go there. I need her alive and well so that she can sanction this alliance of Trent with the Crown. Her people, I know, will not come to me as quickly or completely without her blessing. And I care not how you give it, madam, but I will have the appearance of your allegiance, as well as your money."

Clare straightened her spine but desired nothing more than to sink to the floor in relief.

Henry narrowed his eyes on her. "I will be much kinder than I should be to you. I will grant you a measure of peace, which you have never given me. You will marry Earl Chandler, madam. You will remain where I can watch you—far inside my kingdom."

"I tell you, Sire, you need not marry me off to—"

"You will marry him."

"But—"

"There will be children, madam, to keep you here."

That made her thoughtful, but for only a moment. "If a woman wants to leave a man, she can find ways to do it and make his life a living hell."

Malcolm Summersby fidgeted in his chair.

Clare went on. "She can turn his children against him—"

Henry found that very amusing. "Aye, but you will not."

"You know me not, Sire."

"Not in the flesh but in the spirit. You forget, Nightingale, I have read your works. Such prose that your head and hand can craft about women and men as noble creatures does not come from a person who believes the worst of people."

"Yet of that same person you believe the worst!"

His face grew dark. "You were misguided by your father. I merely set you aright."

"And you think I will come to be grateful to you? I am no vain and silly woman who—"

A hideous cry of an animal in agony rose on the wind.

"My God," Clare prayed, "what is that?"

Jordan cringed.

Henry grinned. "Madam, let me remind you where you are and to whom you speak. That man you listen to forgot himself, and he pays for his arrogance. You see if you go too far with me, you, too, will suffer for your independence!"

"I . . . deserve . . . that?" Clare reeled with anger and fear.

"You take what I give! Husbands and—!"

"Nay!" she shouted back.

Jordan's hands clenched. "Your Majesty, this arguing solves nothing!"

Henry spun. "Would you care to join her in a black hole?"

Clare shook with anger. "Nay! He has done nothing!"

"Nothing?" Henry asked her at high pitch. "I vow I'll shorten him an inch or two—"

"Never!" she shouted back. "I will marry Geoffrey!"

"A wise choice." Henry sagged suddenly and swept perspiration from his brow. "Get her from my sight. Take her *away!* Take her—"

"Harry!" Jordan was yelling at his king. "Not with Baldwin! You will not hurt her!"

Baldwin? Baldwin was here? Why? Where?

A greater cry of torture rose into the air and suddenly, Clare knew where Baldwin was, if not the reason.

"Of course, Jordan," Henry offered smoothly enough to make Clare's flesh crawl, "I will not hurt her now. I'll have her money to soothe the wounds her father and she delivered to me. Take her outside."

Two men at arms rushed to stand at either side of her. Young and nervous, they tried to look at Henry but somehow could not quite do it.

"Where . . . ?" asked one guard of the king who had turned away to consider the wall.

"Oh, pity's sake, man, give her air . . . and me, too." As Henry turned, his eyes locked with Jordan's.

Whatever message passed between them, Clare had no ability to understand it. She was too horrified. Too frightened.

Of all the possibilities she considered for her life on earth, none of them had ever included imprisonment or physical torture . . . or marriage to a man she did not love.

The two young guards led her from the room. She went, blindly, down the stairs and past the hall.

"Clare, sweetheart." Blanchette limped awkwardly from an alcove near the door to the courtyard. Supported by one helping hand from Geoffrey, she waylaid Clare. "I won't desert you. I will speak with Henry!"

"Nay, Blanchette! Do *nothing* lest you make this worse!"

"I won't let him hurt you! I overheard shouting up there. So did Geoffrey, and he's going to help us!" The girl turned adoring eyes up to the man beside her.

"Listen to me!" Clare grabbed Blanchette's arm. "That man is more distressed by Trent's independence and civil wars and conspiracies than I thought possible. What's more, he is a king used to putting down rebellions—though I do think he hates what he must do. Nonetheless, he takes his power and uses it. Do *not* be falsely led that his soft and aging looks imply no steel beneath!"

Clare's guards shuffled, and one said, "Please, madam, let us go outside before the king comes downstairs and finds you still here. He does not take to laggards—or excuses."

If Clare had learned one thing this morning, she knew her next words to be the safest answer. *"Do nothing for me!"* she gave Blanchette in lieu of a parting, and then led her guards through the door. There, she saw a sagging figure being bandaged about the hands and lifted by two guards from the bloodied ground. She recognized her former captain of the day watch who was now a shadow of his previous self. How had he come here? And why?

No matter either, Baldwin had paid a royal price for his choices. Why? He was a mercenary, pledged to any for the greatest sum. He was no king's man.

That sparked a memory, vague, illusive, but growing stronger.

Baldwin had told her father that the king's men had attacked king's men that first day she had met the Dragon in Trent's forests. How had he known that? Who had told him? The troubling question loomed. Was it true?

"I must speak with Lord Chandler," she told her guard.

But he refused her, offering her only the air of the courtyard. "Lord Chandler is at the king's command, my lady. He will see you when and if he can."

"You must convey my message. His life depends upon knowing—"

Her guard merely lifted a brow. "Knowing what?"

She could not trust him. "I will tell him myself, thank you."

Jordan wheeled to face Henry. This interview had gone so wrong so quickly despite his hope and Clare's vow to remain calm. Clare was not the type to provoke an argument, and Henry usually avoided any . . . unless he was in a blood lust as he was today. But she had tried to protect him from Henry, and in the process, she had committed herself to the one sacrament she wished to avoid.

But there was some element to Harry's madness that Jordan had not anticipated or . . . some hidden fact that he had yet to discover and understand.

What was it?

Henry still considered the oak paneling of the wall. Collecting himself for the rest of this interview? *Aye.* But why? Ever had Henry been decisive, instinctively knowing what to do and when and why . . . until lately when his fear of everyone blossomed into an evil flower for bright bursts of vicious color and then closed until the next unpredictable time.

Jordan scanned Malcolm and Diana. Shocked as they had been by the sum of money Clare had offered to Henry for her release, the couple had not shown any emotion since. In Malcolm's case, he seemed totally devoid of feeling or thoughts except when Clare had discussed the ability of a woman to make her husband miserable.

Diana, however, now came alive as a bowl of worms.

She wove her fingers together and tapped her toe against the floor in her impatience for Henry to recover his presence of mind. She cast bold looks at Jordan, and in her dark-eyed depths he saw not only her eagerness to begin this discussion but the invitation she had ever given him. The sultry beckoning of a woman who wanted a man.

Jordan scoffed silently. Diana's torrid glances had tempted him for a few years after her marriage. During that time he had drunk to forget her and almost killed himself. Diana's continuing interest in him had assuaged the hurt of her marriage to Malcolm, arranged as it was.

Yet, persistent as Diana continued to be, she had never succeeded in luring him to cuckold his friend. Jordan would not commit so heinous a crime against himself and Malcolm. Whatever joys Diana could offer with her passion, Jordan had refused for the sake of order and honor in his life.

Over the past ten years, Diana's pursuit of Jordan had gradually become less of a salve to his wounded pride and more of an irritant. His refusal of her favors seemed only to encourage her. Lately she had become blatant in her advances. Just before he left court to bring Clare to her wedding, Diana had waylaid him in the hall of Kenilworth Castle where Henry was in current residence. Snaking her arms about him, she had tried to insinuate herself into his chamber and, thereby, his bed. He had unwound her arms and pressed her to the wall with a firm refusal.

"Give this up, Diana," he had told her with a little shake. "I will not do this."

"You're going away again. To the Welsh border and those independent de Wallyses. Who knows what can happen to you?"

"Nothing will happen."

"You could be hurt or worse . . ."

"I can control whatever happens in Trent, Diana. I wish I could control you. You must stop these encounters."

"But you want me, darling!"

"Diana, you and I will never—"

"You have always desired me! That's why you never married."

"Hear me, Diana. I have not married because I found no woman who inspired me to a love I imagined could be— nay, *should* be fulfilling."

She preened, taking what he had said as a compliment to what she had meant to him. "While I tire of other men who should be you but cannot match you. Why not grant us both this which we need?"

"*Nay.* Learn the word's meaning, Diana."

"No man has ever refused me! Haven't I shown you that?"

"Was that the reason you seduced them? To show me that you could?" He was incredulous at her perversity.

"Aye, and I amused myself in the process of making you jealous."

" 'Twas long years ago that I stopped being envious of other men who have had you, Diana. Now I am only sorry for them and you—and Malcolm."

She pummeled him with two fists. "I'll make you sorry!"

He caught her wrists. "You are demented."

As he had left her, she cursed him. Vowed she'd see him on his knees, begging for her favor.

On the journey to Trent he had relived that scene and tried to understand why she had preoccupied his mind for ten years. He put it down to the allure of any object of desire which had escaped a man in his youth. For too long, Jordan knew his infatuation with Diana was a remnant of his youth, a period in his life when hope was abundant and joy was in each day's adventure. Losing Diana—or rather realizing he had never possessed her and never could—had robbed him of hope and joy. He'd never glimpsed either again until he met Clare and saw in her exuberance and her persistence a courage he envied.

Diana paled like moonlight compared to the brilliance of Clare.

Yet had he been enchanted with her. How foolish. How shortsighted.

In perspective, Diana appeared the epitome of everything a man thought he wanted—and should not contemplate possessing. Oh, she was petite, perfect in her countenance. Sensuous in her every movement. Even at her age—what was she now, twenty-seven or eight?—and with five children—she looked timeless.

'Twas only in the eyes, black and hard as ebony, where those windows to her nature revealed the real Diana. There a man who had the wits to be honest with himself could see this woman was cold and calculating, tempting many a man to her arms for the sport.

Malcolm knew nothing of his wife's liaisons. Or to be precise, Jordan thought Malcolm knew in some corner of his mind, but he refused to acknowledge it. When Jordan had tried to broach the subject, Malcolm had circumvented the issue. Whenever Jordan reflected on those discussions, he could not decide how well Malcolm controlled those occasions. But his instinct told him that Malcolm knew about Diana and ignored her behavior.

Why that was so, Jordan could only list possibilities. Either Malcolm loved Diana too much to destroy her merit in his sight or he loved her not enough any more to care what she did. Or. . . .

Or possibly he tolerated her unfaithfulness because . . . because it brought other benefits? But what could they be? Personal ones such as freedom from a wife's sexual demands? Nay. Malcolm liked bed sport almost as much as Geoffrey. In fact, when Malcolm married Diana, he had given up a bevy of mistresses to ensure that he'd save his energies for bedding his wife and breeding her quickly. From the evidence of the five children the couple did have, Malcolm could say he succeeded in his goal. But suddenly, Jordan wondered if those children were all Malcolm's! Knowing his friend would recoil from that, Jordan grew more perplexed about the Summersbys' actions and motivations.

Yet his confusion made him more wary of both Summersbys.

It also resurrected memories of the band who assaulted him and his two men on the road to Trent. How had those five men known who they attacked?

Malcolm had known the particulars of his journey. So had Henry. They were the only two . . . unless Diana had learned it from her husband.

Had she?

Jordan put his hands to his hips and strolled about the room. He feigned his nonchalance for the Summersbys' consumption. He meant to trip them if he could, and quickly, too, lest he lose his opportunity and Clare.

Jordan turned to his king, wondering if Henry questioned these two who had been so close to him for the past ten years. They had given Henry money—Diana's money—

and Diana's borderlands as safe haven for the Crown's armies.

But Jordan cared not so much about the Summersbys as he did about saving Clare and setting her free. "Sire," he said to Henry calmly, "Lady de Wallys is an honest woman."

An honest woman echoed in his brain. Diana had not been honest, had she? She had taken men to her bed . . . and Christ, what had she said that night?

You're going away again. To the Welsh border and those independent de Wallyses. Who knows what can happen to you?

"Nothing will happen," he had replied.

You could be hurt or worse. . . .

Captured? Ransomed?

Jordan spun to face Diana, who raised her brows at him. She had the look of a cat over a mouse.

Had Diana planned that ambush?

The king turned slowly. The look he gave Jordan rocked him for its virulence. "I repeat, Jordan, *how* do you know if the lady is trustworthy?"

It took a minute for Jordan to recall who it was Harry meant. "Clare I know here." Jordan put a fist to his chest.

"In less than two weeks you can say you have become so well acquainted with her?"

"Aye, my lord."

Malcolm rose from his chair, headed toward the table where servants had put out a pitcher of wine and goblets. "Snowstorms and convents do much to allow a man to probe"—he let the word hang—"a woman's inner nature."

Anger burst through Jordan's bloodstream, but he did not let it overtake his demeanor. "There is no need for such a slur, Malcolm."

"No insult was intended, my friend," he said congenially. "We do need to know the lady's condition."

"She is healthy."

"And is she"—Malcolm poured himself a cup of dark wine—"whole?"

Jordan considered the man before him whom he had

known most of his life and admired for his steadfastness to Henry and for his boldness in battle and politics. This occasion was concerned with both, yet their subject—Clare's purity—had nothing directly to do with either. "Why do you care if the lady is a virgin?"

Malcolm drank liberally, swallowed, and pondered that. "Do you care? I think you do."

Jordan pursed his lips. "What I think is immaterial."

"What you *do* is more important . . . or mayhaps, I should correct my speech and say what you *did* is more important."

"Clearly what *you* think I did with her is most vital. Get to your point, Malcolm."

"Geoffrey will not care to take spoiled goods."

The insult, now spoken, tinged the air a vivid red for Jordan. To even reply would poison it further and dye it black with hatred. God knew, he had seen enough of that from Henry today. Jordan gave Malcolm only a derisive glare and turned back to his king. "Sire, this is unnecessary—"

Malcolm would not let it go. "Geoffrey is no fool. He likes women. We each know that! Jesus, he could not wait to escape the reception line, Harry, to go frolic with Countess de Wallys's little sister. I care not whether Geoffrey gets a wife who is a virgin or a whore, but I mean to discover if I put myself to this time and trouble, march men over hill and dale, out of my way—out of *Glendower's* path—to effect a wedding when the damn union might dissolve tomorrow for want of a hymen!"

Henry scowled at Malcolm, while the change of the king's moods put Jordan on alert for more insanity. "You grow crude in your old age, my friend. Your point can be made without it. Do it."

"Very well," Malcolm nodded, calmer but not chastised. "Jordan, why would you travel here with the lady and not even bring a maid?"

To answer this would open for discussion mysteries to which he had no conclusions, only conjectures. To state that he could discuss them only with Henry would put Malcolm on more alert that he distrusted him. Gaining any information about Malcolm's loyalty or lack of it was Jordan's most necessary task. In the process, must he also turn aside Malcolm's almost leering interest in Clare's virtue.

"Malcolm, we wished to ride quickly and brought little baggage, even few of Lady de Wallys's clothes. This was fortunate because the weather was poor. But also someone followed us and attacked us."

"Nay, who?" he asked so quickly Jordan saw no ruse.

"My question, exactly. He escaped, but not before he injured her palfrey. The animal died of an infected wound. Meanwhile, my lady became ill. I waited, of course, until she was well rested before I tried to tax her with a ride in winter. Think what you will of what occurred between us, Malcolm, I cannot prove it."

Malcolm would not let the matter rest. "Geoffrey will learn when he takes his bride to bed if she is whole. Then it may be too late to ensure the alliance we need."

"If Clare marries Geoffrey, you will have the ability to march into Trent and occupy it without the malice of her villeins. The Crown will also collect her sizable annuity. What more could you want, Malcolm?"

The man shrugged.

Jordan lost his temper then. "Your dismissive gesture cannot put me off, Malcolm."

"Jordan, this woman comes from a nest along the Welsh marches. Who knows who and what she nurtured there!"

Jordan caught back outrage. From a man whom he no longer trusted, this suspicion of the one woman he trusted completely was laughable. "Clare de Wallys is not perverse. Her words and actions do agree. She may have followed her father's footsteps all these years to maintain Trent's independence, but she is her own person, too. A woman of great courage and creativity. A woman who has inherited wealth but who also earns it!"

Diana picked at the skirt of her gown. "Ahh, it is so sweet to learn the Dragon admires the Nightingale. The pretty Nightingale whose illuminated manuscripts many buy here in England and abroad." Diana met Jordan's gaze with hatred in hers.

He would have her less coy. "What is it that chafes you about that, lady?"

Jordan's formal address made her shiver. "Do not try to insult me, Jordan. I meant that your copper-haired bird may have tried to fly too far and at the wrong time."

Jordan spun to Henry. "What is she talking about?"

Henry looked sad. "I fear the lady seeks a new home."

"Oh, really?"

Henry smacked his lips. "You never could lie well, Jordan. Where does she wish to go?"

Jordan was loath to reveal a secret shared in a moment of intimacy with the woman he loved. "It is irrelevant. She has not escaped."

"Ah, but my Dragon, it is relevant. Where does she wish to fly?"

"Why did you not ask her yourself, Sire?"

"Would I get a truthful answer?"

"If you got one at all, it would be true."

"I tire of this, Jordan." Henry ran a hand atop his hair. "Where does the Nightingale wish to fly?"

He might not be able to lie well, but the truth had always served him well. "Flanders."

Diana thought that immensely funny.

Malcolm scowled.

Henry was clearly shocked. "To live among a group of artists and cloth weavers?"

"I am certain, Sire, she wishes to establish a new workshop among creative people who will become her friends and her cohorts."

"And leave her people?"

Jordan shook his head. "Incredible as it sounds, aye. She probably thought it the best solution to avoid a marriage she did not want."

"Well, thanks to you, she will still marry."

Jordan shot Henry a look that told the king how much he valued his own ironic part in precipitating this union.

Twenty-five years of friendship meant the king understood his man's sorrow clearly, and with his next words, he tried to ameliorate the sin he committed against the bonds of their brotherhood. "I must make her marry, Jordan. 'Tis a better alternative than a dungeon for the lady."

Jordan turned away. It was the best solution for Henry, too. Married, Clare could still write and sell her work as well as tax her villeins, thereby granting Henry the annuity, which would fill his empty coffers. Never had Jordan so despised the means that his friend must employ to rule.

Tired, Henry said, "I do not wish to hurt you, Jordan."

You won't. I'll see Clare free of you yet. I will encourage—hell, I'll help—Geoff and Blanchette to elope. Then after midnight while you sleep, I'll take Clare from her bed. Then she and I will leave you and your kingdom of illnesses and fears. I'll escort her to Flanders or anywhere else on earth she cares to go. I'll ensure she is safe and leave her to the freedom she desires. Then somewhere I will lose myself into the Continent, make my way as a mercenary . . . unless Clare might have me. Would she?

Henry stepped near and put a friendly hand to Jordan's shoulder, but spoke to his guard. "Bring me that boy, Earl Chandler. We'll have this wedding before supper."

Chapter Fifteen

WHERE WAS THE PRIEST?

Clare paced her small chamber, waiting for her wedding and the end—or was it the beginning?—to this tragedy of hers.

Through the hours of late day, she'd tried to think. She'd called for parchment and ink to be brought so that she might attempt to write more of her romance. But she laughed at herself and the irony of her personal story, then put down the quill. Her own romance was truly one with a traditional sad ending, for she would not wed the man she loved. She'd marry the man she must. For her country, she would give her body. On her honor, she would remain faithful to him—and starve in the desert for want of love's succor.

She had been prepared since noon for Henry's summons to the manor chapel. But first a servant came with word that the king did not feel well, rested, and would not rise till at least sunset. The messenger also told her that her request to speak with Lord Chandler had been denied by Henry. Then came another messenger to say that the priest would be delayed. The cleric had gone to say a mass for the dead in a nearby village.

Clare had not dared leave her room, even to go to the chapel to pray. What was there to pray for? Deliverance?

There was none.

She ran a clammy hand down her gown. The green wool was one she liked and one of three she had brought on this journey. To complement it, she had also donned the only frivolous item she'd packed—her favorite crespine, the intricate net made of pearls, which Jordan had appreciated. With shaking hands, she had combed back her hair in a severe style, then woven her hair in a loose knot and avoided a veil. She wondered why she bothered with her appearance.

Vanity was an odd characteristic to surface at an occasion which she rued.

She chuckled at herself. Mayhaps she was more like her father than she had ever thought!

Her humor died with the knowledge that she did not wish to attract Geoffrey Chandler to her. 'Twould be a temporary allure for him anyway, she was certain, and she had never wasted her time on pointless projects. But she would warn him not to seek happiness in another woman's arms. She and he might be locked in this union for political reasons, but she would not tolerate his defection from her because of it. He would have to grow into the husbandly role that was ordained for him, just as she would mature . . . and age . . . and die . . . as his unloved wife.

God help her. She shuddered as she wound her arms around her waist and clamped her eyes shut. She was about to marry a man who had the tendency to act as her father had. A man she could never respect. This union would not be a happy one because of that. Nor would it be one of peaceful coexistence, unless Geoffrey transformed his character. The chance of that was small, for Geoffrey was not a creature who changed his stripes unless he fell in love. And while Geoffrey might be incapable of the depths of that emotional commitment, from all indications now, the one woman who sparked his admiration was Blanchette.

Blanchette. The girl could get herself into more trouble than a litter of cats. Her surprise arrival here and her fawning over Geoffrey were the most flagrant examples of the child's willfulness Clare had ever seen!

Yet Clare was not surprised. She should, in fact, have suspected such a display from the girl who was more like her father than she knew or would admit. That Blanchette would court the attentions of a man who was not meant for her did not anger Clare so much as it made her hopelessly sad, because clearly the girl adored the smitten Geoffrey. But Blanchette's actions made her fear Henry's retaliation.

For Henry of England could appear amiable one minute and in the next, lash out to torture and kill those who opposed him. His friends, like Jordan and Malcolm Summersby, still rallied to his banner. But opponents like his cousin King Richard had underestimated his desire for power. Conspirators like Harry Hotspur had miscalculated his ability to keep it. How could a girl of sixteen years thwart the wishes of a man who would mold circumstances to his command at all costs?

She couldn't. Yet did Blanchette continue to work her own will. Cooing to Geoffrey on the manor steps, watching Clare as she took her air in the courtyard after her audience with Henry. What did the girl hatch? Trouble.

Clare had glanced at Blanchette and recognized a novel facet to the girl's actions. Unexpectedly, her guard de Quincy had remarked on it as they watched her sister. "She cares for the man and cannot seem to hide it. Why would she act so with your betrothed, my lady?"

"She has never found a man appealing for more than a few minutes, and certainly, she has never tried to hurt me. Nor is she stupid to ignore how she might anger the king by attracting the earl Chandler. She must, as you say, truly care for him."

And Geoffrey? Clare longed to ask Jordan that question but feared what sorrows for the two young lovers might come from an answer that the boy could honestly care for

Blanchette. If indeed Geoffrey did love her sister, Clare could forgive him his folly. As long as he did not commit adultery, hurt Blanchette, or anger Henry by any silliness.

And what of love? Between her and Geoffrey there could be none. Love mattered not in politics, only between the pages of a romance. Ah, but even there, the emotion was discounted and its fire doused by men's considerations of how the world must turn. "Geoffrey and I will build a union made of respect. I will see to it," she promised herself as she sat upon a bench near the smokehouse.

Soon after, a guard came to fetch Geoffrey, and he disappeared inside the manor house. Clare had retired to her chamber and paced and waited for the event she hated.

A knock came at the door and she jumped.

"My lady, the priest is here. The king orders you to the chapel now."

Taking up her cloak, she left her chamber, eager to get on with what she must, however she could. The servant, stunned by Clare's speed and single-mindedness, had to scurry to keep up as they traveled the stairs, the hall, and out into the courtyard. That expanse was dotted with Henry's army, their armor glowing in the rose of sunset.

Wryly, Clare thought, these ruffians were her wedding guests. Her father would have hated that! He would have criticized Henry for his poor taste to line a maiden's journey to her new life with swords and daggers. Clare halted, a hand to her chest, praying God that would not become the nature of her union with Geoffrey. May it please her Heavenly Father to temper this man's appetite for other women and to focus him on making a solid relationship with his wife.

But Clare stumbled on a small stone and the certain knowledge that such a reformation would not probably occur. Geoffrey did not love her. Never could. They were oil and water. Coexisting, never blending. . . .

"Clare?"

Tears blocked her clear view of him, yet did she know him. She would recognize Jordan Chandler in the pitch black of hell . . . and this was it. This must be it for the utter desolation she felt.

Jordan's hands covered her own. "You can do this," he whispered, though his gruff voice cracked.

She could not speak. If she dared, she would scream at him that he was wrong. She was not strong or noble or honorable. She loved him and never could lie down with any other man. Not his nephew. Never so callow a youth who would not honor her and never keep her in the manner that she needed. Her hope would wither with Geoffrey's dalliances. She would have to fight to keep her mind pure of a thousand negative thoughts. Like little devils, they would kill her creativity and mar the clarity of the messages she sought to impart.

"I swear no harm will come to you. Trust me. Come with me, sweetheart," he said as if he spoke to the dead.

He was right. She was.

He took her to the church door. They did not halt there, and in her shrouded mind she amazingly understood why. No need existed to read the conditions of the dowry. The important people knew them. She did. So did Henry and Geoffrey.

On Jordan's arm, she took the few steps up into the cozy chapel. Lined in a mellow oak, the walls gave off an amber blush in the refracted rays of afternoon sun. The air bore the smoke of braziers along the walls nearest the front pews where Henry and the Summersbys turned their faces to her. They sat, surrounded by other men, nobles and their men at arms in the green and white surcoats of the Lancastrian king. The fragrance of thick mystic incense hit her nostrils with repugnance. Though the atmosphere was the sweetest she could have planned for her wedding, Clare felt her stomach revolt. The man who stood beside her should be the one to remain by her side, not give her away to his kinsman! Had Jordan not helped her, she was certain she would not have held her head so high or her spine so straight as she walked down the aisle. She would have buckled instead of standing at the altar of her coming sacrifice.

But Geoffrey was not here, and she rejoiced in the remaining minutes of her freedom.

As they waited more minutes, Clare could hear the murmurs of the congregation. Where was Geoffrey?

Clare looked at Jordan. His silver eyes bore into hers. He did not appear distressed or puzzled that Geoff was not here. His gaze conveyed only courage to her. Why?

She glanced at Henry. He met her gaze with equanimity and, she was certain, a sliver of ruthlessness that cut her like a shard of glass. He leaned toward Malcolm, whose wife drew near to hear the king.

As Jordan covered Clare's hand with his own, he and she watched Malcolm leave the pew and the chapel.

The wedding guests began to talk in more normal volume.

Clare could not hear their words but knew what they said by their tones. Sympathy, which had been such an outrage to her father, became her own shame. She felt tears rise again and told herself she would not cry. *Would* not!

She trained her mind to note the golden crucifix atop the altar, the robes of the priest. Please God that Geoffrey did not embarrass her more . . . for she did value her own reputation and had endeavored to preserve its integrity by ethical and moral acts. She could not bear it if he took it from her in little pieces by such petty acts as tardiness.

Presently, she heard many footsteps, the jangle of spurs.

"Sire." 'Twas Malcolm's voice.

"Aye, Lord Summersby," Henry asked, dangerously impatient. "What of Earl Chandler?"

"We could not find him, Sire. I sent this servant to search his apartments." Malcolm pointed to a cowed young man who cast his eyes to the floor.

"Did you search, too, Malcolm?" Henry bellowed.

"Aye, when I did not believe him, I did."

"And?"

"The earl has fled, Sire."

"Fled?" Henry seethed.

Jordan clutched Clare about the waist.

Clare groaned that Geoffrey, this young peacock whom

she did not admire, could find the brashness and the means to do what she wished for with all her heart.

Henry struggled to his feet, his complexion florid as he yelled at the servant, "How do you know he has gone?"

Instead, Malcolm answered. "Chandler left this." He held out a piece of parchment.

Henry was incredulous. "Give it to me! How could he have fled?" he asked himself as he almost ripped the parchment in his frustration. Then he halted and stared at Jordan. *"How* could he have escaped the house and grounds without the guard catching him?"

"I cannot specifically tell you, Sire, though I wish to God I could. But he has lived here all his life. To what he knows of the house and village, none of us can hold a candle."

Henry cursed Geoffrey roundly, then waved forward a guard. "Search for him! I want him back."

"Read his letter."

Those words had come from Clare's own mouth. She knew they had, but somehow she could not understand how she had the courage to say them. And so she repeated them.

A frisson of apprehension ran up her back. In its wake, the realization hit her that among the congregation inside the chapel she had not seen Blanchette!

Fear for her sister and humiliation at Geoffrey's abandonment flared in her blood. Outrage that they may have done something disastrous flashed through her mind.

Henry skimmed the message, his lips thinning, his ire gone to pity. "My lady, you will not like this missive."

"Sire, I care not if I like it, only that I end this misery of not knowing its content. Please read it."

"Nay, madam. Here, you may read it if you like. I will tell this assembly only the summary." He turned to face his retainers more fully. "The Earl Chandler and Lady Blanchette de Wallys have decided to marry and declare they are ready to give up everything for love. Honor, country, family, they say, cannot compare."

Clare was not surprised, but oh, it rocked her.

She held the parchment with shaking hands, and though her eyes did mist, she could easily read the words. In bold letters had Geoffrey addressed the letter to her, Jordan and Henry, in that order. Geoffrey stated his great care for Blanchette and his promise to love her into eternity. He apologized to Jordan for his waywardness and to Henry for any appearance of disloyalty.

" 'But I do swear my allegiance to you, Sire, in every way but this. The countess of Trent is a beautiful, gracious woman, but one loves whom one loves, ordained by a God who does not pay regard to politics or economics. Until the end of time, I will adore my lady Blanchette, and the very thought of existence without her withers my mind and heart with such cold contemplations. I beg you to forgive me. I did this not for treason but only for love.' "

"Come with me," Jordan urged Clare, pulling her toward the vestry door. "Head up. That's right."

How she made it to the little room, she did not know. She understood only that when Jordan closed the door between her and mortification, she went into his arms with a shudder.

"Fear not." Jordan led her to a chair, where she stared at the bare wall and the barrenness of her future. He dropped a kiss into her hair as he left her alone.

Alone, as she would forever be. Condemned to the dungeon Henry cited as her only alternative to marriage to Geoffrey.

This time, when she felt the urge, she did laugh, long and loud.

When Jordan and Henry were finally alone in Geoffrey's main hall, Jordan addressed his friend with urgency. "Give me three lances of men. I know the roads and byways here as well as Geoffrey. I can find him and bring him back."

"You would do that, wouldn't you?"

Only because you would expect me to do this, do I speak the lie. "I swear if I don't kill him first, I will return him to you!"

"To marry Clare de Wallys?"

Never. "To feel your scourge first, but *aye,* to marry Clare and never shame her more!"

"She means so much to you that you would ensure she goes to a man who values her less than he does another? Less than he should?"

"Better than to see her in prison!"

"You *do* love her, don't you?" Henry's smile was sad. Having loved his first and second wife, this man knew how important a spouse could be to a man.

Jordan played on it—and told the truth. "Must I make this situation worse and admit to that?"

"There is no need, Jordan. I see it in every move you make, each look you give her."

"No woman I have ever met compares to her."

"Not even Diana?"

"Especially not her."

"In your youth, Diana was the only woman you considered. She was so much a part of you, she was—"

"A disease, Harry. Sometimes we want what we cannot have simply because of that, and we never stop to see how detrimental the possession would be. I understand my need for Diana was based on rashness, youth, lust rolled into one madness. Diana is many things I never saw when I was young. She is determined to the point of unscrupulous, unethical—"

"Immoral."

Jordan stared at his companion of so many years. "You know this?"

"Who could not? She is a member of my court. Her money which I have needed and her position as wife to my second most valued military commander mean that I have watched her closely over the past ten years. I have seen her change from an opportunistic heiress to the sour wife of a man who loves her more than he should. Diana knows Malcolm's devotion to her and does not return any measure of it to him. She is, in fact, rather proud of her liaisons, and while she does not boast of them to anyone, I think she is less careful than she should be to hide the occasions when she cuckolds Malcolm. Do you think he knows of her indiscretions?"

Jordan was confounded by this turn of the conversation,

when Clare waited to know about her fate. He jammed a hand through his hair. "Harry, I care not about Malcolm's problems at the moment. I—"

The king was not to be swayed. "Diana has paled in beauty and appeal over the years. I do wonder . . ." Harry tapped a finger against his lips. "I wonder if she had married you, would she be a different woman now?"

Jordan knew Harry had a reason for this diversion. "We can be known by the company of friends we keep. So I do suppose we can be understood by examining the nature of our mates." Jordan frowned. "We are far from a discussion of what to do about Geoff, Harry. I cannot let the boy go too long. If he has found a priest to perform the marriage vows without benefit of banns, I want to find him and Blanchette before they consummate their union and destroy any chance of its dissolution."

"Jesus Christ, but you are single-minded! It would never occur to you to let Geoffrey go, would it?"

"Never! He is—"

"The opposite of you?" Harry suggested.

"Aye, but I care not what he is! I only want him back. I want to see him writhe."

"I am certain you do. And so he will, I promise you. He is young, and while some may take that as his excuse, I cannot allow him to do this without repercussions. Others will note what happens here and how I respond. Conspiracies have dogged me for so long in so many nooks and crannies of my realm, I naturally look for them every hour of every day. So many men and women have no inkling that they tempt me to throw them in the Tower of London and forget them!"

Jordan panicked that the Tower would soon house Clare, when he meant for this discussion to gain him Clare in his house, his bed, his arms. "Harry, I beg of you to let me get this bridegroom back."

The king dropped his gaze to his folded hands. "Jordan, I will tell you that I see how you care for the lady."

"And on the basis of that and our long decades of friendship, I do plead with you, Harry."

"For what?"

"To let her live without incarceration. She need not, *must not* pay for my nephew's rashness. Geoffrey should be the one to suffer here. Take him! Christ, take *him* and make him rot in a cell. *He* commits the treason."

"And his little bride? What of that willful girl?"

"I care not for Blanchette. She, too, young or not, wise or stupid, must pay for her folly. Though I know Clare will feel pain at Blanchette's punishment, I will put blame where it belongs. The girl is responsible for her own actions. My concern is only Clare, who has done nothing to deserve this degradation at Geoffrey's hands."

"Mayhaps, Blanchette has not caused Geoffrey to act in so unprincipled a manner . . ."

"But what? What is it you keep from me, Harry?"

"What is it you plead for, Jordan?"

"Sire, you change the subject again and—" Jordan feared for this sudden turn of conversation.

"I beg of you, Jordan, just tell me, friend to friend. What is it you want for your Clare?"

For the first time in his life, Jordan lied through his teeth to this man who had been his friend and his king and had once deserved every ounce of his loyalty. But now, Henry was sick with his princely ills, and lying was the least of what Jordan would do to save Clare. "She wants freedom! She wants to live in Flanders, free to write. Free of politics, wars, Glendower, Trent, and you."

"She has told you this?"

"In an unguarded moment, she did reveal she wants to go to Flanders." *Besides, I could not ask her if she wants to marry me! She is too well guarded. Only Geoffrey and blushing Blanchette could I easily spirit away!* "Clare has not said the rest. I have surmised it on my own, based on other conversations we have had."

Harry contemplated for endless minutes.

Jordan advanced. He had thought that once he proclaimed his usual dedication to the most honorable solution, Harry would take the only other route possible to gain Clare's money and land and demand Jordan wed the aggrieved bride. But Harry had a secret. One that plagued him—and now Jordan, too. "What do you keep from me, Harry?

"I cannot let her go to Flanders, Jordan."

"Why not? She has no political aspirations. She is an artist and she wants to write in peace!"

"Are you certain?"

"Aye! But clearly you are not. *Why?" Christ, tell me before I die here!*

"Days ago my customs collector in Calais intercepted a letter, which was clearly signed by your Clare." Harry waited for a reaction, and when Jordan narrowed his eyes in disbelief, he went on. "The letter was addressed to King Charles of France."

Was this the second letter of which Solange Dupre had spoken to Nathaniel Pickering that morning in Castle Trent? The second letter, which he never learned about and now appeared to haunt him, just as he would marry her and keep her safe and loved forevermore? "What did this letter say?"

"She assures him that all is in readiness, and she comes to him as soon as possible. She hopes he has his promised payments ready, because she must flee her home before the wars begin again."

Shaking, Jordan sank to a chair. "Christ above, Harry. You can't think that she conspired to bring the French to the shores of Wales and invade Cheshire?"

"What else am I to conclude, Jordan? I have no other evidence that any of my people correspond with King Charles. I am too sore beset with riddles wrought by conspirators to do much else than send them all into dark cells—or to the chopping block—for their perversity!"

"Clare is not perverse. Not secretive!" Jordan said it, but feared he stretched the truth. He remembered her efforts to write to Blanchette without his knowing, and the other letter that Solange Dupre mentioned, and Clare's admission that she sought to escape him somewhere along the road here to Morning Star. Yet did he need proof to believe this last and greatest treason. "I must see the letter to read the words! I cannot believe she would be treacherous!"

"Obviously."

Harry was too stoic for Jordan's comfort. "What do you mean to do with her? Nay!" He saw Clare's future written in Harry's eyes. *"Nay!* I will kill her myself with my own bare hands before I let you put her in a dungeon!"

"You would murder her to keep her from such misery?"

"Aye. She is generous, imaginative, nobler than you think. She would die deprived of trees and air and sun. I cannot let you do this, Harry!"

Tired, the king shook his head. "There is only one solution, Jordan."

"Christ!" Jordan felt the blood drain from his head. "You would have me kill her."

"Come back to the chapel. I would have you marry her."

Jordan wheeled about, faced the fire. The torrent of emotions he felt fired his hope that he had saved her. "How can I do that?"

"I think because of the best and noblest reason—you love her. Make no mistake, I give her to you because you think more highly of her than I do at the moment. I have no reason to trust her. Evidently, your heart declares you do."

Jordan turned again. "I will prove to you I am right about her."

"I hope to God you do. For your sake as well as hers. Fail to bring me evidence of her innocence—and soon—or I will put her in any convenient cage I can find. Friendship will not deter me. But I would hope that you and I will go on together, Jordan, for many more years."

Jordan wanted to laugh hysterically. God, the man's illness put his mind beyond redemption.

"Ah, there you are wrong, Harry. If I do not find evidence that Clare is guiltless in this French affair, and you put her away and execute her, I will die myself by my own dagger. Like Geoffrey, I do know that life is not worth the living without the one I adore. I love who I love, Harry. England, you, and Clare." *And now not in that order.*

"I pray God then, Jordan, that you live with us for many long and happy years."

As Jordan and Henry walked from the manor house out

into the courtyard, Jordan set his sights on the chapel and vowed he would serve Clare faithfully, but only by her choice. He pressed a hand to his ribs, where his dagger was in its rightful place.

Aye, you will ask her if she wants to marry you. For you will never force her. 'Tis her life, her heart, which must choose the nature of her future. And if, perchance, she wishes not to spend those days with you, by her choice can she say whether she wishes to go to Henry's dungeon. Thus, will you choose to love her enough to do as you promised . . . and kill her before she dies at someone else's less loving hand.

Chapter Sixteen

"PERMIT ME TO SPEAK WITH HER ALONE, SIRE." JORDAN FLUNG open the door, stepped inside, and sank against it.

His face was so stark, so blank of emotion, Clare felt her heart go numb. "What will Henry do? Does he send a cadre to bring Geoffrey and Blanchette back?"

"Aye. But first we will settle your future."

She refused to shrink back to her chair. "If Geoffrey is already married, there is nothing to discuss about my future. Henry has made that plain. I become his prisoner."

Jordan seemed not to hear her. "What would you want for yourself if you could have it?"

Undone by the surprise of Geoffrey and Blanchette's actions, she had no tolerance left to her for anyone's indirection. "Don't divert me, Jordan! I am already captured by this king. This horror tale we endure is too dire, too fraught with terror and death for me to think of what my wishes are now!"

He strode from the door toward her and went before her

to one knee, taking her cold hands in his warm ones. "My darling Clare, answer me."

He was too calm—and yet some aspect of him seemed too excited as if, once the shell of his serenity burst, he would break free of barriers to wilder emotions.

"Why?"

He traced the backs of his fingers up her chin and along the severity of her coiffure. "Why did you want to go to Flanders, sweetheart? Is there a man there whom you—?"

"A man?" She fought the urge to laugh again, but she had hurt her chest in the last bout. "Nay, my Dragon. No man tempts me." *Only you.*

"Is that true?" He looked at her deeply, as if he had heard that last declaration by her soul. "Aye, I see that is so. It gratifies me in many ways, my Nightingale. So then, tell me why you wished to go to Flanders."

She tore herself from his grasp and stood. Furious at his line of questioning, she paced. "What does it matter why I wanted it? What I want is of no importance! It never was. It never will be! I am not more than—"

"Stop this!" He spun her around by the shoulders. "Do not talk like this! What I ask *is* vital. Tell me what I long to know! Why did you wish to go to Flanders?"

"To set up shop! Why else? To flee all of you with your armies and your arrows and rape and pillage! To find some sanctuary from the storms of men's destruction! I have a right to want that! To need it. I am a creature of the air and the sky, not of your petty squabbles over land and money and . . . and bodies! *My body!*" She gasped at the venom of her hatred, putting a hand to her mouth to end the poison that streamed out.

He clamped her near, his lips against her temple, his arms binding her like fetters. "Darling of mine, it's as I thought."

"Why do you need to know? Don't tell me Flanders now joins some coalition to fight in this war. I cannot stand this continual shifting of loyalties. I fear for you. There are too many conspiracies here. Too many tales! You need to be careful of everyone! I am afraid that Baldwin is here. He may be dangerous. He told my father that there were king's men in our forests that day you were attacked."

Someone pounded on the door. "My lord Chandler?"

"Clare, those men called me by name, yet I knew them not. I wonder how Baldwin learned this."

Her mouth dropped open. "You never told me."

"Lord Chandler!"

"I'm coming, de Quincy! Lord, Clare, I couldn't tell you until I trusted you—and then we had new problems."

"My lord, the king says you must come out now!"

"One more minute!" Jordan called to the man, and gently cupped her face. "We must pursue these issues about Baldwin and Flanders and other countries later. For now, tell me only this. In your heart can you commit yourself to me?"

"What?" She blinked at him. "What are you asking me?"

"Will you marry me?"

She worked at words and could find not one.

Jordan smiled sympathetically. "I know it is a shock, but I ask you, Clare, will you marry me?"

"You? Not Geoffrey?"

"That man is taken already. I stand prepared to assume his place, but only if you think you might find some happiness with me, madam. Would you?"

She touched two fingers to his scarred cheek.

"Happiness as I have never known."

Valiant yet, he clamped his eyes shut and then looked at her, struggling to inhale. "Will you have me?"

"Do you really want me?" she whispered.

"From the first minute I ever gazed upon you. Standing tall in your saddle, brilliant with life and passion, bent on saving me from death. You have, you know. You saved me from a desolate belief that I was too old to feel desire. That my life was over and I had little to live for except peace and solitude."

Another knock, more urgent, came. *"Jordan!"*

"That is Harry, Clare. He fears what occurs in here, and he wants an answer. What shall I say?"

The tears came to her eyes this time and overflowed, rushing down her cheeks. She could not brush them away because she had her arms around her Dragon, her heart taking flight from her chest. "Oh, Jordan!" She flung herself against him and planted the biggest kiss on his mouth.

He was chuckling, catching her into his arms, swirling her to the wall. "I suppose this means you will?"

"Aye!" She was laughing, and this joy could never equal any other she'd known.

"Now!" came Henry's demand.

"Now?" Jordan asked.

"Quickly, before you change your mind," she answered.

"Never!" he growled as his lips seized hers and his one arm snaked out to open the door.

Clare cared not if the entire court stood gaping at the portal. For this embrace and this mad kiss, she would have stood at the gates of hell to feel the Dragon's fierce claim of his mouth on hers.

But it was over too soon, and she stood, shaking and silly with happiness, looking up into Henry's expression of approval and yet . . . disapproval. Why would that be? "Come along," he ordered, casting her doubts temporarily aside. "I wish this wedding done, the bride well primed with wine and the bedding complete."

Clare's delight to marry her Dragon could not be diminished, not even by a king bent on bluntness such as this. She wound her arm through Jordan's and told him she was ready.

In as much time as it took for Jordan to propose, the ceremony was pronounced and done, or so it seemed to Clare. She could, in fact, have said she floated. Buoyed on a cloud of euphoria, she went to the main hall where Henry's officers and the villagers sat down to drink her health and Jordan's. At the banquet table she picked at bits of a feast that was to have celebrated her union to Geoffrey. Next to her was the man she had preferred from the start of this odd courtship. She smiled up into Jordan's ecstatic features and would not allow the sadder view beyond of brooding Malcolm and his wife, Diana, to mar her wedding.

Nay, nothing could hurt her now. She only wanted to be done with these preliminaries quickly so that she could claim her wifely due. Her husband. Her Dragon. The very idea had her nibbling at the cheddar and wafers, but imbibing the red wine with a gusto that was new to her.

Jordan did not drink the Bordeaux, but she did not find it an insult to their union. She wanted him whole and happy. If wine made him sad or mad, he should avoid it. She only cared that he was hers. *Hers.*

"Clare?" he leaned closer and kissed her cheek.

She could not get her fill of marveling at him. His dark bold looks. The scar. The length of his hair, which now she had the right to unleash from its tether, comb with her fingers, and tame. There was even more of him she longed for—and not in any domesticated way. His mouth. Moist and seeking on hers. His skin. Bare and brushing against hers. All of him, tonight and every night.

"Clare!" He grinned.

She smiled.

"You are deep into some thought again."

"Hmmm." She sipped her wine.

"Don't drink too much of that, my wife," he leaned over to warn her. "I have a thing or two to say tonight and much more to ask you, and I want you awake and aware of me."

"My lord," she said with a tilt of her head and a hand running up the brawny contours of his upper arm, "I have been awake and aware of you for many weeks. Do not think that tonight, of all times, I intend to fall asleep and miss what I have longed for every moment since I met you."

"Christ, Clare." He grasped her hand and dropped a wild kiss to her knuckles. "How am I to endure these silly mummers Geoffrey hired?"

"These people will talk if you don't."

"I care not for them. Only you, ever you."

She stared into his mellow eyes. "Did I ever tell you that for a Dragon, you are a creature who makes heavenly delights of human words?"

"In my whole life I never hoped to find someone like you, madam. Don't you think that now I have found you, I would give you all the charming phrases I never thought to use on any lady love?"

"You take my breath away."

"I promise to give it back to you and more."

"I cannot wait," she said, scarce above whisper.

He squeezed her hand and looked away at middle space. "You are one sore temptation, my lady."

Malcolm came near, his movements wobbly, and sloshed wine into Jordan's empty cup. Clearly, he had drunk too much of the stuff himself. "I don't think it's proper manners to let your wife go unsung, Jordan. Surely you can take a sip for this illustrious occasion!"

Jordan examined him. "Nay. I cannot, Malcolm. My joy in my bride will come with other proofs of my affection."

Diana, tight-lipped, rose from her chair and moved between her husband and Jordan. Yet did she come so near that her breasts were very close to Jordan's eyes. "Drink, Dragon. You must also dance. These players are almost done." She inclined her head toward them in dismissal as if she were the hostess here.

Henry, who sat on Clare's left, interrupted. "Nay, play on. I like this presentation. One gets so few entertainments anywhere." He put a hand to Clare's arm, but spoke to Diana. "Leave the new couple to themselves, my lady Summersby. I am certain you remember what it is like to be in such a state."

Bliss, Clare concluded. Such happiness Clare admitted she had never experienced—except for the presence and actions of Diana and her husband, both of whom must know from years of acquaintance that Jordan did not drink wine. So why press him? It was a vicious ambition on their part.

"Aye, Sire," responded Diana, none too pleased at his suggestion. "But for these men who do question the loyalty of the Dragon's bride, a show of her complete cooperation is what they need."

"A show?" Jordan speculated and suddenly rose like a flame. "They shall have a glimpse only. What do you think they'll say to this?" He scooped Clare out of her chair into his embrace with the force of a blaze. As she grabbed a fistful of his tunic to balance herself, her world tilted and spun as he crushed her to him and kissed her breathless.

Her surprise could not equal his ardor. She melted against him with a joy that presaged what her marriage bed might hold in the way of wonders.

Jordan was smiling at her, triumphant and bold, as she realized the crowd assembled hooted and stood, then cheered lustily or banged their goblets on the tables for another.

For his display and proof to Diana, Clare had another. Calmly, she threaded her fingers into his hair, loosening his leather tie, and asked him and his cohorts, "What will they say to this display of how the Dragon's bride regards her husband?" For answer, she put her mouth to his and gave him the wealth of pent-up affection she had felt for him for the long tortuous weeks she had known him.

He groaned and clamped her closer, taking the kiss deeper than she ever imagined a love could go. Time and air ceased to exist for her. She felt only her body and his, so dear, so needy. She drove her fingers up his scalp and moaned for more when he tore away.

"Not here," Jordan told her, and put his lips to her cheek. "God, Clare." He trembled. "Not here!" He turned for the stairs.

Clare went blind to anyone else. The noise reached her ears, and she vaguely understood it was a cacophony of whistling, stomping, and bawdy declarations.

Only Diana called out in objection. "My lord, you cannot take her like this! Custom requires the bride be stripped and dressed for—"

Clare ceased placing little kisses down his jaw as he slowly faced the woman and addressed the revelers. "Forgive me, my friends, but mark well my words. *This woman is mine.* I married her before you, as is the custom, and I have shared her with you for hours longer than my patience. But that time has ended, and from this minute forward, I tell you that I alone say who touches her and how and when. Tonight and every night until the day of judgment, no one strips her, dresses her, or puts her to bed but me."

A clamor of approval rang around the room.

"And who inspects the sheets?" Diana chided him in such a voice that it could not have reached the others, though it did frighten Clare so much she shook. The question scourged Jordan's remaining good nature.

He clutched Clare closer, looked Diana squarely in the eye, and mouthed his response with vehemence. "No one."

Bleary-eyed Malcolm appeared behind his wife. "We should see if she's a virgin——" He was tittering.

Jordan was quaking with restrained anger. "I know even now. 'Tis all that's required." He glanced once more at the revelers. "My friends, I bid you good night."

The crowd went wild while Clare's heart and mind flooded with appreciation for this husband, this lover, this hero who surpassed any other, real and fictional.

Jordan took the stairs, then headed for her chamber. He shouldered open her door and nudged it, then closed it with a kick. The bolt banged into place.

Alone with Jordan and nothing to separate them was a condition she had yearned for, yet she inexplicably went still. Joyous as the enormity of what she was about to do with him . . . commit her body to the union she had pledged her heart and soul to this afternoon.

He must have thought her quiet was fright because he, too, went very still. Then he let her slide down his body. "Come here," he tugged her toward the bed, and shy but eager for more of his passion, she went.

"The servants must have decorated it while we were in the chapel," he said as he brushed dried rose petals from the red velvet counterpane, then had her sit on the edge of the bed. "Listen to me, darling," he took the pose he had when he'd proposed in the tiny vestry room—on one knee, her hands in his, his kindly eyes surveying hers. "I have much to say."

This sounded like no declaration of his affection, but

something quite different and far too reasonable. She didn't think she wanted to hear it, whatever it was. "I'm tired," she said as an excuse, surprised she was allowing him to escape from her—and hating her cowardice to let him. "I don't want to talk with you," she said more truthfully. "I want no words now." *Only acts of love.*

"Please," he urged her with sadness in his features. "Let me get this out before my discipline and courage fail."

Compassion for him flowed through her. "When has the Dragon ever lost those?"

He cupped her nape. "When he is married and his wife is the most beautiful creature he's ever seen, the Dragon can be humbled."

"Jordan—" she whispered, overcome at his endearment, and wound her arms around his neck.

But he would not take her to him. "Nay, listen to me, Clare Chandler. You are mine now in the sight of God and those men and women. But that was a ceremony caused by necessity to keep you alive."

A horror appeared at the threshold to her happiness. 'Twas the specter of falsehood. "Do you imply you do not care for me? If you wed me out of pity, I don't want you."

"Clare, Clare. I wed you out of need, my darling."

She stiffened.

"Turn not from me! Hear me out. I would not let Henry hurt you. But so, too, I will not take you here in this physical way to be my wife, unless you want us to be joined!"

She licked her lips. Her throat grew thick with sorrow. "Why would I not want you in all ways, my lord?"

"Because you want your freedom more. Because I will not rob you of it. Because the greatest love I can show you is to let you leave, if that is what you want." His alarmed eyes met hers. "Is it, Clare?"

He went on when she could not. "I want your happiness above all else in this life. And if you want your eventual freedom from me, when times are less precarious politically—mayhaps in a year or two—I will allow you— hell, I'll *help* you to leave me, if you like! I am not so foolish to have you, ravenous for you as I am"—he ran a hand over her pearl crespine and down her throat and arm—"that I would demand you stay with me and thereby ruin the rest of your life. If it is Flanders you want to seek or any other place, then in the future—"

She placed two fingers over his lips. Marveling once again at his heroic rectitude, his unswerving righteousness, she said, "Ask me without the politesse, my husband. What do you wish to know?"

"Christ in His Grave, Clare!" His whole body shook as he grabbed her shoulders. "I cannot have you in this bed and not want you a thousand times until I die. And I will expire if I taste you and then you want to leave me to be free! I could not live without the sight of you or the feel of you forever in my arms!"

These were words too precious to have come from one of her books. This man was too rare to be true. Yet he was real and, by God's bounty, hers.

He groaned, his expression wild with pain. "Don't you see? I love you, Clare. I love you. Answer me! Shall I show you the human ways I adore you or shall I leave you to yourself? Whatever you wish is also my desire."

Ah, this was a grand love affair, the scope and depth of which she never could have imagined. Its magnitude and radiance humbled her, too, and tears appeared to mark its presence and its power. "My incomparable man. My Dragon. I am yours. In name. By right. Please do me the honor to make me yours in the flesh because I will never leave you. I do not want to go anywhere alone again!"

When he crushed her to him with a cry of joy, he had tears in his own eyes. "Clare. My wife." He held her like that for countless minutes while she reveled in the glorious sensation of finally having him to herself until death did them part. Or mayhaps, longer.

"Clare," Jordan mouthed her name, a husky chord of need against her ear. 'Twas prelude to a new music she felt trill along her skin as one of his big hands trailed up her calf and pushed her gown along her bare thigh. "My Clare, how I mean to have you will not scandalize you, I hope. I have thought so often and so intricately of how I would lay you down, I don't know if I am capable of reason now."

"Oh, please don't be reasonable." She ran her flat palms up his arms, across his shoulders, and down his massive chest. She nuzzled her nose into his tunic. "Lord knows, I have no plans to be."

He laughed then. A great booming chuckle that made her grin at him.

"That hearty laugh is another feature I love about you, my husband."

His gaiety died. "Do you love me?"

Caught in her own admission, she nodded soberly. "You take my breath, my heart, mind, and show me such perfection in a man as I could never craft with ink and parchment." She spread her hands out as if she spoke of the seven wonders of the world. "Aye, my noble Dragon, I do love you. There is no man above you, and I shall go to my grave happy to have known you, but ecstatic to have wed you."

He stared at her, his eyes smoldering silver fires as he framed her face in his hands and whispered, "My beautiful wife, lovely bird, sweet bard, I adore you to the ends of the universe."

She cried again then, soft warm tears of delight until he urged her to her feet and untied the bows of her gown at wrists and neck. Grasping great swaths of fabric, he told her to lift her arms, and in one sure stroke, he took all her clothes away.

Memory of her ambition to be undressed by him flared through her. She had wondered what he would do and say in such an encounter. Now she had answers, and long-standing curiosity about how her nakedness might affect him overcame the modesty she felt. His strong features mellowed in the amber candlelight. His eyes examined her leisurely while one of his forefingers traced what he admired.

"Your throat is longer than the gown gives credit, my love. And I have always liked these hollows between your shoulder and clavicle." He bent and dropped a kiss into each, his tongue darting out to leave a wetness in each spot. His nostrils flared. "You were right the night you told me on the wall walk that your breasts are cushions." Each of his hands supported one and lifted, while his thumbs found her nipples and circled them.

Breathing became unimportant.

"Your nipples are the color of ripe peaches." His fingers stroked her. "I told you I could shape them into hard little points, didn't I?" Fascinated, she watched until in embarrassment, her eyes drifted closed.

"Nay, beauty, observe everything when I make love to you. That's right, open your eyes and behold what you do to me. Do you have any idea how I need to see you melt for me?"

She shook her head.

His expression grew taut. "Let us both discover if I can also help you burn." He hovered over her and arched her up so that he sucked one aching nipple into his mouth.

She reeled, her fingers tearing at his tunic, as he shifted to the other breast and laved its crest with searing dedication. "Oh, Jordan, let me do the same. Take off your clothes."

He was laughing lightly as he laid her back on the bed, came between her spread thighs, and ran his palms along the insides up to her very core. "Is that what kissing your breasts gets me?"

"Nay," she teased, sat up, and hooked her arm around his neck to bring him down for one deep kiss. "It's what I get."

"Ah, me. Not even hours from the wedding and I have myself a demanding wife."

"I'll make you happy," she promised in a serious vein.

"Aye, you do, madam. Let's see what rewards I reap if I make you ecstatic." He leaned away and removed his tunic.

She shifted, then pushed back along the full expanse of the bed to go up on one elbow. "The rest, my lord." Her eyes went to his hose.

If she thought she had lost her senses before, her mind churned with frank appraisals now. She had seen some men naked on numerous occasions, sick or well, sober and drunk. She knew arms could bulge, chests ripple, and legs flex with corded power. She knew how males appeared longer, leaner, harder than most females. She knew, too, what other attributes males possessed. She even knew the look of animals, horses especially. But never in all her days had she seen a man so well formed as her husband. Nor so well hung. Or to be exact, so rigidly standing. Her mouth went dry, and then she salivated to think this man was soon hers.

He watched her. "I won't hurt you."

She tore her gaze to his. "I never thought other."

"The intrusion can cause pain. If a husband is careful, he brings forth little or none. I will work for that last."

"I trust you."

"Do." He reached down and grasped her foot. Gently, he began to massage the bottom and then to wiggle her toes.

She giggled. "Is this how dragons make love to virgins?"

"Nay, maiden mine, like this!" He grabbed her other ankle and pulled her down the bed to the edge where he glided her legs up his torso and tucked her ankles around his neck. His hands slipped between their bodies and she whimpered as he trailed fingertips along the folds of her womanhood. He elicited resounding liquid declarations of her appreciation for his acts. "Darling, you are very wet."

She gulped. "Is this good?"

"Aye, wonderful. It means that you want to be laid into a nest of love, pretty Nightingale. 'Tis an ambition I have had since first I saw you in winter's snow. Do dragons mate with nightingales in your stories?"

"Until tonight, only in my imagination, my husband."

He inserted one finger into her needy body, and she moaned. "No longer in just your fertile mind, my beloved, but soon in your sweet flesh."

She arched in ecstasy as his fingers illustrated how this was done by thrusting, then parting and petting her. "I remember the other night"—she said between panting declarations of her delight—"against the wall—your mouth."

"Ah, you liked my tongue on you?"

"'Twas delicious."

"My thought exactly." He grinned wickedly.

"Can we?" She blushed. "Again?"

"When, where, however you like. Say the words. Name the ways."

"I want you inside me," she whispered, the erotic idea sending her hands diving to her crespine in abandon. She felt the hard pearls as the only little gems left to her reality. "I could never erase you from my mind. I wanted you so. Not anyone else. I need you now—oh, my Dragon— everywhere." Her hands drifted down across her breasts and waist down to her nether hair.

He watched her with narrowed, appreciative eyes. "Have me at all times, in any way you desire, and I promise to meet you, joy for ecstasy. To begin that journey, learn me this way first." He pushed her legs from his chest to the bed, and sat her up. Then he took her hands and had one sheath him, her other cup him.

"An impressive lesson, Dragon." She was thrilled, en- thralled. He sucked in air as she nuzzled her nose into the thick springy hair of his belly. "Make me your wife, now, please, before I cannot think—"

He massaged her neck, her back and then cupped her head as he bent to kiss her. "My exotic bird, don't you see? I want you mindless."

"I want you mine."

" 'Tis so now. Don't you know it has been so written since the dawn of time?" He lifted her and arranged her on the center of the bed to loom over her.

"I think you are a poet, Dragon."

"I weave words only for you. You inspire me, wife, for this is my first romance and I will forever be your only lover." In demonstration, he kissed his way down her throat to nipples and ribs, her belly, hips, and then her very center. He nuzzled her gently and suddenly rolled her lips apart. The rush of cool air to her hot body excited her unbearably. "My Clare, once more I wish to taste you as a virgin, and then there will be countless years when I sample your wifely fulfillment. Open for me. Let me love you, inside where I yearn to be, into your heart and soul."

She cared not, knew not what she was, where she'd been, or what if anything she wanted more than now, this, him.

She understood only as he nibbled her and licked her that she could really live like this, in his care, in his arms and his bed for eons.

His lips and tongue and teeth built a tempest in her loins. She felt the fire and the stirrings of a storm so huge, she grew not afraid but ran toward it. With open arms, she thrashed upon the bed and bucked. He lifted his head and hovered over her.

"My dear wife," he crooned as he put a hand to the part of her that ached for more of him, "here"—he inserted two fingers—"we shall be joined now on earth as in heaven. Let me in," he pleaded, and showed her how he would enter her with a few short supple strokes. Then he removed his hand and at the entrance to her body, she felt his hot intent.

When she had held him moments ago, she knew he was a hard bold man. Now as he made his careful way into her body, she learned that he was fire and might, a brazier to take her from the misty imaginings of fantasy to the real wild shores of human love. And when he could go no further because of her physical impediment to their union, he paused to arch back. Filled almost completely by his sweetness, she ran a fluttering hand down his furry chest and realized he perspired in agony of self-discipline. For her.

"My love, my love," she murmured, "do not stop."

"Through the years I will give you as much happiness and as little hurt as I can control. Know always, madam, that surpassing all else, I love you." And with that, he glided forward through one pinprick of pain to seat himself fully inside her.

The bursting sensation felt like a bud opening, spreading, closing around a welcome shaft of heat. Satisfied and not with this fullness, she undulated against him. "This is too sweet to temper," she urged, and he drew back, a question on his face.

Then he smiled, a searing appreciation for her lining his features, spreading his handsome lips, and firing his mellow eyes. Below, he pulled away a little and returned to his complete claim of her. As she raked her nails along his shoulders, he whispered in her ear. "You like this. Why did I know you would? Come this way, darling. Fly with me."

He taught her then to move with him, flutter, float on air, rise on currents, and then soar. Beyond the moment and the circumstances, above people who would envy them or hurt them, he demonstrated how this Dragon did adore a Nightingale. He showed her landscapes she could have never mapped alone. Mountains of jagged wonder, valleys of harsh need, and hungers for the heights to which only he might clasp her up and take her. She named this new land paradise.

She landed on a pinnacle, too high to contemplate, too cozy to leave. She snuggled closer to him, sighed, and kissed his chest. Beneath her lips, his heart told tales of his own flight. She listened and felt whole, astonished she had never known the lack of him before she met him. To tell him in mere words would somehow diminish the essence of what she meant him to understand. So, in mortal recompense, she moved against him, as if through her skin she could impart the substance of her knowledge.

In complement, he hugged her tenderly and dropped a kiss into her hair. Tears appeared again, but she squeezed them away. One hand of his came up and brushed them from her cheeks. "May I ever cause you to shed tears of joy."

Chapter Seventeen

"Now I'm very hungry," Clare told him minutes later.

Jordan rolled her to her back and settled between her thighs, a new nest that fit them both snugly. As if to tell him so, Clare curled one long leg around his hip and skimmed the sole of her foot down the back of his calf.

"Do that more, and I think, wife, you will make me more famished." Though contented minutes had passed since their first flight to passion, for him to recover the ability to launch into another foray, he sought restraint so that he might not hurt her. But against her moist lips, his body aspired to its own ardent intent.

She arched a brow. "I feel how great a need that is, my lord."

He rearranged his manhood so that it pointed upward in the direction which would influence her with a subtle pressure. "You are so lovely, like an exotic bird. Do you know that in that coil of pearls, your face is a sculptor's ideal in clean line and proportion?"

She shook her head, embarrassed, gladdened. Her innocence urged him on to compliment her freely as God ordained. "Your beauty strikes a man."

"Nay—"

"I weave no tales for you." Jordan would enjoy the fruits of his own labors and give his wife sweet talk. "Though you may not have noticed, madam, those men at our wedding feast stared at you, nudged their friends, and commented on this Dragon's good fortune to wed his bride. But I offer myself as your best example of one who saw you and went dumb with your brilliance."

He left unsaid the name of Geoffrey, to whose fickleness Jordan owed gratitude for the glory he held in his arms. Though that young man would certainly pay for his love of Blanchette, Jordan would work on Henry to ensure the king absolved him of his crime. After all, Geoff would not have fled—might not even have gained the courage—had not Jordan suggested it and offered his assistance for the lovers' flight. His heart swelled with joy that he had worked for Clare, her happiness, and his. To make her his wife, to take her to bed, to cuddle her like this was more than he thought heaven allowed a humble man. Now that he possessed her—and she owned him body and soul—he could not ask more of God than this continuous ecstasy. To that end, he pondered when to tell her of his manipulation to get his nephew and her sister out the door and on the road to the same connubial bliss he and Clare celebrated. If he did it now, she'd become afraid. But he liked this union, and he wanted her moaning with delight, not fear. Gluttonous as he was for her, he slid his body easily into her ready little passage. Her walls gave and then closed tightly around him.

He broke out in a sweat. She raised her hips and he groaned. "You learn quickly, madam."

"I want you quickly."

"I can oblige you."

"How fast?"

He reached over to bring a half-burned candle closer to the edge of the bedside table and whispered, "Time me." He braced both arms on either side of her and thrust in such a pace, he cantered. Restraining the urge to gallop into this elegant terrain, he clamped shut his eyes and concentrated on the landscape he traversed. She was hot. She was lush. She was wild.

But when he was ready, she was not. She was a novice to this land they claimed together, and when he pulled away, she grabbed at his shoulders.

"I go nowhere without you, wife." He sat up, filled her to her hilt and reveled in her writhe as she watched him lick two fingers and thumb of each hand and put them to her nipples. She bowed upward in mute appeal. "You see? Your body comes with me naturally."

She glanced down at herself, her amber eyes widening at the sight of his fingers grazing her, circling her, tugging her into sharp greedy cones. Restless, she began her own pace and instinctively encouraged him to ride.

He bent and pressed both globes together, running his tongue from one peak to the other, letting her set the rhythm below.

She flung her arms wide. "If I'd known marriage was like this, I would have come sooner!"

He chuckled. "Come now, then." He leaned back, firmly in her saddle, cupped her hips, and set his tempo to both their satisfactions. She throbbed this time with a sturdy pulse that brought a grin to his mouth and a pounding expression of his appreciation.

Fascinated by this strong and tender creature he could call his own and no other's, he ran gentle fingertips over her forehead, brows, nose, her giving mouth, and then, her firm and creamy breasts. He nuzzled her tempting collarbone and got his reward of her purr. Against her skin that was fragrant with the musk of their mating, he told her, "I'll go down to the kitchen and bring you some supper. You ate nothing."

"I could not," she confessed with a lick of her lips. "I had an appetite for only you."

"You were satisfied, I think."

She pouted. It was a feign that brought a hoot of laughter from him. She could never be like Blanchette, even if she tried. "Mayhaps, I am too untested to judge, husband." Her hand found him, curled around him, and stroked him from rest to awakening interest.

He made an animal sound in the back of his throat. "Clare, my sweetheart. I ignite like dry tinder with the spark of your touch. We cannot do this too often at first because you are so . . ."

But she had already ceased her caress. Instead, she had raised her hand and stared at it. He put a finger to hers to tilt her palm toward him.

His heart went out to her at the sight of the long pink stain. " 'Tis but the evidence that you belong to me and I to you, beloved. There is nothing wrong with you."

But there was. Her eyes declared it brightly.

"What hurts you, Clare?" he asked, though he suspected the cause was Diana's surly reference to Clare's purity. Yet he needed Clare to voice her fears to ensure the intimacy he craved from her. "You must promise always to tell me, else I cannot fight the ghouls which roam and might attack you."

"Why did she say that about wanting to inspect our sheets?"

"Lady Summersby may have drunk as much as her husband, though even if I were certain of that, I would not offer it as an excuse. She is audacious and becomes more unreasonable these last few years since Henry sits the throne."

His last few words hit him hard. He had not thought of Diana's behavior in terms of when it became more outrageous. Why that timing should bother him—or even be significant—now made him wonder what Diana did besides pursue him and other men for her bed. Why the woman should attack Clare not only angered him but gave birth to an unnatural fear that Diana could hurt his wife—and the next time do it with more than words.

"Of what importance is Diana to Henry?" Clare asked, staring into nothing. "Does she—?"

"Sleep with him? Nay, love. He is one of the few men I know who keeps to his wife, whom he adores. To Henry and Malcolm, Diana brings two things. Money and land. Both of value in this war against Glendower. She has been known to give a few good strategic points on military activities along her border and so, at her request and to keep her happy, Henry allows her to come with Malcolm and the rest of us on some of these expeditions."

"So then does she—?"

"Sleep with others?"

"Aye," she said, but searched his eyes.

"Not me. Never me, my love."

"Why then does she dwell on my virginity? Her words made me feel unsuitable for you. I know that many rumors exist about the heiress of Trent who would wed no man, but I hope none of them hinted that I was immoral."

"Never, darling. Gossip pronounced you merely aged and willful and solitary."

She gave an indelicate laugh. "You are sugaring the truth to make me feel better."

"Nay. But this last fact I will not candy, though God knows, I wish I could. . . . Clare, I once thought I loved Diana. That was years ago. Before she was married to Malcolm."

"She was the woman you told my father about that night you met him," Clare said without question, but sadness.

"Aye. I lost much when I saw her marry Malcolm. In that situation, I had come to care for her when—like this time, I met her before her betrothal and grew enthralled with her. She was a rich, powerful heiress and I . . . I was the man who led a contingent to escort her to her wedding."

He caught the lightning of Clare's surprise. "Ironic, isn't it? But true. In that situation, there was no possibility of Diana escaping the marriage Henry and her father had ordained. With Diana's and Malcolm's wedding came the end of my youth. I lost my naive belief that all things come aright for those who are steadfast and true. Afterward, I lost my self-respect because I drank until I did not recognize myself."

"But you did not lose your sterling character, my love." Clare cupped his cheek. "You remained loyal to your king and your ideals. Your reputation as Henry's Dragon shines without blemish. You may have misplaced your self-respect with what the wine did to you, but you stopped drinking. As a result, you have more than gained respect from others for your noble years of service to your liege lord and England."

He traced Clare's lovely jaw. "I lost such hope for any personal happiness that I had not even a desire."

She took his hand and kissed his palm. "I hope you have gained it back."

"Aye!" He gathered her close. "I thought I could never love again. But then, I was so very wrong because I had never loved before." Her glowing eyes burned with this new compliment to his regard of her. "How I adore you has not primarily to do with this . . ." His big hand claimed throat and breast, hip and thigh, and very core. "But first to do with this." He laid his hand against her temple and then against her heart.

She wound her arms about him. "Make love to me again." She invited him with a sinuous embrace. "Together, we will grow stronger and allow no one to hurt us. No one to rip us apart."

He did as she asked then, sinking into her in desperation for years of loneliness and then in slow exultation for the companionship they two would share.

She met his moods with an eagerness that cauterized his wound and a sensuality that salved it. Moving with her, he felt rapture lift his mind beyond his earthly bounds. "Don't leave me!" he blurted, and startled himself.

He paused, knowing where that fear had been born.

"Where would I go?" she asked him.

France?

"Without you"—she kissed him atop his heart—"I would be without my best inspiration."

He thrust inside her, seeking vigorous reassurance she was his forever. This time she pulsed to completion with him, brisk and fierce. He clutched her close, but his fear, spawned by his knowledge that she had once written a letter to the French king—and had not told him why, resurrected like the dead. He would ask her and learn the answers. He moved away.

She undulated against him. "Don't go, please. This affection is nothing like I've ever thought to have."

He hesitated, overcome with the need to do her will.

"What ails you, darling?" She rose, placing her hands on either side of his head and kissing him deeply. When he did not respond, she stared at him. "You should share your private thoughts with me as I have done with you."

He tried, but she whispered, "Let me guess. You wonder if I might fail you."

Did she see inside his mind? How could she hit the mark so accurately?

"My father declared that night you two met that you had only given loyalty and never received it. Oh, my Dragon, I can say I will not desert you, but give me a chance to prove it. Let me show you that as strongly as you give devotion, so can I in equal weight return it to you. Let me demonstrate for years and years that the adoration you have displayed to me, I give in kind to you, my husband."

He caught her to him then. "You pick the right words to say to me." He pushed her back against the feathery mattress and kissed her so that she sighed into his mouth.

She smiled, her eyes closed, happiness drifting over her features as her hands glided over his shoulders. "I hope we have babies. Lots of chicks. We will drive you mad with husbandry of every kind."

His heart tripped. "And if I can't? I may be too old for getting children, Clare. I have no evidence that I was ever capable."

Apology stood in her eyes, while her fingers purled down his chest to his nipples, made tighter by her touch. "Marriage—*our* marriage will be made of many desires, and perhaps some will never come to be. But I cannot fear the latter because I now have you with whom to face the future."

"But if you want babies—"

She grinned and brushed her hips against his. "We won't get them unless we try often, will we?"

"You tease dragons, Nightingale?"

"My newest vocation."

This time he took her to another peak, as high but different from those others. This one offered a rapid climb, stunning points, a plummeting descent.

The bedside candle had begun to gutter when he rose from her sated body to peck her on the cheek and promise to bring her other sustenance. Reluctantly, Clare let him go with a contented expression.

He was loath to leave her. But the need to discuss this issue of France required time to clear his mind for the subtleties that topic would require. Because he loved her, he would choose his words carefully, lest he insult her or hint of any disloyalty to king and country. His feelings for her decried such desecration. Yet he needed to know every bit of her thinking about Charles and France.

Her future depended on how he handled this. And he had little time to follow the tangled strings of conspiracies. Henry had declared no deadline to his search, but Jordan knew he would expect answers soon. Mayhaps even in the morning. For Henry might be kind and brotherly, but he was above all else the king and firmly committed to that function, no matter friendship, kinship, or money. Henry would put Clare in his dungeon or beneath his ax without remorse or apology.

But Jordan would not allow that to happen. He sought his hose from the floor and pulled them on. He would save her from degradation. Her letter to the French king and her intentions toward that man and his country would never end her life. He would not allow it. Before that happened, he would abduct her from any dungeon and they would fly together abroad!

He jerked on his clothes, ripping one seam of his tunic in his anger. Gently closing the door, he saw the corridor was empty. In this manor house made mostly of oak, Geoff burned only one brazier at night. Jordan descended the stairs to the grand hall. Most of the guests had gone to their beds upstairs or their tents outside. Only one man—de Quincy—remained at a far table, slumped across it, his wine goblet overturned. The fire had mellowed so that the hall shimmered in a spectrum of silver and yellow shadows.

Jordan made short work of assembling Clare's nighttime feast. Finding a whole almond capon and a pot of raisin pudding, he outlined his questions for his wife.

When the door opened, Clare stretched like a cat upon the sheets. "That was quick. What have you brought?"

"This." The point of a misericorde nicked her throat. She wanted to cry out in fright but the pinprick stayed her, made her prudent if not wise. Who—?

In the faint rays from the candle Clare detected at first only a huge specter swathed in a cloak, hovering over her like death. Then the light offered clarification.

Diana.

"Get up!" She flung back Clare's sheets and peered down at the sight.

Clare did not flinch. The cool air brought needed reality. Only her nipples constricted.

Diana sneered. "Too tall, too muscular to be ideal. Did he tell you that? *Get up!*" She gestured with the dagger so that Clare had to rise with it or be slit.

Diana's black eyes remained on the sheet. "He made certain his nightingale sang for him, didn't he?" A slash of pain darted across her face. "He was mine and you had him. Go!" She nicked Clare again and, with her other hand, pushed Clare toward the chair where her cloak draped. "Put it around you."

Behind Clare now and holding her one arm in back of her, Diana held the stiletto to Clare's back. Clare felt the power in the smaller woman's frame. Petite Diana might be, but she was also toned and fierce. Besides, she possessed the only weapon here. Clare must employ her own. Her wits, her words. "Where are we going?"

Diana chuckled. The sound was sinister. She leaned up to coo in her ear. "Where do you think we go? Where you wanted. *France.*"

"*What?* How do you know I—?"

"Henry's customs inspector caught your messenger with a letter to Charles. Such proof of your treachery I could never have invented. Put the cloak on, damn you."

"But if I'm going to France,"—Clare licked her lips—"I will need more. It's cold outside."

"I care nothing for your health."

Clare fumbled, dropped the heavy wool. Diana's knife followed her reach to the floor and up again. "Why do you want me to go to France?"

"I want only to get you away so that Henry *thinks* you have defected." Diana pressed the point of the dagger into Clare's skin so that she jumped at the puncture. "The cloak, hurry."

"If you wish Henry to believe that, then I must have clothes. My leave must appear to have been planned!"

"Do it then, efficiently."

Clare forced her mind past fear to reality. What were the odds here?

She donned her undertunic and considered she had only one opponent with one weapon. Her heart did not gain any confidence from her logic. She pulled on her gown. Was there another person up and about? Could she scream for help? Not with this point aimed for her gullet.

Diana anticipated Clare's delaying tactic and dug her knife in. "Put your hands through! *Now!* Wherever your husband has gone, I'd guess he's not far—"

Please, God.

There was only one stairway down to the main hall. If Jordan were retracing his steps to the kitchen, he would cross their paths. If people were still awake and aware in the great hall, they might help her. But if they were no saving graces, mayhaps she could stumble, trip Diana, and escape. Any struggle with Diana would be a contest, but Clare was bigger—and she could win if only she could divest Diana of her weapon.

She bent and fumbled for her slippers.

Her heart took hope.

Until she rose and came face to face with Solange Dupre. The woman grinned, looked her up and down, but spoke to Diana above a whisper. "The horses are secured in the trees beyond the main gate. Only that one fool we saw before still sprawls over a table in the hall. The rest are drunk and gone to bed."

"Didn't you find Baldwin?" Diana asked her, worried.

"*Oui,* he is in chains. I could not free him. But he is worthless to us. Henry has tortured him so he cannot walk or use his hands. He sits and whimpers like a little dog."

"But they'll kill him."

"His cock is bigger than any other man's?"

"Christ, I would not bed him. He is my bastard brother!"

Solange lifted a brow at Diana. "My king did wonder that you made him pay so high a price for this man's spying these past ten years."

"Tell him when you see him next week, I care not. The information was good, no matter the sum of gold."

Solange stuck her own dagger to Clare's breast. "We must flee, *comtesse.* Our escort will not wait through the night!" She smiled sardonically. "I wish to turn this bird loose to them. I think I will watch. They'll teach her things a dragon never learned." Her nostrils twitched. "She smells right for the occasion."

Clare swallowed the acid of her outrage. "Baldwin, Nathaniel Pickering, and you spied in my home."

Solange stuck her dagger in a sheath at her waist, grabbed Clare's hands, whirled her about, and bound her wrists with what felt like strips of leather.

"*Certainement,* more than that."

"You plotted so that Trent did not ally with Henry."

"We did, but it was difficult. Your father suspected, and we could not let him tell you!"

"You killed him!"

"It was a good plan. I told Baldwin about the uses of arsenic. I took it from your storeroom—a purer, more abundant source than the supply in the workshop, *non?* Baldwin gave it to your father. He had the access to the bedchamber." Solange spun her around and stuffed a rag into her mouth. Diana bound a strip around Clare's head to hold it there. Solange slid her knife from her belt. "We go."

Clare faltered, gagging.

Diana prodded her shoulder with the knife, pushing her toward the stairs. "If you do not walk, I swear it will not matter that I must show Henry how you betrayed him. I'll carve you up the minute I get you to my men. I have no reason, Clare de Wallys, to be merciful to you. You lived a life of freedom which I wanted. Then you wedded the only man I ever needed. I will not see you rob me of my only satisfaction. *Walk.*" Diana thrust her forward.

They took the steps, Solange first, sliding against the carved oak, one careful soundless move at a time.

At the bottom Clare saw a figure of a man across the room, his head cradled in his arms. 'Twas de Quincy, and he snored.

Solange urged them, waving her dagger toward the door to the courtyard.

They were out the door, down the steps into the velvet cloak of night, Diana pushing Clare across the courtyard when Clare heard the first bellow cut the air.

"Halt!"

"Like hell, Jordan." Diana seethed and jerked on Clare's wrists, wrenching her arms at the sockets so that her breath snagged. Diana half dragged her toward the nearest huts. In the shadow of the walls, they might blend with night. But more men roused from their tents, and the clatter gave Clare hope as Diana inched her along toward the gate.

"In here!" she ordered Solange, and she thrust Clare through the door.

Solange was cursing in French. "The smokehouse."

In the pitch black, Clare sank against the wall. She saw nothing, smelled only the overpowering aroma of curing meat. Her eyes smarted with the smoke. She was pushed against the rough woods, bumped her head on a hanging carcass, and listened to the jangle of men running across the cobbles.

They were scattering as if they knew not precisely where to run. Clare moaned at the agony of her arms pulled at so odd an angle and recalled how once she had seen Jordan fight with a man and kill him, though Jordan's arm was totally misplaced. If Jordan could prevail, so would she.

How?

She tried to see. The smoke was so thick, her eyes watered. Breathing dried her throat and lungs. If they didn't leave here, they would die without air. The three low fires that ate it glowed like evil cauldrons in small hollows in the earthen floor.

What if . . .

Her usual game.

"We must go," Solange rasped.

Diana coughed. "We *can't* until they leave."

"We will die!" Solange was angry.

Smoking required low, long-burning fires. The challenge to any manor cook was to keep the fire smoldering with huge chunks of hickory wood and little air. Only *more* air or a new fuel made the flames dance higher.

Then once more she heard Jordan. He seemed far away, upon the manor steps mayhaps.

"Come, come," he spoke as blithely as if he enticed a man to surrender his winnings at dice. "I know not precisely who you are, but you must bring my wife back to me. I know you've abducted her. She would not leave me of her own accord."

Diana snorted and pressed her knife to Clare's jugular as Clare let out a sob.

"I know where you are," he asserted. He walked down the steps in purposeful even movements, coming nearer, yet far enough in the center of the courtyard that Clare wondered if he spoke the truth. He murmured something to a cohort who then ran back up the steps into the manor house.

Diana quivered. "He will disperse them and we can run."

"Kill her now and make our journey easier!"

"Nay, Henry must have proof that she conspired against him. . . ." Her voice dwindled to no more than a scratch.

Clare feigned weakness, lolling her head against the rickety wall, sagging sideways. Toward the door.

Men rushed past.

Diana was coughing continuously. The point of her dagger wavered. Clare lurched away. She thrust open the door. The rush of crisp air made her chest expand. Behind her she heard the two women cry out.

Diana slashed at Clare. Her move was weak, but her mark was true. The knife burned down through Clare's thigh as she lay across the doorway, letting in the air, sweet air.

Behind her Clare heard the crackling hickory of the three fires fanned to life. She felt the billows of the flames rolling along her skin.

Diana scrambled up off Clare. "My cloak!"

Solange pushed Diana. They stumbled over Clare. Fell against the door.

It drifted open.

Clare tried to get to her knees.

A gust of flame roared over them. Its power and heat knocked Clare to the ground. Her wounded leg dragging, Clare slithered from the others. The pain of flames consuming clothes, skin, and hair brought her to the edge of a broiling void. Her last thought as she felt the fire eat at her was that hell could not be far away, and, surely, God would never send her Dragon there.

A cry tore from Jordan when he saw the two flaming figures vault into the courtyard.

"Clare?" Was one Clare? He sprang forward.

Malcolm grabbed his arm, pointed. "There!"

The sight he witnessed sliced his heart from him.

A burning brazier crawled from the smokehouse. *Clare!*

But the hiss of Malcolm's dagger rising from its sheath made Jordan reel toward the man.

"Nay!" Jordan locked with his friend in hand-to-hand combat. "You cannot kill her!"

Malcolm pushed at him. "Diana is a traitor. I murder *my* wife, not yours!" Tears ran down his cheeks. Shock made Jordan's fingers still. Malcolm spun, lithe and sure, let fly his knife across the courtyard to skewer the fiery torch, which sank slowly and then thudded to the earth.

Jordan witnessed Diana's death at a run, terror whipping

through his head. He scrambled the last few feet in the dust, some logic telling him not to leap upon Clare, not to crush her, but to cover her, smother her, tumble her over . . . and over. . . .

He rolled and rolled with her until his only thought was that the sparks had died, and he prayed that she had not gone with them. "Clare," he appealed to her and God, gathering her gently in his arms. "Stay with me, my love," he pleaded. But her clothes were cinders floating from his fingers.

She drifted a hand along his cheek. "Stubborn man, you never would let me go."

He caught back a roar of outrage. He struggled to his feet, scooped her to his chest, and ran with her toward the manor house. Dodging men at arms who hurried toward the two women, now but blots upon the cobbles, he sidestepped his king.

Henry stood motionless at the door. His face was lit by one torch he held aloft. With melancholy eyes, he surveyed Jordan bringing in his precious burden.

Chapter Eighteen

HELL FELT MUCH AS SHE'D PREDICTED. AYE, 'TWAS HOT. Prickly. Too tender to let the wicked rest. She would moan and squirm. She would try to roll over to her back. A stab of pain would flare from her left leg. And she would realize she was bound, loosely but securely, by the wrists to the bedpost. She would wonder if this were her only torture, only to feel the skin of her back burn and itch.

A devil's disciple would draw near and in an urgent voice cajole her to accept his spoonful of a bitter liquid to help the calm creep into her limbs. The creature had supple fingers, too, coated in ointments that accosted her abused sense of smell. She swore she wanted lemons and flowers, a delicate tisane of rosemary. "And damp that fire in the hearth," she whispered to him.

"For a good physician, my love, you are an irascible patient."

She huffed at him. She even thought of batting his hands away, but they were angelic, smoothing hurts, drifting over her sore and aching places into hollows and crevices no one had ever touched except herself . . . and her husband.

"Jordan?" She searched for him here in this despicable place.

A trick of the devil, wasn't it, to have him appear?

"Aye, sweetheart. What do you want?"

"Hold me."

He would bend down and put his flesh so close to hers that through his clothes she could feel his body heat radiate atop her fiery skin. He was a tantalizing illusion. "This is as close as we can come for now."

Was this death? Or the recurring dream of being consumed by fire and searching hopelessly for Jordan? "I am lonely here without you, Dragon."

He moved to kiss her fingers and vowed, "You are not alone. Recover quickly so that I might prove it."

Rejected, she tried to thrash.

He restrained her with words. "I will take the bonds away if you promise not to roll to your back and break the blisters."

Freed, she ran a hand up to her hair and cried when she felt a wealth there. The searing memory of suffocating smoke and fast flames jolted her mind. "How is this that I still have hair?"

"You wore your pearl crespine. The fire singed a few curls, but that's all."

Her hands covered her cheeks. "My face."

"Unharmed. You are as beautiful as before."

Fully aware now, she panicked. Her lips trembled. Her fingers flowed down her naked sides. "And my body?"

"Healing. Do not touch my handiwork." He picked her hand away from the bandage around her thigh. "I see myself succeeding in this new calling to take care of you, and I will not have you spoil my progress by your explorations. Keep your hands still." He demonstrated how he wanted her spread like an eagle on the bed.

Return to reality rushed swiftly to her mind thereafter. She could note the passage of hours and her progress by the increasing fatigue of her husband, her vigilant monitor, her

Dragon at the door to her chamber. Barring entry of any ill. Refusing Malcolm an audience with her, lest that man speak of Diana and horrors too fresh for Clare's recovering state of mind. Questioning a guard who knocked late the next morning and announced through the door that Jordan's nephew, Earl Chandler, and his countess, had been found and brought back. "The king requests your presence in the hall, my lord."

The probability that the couple would pay for rashness with their lives had Clare struggling up from her bed to go.

"Nay, Clare. You will return to your rest. This is my task to save these two."

"But I must speak for Blanchette. She is naive—"

"Geoffrey, too. But I promised Geoff I would support him in this marriage, and so I will."

Amazement did much to kill her fear and inspire awe. "You promised Geoff you would speak for him?" Her husband nodded. "*When* did you do this?"

Jordan's lower lip rolled down. "Before he left."

"You defied Henry?"

"To marry you, to save you, aye." He combed her hair over her ear. "I had been loyal for thirty-eight years, and what had it gained me? Nothing worth living for. When I saw that at Henry's hand you could be hurt or worse, I went to Geoff and offered him the means to escape. I went outside, noted the position of the guards. Morning Star Manor used to be my boyhood home, remember. Geoff needed only a clear path to allow him and Blanchette to ride through. He welcomed the opportunity. He loves her, Clare. Almost as much as I love you."

Joy made her giddy. Fear washed it from her. "I know you will save them," she assured him.

When Jordan returned, she balked at the strain on his face. "What will happen to them?"

"Henry is angry, as I expected. He is so sore beset by contestants for power that he sees conspirators in anyone now. But he does have some reason left, and I have argued that the four of us are happier for being well matched. And contented people do make contented subjects."

"Did you tell him you helped Geoff and Blanchette escape him?"

"Nay. I suppose it is a mark against my honor not to be totally honest with my liege lord, but I thought to tell him would cause more problems. Henry sees conspiracy everywhere in places they do not exist. In this matter of your marriage and loyalty, I sought not to take his power from him as to temper its influence with the woman I love. I saw in Henry's actions a virulence against you that was not merited. I wanted you, madam. And I wanted to retire to a peaceful life with you. I worked so that I might have you—and in the bargain, your sister and my nephew gained each other."

Jordan's logic was sound, but she heard some mysterious note in the harmony. Why? Because Henry was too besieged a ruler to accept simple reasons for complex actions. She opened her mouth to ask Jordan when he rushed on.

"Henry is a good man at heart. He wishes to speak with you, if you are able. If you wish it. Do you? He is contrite and wants to show it to you before he marches out to meet Glendower."

"Please let him in. I want him to understand why I once wished to go to France. Diana knew, and I think, from the way she hated me and sought to use me as her camouflage for her disloyalty, that Henry must have also."

Across the room, she realized her husband yearned for the explanation, too. "You knew I wished to go to France?"

"I suspected you wished to flee. I knew not where until you blurted out about Flanders night before last. Then yesterday, Henry revealed he had evidence—letters from you to Charles—that you wished to go to France. I did not assume your motive was political. But when de Quincy found William Baldwin in the smokehouse minutes later, Baldwin had pages of a letter on him, which incriminated someone of being a friend to the French and Glendower as well."

"Amazing. Who wrote it? How did Baldwin obtain this?"

"When Baldwin was under Henry's order for torture, Baldwin revealed that he had been given it by a French spy here. He would not say who that spy was—until this morning when he learned Diana died."

"How?"

"In the fire. She will not hurt you again, nor others." Jordan swallowed his sorrow. "She was very devious for so long and none of us knew. . . . Baldwin admitted he worked for her secretly for years. She is his half sister, and he loved her and spied for her, even though he was employed by many noble lords as a mercenary soldier. You should know, too, that this morning he also revealed that he followed us and wounded your horse. He also says he was ordered by Diana to let those brigands attack me in the woods."

"To keep you from securing the alliance between Trent and Henry."

Jordan nodded. "Diana was nefarious—using her position and knowledge of Henry's actions to foil him. She used much to her advantage so that Henry had many reasons to distrust you, but not all of them were Diana's fabrications." Jordan grew grave. "Henry told me before our wedding that one of his men arrested your agent in Calais with another letter in hand. This one you had written, for it bore your bold script and full name. Diana and her conspirator, Solange Dupre, rejoiced when they thought it could be used to cast further doubts in Henry's mind that you could be trusted. Malcolm has told me just now in Henry's presence that he suspected his wife of collusion with the French and Welsh but had no proof until he saw how she rejoiced here that you were being blamed for the French invasion of the English forts along the Welsh and Cheshire coasts."

Clare was stunned. "How the most innocent intentions are misconstrued is a human foible of giant proportions. I did write to Charles, accepting his offer to work at his court, never thinking anything about treason, only art. I soon changed my mind, however. Wishing to preserve Trent and hoping to align with Henry, I wanted to go to Flanders. Truly I did. Oh, Jordan." She felt tears rise. "You thought I wanted to go to France."

"I was never certain when or why you wished it. I wanted to learn from your lips alone the sequence of your thinking.

I would have opened the discussion with you when I returned from the kitchen the night we were wed, but you were gone." His voice hitched on a despairing note.

"You thought I had left you?" That he could have suffered from any doubt that she had loved him completely stabbed her like a thousand tiny knives.

"Nay, love, I knew enough of you by then to understand that wherever you walked without me, you had gone against your will."

She let her eyes declare how completely she adored him. "Did you know it was Diana who had taken me?"

"I was not certain if it were she or Malcolm, or both of them in a pact. I had reason to distrust both, as I told you the night your father died. I never knew who had taken you until I saw Malcolm run out of the manor at the call to arms. He . . ." Jordan glanced toward the window and flexed his jaw. "He killed Diana."

Clare felt weak with heartache.

"He used his dagger to spare her the agony of burning to death. He loved her . . . loves her still, though she betrayed him in every way." He swallowed. "I ache for him. He mourns her, he hates her. He left minutes ago, taking her body home with him, not to Montaigne and her people but to Summersby and their children. He says he'll never tell them about what she did. He says to let her soul haunt the place will be just punishment." Jordan licked his lips, focused once more on Clare's eyes. "He told me to relate that he regrets whatever pain he and his wife may have caused you."

" 'Tis not I who needs that succor but you, my love. Did he say the same to you?"

"Aye. It was almost more than I could bear to see him so bereft when I am so blessed with wife and life and love."

Tears streamed down her cheeks then. "Let Henry in. We'll cauterize the wound and let the healing begin."

When Henry stood at her bedside, he was dressed to travel in light mail tippet over which he'd donned a jupon surcoat in Lancastrian green and white. His manner was as regal. "I have often discovered I was wrong. Never have I been more distressed that it is so as now, when we find it was not you who wished to ally herself with the French and Glendower."

As an apology, it was the fullest she supposed Henry could manage. She would more than meet him halfway. After all, she had her future to consider, and she wanted it to be a peaceful one in his kingdom. "Diana's abduction of me was to give you the impression that I was responsible for the French alliance with Glendower. Never, Sire, did I ever plan to conspire with him. My first intention was to go to Paris and write for King Charles in his court. After Jordan arrived and I began to find my own castle infested with conspirators, I came with Jordan to hope to persuade you to accept my alliance and my allegiance, but to let me go to live alone in Flanders. When you arrived early and my escape was blocked by Jordan's dedication to you, my goals changed."

"From my sources in the Louvre I had heard that Charles wished to employ you at his court. I did not know if he wished you simply to write for him, as he has other artists work, or if he meant to repay you for years of keeping Trent neutral."

"I can understand your confusion." But she would not excuse him from the trouble it had caused.

He must have sensed her thoughts, because his next words changed the subject. "I hope you did wish to marry this man."

Her gaze drifted to her husband. "Once I did met your Dragon, Sire, 'twas little I could do to tame my heart to seek other courses. To live in love with this man is precisely the story I would have written for myself."

Henry inhaled. "I will attempt to make amends to you for this."

A sharp fear stole her next breath. Could Jordan come with her or would Henry take his Dragon on to other battles? "I will ask one favor, Sire. You might let us retire to the country to continue our lives in peace."

Henry slapped his leather gauntlets to his thigh. "A wish I have already granted this man before the two of you met. I take my leave and wish you well. Mayhaps, this battle I fight will win us all the peace we crave."

When Jordan closed the door on him, he turned to face her, his own eyes glistening. "I think that ends the story of the Dragon's devotion to his friend and king, my Nightingale."

"He will allow you to retire! Is it so?" She dared to hope.

"He promised me this before I ever went to Trent. Now no strings could bind me to him. I am yours. Will you have me, day in and out?"

She opened her arms. "Until time becomes immaterial. Come, my heroic Dragon, breathe your fire on me and warm us both for eternity."

Epilogue

"PAPA! MORE NUTS AND DATES FOR JEROME!" JORDAN'S SEC-
ond son, Jerome, bounded upon Jordan's lap as he dipped
his fingers into his father's portions. The child had an
appetite that rivaled France for voraciousness. Jordan let
the three-year-old gobble the sugared walnuts and dates but
cocked a wistful brow at his wife. Clare grinned and
returned to her supper conversation with Blanchette.

He'd let his children eat. His guests, too. But by the mass,
they had better be quick about it, for Jordan had better
things to do and say to his wife, who had given him
indication of her birthday present which took his breath—
and inspired his fear.

Another baby.

God, preserve him. He glanced about at his flock of six.
'Twas enough. Three strong boys, including strapping Jerome, who imitated his older brother, Giles, in appetite and

friskiness. Three pretty girls, potential beauties like their mother. Every one of his chicks intelligent, irrepressible. Wearing him out so that he sought his bed each night, glad, sated with the daily rewards of his retirement to domestic life. But he also sought his wife in that same bed. And though in her arms he did ever find a newer facet of their love in which to rejoice, he worried that time was catching up with him . . . and her.

She had lost their last babe. At thirty-five, she was still agile and athletic, if a bit rounded. She rode with him over this small manor and her wider realms of Trent, never shirking her duties or her concerns for their people. Seven pregnancies in twelve years might have debilitated many women, but not her. Energetic, she worked late at night, early in the morn, whenever her fancy took her. She loved her work, his famous Nightingale.

Her fame and fortune had only increased in the years of their marriage. Soon after their wedding, she had published two new books. The first was King Richard's memoirs, which debuted with Henry's blessing. Clare and her assistants produced only a dozen copies of the piece, purchased mostly by those who had once supported Richard and sought to find inside the pages the proof that his cousin had killed him. When rumors went around that Richard wrote about starvation at his own hand and had only suspicions of Henry's attempts to kill him, requests for copies of the memoirs died.

Clare's second work, produced just before their first child, Giles, was born, was the one that made her reputation. *The Nightingale's Song* sold so many copies that her workshop could not keep up with the demand. She had licensed another manuscript shop in London to create more in her name. Meanwhile, she also heard rumors that others reproduced the tale without her permission—and without sending her any commissions on the sales. Although she might have sought out the culprits, she decided not to waste her time in negative—mayhaps futile—activities. His Nightingale declared she preferred to spend her days in positive ways as the Dragon's mate and the mother of his children. His many children. . . .

After she miscarried their last child, he had promised himself to give her no more. But abstinence was not a solution he contemplated. He could never stay away from her, but he had tried not to plant the seed of another child. 'Twas useless to attempt such restraint. He loved his wife as he did when first he met her. With a white hot passion, they burned together long and sure whenever their bodies joined. His attempts to pull away from her were so much fantasy.

His fear about her future ability to carry a child had come to him only in these past six months during her recuperation. For the twelve years of their marriage, Clare was so healthy that he had worried little that she would suffer in childbirth. Confirming that, her first delivery was swift and hard. Giles led the way for the others as he rushed to enter the world within five short hours of Clare's first pang. Giles greeted them with lusty cries.

Each of Jordan's children gave him cause for laughter and provided good companionship, purpose to an already meaningful existence with Clare. But the possibility for more frightened him out of his skin.

He was growing older. Ancient was more the truth.

Fifty might be half a century by some people's reckoning, but few lived to count the numbers. He had and he expected that no time soon would he stop. Nor did he wish to leave Clare.

"Want your pudding, Papa?" Jerome asked, and held the spoon to Jordan's mouth. Lest the sloppy mess dribble to the linen, Jordan obliged his son. "There. That'll make you happier."

Jordan wished a change of mood were that simple. "Why not share it with your cousin Alyce? She's eaten her own papa's dinner and needs a little more, I think, don't you?" Jordan nodded down the table toward Jerome's favorite playmate, Geoffrey and Blanchette's third and youngest child, who sat upon her father's knee.

The little boy gurgled in delight, creamy pudding ringing

his lips. He scrambled down toward his cousin and his uncle's willing arms.

Geoffrey and Blanchette took and gave with boundless affection to Jordan and Clare's brood, and the generosity was returned. The two Chandler families visited each other often, their broods of children finding their best friendships formed with their cousins. So, too, had the four adults formed a mutually enjoyable relationship, built of trust and devotion.

Geoff and Blanchette bore much gratitude, too, to Jordan for his help in spiriting them away to marry against Henry's edict. The king had never extracted a price from them for their folly—and for that, too, they gave great thanks to Jordan, who had convinced his friend not to take petty revenge on two lovers. Jordan had argued that the tale of Geoff and Blanchette's romance—coupled with the Dragon and the Nightingale's—could bring more benefits to Henry's countrymen than punishment could ever inspire. Henry had taken the advice and let them live in peace.

Most of these twelve years, Jordan had witnessed a blossoming in his life. The relationship he and Clare shared grew richer. Clare remained countess of Trent and had named Jordan her earl, though he took only a minor part in the administration of her fiefdom. He had his hands full with his barony and the greater piece of land Henry gave him as earl of Preston.

Clare oversaw the prosperity of Trent. Now that Glendower was gone these last eight years or more, Trent's people profited by herding more sheep and carding more wool. In the villages numerous rumors surfaced about Glendower's death, but no proof could be found that either he lived or died. The Welsh, Jordan suspected, wished to keep the myth alive that the last Prince of Wales still strode the earth—and in their minds, that kept the English from their gates.

Death came in many guises. Malcolm's, two years ago of a lung ailment, was marked by increasing isolation and bitterness. Since the day Malcolm left Morning Star Manor, he had not returned to court and spoke nor wrote to anyone except his children. He died, Jordan learned from Malcolm's heir, in a dark and dingy room similar to the one Aymer had inhabited in Castle Trent.

Henry died two months after Malcolm, irritable and morose. Jordan prayed that his friend had at last found surcease from the daily pressures of ruling a kingdom whose troubles ate him alive. The country certainly breathed fresh air after the old king had departed.

Hope reigned as virile as Henry's oldest son. That ended last month, however. Jordan feared again for England as Hal had assembled a vast armada of fifteen hundred vessels and then days ago sailed it from Dover, his attack on France imminent. King Charles still lived, quite old, mad, and ever at the mercy of ambitious courtiers who argued to invade England. Evidently, few French had learned twelve years ago that England would not bow to them. But Jordan had the impression Hal would teach them what his father could not.

The young king Henry the Fifth of England possessed a characteristic his father never could claim—a positive outlook. With it, Hal talked his way into any new adventure, making any dream sound like reality. In truth, if Hal were not a king, he could have been a writer and persuaded just as many people to belief in his fictions. Had he done so, today Hal might be richer than Clare!

Instead, as his father had tried to persuade her to do, Hal paid her to compose stories for him and his other family members, too. He encouraged Clare to continue to write in English of the common classes. He himself used the language in his court and refused to parlay in old Norman French, which had been the norm since William the Conqueror.

Clare became so renowned for her English prose that her orders multiplied, and she contemplated opening another shop in Chandler village and putting her trusted assistant, Ella, in charge. Ella, who had once apprenticed to the spy Solange Dupre, had proven her loyalty long ago when she had written the note to Jordan to leave Trent and take Clare with him. Coming from Blackpool in Lancaster and faithful to the Lancastrian King Henry, Ella had long suspected Solange of duplicity, and when she overheard odd things from the Frenchwoman's lips, she hastened to do what she could to save her lady from the spy's machinations. It had taken her years to admit it, but the truth had slipped out one day when she and Clare discussed the events that led to the creation of *The Nightingale's Song.*

In truth, his wife would probably open this new shop, though he wished she would not work so hard. Clare seemed compelled by an inner fire, which he had no business dousing. He counted himself fortunate for her gift of love. The peace. And their babies.

He pushed his chair back with a scrape, surprising the rest of the party. "I need air," he muttered as an excuse. He headed for the third story of his new manor house and the garth he and Clare often walked to view the stars and the blooms on her geraniums.

"May I ask you to put Lionel to bed, Blanchette?" Clare handed over her youngest child to her sister. She followed her husband from the hall and climbed the stairs to their garth.

He stood near her red geraniums, fingering the petals. He came here often, as did she, to retreat from their gaggle of children or simply to gaze across their horizons. Ever an easy man to live with, Jordan balked at little. When he did, she felt it like an arrow in her heart.

Tonight at her announcement, he was not happy. Even now as she strolled toward him, he sighed but circled his arms around her, burying his lips in her hair. She knew enough to enjoy the few minutes of silent communion he would take before he spoke. "I must apologize to you, Clare. I did not tell you how pleased I am about the new baby. I am . . . Nay, wait, let me tell you all. I have become so accustomed to the smooth rhythm of our days, I rue the interruptions. I fear the changes, too. Each year I fear them more. I shouldn't. They give our lives texture. They present fresh challenges, like a new chapter in one of your adventures."

"I have never written a tale I enjoyed more than life lived with you."

"Nor I with you, wise Nightingale."

Reveling in his acceptance, she had to ask for more. "And you won't withdraw from me because you fear I might die in childbirth?"

She could feel his every muscle quaver. "I won't promise to be calm about watching you endure any suffering. That fire you survived was enough for you and for me. There is so much peace in our lives that I dread any situation as one with the possibility of disaster." His hands smoothed her gown along her back, where a few scars remained to mark the night Diana forced her from their bed. "We will live our days into an envious old age, I think."

"I know it. People will see us as we hobble along. 'There go the extraordinary Chandlers, they'll say, venerable and irritable.'"

"Mmm. So prolific, too."

He kissed her with unquenchable desire. "But we won't care. We'll smile together, cackle, and say that 'twas love that made it so."

Hand in hand, they walked from the garth toward a future made of hope.

The Nightingale's Song

Through winter's dusk, a staunch king's man
rode forth to me with royal plan.
The Dragon breached my land, home, joy,
To betroth me to one prideful boy.

Then the Dragon, beset by outlaws,
gained rescue from their claws
by my own Nightingale's quick throng
of six women, brave and strong.

He praised me for my bevy's valor.
I nursed his men's wounds, erased their pallor.
I wished them well. I bid them go.
The Dragon spoke the hated plan which I did know.

"This child, my nephew, you shall wed."
"Sirrah," scoffed I, "I seek no bed."
Instead I vowed I'll be free,
to France—or Flanders—I would flee!

But as I came to know him more,
This fierce Dragon of worthy lore,
I rued him not, nor feared his touch.
I knew I cared for him too much.

But foes conspired to attack us,
plotting murders in the dark.
The Dragon led me from my lair,
Unto his king we fast repair'd.

The Nightingale's Song

Torn by love's grief at umber hour,
The Dragon came silent to my bower.
Stark in his need, he built the fire
with honor's ash for love's desire.

"Bid me stay or make me go,
but tell me quick what I must know.
Can you love me? Will you have me
for one hour of bliss?"

I rose, a rebel to sire, king.
Cast off future, gown, and ring.
"Dragon, I do want you. I will have you.
For eternities of love."

He kissed me and my world reeled,
while the night disrobed for dawn.
He showed me how love brought joy.
But he did not tarry long.

My foes came to my chamber
and tore me from my nest.
"Your flight, thrush, will show the English king
that you loved France the best."

The Dragon came upon them
As they abducted me into night.
"Come," he crooned, "I'll have this bride.
You've nowhere to run. You cannot hide.
I'll stalk you to the fires of hell.
I'll see to it, the king will tell
all future traitors of how well
you and your friends did fail."

They feared his words and his king's ire.
They tried to run. But, lo, the fire
of their misdeeds roared higher
than their dishonorable aspirations.

For years, with my Dragon's chicks about me,
I oft tell this romantic tale
Of how the fierce Dragon, brave and courtly,
did adore the Nightingale.

—*The Nightingale*
  (Clare de Wallys Chandler,
  countess of Trent and Preston, Baroness Chandler)

Author's Notes

IN 1403 CLARE DE WALLYS STOOD ON THE THRESHOLD OF A NEW age of literacy. Yet another sixty or more years would pass before the invention of the printing press made books more widely available—and affordable.

In Clare's time, "books" were still truly manuscripts. Hand-produced and individually illustrated—or illuminated, as those in the period would have said—these works of art were created by groups of people. Some were men in monasteries and they wrote in Latin. But increasingly, as the necessity and joy of writing and reading the vernacular spread among the middle and lower classes, others began to do the work of producing books. Some of them were women.

Here I took the example of the famous Christine di Pisan, who made her living from writing. This woman ran a shop, obtained patrons who funded the production of her manuscripts, and employed women to do the work.

Her clients were princes, merchants, and anyone else able to pay for the expensive supplies of vellums, pigments, and ink, plus the labor of planning, cutting, and bindings. Her products included histories, biographies, textbooks, books of prayers, poems, and what we today call romances. She produced any type of work that earned her money to support herself, her children, and her scribes, clerks, and illuminators. We would say today that Christine was writer, editor, marketer, public relations expert, and publisher all rolled into one.

Christine di Pisan bears other similarities to Clare de Wallys. As I say here in *Nightingale's Song,* Christine was asked by Richard II to come to his court to work. Perhaps Christine understood the precarious nature of his power. Whatever her reasons, she refused his invitation. Nor did she accept the invitation to attend Henry IV at his court.

These facts, coupled with our lack of knowledge about who wrote some of the most prized stories in Chaucer's England (including the famous *Sir Gawain and the Green Knight,* which was written by someone in the vicinity of Cheshire, England), led me to conjecture that a woman could have written some of them.

More women in that period—especially titled ladies and merchants' wives and daughters—learned how to read. Many became patrons of such workshops as Clare's. Some women collected so many books, they became noted for their libraries. A few of them were renowned for their collections of romances!

I hope you thrilled to Clare's romance, and I invite you to indulge yourself in my next one for Pocket Books. *Never Before* begins a Victorian series I have longed to write about American heiresses bound for Britain—and the possibility of gaining titled, handsome husbands. To their dismay, life among the aristocracy is not what they expect, and love often becomes a thorny proposition.

I enjoy receiving your letters! Please write to me and include a self-addressed stamped envelope for a reply:

Jo-Ann Power
4319 Medical Drive, Suite 131–298
San Antonio, TX 78229-3325

JO-ANN POWER

You and No Other
❑ 89704-7 / $5.50

Angel of Midnight
❑ 89705-5 / $5.99

Treasures
❑ 52995-1 / $5.99

Gifts
❑ 52996-x / $5.99

The Nightingale's Song
❑ 52997-8 / $5.99

Available from Pocket Books

**POCKET BOOKS
PROUDLY PRESENTS**

Book One in the "American Beauties" Series

NEVER BEFORE

JO-ANN POWER

**Coming Soon
from Pocket Books**

**The following is a preview of
Never Before. . . .**

Dublin, Ireland
March, 1875

He had lost her! He beat his hat against his thigh as he emerged from the clubhouse stands. Lost her! For the sake of money! Strong legs. A long mane and gorgeous tail. To have mated her would have brought him the greatest delight he'd had in a decade. And for want of a few pounds, she now belonged to another. Ah, hell. Why was he surprised?

During the last decade, he had lost his inheritance. His savings. Damn!

In a fit, he sent his hat sailing across the yard. Missing members of the crowd, the black felt spun toward the nearest trash barrel and dropped in.

Rhys Kendall congratulated himself.

His words died as he spied the new owner of the horse he had craved. She marched up to the bursar and pulled open her reticule. From its abyss, she took out two eye-popping items. The first was a pistol that looked like an American derringer. Its partner was a roll of bills so big he would have trouble putting his fist around it.

Did she carry the weapon to protect her from thieves? She should. But now that Rhys got a closer look at the rosewood-haired beauty who had bid against him, he decided she needed the gun to ward off admirers.

She was unescorted. Utterly, oddly alone. A bright sprig of green amid a somber plain of men, she was dressed sensibly for the sale in a riding habit. Most ladies came to the Dublin Spring Horse Trials and Sale dressed to impress, unless of course, they were unmarried and then they came dressed to lure.

He wished this one had not dressed at all. Her hair was nearly the same color as the bright bay she'd bought. Faceting the sun in a rainbow of reds and browns, her unfashionable fat braid was topped off with a pert—but slipping—straw hat. The sheen on that braid made him rub his fingers together with the itch to unwind it, brush it and wrap it around his wrist. His waist.

His mouth watered at the rest of her. Her legs had to be as long as his. Hard but sleeker. She would fit him. Especially when he lifted her to him naked and moist . . .

He cleared his throat. Glutton for punishment, he ran his gaze up the curve of her bottom and around to her firm breasts. He bit off a few rueful words, nurturing a hunger for what was forbidden to him. *And she most certainly is beyond your means, old man.* Because from her purse and her clothes to her independence, she was a woman with money.

No match for him.

His eyes snagged on a movement to his left. From a group of people, a short man pushed through to halt at the sight of the same woman Rhys admired. The fellow narrowed his eyes at her and checked a time-piece from his pocket and snapped it shut.

Suddenly, the lady chuckled and clapped her hands in response to the bursar.

"Oh, wonderful!" Rhys knew she said, and then her hat fell over her eyes.

She swore an oath and ripped the thing off. Her braid unraveled. A few pins scattered. She shook her hair free of more, and she paused. Amid the crowd, she found his eyes.

She appeared bewildered, recognizing not only that he had been her competitor for the mare but also that he had been studying her. Blinking, she wondered why. But dismissing the issue, she marched herself over to deposit her hat in the trash barrel. Though she didn't dust her hands, Rhys noted the little flick of her chin as if to bid the bit of trouble good riddance. Then she stopped and peered into the trash. She frowned, turning her face toward him to examine his empty hands and his bare head.

She reached inside and retrieved his hat. Nose wrinkling, she held it up by two dainty fingertips. The remains of a watercress sandwich dripped from its brim.

"Yours?" she mouthed.

"Not anymore," he replied, shoulders shaking in laughter.

She opened her fingers and let the hideous thing fall back inside the barrel. This time, she brushed her hands off and tossed him a grin that made him wish he were a rich man.

Then she turned to retrace her steps, get her chit for

her horse, and walk toward the stable block. With every step, her rippling hair tapped against her trim derriere.

Rhys wrestled with the urge to follow her.

Into his reverie darted the little man who had found her so intriguing before. Rhys watched him limp after her. Why would a worm like that trail a woman like her?

Rhys felt a stab of fear. He quickened his pace. Noting the sway of emerald green, Rhys tracked her progress while the man wove through the crowd behind her like a garden snake. Until suddenly, he paused, jerking around and flattening himself against the stable wall. With a stunned expression spreading over his pockmarked face, he ran in the opposite direction.

Rhys memorized his thin mustache, his sharp nose. He made certain the fellow was well gone before he spun to check on the lady in green—and bumped into someone.

"I apologize—" Rhys offered, but the rest died on his lips. He was face to face with the one man who was responsible for everything he had become this past decade—angry, hungry, poor.

"Brighton."

"Rhys." Skip Brighton was just as shocked. Rhys knew it from the way his face went white. "Hello. I never thought to see you here in Ireland."

"I will say the same."

"I come to Europe at least once a year."

"I know."

Skip sighed, looking sad and definitely older than his forty-five years. "We arrived last week."

"I will inform my solicitor he is flagging in his duty

to inform me well in advance about your travel plans."

"It's not his fault. I came to Dublin unexpectedly."

"All the more reason to be vigilant. I claim the *droit de seigneur* to shoot all wolves invading my territory."

"Or attempting to buy it?"

"That, too." Why in hell a pirate like Brighton would try to purchase Kendall Manor baffled Rhys. Skip wouldn't want to settle down. He never had. Not when his first wife was alive, nor his second. Even when he was smuggling cotton and artillery between England and the South during the American civil war, Skip Brighton had never endeavored to buy property in London. Nor would Rhys ever allow him to buy his own estate. Skip Brighton might be Rhys's second cousin, but Rhys's pride demanded he keep the rarest jewel of his family from the man who had taken most else from him. He'd never give Skip the satisfaction to possess the family town house and gloat that he'd gained it at Rhys's further indignity.

Skip offered a fleeting smile. "It's true, Rhys, that I never was a man to stay anywhere for long, but now I feel the need. I learned your London residence was for sale and I made the offer to buy it because I thought it would be . . . shall we say, fitting."

That insult made Rhys ball his hands. "If I starved in the street, I would not sell you the dirt from my shoes, Brighton."

"That's a shame. I thought it was a fair price."

No, a much too handsome one, Rhys admitted with bile. "To anyone but you, it would have been the selling price."

"Too bad my money's not as good as other men's."

"Your money was gained from my people's loss, Brighton. I'll never take a bloody penny from you."

Skip nodded, tightened his jaw. "Old habits die hard, don't they? We must be careful lest we die unreformed. That would be the biggest tragedy, wouldn't you say?"

Rhys's hatred for this man went from boil to simmer. Was Skip getting tenderhearted as he aged? Impossible. Yet Skip's next words told Rhys that just might be so.

"Well, I must tell you I am happy to hear you recover. My friends in London inform me that your factories are producing fabric up to their capacity."

Rhys put up a higher guard against the cunning of this marauder. "They are. We'll earn a profit this year for the first time since your southern states seceded from your union. I'm importing Indian cotton now."

Skip's hazel eyes faceted in unreadable shades of gold. "I'm glad to hear it."

Damned if Skip didn't sound sincere. But Rhys could not forget that the ruin of Rhys's mills had much to do with Skip's treachery during the American civil war. Rhys was already stepping away. "Excuse me."

"I hope we meet again," Skip called after him.

"You hope in vain," Rhys muttered to himself, his anger raging. He much preferred the way his blood had heated when he'd been admiring the woman in green. He had to find her and assure himself that the slimy creature who had followed her hadn't decided to trail her again.

He'd bet his meager monthly income that he knew where she'd be. With her new possession. He turned in the direction of the stable block where the animals were housed in preparation for their departure with their new owners.

She was alone, at the far end of the open stable, crooning to the draught horse. Rhys strained to hear her voice, low as a June breeze and just as warm.

Rhys felt the fires begin again in his blood as the horse nuzzled the woman's breast. The material of her riding jacket caressed her torso like a kid glove. She didn't wear a padded bust improver. Who would want her to?

Not me. He'd want her free. Hair, breasts, legs.

He rolled his eyes to the rafters, amazed at himself for desiring a woman so physically when brains usually appealed to him first in a female. Of course, since few of the feminine gender were encouraged in England to divulge the true depths of their gray matter, he had not been amused by many women other than his mother and the Kendall village witch. Both ladies had tutored him on herbs and wine and human nature, spoiling him for less scintillating company. Since both women had died when he was fourteen, he had for the next twenty years of his life sought out intelligent companionship. Except, of course, in bed, where conversation was limited—and wit was displayed by what one did with one's body, not necessarily one's tongue. Although with this sprite, Rhys would like to use everything he had.

What was the matter with him? Moonstruck was not in his repertoire with women. Rhys straightened.

At the other door, a shadow moved.

No. *Limped.*

Something small glinted in the man's hand. A gun.

Rhys charged forward. Across the length of the stable, even Rhys's speed could not compensate for the fact that the culprit need take only two steps to gain the barn door . . . and hurl himself through it.

In the same second, the woman whirled, astonished.

The horse shied, whinnied. Straining at her tethers, the animal tried to rear and defend her new mistress.

Rhys halted at the door. The worm of a man had vanished.

Rhys spun with the need to find the woman, comfort her.

Instead he heard the cocking of a pistol. A hard circle of steel bored into his coat.

"Don't move," she ordered him, her voice deadly calm.

"I wouldn't dream of it. Put that away, though. I'm not the one you want to use it on."

"No, no, of course not." He could feel the pistol wavering in her trembling hand.

He placed his hand atop hers. "Give it to me."

She shuddered and wobbled forward. Suddenly, it was the most natural act in the world to wrap her in his arms.

His brains became mutton when his loins registered what a prize he held in his embrace. "You're safe. You're unhurt. He's gone and I've got you." He possessed all of her, like his first dressage trophy he had hugged to him when he was eight and insisted he sleep with it each night for weeks. He speculated that were he to take her to his bed, he would not let her leave him for months. "I'm very glad you had your pistol at the ready," he whispered into the velvet wealth of her hair.

She made a sound of agreement, her face to his chest.

"Deters any highwaymen." He wanted her to laugh. She choked between a sob and a chuckle. "I always carry my pistol."

"Really? Ever prepared, eh?" He drew back and looked down at her. She brought her face up, their gazes locked, and he discovered gold. Oh, her eyes were definitely hazel, brown as earth, green as grass, but studded with golden nuggets, now hard with fear. "Why do you need a gun in your purse?" Did she have any idea why that man followed her?

Her eyes darted to the barn door and back up to him. "I learned to keep one with me during the war."

That jarred him. So did the cadence of her speech. She was American, and the conflict she spoke of had to be their War Between the States. She would have been terribly young then. "How old were you?"

"Nearly six when the southern states seceded. Almost ten when Lee surrendered to Grant."

Rhys chastised himself heartily for being attracted to this charmer who was, therefore, no more than twenty years of age. He didn't fall for many women, hardly any women, actually. He'd sworn himself off dalliances to protect his heart from pains, his reputation from stains. He'd removed himself from the endless circuit of balls and dinner parties as much to declare publicly he was not husband material, as to protect himself from finding a woman he might want but could never keep. Not in any style to which her hope or his affection might wish he could afford. He wanted to hoot in irony that he was having his wits scrambled by this very young lady who knew horses, hated hats, welcomed his protection—and was a tempting fourteen years his junior.

She stepped backward from his embrace. "Thank

you for your help. I'll take my pistol now." She put her hand out.

In it, he placed the gun, but did not let go. "Did you have any idea that you were being followed?"

That brought a bewildered look her eyes. "No. Was I?"

"I saw a small man with a limp watching you when we stood near the bursar's post."

"But you were watching me—and following me, too."

"Ah, yes. But I did not draw a gun in your presence."

"I'm grateful. Thank you." She squeezed his fingers in a reminder that he still held her hand.

"I'd like to ensure your safety. Are you with someone? May I escort back to the clubhouse?"

"Yes, thank you. I'd like that." She tilted her head. "Should I address you as 'sir' or 'mister' or 'my lord?' "

"Rhys."

"Rhys," she repeated, and he longed to hear her say it often and in secluded dark rooms. "That's a very odd name."

"It's Welsh. Traditional name for boys among my mother's family. The family name is Kendall. A wee bit of Scots. We come from the northern borders of England. What's yours?" Instinct told him that he needed to be able to find her. Common sense shouted that he ask nothing of her.

"Ann—"

"Ann, full of grace," he murmured, floored by the aptness of her name.

She tilted her head in question.

"Full of grace. It is the meaning of your name."

"I never knew."

"I did. The first minute I looked at you."

She did not breathe. "You are very complimentary."

"It's an act I perform with utmost discretion." He grinned at her, offering his arm. "Come along. I'll see you out of here. You've made friends with your mare and you can send your stable hands to come fetch her."

"Yes, thank you. My party are at the clubhouse, having tea before the next round of bidding." She hooked her hand over his arm, and the effects of her frightening experience had her gripping his arm a little too fiercely. But he didn't object, because it brought her body close to his.

As they walked, her hair caught the rays of the sun like flame. "Where do you stay in Dublin?" he asked. *Who are you with? Your parents? Your husband?*

"We're at the Imperial Hotel."

"The finest establishment in the city. But it has no stables. Where will you keep your mare?"

"I'll put her two streets away from our hotel. Have you heard of Rooney's?"

"Tim Rooney will take great care of your mare."

"Good, because I have a shopping list for Ireland and London."

"So you'll purchase more than one mare? I'm glad you told me. I care not to bid against you a second time. It's humiliating for a man to lose to a lady with so much money," he teased her, then became serious. "But why do you carry cash? That fellow who followed you probably wanted to relieve you of it." They took the dusty lane toward the whitewashed two-story clubhouse. He hated to come to the end of the road.

"Maybe. But I like the feel of currency. Makes me think I'm secure. That's a result of what happened to us during the war, too. You see, when you are tired and hungry, you take what money you have and spend it quickly, before it disappears."

That feeling Rhys knew too well. "Did you live in the Confederacy?"

"Yes, Virginia."

Skip Brighton hailed from Virginia. Odd to meet two people in one day so far from their home and at the same event. Unless they knew each other. Unless this lovely creature had become Brighton's third wife. Riled by that thought, Rhys patted her hand, but it was her right hand. If she wore a wedding ring, it would be on her left.

They had reached the entrance to the clubhouse, and when Ann informed him that her party had a box in the second tier, they began to climb the steps.

"Tell me where you go after Dublin," he urged.

"London." She paused to consider his mouth, his eyes. "Do you live here in Dublin? You don't seem to speak like other Irishmen I've met."

He didn't want her to meet any other men who might enchant her with blarney. "I visit Ireland only for this horse show to sell or buy animals for my farms in England."

She looked away. "Then you don't go to London often."

"Not unless I have good reason."

They had reached the second tier of boxes. One buxom young woman with russet hair waved at Ann. Beside her stood two other ladies and a shocked Skip Brighton.

Ann's gaze trailed Rhys's. "That is my father. Do you know him? He's smiling at you but . . . Is something wrong?"

"I know him well." Too damnably well.

Skip Brighton worked his way past three young women, each as distinctive as a feather from a unique bird. The well-endowed redhead looked like a flamingo in rose ruffles, the blonde was a dove in tailored gray, while the last resembled a pudgy raven in a flurry of peach organdy.

"There you are, Ann," Skip said, his attention on Rhys as if they were friends. "You two have met. Rhys, nice to see you again."

Rhys turned to Ann. "It was the highlight of my day to have assisted you, Ann. I will send round to your hotel a listing of the best horse trials in Britain. I wish you well in your endeavors in breeding. You have great taste and a way with animals. Good day." It was the hardest task he'd ever done to turn and walk away.

"Goodbye" was what he'd meant. Ann knew she would never see him again. She was certain the reason was that Rhys and her father did not get along. Or to be precise, Rhys hated Skip. While part of her was not surprised because so many men despised the man who had made millions at their expense, Ann added this grievance to her list of others against her father.

"Who was *that?*" Colleen came to Ann's side.

"His name is Rhys Kendall," she replied. He was so tall that she could watch his departure easily. His broad shoulders in the charcoal frockcoat were stiff. His gait was swift.

She had met scores of men filled with bitterness. Each had been fresh from a battle. This meeting between her father and Rhys seemed less bloody than one that battered men's bodies, but this one ravaged one man's mind. Rhys's.

What had her father done to Rhys? She would find out.

Colleen hummed. "He is the best-looking man I've seen so far. I wonder if he's married and rich."

Ann inhaled and pivoted. "I have no idea."

Her father caught her gaze and said, "I do."

"Is he anyone we should care about?" Colleen pressed.

"You could say that, Colleen. Even though he is poor, he is a bachelor. Rhys Westport Kendall is also His Grace, the sixteenth Duke of Carlton and Dundalk."

"So if a girl had money," Colleen concluded, "she might make the perfect wife for him and become his duchess."

"Precisely my idea," Skip murmured.

Ann did not bat an eyelash, but turned for the family box, her father's words sounding warning bells in her head.